TAN VAN HUIZEN

THE KEEPERS

Black Rose Writing | Texas

ISBN: 978-1-68433-952-5
PUBLISHED BY BLACK ROSE WRITING
www.blackrosewriting.com

Printed in the United States of America
Suggested Retail Price (SRP) $20.95

The Keepers is printed in Garamond

*As a planet-friendly publisher, Black Rose Writing does its best to eliminate unnecessary waste to reduce paper usage and energy costs, while never compromising the reading experience. As a result, the final word count vs. page count may not meet common expectations.

PRAISE FOR
THE KEEPERS

"Out of horror-rich New England comes a unique and original voice in Tan Van Huizen and his debut novel, *The Keepers*. A blend of visceral and folk horror, its characters are well developed through the author's capable hands, penning gritty dialogue and tension-building action. Van Huizen is a gifted storyteller and an author to watch."
–Andi Marchal, author of *Vykup: A Novel of the Koldun*

"Van Huizen has mastered the art of portraying visceral horror juxtaposed against his rich and fully developed cast of unique characters. This novel will keep you in your seat until you finish and stick with you long after the last page is turned. I highly recommend *The Keepers*, even for those that are not fans of horror. This book is so smooth and ingenious, it is a complete delight to read."
–Deborah Wynne, Award-winning author of *Opening Act: Pirouettes and Promises: Book One*

"*The Keepers* is an amazing novel that centers around the Hockomock Swamp. From the rich background of even his minor characters such as the bereaved mother Priscilla Hooke, to the centrally cast and pathologically cruel chief of police, Elias Hicks, the reader can't help but feel everything from wrenching compassion to horrific revulsion. *The Keepers* certainly contains enough horror to satisfy the fans of that genre but with a compelling plot and well-rounded characters it should also appeal to fans of mystery, paranormal activity, history and spirituality."
–Jill De Burgh, author

"The strength and chilling intensity of *The Keepers* is in the characterization. Individuals are well-observed, oddly sinister, and teetering on the brink of lunacy like Henry James, or defeated, world-weary specimens with a touch of low, animal cunning, such as Cam and Darrah. *The Keepers* is an excellently written horror story, absorbing the reader into a gripping and darkly atmospheric story with an old-school Stephen King vibe. It has a cast of wonderfully realized characters, making this a horribly compelling read."
–Ryan L., The Book Review Directory

"It's funny how I got so involved with the characters, liking and disliking them, and how I really hoped Chief Hicks would get his in the end. *The Keepers* is definitely a page turner. I loved all the characters, descriptions, and setting." **–Denise Lacroix**

"*The Keepers* is a gripping piece that has a grittiness to it that you can't rinse off (in a good way)."
–Mercedes Griffith

"I was immediately lured into *The Keepers* by the historical base and richly detailed characters. This finely woven story telling of an ancient evil that lurks in a sleepy Massachusetts town that's steeped in history and full of mystery. This story takes you on a heart pounding journey to uncover the dark and deadly truth behind the facade. I absolutely loved this book and it's gritty horror storytelling. What are you waiting for, go buy it!."
–Rhonda Kohman, poet

"I didn't know what to expect when I started to read *The Keepers*. What I found was a story that captured my attention and held it until the last sentence. The characters were believable, and the story was exciting. At times I couldn't put the book down. So I got a cup of coffee and a few donuts and read the last 60 pages without stopping. As I finished the last few words in the last sentence, I was ready for the sequel. So pour yourself a cup of coffee, grab a donut and enjoy. You won't be disappointed."
–Steve Koller, educator

"It was very good! After reading the book, I am hoping, and believing, that there is another one or two that will tie up the loose ends. Non-fiction type of books are what I usually read, so I was somewhat surprised by how much I enjoyed it! Not that I am going to completely change my taste. My wife says I read to learn, not for enjoyment. *The Keepers* was enjoyable."
–Don Koller, educator

This book is dedicated to the people of the fallen night.
It is with reverence and heavy heart we honor and remember you.

FACTS

The Hockomock Swamp (Hockomock, the Native American word for 'place where spirits dwell') is a vast wetland encompassing much of the northern part of Southeastern Massachusetts.

During the seventeenth century, the Hockomock Swamp served as a fortress by the Wampanoag against an invasion by early English settlers. It played a major role in King Philip's War [1675-1676] as a strategic base of operations for Metacomet (Sachem of the Wampanoag, also known as King Philip by the settlers) to launch assaults upon nearby English villages.

The early English settlers feared the Hockomock. They thought swamps were places of evil; a place possessed by Satan to conduct his evil works. They referred to the Hockomock as "The Devil's Swamp" or "The Devil's Bowl."

The Bridgewater Triangle is an area of 200 square miles within Southeastern Massachusetts. It is a site of alleged, paranormal phenomena, ranging from UFOs to poltergeists, orbs, various bigfoot-like sightings, giant snakes and thunderbirds. The Hockomock Swamp lies within the boundaries of The Bridgewater Triangle. Some believe it is the nexus of the Triangle's disturbances.

The swamp's environment is part of the northeastern coastal forests ecoregion. It is the largest, freshwater swamp in the state spanning six territories: Bridgewater, Easton, Norton, Raynham, Taunton and West Bridgewater. Some residents still sleep with their lights on. I know. I'm one of them.

Titicut is the name of the fictional town in this story. It is also the Wampanoag name for the Taunton River, which begins in Bridgewater, Massachusetts and winds 37 miles to Mount Hope Bay, a tidal estuary bordering Rhode Island. The bay was once part of the Wampanoag nation, and the site of past events of King Philip's War, 1675. Per capita, King Philip's War was the bloodiest war in America's history.

EPIGRAPH

"The oldest and strongest emotion of mankind is fear, and the oldest and strongest kind of fear is fear of the unknown."
   –H. P. Lovecraft

"Do you remember," said O'Brien, "the moment of panic that used to occur in your dreams? There was a wall of blackness in front of you, and a roaring sound in your ears. There was something terrible on the other side of the wall. You knew you knew what it was, but you dared not drag it into the open."
   –George Orwell, 1984.

"Fear, the greatest of which, builds with anticipation and plunders the rational mind of all reason, swallows all common sense."
   –Unknown Author

"Our fears become terrors when allowed time to ferment in the wilds of imagination."
   –Tan Van Huizen

"Whoever sacrifices to any god, except the Lord alone, shall be doomed."
   –Exodus 22:19

THE
KEEPERS

PROLOGUE

By the year 1620, nearly a century after the first firebrand speakers of the Protestant Reformation quaked the ground beneath the Roman Catholic Church, a small sect of fundamental adherents, guided by the hand of God, set out into the wilderness according to His counsel and of His will, to worship Him in the unadulterated light of truth.

The truth, as the adherents believed, God almighty, was the supreme power over all creation. He reigned over light and dark, good and evil, the living and the dead. He was the creator of the past, the present, and by His divine providence, the creator of all things yet to come.

The adherents were His faithful servants; they were a congregation of newcomers who voyaged across a formidable ocean with rejoicing hearts, secure in His charge to face the savage pagans in their unholy wilderness and carry forth His creed.

"It is God who arms me with strength and makes my way perfect. He makes my feet like the feet of deer and sets me on high places. He teaches my hands to make war, so that my arms can bend a bow of bronze. I have pursued my enemies and overtaken them; neither did I turn back again till they were destroyed. I have wounded them, so that they were not able to rise; they have fallen under my feet. For You have armed me with strength for the battle; you have subdued under me those who rose against me." Psalm 18:32

At the end of days, the adherents believed good would always triumph over evil by His will and His worthy purpose, but not without rigorous testing by the dark forces. Only those pure of faith, who stand as righteous soldiers in God's army, who wage war against Satan's damnable lies and false promises, who with fidelity follow His commandments and rise against evil's advancement and influence over good, shall be the inheritors of God's Kingdom and worthy of predestination.

Ever since Eve succumbed to the Serpent's artifice, God has used Satan's wiles to test His flock. After all, it was God, the creator of all things and supreme power over all creation, who permitted Satan to roam the earth and tempt His flock with wickedness, might the beast uncover those heretics who would abandon God's word and sell Him for a few pieces of silver.

Just days before the adherents made landfall, in the year of our Lord 1620, armed with bibles, muskets and purpose of industry, the adherents signed the Compact of Governance. It would ensure their survival and self-destiny, that no body politic, no foreign nation, no imperial ruler, no false prophet, nor pagan warriors under the adversary's command, shall hold or exercise sovereignty over God and His faithful.

Women and children, as was their Godly station, bore witness without reservation the reading and signing of the Compact of Governance. One by one, men of good standing congregated before their brethren amidships and pledged an oath to uphold the document, before they signed it by faith and by witness.

A half a century later, in the year of our Lord 1676, nearly two generations after the first adherents made landfall in the new world, a second compact "The Compact of the Covenant," was signed in secrecy by a splinter group of faithful adherents known to the congregation as church elders.

The elders handled Christian governance, surveillance, and admonishments. They were The Keepers of the faith, guarding against God's adversary, and punishing those who were thought corruptible; those who were likely servants of Satan's works.

What the elders witnessed deep within the wilderness in 1676, three days after the last of the first men were sent to their watery graves, shook their foundational beliefs to the core. It awakened the horrifying possibility that God's adversary could ultimately prevail.

Over the next three centuries, The Keepers of the covenant would meet secretly below the old meetinghouse to carry out the tenets of their creed. As church elders, their charge was now twofold: protect the faithful against God's adversary and to appease the warring spirits in the realm of the dead, known as people of the fallen night.

On Friday, September 9th, in the year of our Lord 1983, The Keepers would meet again.

CHAPTER 1
IN THE BEGINNING (COFFEE WITH LARRY)

"That's a large, Dunkin' regular and two glazed sticks, Officer Stevens," Susie Bradley, the girl behind the counter, said.

"Nice to see some of our youths still know the value of work," Officer Stevens said, handing over some loose change. "Say hello to your mom and dad for me. And here is a little extra for your tip jar."

"Thank you, Officer Stevens. Are you going to the Harvest Fair this year?"

"Sergeant Guthrie is the defending pie eating champion three years running. They don't call him 'Sergeant Gut' for nothing ... I'll be there to make sure it won't be a fourth. You can bet your bottom dollar." His eyes twinkled above his rounded cheeks. "Especially if it's rhubarb. I just love Betty's rhubarb—"

Police dispatch: A possible 10-46; abandoned car reported on Turnpike, two miles past the old service station, heading east.

Juggling a large Dunkin' and two glazed sticks, Officer Stevens somehow squeezed the button on his radio while exiting the shop. "This is Stevens. ETA in about 10 ... I'm on my way."

Stevens took a draw off his coffee and opened the door to his cruiser. He reached down among the scattered papers to find the cassette tape of Lawrence Welk, Barb his wife gave him for his birthday. He tore open the package with his teeth when a note dropped out written in Barb's hand.

Happy Birthday, my big and burly LOVE MUFFIN. Got my apron on and making your favorite tonight. Get on home when you can... Love, your CREAM PUFF Barb... P.S. You might need a bigger drawer.

Shaking his head, he chuckled and popped in the cassette. "I love that woman." He eased back and allowed the dulcet sounds of that champagne music wash over him ... *A one and a two and a....*

Police dispatch: "Come in, Officer Stevens."

1

"Stevens here, over."

"Just a heads up, Officer. The vehicle is an early '70s El Camino, approach with caution. There were earlier reports of a disturbance in that area, but you know how that goes, probably just a couple of teens dragging their hotrods."

"Copy that, over."

Stevens placed the handset back on the dash and made his way through the quiet neighborhood streets before turning down Turnpike, where days can pass without seeing a soul. It was flanked on both sides by wetlands. Dead, leafless birch trees, milkweed grass, and an abandoned gas station, long out of service, were the only inhabitants to grace the forgotten landscape. About all you could hear on that road was the crackling of high-tension wires and that lonely "KAWW" sound that black crows make as if to warn or embrace their desolation.

The vehicle was seen two miles up. Stevens angled his visor down to shield his eyes against the sun's glare and approached cautiously, as advised. He squinted through the rear window, but it was tough to see. No one was behind the wheel.

His eyes travelled over the vehicle and noted it was indeed an early 70s El Camino. The left blinker was flashing, and the vehicle had a damaged quarter panel.

"Dispatch, this is Stevens. I have a reg on that abandoned vehicle."

"Go ahead, officer."

"Massachusetts plate: Charlie, Johnny, Zebra, 7, 3, 9. I'm gonna have a look."

He stepped out, tucking his nightstick behind his back in a non-aggressive posture, and made his approach. Besides the damaged quarter panel, he noticed the cargo bay dented in, possibly from a prior incident, and the bed was nearly rusted out. The rear tires were warm and tacky to the touch, and he could smell a mixture of gasoline, brake fluid and burnt rubber cutting through the air.

He stood and surveyed a fresh set of skid marks. Stevens knew coyotes, deer and fisher cats were in the area. Perhaps one bolted in front of him at the last moment.

He walked up to the driver's door and reached through the window to turn off the blinking signal, but before his hand grabbed the lever, a black crow burst through and knocked him clear off his feet. "Jesus, Mary and Joseph!" He reached behind his left ear to feel a trickle of blood. "He clipped me. The damn thing came at me through the window."

Stevens steadied himself to his feet and heard an agonizing wail emanate from somewhere inside the vehicle. It sounded like an animal sick with pain. "Don't move! Hold it right there!" he said, while drawing his weapon. He rubbed his eyes to gain focus, but still could see no one. He inched closer, stepping cautiously, until he could peer inside. And there, tucked in a fetal position under the dash, a frightened man was crying and shaking, his eyes wild with fear.

"Hold on. Don't move. I'm going to get you out of there, but you have to remain calm. There's no reason to be afraid. Take a deep breath and just relax. It's over. It's all over. I'm going to open the door, slowly. No sudden movements. I don't want anyone to get hurt."

Stevens readied his revolver and slowly opened the door. "That's it. Nothing to be afraid of." He reached in and, with his left hand, freed the man's legs before lifting him up carefully where his shoulders and head slumped back in an almost lifeless manner when Stevens realized who the man was. No words were spoken. None had to be.

A moment slipped away as he blotted his upper lip with a hanky and regarded the terrible crows gathering overhead. He radioed dispatch, saying only two words. "Carl Jenkins."

CHAPTER 2
HIGHWAY ROBBERY

It was the last Friday of summer break and Coach Mitch Daniels was getting his team ready for the upcoming football season. School was starting on Monday and the first game against King Philip High was in a couple of weeks. Daniels had his boys running double sessions, two-a-days with suicide burns, pushing them to avoid being embarrassed again at this year's season opener.

Other than the jocks and Coach Daniels, Titicut High was nearly empty. Some of the cheerleading squad was there going over formations, discussing which girl went skank over the summer and allowed which boy to steal home. The school's custodian (known as Mighty Mouse) was also there. No one knew where he got his nickname. Assistant coach Ryan once took credit for the name, saying, "With that squeaky voice and the amount of times he'd been thrown out of senior parties with his tail dangling between his legs, what else would you call a rodent with slicked-back hair, the ears the size of Dumbo's?"

Whatever the case, you knew Mighty Mouse was lurking at school somewhere because his green shit-box was parked in the lot, haphazardly, on the east side of the building. Cam Jenkins and Randy Coltaire knew he would not be a problem. Mighty Mouse hated the jocks as much as they did, and besides, they knew he was a creature of habit. Being the Friday morning after Thursday night's two-for-one pitchers at Dave's Bar & Pizza, there was no doubt he was curled up somewhere on the second floor sleeping one off. The only way Cam and Randy might run into him is if he was locking up or he was scrambling downstairs to the girls' locker room, hoping to catch a glimpse of the cheerleaders in the shower.

Cam and Randy rode along the wooded trail at the far end of the complex, making sure not to be seen. The plan was, once they reached the student footpath, they would jump off their dirt bikes, cut the engines, and roll them the rest of the way. Ransacking the lockers would be easy money. They were confident that the practice squad would be sufficiently occupied because all were too busy trying to impress Coach Daniels to notice their presence. They took one last drag on their cigarettes and began traversing the footpath like two panthers closing in on a target.

"It will be like taking candy from a baby," Cam said.

"You know it," Randy said. "I mean, look at them down there. They've got their heads so far up Daniels's ass they won't know what hit them. Fucking, easy money man."

Both wore shit-eating grins, the kind only rebellious teens wore that never thought about tomorrow, only the thrill of now. They would do the deed and fly like the wind.

"All right, tie off," Cam said, slipping his T-shirt over his head. "Make sure you cover your nose, mouth, and chin. Keep it tight right beneath the eyes." Randy took off his T-shirt, revealing a bruise the size of a piston head.

"What the fuck is that?" Cam asked.

"My old man is back in town," Randy said, looking at the bruise. "I guess he got bored."

"Jesus, Randy. Jim's a fucking dick."

"Jim's a pussy, but I got him back good, you know. Hit him where it hurts. Once I knew he was adios for the night, I lifted a couple of ounces off him and went out to the garage to fire up a spliff."

"You best not be around if Jim finds out," Cam said. "He'll do you worse than a piston-sized bruise."

"He could try, but I'm ready bro." Randy lifted his pant leg and exposed a hunting knife sheathed to his ankle.

"Fuck, that blade could take down an elephant."

"Elephants and dickheads. And I don't plan on missing."

They rolled the bikes down the hill and hid behind the equipment shed. From there, they would rush the brick facade and hoist themselves up through the window, dropping themselves right into the locker room where they'd pop the locks, clean out the lockers, and fly like the Blue Fucking Angels. WAM-bam-thank-you-ma'am.

"Okay, you ready?" Cam said.

Randy nodded.

"Let's go."

They sprang out from behind the shed and sprinted toward the wall. Cam got there first and leapt up, grabbing the brick sill of the window. In a single move, he swung himself up like a pole vaulter, boots first through the opening, then turned around and reached for Randy's hands and pulled him on through.

Randy tossed Cam the bolt cutters and made his way to the door while Cam went down each row and up each column, popping every lock. The heavy-gauge bolt cutters snipped through the steel loops like a knife through warm butter, making quick work of it.

"Easy money," Randy said. In less than a minute, they had about thirty-five lockers open and began ransacking each one, looking through jackets, shirts, pants, books, and shoes.

"Check the shoes," Cam said. "No one ever thinks about the shoes." Cam tossed one of the gym bags to Randy and told him to fill it. Randy stuffed cash, watches, rings, cigarettes, a couple of AC/DC concert tickets, a few joints, everything he could get his hands on and stuffed them inside the bag. They moved rapidly along each column and row of lockers, grabbing all that they could.

Cam opened one of the last lockers and reached for a wallet, when he saw a picture taped inside the door. It was Colleen. His hand retreated, pausing for a moment, his surprise turning to anger. Frozen as if his Timberlands were hardening in concrete, he gazed at the picture, smiling back at him. It was the same smile Colleen laid on him in the cafeteria when they bumped into each other in the lunch line last spring. He opened the wallet that was tucked in the heel of a shoe and saw an ID of Jake Tanner. *She's Jake's girlfriend?* he thought to himself. *A fucking jock?*

Colleen Fitzgerald was high class from Westchester County, New York with plans and a future. Cam had neither. Like his father, and his father before him, Cam was a townie in the making. And as far back as he could remember, a Jenkins had been planted down in the Titicut territory. "Ever since the newcomers," his granddad used to say, bending his wizened elbow to a shooter of Wild Turkey, "the Jenkins' men have worked this God-given land."

Cam felt as though he was standing in quicksand when he heard Randy shout, "Come on, man, snap out of it. I can hear them coming!" The voice echoed and pounded inside Cam's head, returning him to the reality of the moment, while Randy quickly zipped up the bag and ran to the window. He hoisted himself up, but slipped a little on the wall. He struggled to find his footing as Cam came up from underneath and grabbed the bottom of Randy's boots, lifting him until he pulled himself through. "Hurry. They're coming!"

Cam glanced over his shoulder as he reached for the sill. He could hear cleats clicking on the other side of the door grow louder and draw closer when it stopped, and the door swung open. It was Jake Tanner and a slew of other teammates standing ape-like, their faces piping red with sweat and fury.

For a split second, there was silence; a sort of standoff so often seen in movies where two dueling gunmen stand knuckle down before drawing their weapons. But the silence did not last. A hot, metallic, "Get the Motherfuckers!" rang out as they charged after them. Cam kicked a laundry cart at the angry mass, barely escaping the outstretched arms, grabbing at his legs. He kicked one of them in the face as he jumped up and pulled himself through the window, struggling against the beefy arms clawing at his boots.

Randy mounted his bike and drove his heel through the kick-start. The powerful, two-stroke engine cranked over and ripped through the air. Freeing himself, and only a second behind, Cam leaped upon the seat of his bike and secured the gas tank beneath his crotch. He fired up the high-compression engine with a lightning-quick boot heel, spewing thick, bluish smoke into the air.

With enough torque to shoot a cannon, Randy pulled the hole-shot and jumped out in front of Cam. The heavy knobs chewed up the soil and grass, spitting out mounds of fresh till. They looked over their shoulder and saw the players burst out of the exit doors shouting at the top of their lungs. But the only thing Cam and Randy heard, as they tore across the end zone, was the winding of gears and the maniacal beat of their own drummer playing louder and faster as they powered through the hash marks. The chase was underway.

CHAPTER 3
BAD GIRLS JUST WANT TO HAVE FUN

In the partially unfinished basement of her uncle's summer home, Nicole Guthrie rolled off the cot onto the cold, concrete floor, dry heaving and hacking up a lung. She grasped her head between her hands and squeezed, desperate to stop the hammer like pounding.

She stretched out, kicking over a few empty beer cans, as her naked body delighted in the sweet relief of her cooling flesh. She wondered, lying there in a near-catatonic state, how many girls like her made promises to the man upstairs, swearing to never drink again, promising to be a good girl if God would only see them through. But she wondered even more, as she tucked her wobbly knees up under her chin, how many broke them.

Her lip curled into a funny smile knowing she could keep the God option open, tucked away in her back pocket, that is, if she had back pockets and knew where her pants were.

Niki slowly peeled herself off the cold floor and scooted over on her bare ass. She rocked herself to her knees, bracing her hands on the side of the cot, and pulled herself up on her wobbly legs as careful as a Flying Wallenda. She had walked this tightrope many times before and had always made it to the other side, her scuffed up knees and bruised reputation notwithstanding.

To find her balance, she closed her eyes for a moment and felt the carousel in her head dissipate, just enough so that walking seemed at least possible.

Grabbing a beach towel and cinching it around her waist, she made her way across the room, pausing to see her reflection in one of those mirrors, the kind you see hanging in bar rooms and pool halls advertising American beer companies with half-naked women in suggestive poses.

She rubbed her eyes to get a better look and saw a beat up whore staring back. Young and bodacious yes, but she looked worn and used with powder-blue eyeshadow smudged around her puffy eyes. Her hair fired off in different directions and it felt sticky to the touch. Sticky from what? She did not want to know. She wondered if Phyllis Diller ever looked so bad.

The pounding in her head began to wane. It was still there, dully, but the Neil Peart drum solo was behind her. She drew open the drapes and stepped out onto the private deck that overlooked Buzzards Bay. The morning sun was shocking and bright, but it felt good on her face as she closed her eyes and tilted her head back and breathed in the salt air. She enjoyed the westerly breeze passing over her skin with the coolness of silk, but the shrieks of morning gulls pounded her ears with all the driving force of a sledgehammer.

It had been one hell of a summer, she thought, gazing listlessly at Cuttyhunk Island in the distance. Come Monday morning, she would be a senior in high school and grinned at the endless possibilities of owning a new freshman class of naïve, goody two-shoes.

She looked down at her sunburnt toes to see a cooler full of beer and wine coolers and popped open the lid. She reached for a cold brew and held it to the back of her neck for a glorious second, before pulling back the tab and hoisting the can to her eager mouth. The bubbles on her lips tickled as the golden liquid passed over her tongue and down her throat. Her smile turned to a shit-eating grin, happy in the knowing, proud even that she had not exercised the "God Option." Her promise to the man upstairs to be a good girl and never drink again remained open, a card not yet played. She would broker that deal another day.

"What time is it?" a boy's voice cracked, coming from the backyard.

"What? Who is that? Oh shit ..." Niki ran down the steps and across the pool apron to see a fluff of messy, blond hair sticking out from the hammock.

"Who are you?" she asked.

"Shit. I thought my memory was bad."

"Just tell me your name?"

"It's Kevin. Hey, are these yours?" Kevin pulled a pair of dungaree shorts out from behind his head. They were Daisy Dukes, a size too small, frayed and worn with a red tongue patched over the left cheek.

"Cool, The Rolling Stones—" Kevin said.

"Give me those." Niki snatched them from his hands and slipped them on under her cinched towel.

"Hey, have you seen my bud?"

"Your bud?" Niki said.

9

"Yeah, Brad. Have you seen him? Six-foot-tall, with long dark hair, shooting Jägermeister and belting out Rebel Yell at the bar last night. Your friend was sucking face with him."

Like a sudden tremor tearing a chasm in the earth's crust, Niki's memory erupted from the dense, gray matter of her pickled brain. "Darrah!"

Niki shot up the back deck and threw open the slider with one quick hand. She dodged through the empty cans and bottles and bound towards the bedroom on the other side of the basement, poking her head inside the door. Not there. She ran up the basement stairs, cut through the kitchen, and stumbled up to the second floor. She checked the spare bedroom, but no Darrah. Sprinting down the hall, with her head tossing like a weighted gyroscope, she glanced through the open door of the bathroom and saw no one, but stopped. She heard something. The sounds of moaning and a waterbed sloshing. Niki threw open the door to see Darrah's ass bucking up and down, her jet-black hair sweeping behind her.

"Finish him off," Niki said, watching the beads of perspiration glisten like diamonds on Darrah's dark skin. "We have to get out of here. We're meeting Cam and Randy."

"You got it, Niki." Darrah pushed herself off and rolled out of bed. "I'm done with this boy scout, anyway."

"Hey, what about me?" the boy pleaded with a 'you owe me' look in his eyes.

"If you think this was about you," Darrah smirked, throwing the boy's dungarees at his face, "then you're dumber than the rest of them. Let's get out of here Niki, this guy bores me."

CHAPTER 4
TAKE IT ON THE RUN BABY

Cam and Randy entered the zone, that tunnel riders enter where everything around them disappears and all that is seen in the distance is the checkered flag.

Power shifting through the gears, they surged forward to the south end of the building. They passed the equipment facility before turning west, where they saw Mighty Mouse flashing the sign of the horns and cheering, his tongue hanging out and pumping his fists.

As they both screamed by, Cam pointed at the berm of dirt. He twisted back on the throttle and shifted his body weight forward and to the left, powering through the huge mound with his rear tire at a forty-five, chewing and spitting up a rooster tail twenty feet into the air.

Randy tracked Cam out of the berm and sped up on the long straightaway, heading across the practice field. They could see Jake Tanner and the rest of the jocks shouting and flipping them the bird, and could see Coach Daniels running into the building, no doubt to call the police.

Cam and Randy knew they were in the clear. They would only need to stay off the main roads to avoid being captured by the town cops. "The Bozos in Blue," Randy called them.

They didn't have anyone friendly to them on the force, not with their juvenile records and the constant pain-in-the-ass Cam's father had been to the police, but they didn't much care. They were supremely confident in their abilities to ride. The thought of getting caught by the "Bozos in Blue" never crossed their mind.

All teens have delusions of grandeur to some degree, but Cam and Randy's ran hotter than most: It was an, "In Your Face" kind of grandeur with a side order of "Whatcha-Gonna-Do-About-It."

With a twist of the wrist, they surged up and over the small crest, looping up the hill onto the narrow, student, walking path and burned through the thick canopy of trees. With the scene of the crime disappearing behind them, it was now only Cam and Randy riding in tandem like they had a hundred times before—for the pure rush of it.

Downshifting out of the tree line, they blasted across the tracks and took the power lines, climbing the heavily scarred access road cut with deep ruts and gullies. They reached the top of the hill and gunned it, chewing up and spitting out rock and dirt with each shifting burst of speed.

They flew over the next hill, catching air, where in the distance Cam noticed a police cruiser about three hundred yards ahead at the bottom of the hill. Quickly downshifting, he spun around to grab Randy's attention, both coming to an abrupt stop.

They both sat idling, their hands poised on the throttle and ready to fly if the cruiser made any sudden moves, but it remained still. Eerily still. All they could see was the sun reflecting off the chrome grill and the black, tinted glass. Not even a figure could be seen. Only a solitary cruiser, oddly out of place.

"What the fuck is he doing?" Randy asked. "There's no way the cops knew we came this way. And there wasn't enough time."

Cam placed his hand down on the bag of stolen goods and made sure it was secure before he peered back at the cruiser.

"I have no clue, and I don't want to find out. Come on man, we have to get the hell out of—"

"Wait," Randy said, "maybe he's just finishing jerking off and then he'll move on us."

Cam snickered. "Captain Cop choking his Tennille. That's about all they're good for."

"Shit. We have to make a decision fast." They both focused on the cruiser and looked for a tell: a window rolling down, a door opening, a trunk popping, brake lights, sirens, the static sound of a CB, the smell of bacon wafting from the tailpipe, anything that would indicate there was someone behind the tinted glass, watching their every move.

"God dammit," Randy said, revving his bike. "Why the fuck is he just sitting there?"

"I don't know, but there's no time to jerk around. We can bury this asshole in the dirt if he comes chasing." Cam reached down and grabbed a rock and threw it at the cruiser. It skipped a couple of times before taking a bounce off the hardpan and smashed into the left headlight.

"Shit, Cam! What was that?"

"Just watch and get ready to fly." Their hands tensed over the throttle, focusing dead ahead. "Come on, mother fucker," Cam said. "Put your dick in your pants and let's rock." But like before, there was no response. After smashing the headlight, Cam was convinced there was no one behind the wheel. He would have hightailed it after them if there was. "Come on man. Let's get out of here."

They revved the engines and started down the hill when suddenly a glare of blue lights flashed and sirens wailed. The cruiser's high beams blasted their eyes and a commanding voice roared out over the loudspeaker, telling them to halt.

"Go! Go! Go!" Cam said, "When we get to Walnut Creek, follow my lead!" Cam looked over his shoulder to see an oversized, chrome grill, like the teeth of a giant, staring him in the face and bearing down. Shifting into third and fourth, they flew over the hills and blasted through the deep trenches.

The cruiser was kicking and jumping and bottoming out. One of the hub caps popped off twenty feet in the air as his front quarter collapsed. Cam smirked, but knew the cop was determined. Come hell or high water, he meant to bring him and Randy in. And a few hundred taxpayer-dollars' worth of damage to the cruiser would not stop him.

They pushed towards Turner's Pass as the railroad tracks were just around the next bend that ran parallel to the old logging road. Cam knew the road was overgrown, making it difficult to see where the road ended and the creek began. He would draw the cop into a kind of mousetrap where he and Randy were the cheese, and the creek was a loaded spring ready to snap. They just needed to sandbag it a little and let the cruiser catch up for his plan to work.

Cam pressed his palm towards the ground, indicating to ease off the gas, but not too much; they needed to maintain enough speed to create the illusion that an all-out chase was still underway. Looking behind, he saw the cruiser overshoot the turn and cut the wheel hard. The vehicle skidded up and over the side, taking out a few small maples, before it straightened out and barreled towards them. With lights still flashing and sirens blaring, he was closing in. The creek was just ahead.

Taking measure, Cam looked over his shoulder one more time and tapped the side of his head twice. The time was now. Their adrenaline surged and their nerves tightened in what seemed to play out in slow motion like a dying phonograph: 500 feet, 400 feet, 300 ... 200 ... 50... and in an instant like gunpowder exploding, Randy broke right; Cam broke left. The road dropped out beneath the wheels of the speeding cruiser, sending it flying through the air like an Evel Knievel jump gone bad. To witness this maneuver from the sky, it would have looked like the Blue Angels rolling out of formation at ninety degrees, with one plane nosediving towards the ground.

Cam slowed to a stop and pulled the T-shirt down off his face. He looked at the cruiser sinking beneath the rushing water and lit a cigarette. Randy, who was on the west side, sat perched on his bike high on the bluff and gazed down at the huge plumes of steam belching from the radiator. Cam drew down his smoke and flicked it into the water below. He gestured over to Randy to move out as he returned his eyes to the creek and watched the cruiser list.

Riding off along the high end of the bank, behind them, a single arm dressed in police blue struggled to pry open the driver-side door against the surge. Cam and Randy never looked back.

CHAPTER 5
HELLS BELLS

With a sleek, dark thigh—the kind only delivered with a blend of tropical oils and the unadulterated worship of the sun gods—Darrah kicked the cooler's lid shut and hoisted up an end.

"Come on, Nik. Let's ride out the summer."

"From where I was standing," Niki said, "it looked like you were 'riding out the summer' just fine. Bare-assed on top of Brad."

"What, that boy scout?" Darrah said, her teeth hot white against her complexion. "Whatever, Nik. Just help me get this cooler in the back seat."

Pure muscle with sex appeal is how Darrah described her '79 Trans Am. Equipped with a T-top and enough horsepower to rip a hole in the sky. It was black and shiny with a gold phoenix emblazoned across the hood that seemed to shout... *Catch me if you can.*

Darrah opened the door and slid her bare thighs over the seat. The feel of leather gliding under her silky skin always gave her a slight thrill, but it was the rumble of the four-barrel that shot vibrations up her legs and made her want to drive fast; really, really, fast...

Darrah turned it over and jumped on the gas. The raw, unadulterated power pulsated beneath the shape of her calf when she dropped the hammer.

Niki shot back with tremendous force. The explosive power glued her ass to the seat like a drunk's to a barstool.

"Oh, my fucking God, Darrah ... my stomach just kissed my boobs." Darrah jerked the wheel and spun a one-eighty, leaving a stretch of baked rubber. As the Trans Am came out of the fishtail, Niki managed to pull her knees up under herself and knelt to grab the visor, her blonde hair blowing wildly behind her.

"Wooooo Hoooo!"

"Hold on Nik, you may lose your top!"

"Go for it!"

Niki's arms stretched tight as the machine lurched out from the cloud of smoke. Darrah put on her Wayfarer sunglasses and pushed in a Rolling Stones cassette. She leaned her head back comfortably against the seat, checked her side mirrors, and planted her painted toes down on the pedal. "Hold on Nik!"

The speed increased rapidly as Darrah found her line and blasted up Route 88. The two-lane suicide trap ran dead straight for eleven miles without any barriers or grass medians of any kind. There was only the sun, the road, and a breath of alcohol between you and whatever vehicle was barreling down from the opposite direction.

Niki pulled her head down from the T-top and planted her butt squarely in the leather seat, exhilarated.

"Holy shit!"

"Fast enough for you darling?" Darrah said, snapping on some gum.

"Have you seen my hair? I look like Jon Bon Jovi with lipstick."

To say Niki's hair was windblown was perhaps the greatest understatement since a Boston weatherman called for "a little snow" the day before The Blizzard of '78, which buried all of New England in three feet of heavy pack.

Niki ran her fingers through her wild mane the best she could and reached inside the cooler for a beer.

"What's your pleasure?"

"Seagrams," Darrah said, lighting a cigarette.

"One Seagrams coming up." She reached through the sloshing ice and grabbed a bottle.

"Ready?"

"I'm ready," Darrah said.

"Brace yourself. Here it comes."

Niki proceeded to work the bottle between Darrah's thighs.

"Oh my God!" Darrah squealed, her legs bouncing. "That is so fucking cold!"

Darrah gave Niki a playful shove and lifted the Seagrams to her lips. She sucked down a few long swallows, beads of moisture dripping from the bottle onto her skin.

The cassette advanced to the next track with the unmistakable vibe of Mick Taylor's up-tempo guitar licks pouring out on the track "Bitch."

"Fuck, Darrah, I love this song. Turn it up."

Darrah switched the wine cooler to her left hand, and with a rather skillful twist of the wrist, turned up the volume with her right. She began to tap her left foot and flicked the cigarette butt out the window.

She lifted her left leg and guided the steering wheel with her inner thigh while gesturing with her hands as if playing a trumpet to the big brassy sound until she noticed a car up ahead.

"Look at what we have here," she said, tasting her lips. "We have ourselves a John-Boy, twelve o'clock."

Niki saw the rear of a station wagon roughly three hundred yards ahead; it was fully battened down with beach chairs, floats, and two children's bicycles hanging from a rack. Ahead of the wagon, perhaps two hundred yards away, a green traffic light dangled from the cross wires, soon to turn yellow.

Nicki hoisted her butt up on the passenger-side door and grabbed the center T.

She unsnapped the button to her cutoff jeans and tugged them down off her hips. "You got it Darrah, you got it!"

Closing in, the speedometer's needle passed seventy-five, now eighty. The nose of the Trans Am closed the gap rapidly, becoming uncomfortably close. Blurry bumper stickers, plastered all over the rear window of the wagon, now came into view.

Darrah sat cool, anticipating just the right moment the traffic light would switch from orange to red. The idea was not only to pass the wagon and gun it through the intersection, but to pass close enough so the driver (in this case John-Boy), would be delivered a ham sandwich, hold the mayo, like a waitress delivers a car-hop tray from the Dog & Suds.

The light turned yellow.

"Get ready," Darrah said, "hang it low!"

"Wooooo Hooooo. Hit it!" Niki dropped her full weight, stretching her arms like tightropes against the T-roof. Using her calf muscles for extra balance, she arched her back and dropped her ass. She looked like one of those girls on a truck's mud flap. With a slight turn of the wheel, Darrah pulled out from behind the wagon and crossed over the centerline. She eyed the line carefully on her right quarter, while simultaneously watching for the traffic light.

The speedometer's needle passed eighty-five, ninety. Niki held on tight, fighting the force of the wind rippling the skin on her face. Her hair sprayed out behind her like a storm swell and felt a surge of adrenaline. She could see the hands of John Boy's watch resting comfortably on the door, his wrist hairs blowing over the band. The traffic light turned red. Darrah buried the pedal, pushing the needle past ninety. As she gunned it past, Niki bounced her ass up and down, making contact with the back of John Boy's hand; it looked like some kind of meat puppet on a pogo stick. Mrs. John-Boy, in the passenger seat, gasped in fright. The two boys in the back seat let out a raucous cheer before the station wagon swerved onto the shoulder and skidded to a stop.

Blasting through the red light, Darrah and Niki laughed hysterically as they glanced over their shoulders at the stalled wagon.

Wiggling her shorts back up over her rump, Niki sat back in the seat, feeling pumped.

"You should have seen John-Boy's eyes bug out of his head," Darrah said. "It was a perfect moon landing."

"Oh my god, Darrah, Mrs. John-Boy was like, 'Oh my word, oh my word, a naked buttocks.'"

"I saw the horror in her eyes. How about the boys hanging their heads out of the windows, their tongues drooling like dogs in heat?"

"Boys will be boys, right?" Niki said.

They settled back in their seats and enjoyed the sun streaming through the T-top and listened to the music. Niki kicked her feet up on the dash and began to paint her toenails with a sparkly fluorescent yellow. She turned her calf in and out and admired how sexy the color looked glowing next to her golden skin. "Randy is going to like that."

Darrah raised an eyebrow and smiled, then glanced at the fuel gauge redlining empty. "Ah shit! Thirsty again."

"There's a station at the next intersection," Niki said, "take a right and enter on the left."

"Nik, can you reach under the seat and find my purse? I think I have two twenties in there." Niki reached under and pulled out Darrah's bohemian-looking purse, fringed in reds and blacks, and placed it on her lap. She began to sift and sort through makeup, some loose change, cigarettes, roaches and clips, a condom, but could not find the bills.

"Are you sure it's in here?" Niki asked.

"It's gotta be there, Nik, keep looking. Actually, just grab the wheel." Niki grabbed the wheel and Darrah reached in the purse and ran her hand through. "Shit! No money. I don't believe it."

"Fuck, Darrah, are you sure you had it?"

"Yes, I'm sure, only—"

"Only what?" Niki asked.

"When I was dancing with that Boy Scout last night, I may have left my purse at the bar."

"Fuck, he stole your money."

"No, he didn't steal it."

"How can you be so sure?"

"Because, I would have found it this morning when I rifled through his pockets. Shit! Now what?"

"Bang a right at the gas station, I got a plan."

Darrah swung in from the side road and pulled forward so she could see through the windows of the gas station. It appeared empty except for some dweeb-ish looking teen working the register.

"You got that look in your eyes," Darrah said, her lips pulling back slightly. "I can see that brain of yours working overtime."

"Easy target, Darrah." Niki pointed her finger. "Look behind the cash register. A high school dweeb, no older than sixteen. He won't know what hit him."

"Like taking candy from a baby."

"Pull ahead and fill it. I got this."

While Darrah pulled up, Niki fixed her hair and applied some baby oil to her skin. She thickened her lash with a sweep of mascara and juiced her lips with some gloss. "Be ready," Niki said, stepping out of the car. "We may need to book it out of here in a hurry."

Darrah gave a nod and stepped out of the car, watching Niki strut towards the station's door, exaggerating her hip movement with every stride. Before Niki went in, she could see the boy through the station's window nervously pushing his bangs off his face. She flashed him a smile, but he awkwardly looked over his shoulder dumbfounded she could be smiling at him. He did not get many looks from members of the opposite sex. And from girls like Niki? Never.

"Well, hi there," Niki said, the bell on the door clanking open and then shutting. The boy's eyes darted left and right and clumsily said, "Um ... hi."

"See my girlfriend out there. Yes, right there. It's okay to look." The boy turned his head, hesitantly, to see Darrah squatting, checking the tire pressure while the tank filled. Darrah smiled at the boy and waved. His gum fell from his mouth and plunked on the counter.

Niki pinched the gum between her fingers and placed it back in the boy's gaping mouth. "She sure is pretty, huh?" The boy fumbled for words; his eyes never lifted higher than Niki's halter top. "What's your name, sugar?"

"B-b, Billy," he stuttered, his face turning red.

"Well, B-b, Billy, I think you're awfully handsome." She reached up and cupped the side of his cheek. "Don't you think I'm pretty? Hmm?" She tugged down on her halter, exposing all but her nipples. She then reached for his hand and placed it on her chest, guiding his boyish fingers over her supple skin.

Billy swallowed hard and his hands trembled. His eyelids dipped and was about ready to faint, when Niki said, "I think you like that." She glanced down and pointed at his crotch. "I know he does."

She drew a seductive finger along the counter and turned with a swerve of the hip. "I need two packs of Marlboro Lights and a couple lighters." She walked over to pick up a bag of ice and some ginger ale and returned to the counter. "How much do I owe you, Billy?"

He pushed his bangs back off his forehead and punched the return on the cash register. "Um, let's see. Ten dollars in gas, two packs of Marlboro Lights ... Um, ginger ale, ice—" Niki reached up and pressed her finger across his lips.

"Sh..." She reached for her pocket to get some money, then stopped.

"Wait. Can I use your bathroom?"

"Um, sure, it's right over there." She could feel his eyes bore through her cutoff shorts as she strutted to the bathroom.

Placing her hand on the doorknob, she pretended it would not budge. "Can you help me, Billy? There's something wrong with this door." Billy looked outside at the pumps and saw only Darrah sunning herself, smoking a cigarette, and waving at him. He waved back awkwardly and thought about the open register.

"Come on, Billy, I really need to go." He hesitated, then thought about how much trouble it was to cancel out the register, only to run everything through again. And besides, what was the worst that could happen?

"Coming," Billy said, stepping toward the bathroom with some urgency. She placed her hand on the back of his shoulder while he turned the knob rather easily, opening the door.

"Wow," Niki said. "You're so strong." Billy looked a bit surprised, when Nicki immediately pulled him into the bathroom and closed the door. She pressed him up against the tiled wall and kissed his lips and neck. Her hands moved over his sparrow-like chest and worked them down to his belt, feverishly loosening his buckle, before yanking his trousers right down to his greasy sneakers.

"Wait," she said. "I need protection. You don't want to be a daddy, do you?"

"Um, Um, no. What's happening?"

"I'm about to have sex with you, Billy, that's what's happening."

Billy's eyes were the eyes of a puppet. He stuttered and stammered, unable to speak, until he felt silky fingers gliding along the length of his erect penis. "Jeepers Creepers!"

"Hey, you know what? You sell single condoms. I saw them behind the register: ribbed, studded, and lubricated. Oh, and even glow in the dark. Now, how exciting would that be?"

Billy felt his Adam's apple ripple and his penis twitch.

"I want you to keep your eyes closed and the light off," Niki said. "You're in for a big surprise."

"When can I open them? I think I saw a spider."

"You don't want to ruin the surprise, do you? You can open them the moment you feel something moist and hot." Niki tugged up her shorts and closed the door behind her. "Remember, keep your eyes closed, Billy, and I promise you a big, big surprise. Just think how much you can brag to all your friends. I'll be right back."

With a goofy smile, Billy closed his eyes and dropped his head in his hands and sat in the dark. *My friends are never going to believe me*, he thought, *GEEZ I don't even believe it*. He leaned back timidly and found himself wedged between the toilet and sink, but he was smiling. Billy was in love.

Niki quickly emptied the cash register drawer. She glanced at Darrah through the window distracting a couple of men that pulled in for gas. Niki grabbed several cartons of cigarettes, lighters, snacks, a sheet of lottery tickets, and all the Trojans she could. "I found the condom I want you to use, big Billy. I'll be right there."

With every passing second, Billy's excitement grew, but he felt vulnerable and scared. The smell of urine and old meatballs made him dry heave. His hand slipped into the toilet water when he heard, "I'm coming, Billy."

THE KEEPERS

Those were the last words Billy heard. As he sat there in a sticky mess, alone in the dark, wedged between the sink and the toilet bowl, he listened to the door clink open and then clink shut before he heard the humiliating sound of tires squealing.

CHAPTER 6
CAN'T YOU SEE THE SIGNS?

To prevent Carl's urine-soaked pants from seeping through the back seat of the cruiser, Officer Boo Stevens laid a vinyl tarp down before he guided him through the door and cuffed his hand to the center ring. "For your protection, Carl, you understand."

The tow truck was on scene and just hooked the El Camino. The operator pulled up alongside and said, "It looks like there's some body damage around the front quarter and the wheel well. And I think there's a bent tie rod or two.

"Alright Sonny. Haul it to the station and unload in the service lot."

"Copy that."

Sonny arched his head forward and took a close look in the back seat. "Is that Carl Jenkins? Hey, Carl. Officer Stevens, you have to cuff him like that?"

"Chief's orders, Sonny."

"Well, that's that, then," Sonny said matter-of-factly. "Hey Carl, let's work somethin' out on that fuel pump. I can get that '57 Chevy of yours hummin' like a bird." Sonny knew it was unlikely Carl would respond. He saw that glazed look before, like no one was there. It was the same look others had in Nam.

"I'll talk to you later, Carl. You take care now." Sonny thumbed a plug of tobacco deep inside his cheek, while Officer Stevens tipped his hat and drove off.

Looking in his rearview mirror, Stevens noticed Carl was conscious, but barely. He popped open the glove-box for a pack of cigs, he always carried with him, and passed one through.

"Smoke?"

Carl nodded and leaned forward, pinching his lips around the filter as Stevens lit it. He let Carl smoke it down some before taking it from him and tamping the butt in the ashtray.

"Now, Carl," Stevens said, "why don't you tell me what happened back there? How in God's good name did you end up under your dash?"

Carl's eyes drifted towards the window and they shut before his head snapped back. "Come on, Carl, stay with me. What happened out there?"

In a low whisper of a voice, barely audible, Carl said, "They came out of nowhere. Their teeth dripping blood. Then, there was only darkness."

"Darkness? You mean you blacked out? Is that what you mean, Carl? Stay with me now..." Carl's eyes closed, and his head fell to the side when a transmission came over the radio.

Possible 10-26 at Titicut High School, officer please respond. A second transmission immediately followed.

Officer Stevens, I got that reg for you — Mass plate: Charlie—Johnny—Zebra—7—3—9 registered to Stevens, Carl Stevens.

"Thank you, Polly, copy that. Carl's in custody now. The vehicle is being towed back to the station."

"Copy that Officer Stevens, you're welcome."

Boo sped up and took a left on Park Street, then headed towards the center green when a third transmission came over the radio in as many minutes.

A possible 10-31. Officer Harding is not responding to his radio. Last seen entering the cutoff road at Trader's Bluff, heading towards the high-tension wires.

"Lots going on for such a small town," Jenkins said, his mouth twitching like he had an itch.

"Glad to see you're back, Carl," Officer Stevens said. "It's the last weekend of summer and the kids like to raise hell before they head back to the classroom on Monday. Happens every year."

Stevens adjusted his rearview mirror until his eyes met Carl's and followed up on a previous line of questioning. "Before you nodded off, Carl, you said something about there being nothing but darkness back there. What did you mean by that?"

Carl maintained his glassy stare. His eyes were still locked on Boo's as if he did not hear the question. "Look Carl, I'm not trying to bust you on this. I'm your friend here talking. Now, the chief, well, that's another matter, but you can always talk to me. I know things have been hard on you, but sometimes that's the best time to talk things out."

Boo thought he saw a softening in Carl's stare; there was some kind of understanding in the eyes. He tried again. "Carl, tell me, what did you see back there? What made you swerve off the road and piss your pants?"

The soft stare turned egg white. Carl's eyes rolled up under his lids and he convulsed. "Carl, you alright? What the hell's going on? Are you going to get sick back there?"

Stevens maneuvered his arm behind the seat and rolled down the window; he got Carl's head moving towards the opening. He grabbed the Dunkin' Donut bag and passed it back to him. "Carl, stick your head right in there and breathe in deep. Go on, breathe."

Carl fumbled with the bag, but managed to get it over his mouth. "That's it, deep breaths," Boo instructed. "In and out. In and out. That's it. A few more times. You're doing good."

Stevens could see the bag contract and expand and could see a calm wash over Carl as his chest cavity relaxed and his body became laggard.

For the moment, Carl's demons were silenced and the lunatic in his brain sedate. The calm flowed through his body like a river of Valium. He removed the bag and revealed the gentle smile of a man at peace, a man whose brain, like scattered pieces to a psychedelic puzzle, finally assembled themselves to a complete and vivid picture. If only for a moment.

Carl lay his head back against the seat and turned to look out the window. He watched the blue-sky filter through the canopy of oak trees that lined the center green planted over three hundred years ago.

Maintaining his peaceful gaze and speaking aloud as if speaking to no one in particular, he said in a clear voice, "You asked me what I'd seen out there today. What could make a man lose himself like I did. Well, it's always the same, Boo, only today was more terrifyingly real like a coming storm you can't stop. What I saw out there today was the end, and it's coming for us all."

Officer Stevens swallowed hard and fell silent. He drove around the square and headed towards the station on the west side of the swamp. He sped past the dense cedar and thickets of maple that ran along that stretch of road and turned into the entrance way of One Police Plaza — a virtual fortress of white concrete structures rising from the plaza grounds like battering rams. But it wasn't always this way.

Prior to 1974, police and fire departments were on the east side of town, housed in a refurbished, grain warehouse, but that all changed when Jacob

Briggs, town selectman, stood up in an open town meeting to propose that police and fire be relocated on a tract of land that sat undisturbed on the western side of town.

It was a brash proposal; the town's residents knew the land had been in the Briggs family since 1623, (granted by royal charter), only two years after his ancestor, Clement Briggs, arrived in Plymouth Colony.

The cynical among them, which included all but a few, thought the proposal terribly convenient for Briggs, that if passed, would line the young selectman's pockets with taxpayer money. New Englanders, if nothing else, were proud Yankees and knew the value of a dollar; and although they were already suspicious of the young selectman, (a trait born of blood and custom), they were even more suspicious of their hard-earned tax dollars ill-used in service to Briggs with kick-backs and favors owed.

Only three days following the proposal, it was passed. The new facilities would be built on Briggs' land and construction would begin in the spring and continue at breakneck speed until its completion. It was found out, quite by accident, not only did Selectman Briggs lose on the deal, (nine cents on the dollar, a deal a New Englander could get behind), but he was left broke and in arrears.

Word had it, Briggs was so despondent he went into seclusion, but less than a year after One Police Plaza was complete, a wallet, a pair of shoes, and a few scattered teeth were discovered by an amateur photographer deep within the swamp. Forensics positively identified the teeth as belonging to John Clement Briggs. His body was never found.

One Police Plaza was more of a complex of strongholds, rather than a structure to house those who serve and protect. No matter how many times Carl had been brought in, he could not help but be astonished at the buildings resembling fortified bomb shelters.

Officer Stevens drove past the many municipal buildings and alongside the structures that housed the first responders and emergency response teams. Police headquarters loomed large just beyond. The building seemed to swim up on you like a tidal wave, creating a disconcerting, frightening appearance when the sun rose against its eastern facade.

Officer Stevens drove around to the rear entrance and parked in the receiving area where detainees were taken into custody. He opened the rear door, unlocked the handcuffs, and guided Carl's head, making sure he found his balance.

"Okay, Carl Jenkins," Stevens said, gesturing his arm towards the door, "I think you know the way."

Carl rubbed his wrist and took a moment to look at the expanse behind him. His eyes travelled up along a massive steel frame that shot up over three hundred feet into the air.

"Communications tower," Stevens said with an air of pride. "We are always thinking about the safety of this community, Carl Jenkins. Now, let's not keep the chief waiting."

Stevens punched in a five-digit code on the security panel. A second passed before the light turned green releasing the lock. "After you, Mr. Jenkins." But before they passed through the receiving door, a tow truck pulled up alongside. "I offloaded the El Camino right over there in section B," Sonny said, tossing Officer Stevens the keys. "Stop by the garage, Carl. I'll keep a hold on that fuel pump."

Stevens guided Carl through the doors into a small, back hallway leading to the holding cells. The cells were on the left-hand side, opposite a few private offices for senior officers, including Chief Elias Hicks, as well as a break room and an interrogation room. Passing thru, Officer Bruce Durst walked by drinking a coffee.

"Where you off to, Bruce?"

"Responding to a burglary down at the high school," Durst said.

"No word from Officer Harding?"

"He's not answering his radio."

"Keep trying. The electrical interference from the power grid really likes to mess with them radios. Right this way, Carl."

Stevens opened the first cell door on his left, located directly across from the chief's office. "In you go, Carl. The chief will be with you in a minute. And just some friendly advice. If I were you, I'd keep the 'everything turned black, and they're coming for us all' stuff to yourself, hmm?" Carl moved to the back of the cell and sat on the hard bench that ran the length of the wall. He relaxed his head back and watched Officer Stevens through the iron bars entering the chief's office and closing the door behind him. There was a highly polished brass sign plated to the door which read: Elias Hicks, Chief of Police. You May Pray To God But I Cast All Judgement.

For the moment, at least, Carl felt safe from his dark visions, but he still needed to face Hicks. That was sometimes worse. Although Carl was not a man of God—He hadn't done much good for him lately, he would say—there were times like these, especially facing Hicks, he felt it never hurt to cover all the bases a man could cover. He peeled his eyes back from the brass sign, folded his hands beneath his chin, and prayed for merciful judgement.

CHAPTER 7
MARSHMALLOW CLOUDS
AND MARMALADE SKIES

Jenkins Field was a stretch of land that used to be a working farm until 1946. It was around that time, VE Day, nearly a year on, when things took a bad turn.

Cam's grandfather returned from the war riding a wheelchair, unable to perform the duties of a farmer. He had ideas of leveraging bank money to buy new equipment and hire a couple of hands, just enough to carry the operation until the farm began earning money. But in the end, the bank said no.

The family began to sell off parcels of land to pay their bills until there weren't any other parcels left to sell, at least none that someone wanted to buy. And when that happened, the money eventually ran out, leaving Cam's grandmother to go find other work.

For a time, she worked at Linfield Convalescent Home and later worked for old man Wilbur pickling cows tongues and pigs' feet. The very idea that someone would eat these cleaved animal parts, soaking in brine, resembling one of Dr. Mengele's evil experiments was a disturbing and nauseating thought. But as she would say, "Not that pretty to look at it, I grant you, but you fix them up all sweet like with candied yams and they're damn good eating."

The acreage surrounding the homestead stretched out towards a dense tree line at the rear. The barn, far off the main road, was set behind the house surrounded by heavy branches and untended fields. Years of unfettered growth and neglect provided the perfect cover for Cam and Randy's comings and goings. They were nearly invisible. Just the way they liked it.

Riding into the field, Cam could see the corrugated metal of the barn's roof just ahead. Below the gable, with his tail wagging frantically, Cam's dog, Whitey, sat at attention like a sentry with his head and chest high. Over a mile away

Whitey could hear the whine of the two-stroke engines whenever Cam was on approach. And whenever he did, he would take his position in the loft and stand watch until his master returned. He would stay there, poised, until he knew Cam saw him and then....

Off with a jerk of the head, Whitey's legs were already pushing at full stride when they hit the ground in a flash of fur. He bound towards Cam and Randy, hurdling over branches, and wound his way through the tall grass.

Ever since Whitey and Cam found each other, it was the same routine: Cam would return and Whitey was off like cannon fire; seventy-five pounds of coal-black gunpowder, all but a single, white foot, shooting out from the loft.

It was because of Whitey's unique color markings and because of an exchange Cary Grant and Audrey Hepburn had on the big screen in '74 that led to Cam naming him Whitey.

During that hot, New England summer, Carl brought Cam to the drive-in theatre for the evening's double feature. The opening picture was a movie called *Charade*, starring Cary Grant and Audrey Hepburn. During an exchange, Hepburn's character is trying to determine if Grant's character is trustworthy:

Hepburn: *Alex, how can you tell if anyone's lying or not?*
Grant: *You can't.*
Hepburn: *There must be some way.*
Grant: *There's an old riddle about two tribes of Indians. The Whitefeet always tell the truth and the Blackfeet always lie. So, one day you meet an Indian, you say, "Hey, Indian, what are you, a truthful Whitefoot or a lying Blackfoot?" He says, "I'm a truthful Whitefoot." But which is he?*
Hepburn: *Why couldn't you just look at his feet?*
Grant: *Because he's wearing moccasins.*

Years later, Cam would remember this exchange when he needed to give the dog a name. He was Cam's *Whitefoot.*

It was late morning and the September sun had just lifted above the forest canopy. The light cast a glow across the swishing fields of goldenrod and the air was sweet and calm. It was a tranquil scene, so often captured on New England postcards, a stark contrast to the chaos that went down at the high school earlier, where a burglary turned into a high-speed chase leaving a cop at the bottom of Walnut Creek.

Now, seeing the familiar tuft of black fur barreling towards them with a pinkish tongue hanging out, Cam and Randy cut back the speed allowing Whitey to circle around them like a herding dog circles sheep. They motored their bikes near idle, riding over the soft bed until they killed the engines and pushed them into the barn.

Cam tossed the gym bag full of stolen goods onto the workbench and immediately fell into a pile of hay wrapping Whitey up with both hands. They tossed around like a couple of kids playing in a leaf pile. Whitey licked his face, neck, back, and shoulders, and hopped up and down like a rabbit. Cam could barely breath from the onslaught.

"Whitey thinks you're a Slim Jim, man," Randy said. "You're nothing but a piece of meat."

"Good boy, Whitey, Good boy," Cam said, barely getting the words out past Whitey's sloshing tongue. Cam finally managed to work himself free from the bouncing fur and reached his hand inside the cooler.

"Heads up!" Cam said, tossing Randy a beer. He then grabbed a cold one for himself and proceeded to spill the stolen contents of the gym bag onto the workbench.

They separated the cash from the rest of the pull and counted out seventy-five dollars. The non-cash items were counted one at a time: one swatch, a pocketknife, a couple of necklaces, several school rings, money clip, a loose joint, a couple of concert tickets. And then Randy palmed a gold necklace with a locket.

"Hey, Cam, get a load of this." Randy tossed Cam the locket. "You know that dumbass, Jake Tanner? It's a picture of himself inside. Take a look."

Cam studied the locket, looking at the cheap but ornate inlay. He then flipped it over to read the words inscribed on the back: *Colleen, I'm sorry.*

"Colleen, I'm sorry." Cam read the inscription aloud, somewhat bewildered. "Jesus, Jake had a picture of Colleen in his locker. No wonder why. They probably hooked up sometime over the summer."

"I know her, Cam," Randy said. "She's that girl from New York. Her old man is some kind of developer. Bucko dinero. My old man hit him up for some work over there on Red Mill road." He noticed Cam's face turning red. "Come on man, who cares if Joe Football hooked up with her?"

"I don't fucking care," Cam snapped. "It's just—"

"Just what, man?"

Cam tossed the locket onto the workbench with the other stuff and lit a smoke.

"What's up, Cam? You like that tight-ass? That chastity belt of hers is locked down so tight, not even Harry Houdini could pick it. Now Darrah, their ain't a man alive that wouldn't give up his life to Uncle Sam for a sweet piece of that. You're one lucky dude."

Cam gave Randy a playful shove and sat down on a milk crate with Whitey at his feet.

"Dude, I'm not the only lucky one. Niki G just about busts out of that halter top."

"I can attest. I can attest," Randy said. "Hey, you remember last summer at Dave's, when we were all there shooting pool and having a slice? And that dude, Brian, took a beer—"

"Yeah, I remember," Cam interjected. "You mean when Brian and Steve Murphy walked in?"

"Exactly. Remember both of them idiots came in to pick up a couple of pies and ordered a pitcher of beer while they waited?"

Cam burst out again, recalling the memory.

Randy went on. "And Brian, all looking like Frankenstein when he turned his head to check out Niki strutting by, trying not to be too obvious, when his whole body shifted on the barstool and knocked over a pitcher of beer into Steve's lap?"

"Oh my God, Fuckin'-ey. Remember the look on Steve's face when he shot up from the barstool trying to cover his hard-on through his beer-soaked pants?"

"Oh my God, I fucking lost it," Randy spouted. "When I saw him running out of the bar covering his balls. And Niki getting in his face, using her pool cue to lift his hands from his crotch, saying, 'What's the matter, Stevey? You see a pretty girl and you piss your pants?'"

Cam could barely breath over his laughter. "Did you see the look on that idiot's face? That was one of the funniest things I'd ever seen."

"It was, man." Randy said. "By the way, when are Niki and Darrah coming over?"

"Late morning. We got a little time to burn."

Randy knew what that meant and pulled out the cellophane bag from his back pocket and rolled a joint. He turned on the radio and out of the speaker came the sounds of Eddie Van Halen playing the hard-driving riff of

"Unchained" on his Kramer 5150. Randy passed the joint to Cam to take a toke, then grabbed a threshing flail hanging on the barn's wall. He struck his best rock star stance and started ripping the virtual guitar, filling the barn with electrically charged adrenaline.

Cam laid down with Whitey and let the THC wash over his body. From his faraway place he gazed at Randy's fingers flying up and down the flail, squeezing out every droplet of sound. He looked like a man possessed, and perhaps he was. His hands slid over the neck like liquid motion, blurring sound and color as a wash of sunlight bounced off the beads of sweat clinging to the strings, warping any discernible form. A shapeless spectrum emerged, like a cloud-bank of incandescent hues waving into a mind-numbing cadence of symphonic illusion, blending reality with fantasy.

Cam drifted further away, away to a weightless place; it was a place where the sands ebb through the hourglass of time, and where a kaleidoscope of dreams soar on the wings of butterflies over marshmallow clouds and marmalade skies.

CHAPTER 8
OATHS, LIES, AND SCARY THINGS

Five minutes came and went, then twenty, when Carl began to fidget inside the cell. He got up and paced around, and immediately sat back down again, dropping his head between his knees.

He grabbed his left hand to calm his twitching fingers when the door opened to Hicks's office and Officer Stevens exited, leaving the door partially open.

Carl lifted from the bench and watched Officer Boo Stevens make his way down the long corridor to his desk, never acknowledging Carl, like he forgot he was in the cell.

Carl returned his attention back to Hicks's office and peered in through the partially open door. Inside, he saw a pair of black boots perched on a large, walnut desk. An enormous hand came into view, parsing through a couple of pages of reports, when Carl saw Hicks's wrist turn over and a pair of eyes glared down at his watch face.

The chair rolled back from the desk and faced the window. A minute ticked by, then ten; there was no movement at all. No sound. There was no rustling of papers, no phone calls, no interruptions, no scratching a head, nothing. Only a man sitting motionless in his chair and the sound of heart-stopping silence.

For a moment, Carl thought maybe Hicks fell asleep. It had also flashed through his mind that if there was a God, and God was a fair man, that in fact Hicks wasn't asleep at all, but dead as a doornail. Perhaps dying suddenly from a heart attack, or bad karma, or maybe even a blood vessel exploding in his brain rendering him catatonic. It might even open Carl's eyes to at least the possibility that God did not abandon him and was on his side after all. Today, however, would not be that day.

With a simple lift from his chair, the question whether God was on his side, or not, had been answered once again. Hicks stepped away from his desk and passed through the door, where he stood as a pillar of stone and stared down at Jenkins.

"Coffee, for Mr. Jenkins—black ..." The officer in training jumped from his desk and poured a hot cup to the brim. With a brisk step, the officer's eyes glued to the cresting liquid, he made sure to pass the cup to Hicks without spilling a drop. "Thank you, officer," Hicks said, as he grabbed the cup, his eyes never shifting away from Jenkins. He stepped forward and passed his hand through the bars. "Come forward, Mr. Jenkins, looks like you could use a cup of coffee. Black, if memory serves?"

Carl knew Hicks wasn't asking. He got to his feet and approached the way an unprepared student might approach the blackboard after being summoned by his 9th-grade algebra teacher.

Carl's trembling hands wrapped around the cup and raised it to his mouth. As he took a sip, Hicks grabbed a chair and dragged it near the cell and sat down, his weight causing the seat to creak under the strain.

"Go on and take that bench, Mr. Jenkins. We'll talk through the bars." Carl moved to the back and sat down at the far end of the cell, leaving some room between himself and Hicks.

"I don't want to take up too much of your time, Mr. Jenkins," Hicks began, glancing at the file in his hand. "But there are a few matters of concern that need to be addressed. I think we can conclude our business here rather quickly if you cooperate. Fair deal?" Carl nodded as Hicks raised the file to his chin and held it there a moment. "Good. I'm glad you agree. I'll get right to it. Officer Stevens and I had a disturbing conversation. His report mentioned things that happened on that long stretch of road that, frankly, trouble me. Do you know why that might be?" Carl said nothing. Again, he knew Hicks wasn't asking, he was telling. "It troubles me deeply," Hicks continued, "that I have extended you every courtesy and have shown you more patience than even my wife. Darkness? Blood-dripping teeth? The end is coming for us all? There is no boogeyman, Mr. Jenkins. Monsters don't suddenly materialize from the black smoke of your tires. I'll be frank, when I hear people talking about things that aren't there, especially you, I get damn worried."

Hicks turned back and sat down. His eyes narrowed and shifted over Carl when suddenly his countenance changed, and with an easy, almost pleasant smile, he spoke slow and steady with an almost wistful air. "If you'd indulge me, Mr. Jenkins, I'd like to tell you a story about my youngest boy, Edward. At the time, he could not have been more than eight or nine years old; God bless his soul. One night, during the summer, he woke from a nightmare screaming. Loud as hell, like an alley cat. I got up and found him in his room, crying. He was all sniffling and rubbing away the tears from his red cheeks. He had this sort of 'help me daddy' look on his face. Well, once he stopped blubbering, enough to speak anyway, he told me he had a nightmare about ghosts in his closet. He said he could see dark shadows moving in there and they were going to get him. As fathers do, I consoled the little fellow, told him it was normal to have nightmares, from time-to-time, but it was only that, a nightmare, and not something real to be afraid of. So, I fixed him some milk and told him to get his ass back to bed. The next night, I heard the same damn thing, again, but this time it was these painful, long, drawn-out sobs coming from his bedroom. Again, I ran to his side. But wouldn't you know, the boy did not wake from a nightmare at all, he hadn't even gone to sleep yet. In fact, he was still wearing his baseball uniform and was lying on top of the covers clutching his tiny hand around his Little League bat. Can you believe that Mr. Jenkins? I mean, after speaking with him father to son the night before? So, I walked over, rather briskly, and slid open the closet door and said, 'Look. Nothing in there, but clothes, shoes, and a few boxes of baseball cards.' Well, if you could have seen the look on that boy's face, it'd break your heart. Man was that boy shaking. So, I spoke with him at some length to help ease his fear. Now, I was frustrated, God as my witness, I spoke in an understanding tone, womanly even, and tucked him back in bed. As I left the room, just before I turned off the light, I told him how proud I was of him, you know, father to son. Well, he had this look, you know, that sweet puppy-dog look you see when the bitch pleases her master. Anyway, I was so proud of him; the boy promised me during our little talk, scout's honor, he said, that he would no longer fear that which need not be feared. The boy made an oath, Mr. Jenkins, a promise to his old man to see things the way they really are. It was a covenant, you might say, forged between father and son, between the chief of police and the one who swears good citizenship. Well, we had all fallen asleep without further alarm and the next morning we all went about our day as normal. When I got home, I suppose it must have been around midnight, I had a couple of bites of leftover meatloaf, drank down a Miller Lite, and turned in for what promised to be a good night's sleep. As I lay there, awhile, it dawned on me how quiet the house was. All I heard was my wife breathing and the quiet hum of the fish tank coming from my son's room. I lean over, kiss my wife, and say simply,

'I'm proud of our boy. Not a peep out of him.' Well, wouldn't you know, Peg shot her head off the pillow and said, 'Chief, he didn't tell you?' And I said, 'Tell me what?' And she said, 'Edward told me you gave him permission to stay over at Robbie Jansen's house tonight after the game.' Well, my head just about hit the roof, Mr. Jenkins. You see, I knew why he done it. My boy hated Robbie Jansen. So, I flew over to the Jansen house in the middle of the night, dragged that boy's lying ass home, and tossed him into his room like a tenpin bowling ball. A perfect strike against the oak bureau. I slammed the door and told him to stay in there and don't dare come out or I would punch his ribcage with my fist, repeatedly, until each boyish rib of his snapped like a dried chicken bone. Of course, he began to cry, but I waited patiently. I wanted to give the fear time to ferment in the wilds of his pea-brain imagination, enough time that the fear would percolate into the stark raving terrors of a lunatic. I leaned in heavy with my ear pressed against the door. I could hear his painful cries. I began to crack my belt in the palm of my hand. Slow at first. Cracking it just so, with just enough wrist to maximize that tight, crisp snap of hand-tooled leather. With each crack I could hear him jump. I cracked it harder and harder and harder until streams of blood ran from my swollen hand. I then turned the belt against the door and hacked away with brutal force. Over and over and over I hacked. Splinters of wood speckled my sweating face as I barked obscenities and threats through the door. I knew that boy was riding the razor's edge between terror and psychotic break when I burst through the door large and square."

Hicks chuckled hoarsely. "You should have seen the look on that boy's face. Eyes and mouth all affright. Piss running down his leg. Kind of like how Officer Stevens found you, Mr. Jenkins. Anyway, I told him how disgusting he was, you know, cowering there in his short pants stained with pee. I told him to stand at attention and keep his damn eyes closed. I said if he moved an inch, or made a peep, or lacked enthusiasm following my orders, why today would be his last day on earth he would ever walk again without a permanent limp. He was terrified, mind you. Shaking and gasping. I understood the boy was doing the best he could, but I knew he was still being defiant. So, I lunged, grabbed his arm, yanked him into the closet, and cuffed his spindly wrist to the hanger rod. I turned on the flashlight, forced him to take a hold of it, and pushed that light right up, hard, under his chin like. I said now you hold it there, boy. Don't you dare let it slip. You keep it pressed, snug, under that weak chin of yours, and you hold it there all fucking night. Because when the monsters float through these closet walls and appear before your tearful eyes, I want them to get a good look at what a sniveling, defiant, liar looks like."

Hicks was chortling in short bursts now; it sounded like a train whistle forced through the hollow of a barrel. "You know Mr. Jenkins, with that flashlight pressed up hard under his chin, that boy's face looked like some kind of fucked-up, ole jack-o'-lantern. And it wasn't even Halloween."

The laughter seemed to rattle the steel bars. Carl's anxiety filled his mouth and leaked bitter through his teeth. He covered his ears with his trembling hands and tucked his chin inside his knees.

"Sorry for droning on there, Mr. Jenkins, but I promise there isn't much longer to go. You have been awfully patient, and I want to thank you for that. I'm sorry, but you seemed to have dropped your coffee there. Could I have the rookie get you another?"

Hicks grinned as he watched Carl's hands shake violently about his ears, allowing the pretense to fester a few seconds before he continued. "All right, maybe we can share a cup after our little chat. So, here is the best part of the story. Pay attention, Mr. Jenkins, I think you'll like this. I leaned into the boy's ear, real close, so close the white hairs of his earlobe tickled up against my nose and I says to him, 'when they come for you tonight, and I know they will, I want them to get a good look at the boy who openly rebelled against his father and failed to keep his oath.' The boy who had so little respect for the promises he pledged me, he thought he could break his word without paying a price. 'Well, I promise you,' I told him, 'you will never make that mistake again. When the handcuff slices into your wrist and it begins to bleed, and your shoulder feels like it's breaking from the socket, I want the monsters to see the face of lies before they cut you to ribbons.'"

Carl fell to the concrete floor. Tears of anguish stung his cheeks. With ever so slight a smile, one almost impossible to detect, Hicks gazed down at the writhing body of Carl Jenkins. And in a calm, almost soothing voice, Hicks said, "I swore an oath, Mr. Jenkins. With my right hand on the Bible, I raised my left hand high and proud. I made a promise to serve and protect this community; to exercise fidelity in all pursuits; and to bring all who break the law before the hand of justice. It's a covenant of trust I swore to uphold, Mr. Jenkins, even if I have to break a few heads to do so. I'm a law man and I know God is watching: 'I will not violate my covenant or alter the word that went forth from my lips.' That's from the good book, Mr. Jenkins, Psalm 89:34—it will do you good to never forget that. Now, get up. Rise and step forward."

With all the urgency of a drill instructor, the chief's words thumped in Carl's ears like a war drum. Carl struggled to lift his body onto his wobbly feet, his eyes reaching for the strength that stood before him.

Hick's planted his big boot against Carl's chest and knocked him to the floor. He then yanked him up by the belt and dragged him out of the cell behind his powerful gait. "Mr. Jenkins," the chief began, looking down at the writhing body. "I think you and I have reached an understanding today, and I must say I feel damn good about it. And I just know you feel the same way. You know how I know that? Because after my boy, Edward and I had our little chat, I went into the little fellow's room the next morning and watched him dangle there in the closet by the wrist. Shit and piss running down his leg. His face was like a creepy doll's face, all waxen, his mouth stretched open like a landed fish. Well, Mr. Jenkins, that boy had the same look in his eyes as yours do right now. That's how I know. From now on, I believe you'll see things the way they really are and not the shadows of things that aren't. Won't you Carl?"

There was no response.

"Good. Oh, Carl, before you go, do you know that boy of mine never saw another ghost in his closet ever again, God bless his soul, and he never told his mother about his night of 'Enlightenment' if you will, just as we agreed. And do you know why? He knew God, and I were watching. I want you to think about that. Now, go on home Carl and remember what has passed between us."

Hicks tossed Carl his keys and watched him stumble out the rear entrance. When Hicks turned around, he made his way over to Officer Stevens' desk and handed over Carl's file.

"File this under Hockomock," the chief said. Officer Stevens flashed a look of understanding and lifted from his chair. He then walked over to the paper shredder and ran Carl's file through its steel teeth. Years of police reports were chewed up into tiny bits. All correspondence, police logs, witness statements, everything and anything that tied the police to Jenkins was destroyed, like it never existed.

CHAPTER 9
DOGS OF DOOM ARE HOWLING MORE

Feeling a wet tongue on the side of his face, Randy lifted his head from the barn floor and opened his eyes. He saw Cam lying there and gave him a shove, but he did not respond; he had a look on his face that appeared distant, his thoughts dangling somewhere inside his head.

Randy laid his head back down and closed his eyes, while Whitey had curled up around Cam's head and settled in for a snooze; he looked like a black halo hovering above Cam's head.

Quiet in thought, Cam lit a cigarette and took a drag. He blew out smoke rings, watching them slowly lose shape as they drifted toward the rafters, and thought about the dream he had and how unusually vivid it was. He wanted to go back there, hit the playback button in his head and work through in his own mind what felt so real and so very terrifying.

Blowing another ring and recounting the images, it ran through his head like a narrative as if listening to the words of a storyteller:

It was a long time past, but not unfamiliar. The surrounding woods and grounds were real. The fields and pathways leading to the nearby river were real. The sounds of running water and the sounds of twigs and leaves crunching under foot were real. They were the same familiar sounds the boy and his dog heard many times before.

The scent of pine was strong. The rock walls that ran the property and through the township, bordering every road and field, separating one farmer's land from the next, were the same in his dreams as they existed in the natural world.

All remained the same, except there were no houses. There were no barns. There were no power lines. There were no dirt roads or access roads. There were no boats on the lakes or kayaks on the rivers. There were no abandoned pieces of farm equipment dotting the fields. There were no metallic grain silos. There were no fences or barbed wire holding back livestock. And there were no farmers. There was only the boy and his dog, Whitefoot, walking out from the grove of pine along the river, feeling pleasantly tired from a day of rock skipping and hunting for arrowheads.

The boy could see the sun low on the horizon and ready to fall. He knew the night loomed and was glad to be heading back to camp. There, around the fire, he and Whitefoot would gather round the pagan circle of five stones, have something to eat, and recount the day's adventures.

On their way back, it has been told, the boy and his dog found themselves in a meadow of golds, browns, and greens, spanning out before them like a great ocean of wild grass, waving over in greater distances than his youthful mind had yet to ponder.

So overcome by its beauty, they went off together headlong into the endless sea.

They ran freely through the wild grass, ever closer toward the silver horizon that never sleeps. The boy could feel the sun and breeze on his face and could feel the sensation of cool grass between his toes.

Whitefoot was happy and at peace spiriting behind the boy. Both ran openly, nakedly, as free as gazelles across the Sub-Saharan plains, when suddenly the ground dropped beneath their feet, holding them weightless between the grass sea and the rising sun.

They were suspended between realms, terrified by a black thunder rolling across the sky like a tidal wave, barreling toward them and swallowing everything in its path.

The boy felt they were being drawn toward a vortex of nothingness, sucked into the swollen belly of an aching pit. He struggled against the mighty force in a desperate attempt to reach out for Whitefoot, but it would be of no use. Whitefoot slipped beyond the boy's reach, lost forever behind the thick curtain of darkness.

The boy was heartsick. He spent his remaining days, alone, searching the fields, woods, and swamps for his dog. There were times he thought he had found Whitefoot in the black water, only to be fooled by the shadowy reflection looking back. For the boy became the dog; the dog became the spirit; the spirit became the people of the fallen night —

It was then Cam woke up, the last words of the storyteller echoing ominously in his head: *The spirit became the people of the fallen night.*

CHAPTER 10
LOCKER ROOM TALK

Officer Durst just finished questioning the football players at Titicut High School. He jotted down an inventory of stolen property and was now taking final statements and eyewitness accounts.

Each player, coach, and cheerleader interviewed recounted the same story, the same chronology of events; only Mighty Mouse spun a different tale. He claimed not to see a gym bag—presumably to hold the stolen goods. He further claimed not to see the suspects, at any time, either enter or exit the school building, or hear or see them make their getaway on dirt bikes.

"We'll get these punks," Durst said, addressing Coach Daniels. "Tell your boys not to worry."

"I only wish we got a better look at them," Daniels said. "Their faces were covered. But thanks for coming down, Bruce. Hey, are you coming to the Fifty?"

"I'll be there," Durst said. "It'll be me and a few other officers. After last year, the chief wants to beef up security. By the way, what ever happened to that cheerleader? You know the one, cute, long-legged, drunk as a skunk, running out to midfield flashing her titties and howling up at the bonfire."

"Oh, her, Sara Wilkinson. My boy took her to the prom."

Durst belched out a laugh, "You don't say? I thought for sure she'd end up in Titicut State Hospital eating her bed sheets. Your boy, Stan, he sure knows how to pick them."

Coach Daniels flashed an awkward smile as Durst referred back to his notes, his finger running down the page. "Listen, Mitch… the janitor on duty here, what's his name?"

"Mighty Mouse," Daniels said. "At least that's what everyone calls him, why?"

"Well, there's something just not right about him. I don't trust his story."

"No offense, but it doesn't take an officer of the law to know there's something not right about him; them shifty eyes and slicked-back hair, he gives me the creeps."

Officer Durst huffed. "This, Mighty Mouse. His statement is at odds with all the others. I think he's lying to me. He knows something more than he's telling."

"He's a perv too," Daniels added. "Been caught more than once skulking near the girls' locker room. The school kept it quiet though, did not want to send the students into a panic."

Durst rolled up his notes and tucked them inside his jacket pocket. He then unfastened the clasp to his nightstick and nonchalantly said, "I've got a few more questions I'd like to ask this Mighty Mouse. The chief doesn't take kindly to liars."

"Listen," Daniels said, "my star player, Jake Tanner, had a special, gold locket stolen. There is an inscription on the back. He'd really like to get that back."

"If that weasel knows something, I'll get it out of him."

"Mighty Mouse is an ornery son-of-a-bitch," Daniels added. "Not sure how cooperative he'll be."

Officer Durst removed his nightstick, swatting it in the palm of his hand. "You let me worry about that, Mitch. You worry about getting these boys ready for the opener."

Durst turned from Daniels and walked through the side door next to the boys' locker room. Mighty Mouse was inside cleaning up after the robbery and whistling a tune. He was smiling and muttering to himself, something about the jocks deserving it, when behind him he heard the whir of a baton slicing through the air, exploding at the base of his lower back.

White-hot pain shot up Mighty Mouse's spine. He dropped to the floor like a death row inmate drops from the hangman's noose.

Durst stepped over the twitching body and straddled each boot heel on his left and right flank. He crouched down, pulled his head back by his hair, and looped his nightstick around his neck like a garroting wire.

"I know you're lying to me," Durst said, jerking back on the blunt instrument, throttling his windpipe. "And the chief frowns on liars." Crushed gasps of air escaped Mighty Mouse's lungs. His face and neck turned bruising shades of purple like an expanding balloon ready to pop.

"Now, you're gonna tell me all that you know. Understand? If you lie again, I'm afraid them beady eyeballs of yours won't know what to do except pop right out of your skull."

Jake Tanner and Dirk Hopkins suddenly stopped. They were heading into the lockers when they heard Officer Durst's booming voice and the gasping cries of Mighty Mouse.

Jake quickly backed up against the wall and held there, his finger pressed to his lips signaling Dirk to keep quiet.

Officer Durst, hearing nothing of Jake and Dirk, released the crushing hold of the nightstick and watched Mighty Mouse's head snap forward and bounce against the floor as if loaded on a spring.

Spit and bile coughed out as Mighty Mouse lay writhing with his hands wrapped around his neck. His lungs struggled for precious air, fighting the onslaught of oxygen rushing past his bruised windpipe.

"You're gonna tell me right now, you lying son of a bitch, who was on them bikes?" Mighty Mouse was curled up from the blinding pain. He looked like a snail lying on its side, trying to tuck back into its shell. Durst drove a hard boot into the underside of his ribcage kicking Mighty Mouse over on his back. "I'm gonna ask you one more time." Durst leaned over and forced the butt end of his nightstick under his chin. He leveraged his head back until his Adam's apple pointed due north, the skin around his jawline tightened down like a snare drum. "Who was on them bikes? Tell me you son of a bitch! Who are they?"

Mighty Mouse lifted a weak hand. He could no longer hold out. "Okay, okay, okay…." His voice sounded like a thin pipe of dry air.

"Okay, what, son?"

"I'll tell you what I know…"

A sinister smile formed over Durst's crooked lips. "I'm glad we understand each other. Now, understand this. If I catch you holding back, or if you lie to me, you'll pay a heavy price. There are over two hundred bones in the human body, you maggot. Mark my words, I'll snap each one like kindling wood. When I'm done with you, you'll be sucking gruel through a wired jaw. Do I make myself clear?"

"Y-yes sir." Mighty Mouse barely managed the words, but was terrified not to answer.

Up against the wall and out of view, Dirk and Jake listened in horror. They held their position too afraid to draw Durst's attention.

"Let's get out of here," Dirk whispered. "That cop is fucking crazy."

"Wait. Don't you want to know who the fuck stole from us?"

"That cop is nuts. We gotta get the hell out of here."

"Sh, listen. Mighty Mouse is about to spill his guts."

Officer Durst pushed. "Their names god dammit? I am losing patience and I'm about to break your jaw."

"It was Coltair," Mighty mouse said, shielding his head with his hands. "Randy Coltair."

"That's one of 'em. Now I want the other name. Give me the other name, you disrespectful son of a bitch." Winding back, Durst raised his nightstick over his head, his chest barreling, his face turning a horrible shade of crimson.

"NO WAIT! It was Jenkins! Cam Jenkins."

Durst dropped his arm by his side. He looked down at the pathetic sight, grinning. "I'm not going to lie to you, you sniveling son of a bitch, I was hoping you'd give me a reason to break your jaw. I've got a young daughter that will be attending Titicut High next year. If I ever hear you perving around them girls' lockers, ever again, I'll break it in two. Understand?"

As soon as Dirk and Jake heard the names Randall Coltaire and Cam Jenkins, they split for the door and ran outside across the practice field passing right by Coach Daniels.

"Tomorrow, boys. Practice at 10:00 AM. Be here."

"Okay coach," they said, never breaking stride.

"Jesus! Where the hell are you going so fast?"

Without looking back, Dirk and Jake ran into the parking lot and saw Greg Stillson and Paul Cannon, two starting linebackers and huge AC/DC fans, fuming their tickets were stolen.

"Let's go," said, Tanner.

"Go where?" Stillson asked.

"It's payback time. I know who stole our shit."

"What's their names?" Cannon shouted.

"Cam Jenkins, and that scumbag friend of his, Randy."

"Dammit. I'm gonna kill those assholes. Let's go!"

Stillson yanked the keys from his pocket and sprinted towards his truck. "Get in the back. Paul, you're riding shotgun."

They got in the F-150 and gunned it out of the parking lot, plowing over an orange traffic barrel as they turned. The way they were hooting and hollering and throwing their fists, they looked like good, old southern boys on a hunting party. They would grab their baseball bats and makeshift Molotov cocktails. Cam and Randy were about to get their asses beat.

Officer Durst stroked his chin and stopped pacing. He gazed a moment before throwing Mighty Mouse a handkerchief to dab the blood around his lips and teeth. "One more thing," Durst said, squatting down by his side, tapping the nightstick in his hand. "This little chat of ours stays between us. Is that understood?"

Mighty Mouse continued to nurse his wounds and nodded his head.

"What do I tell people about my fat lip and the fucking bruises all over my neck?"

Durst threw back his nightstick. "What I'd tell you about sassing me? You tell 'em you cut yourself shaving. You tell 'em you fell over when you were twirling around naked like some kind of ballerina. I don't give a fuck what you tell 'em."

Durst began to chuckle at the image he just painted. "Listen," Durst said, his nightstick pressed against Mighty Mouse's Adam's apple. "I know what you can tell 'em, something everyone will believe. You tell 'em one of them girls you like to stare at in the showers caught you stroking your chipmunk, and they beat you within an inch of your life." Durst bellowed out an enormous laugh. "You tell them that."

Holstering his nightstick, Durst left the locker room without saying another word, the click of his boots echoing inside Mighty Mouse's head. He made for the parking lot where he noticed Coach Daniels getting into his car.

"Hey, coach. You gotta sec?"

"Sure, Bruce, let me guess. Mighty Mouse squirmed his way out of telling you anything."

"No, I'd say we had a rather productive chat. He must have liked the soft tone of my voice. Listen, Mitch, you know these two boys, Randy Coltaire and Cam Jenkins?"

"Yeah, I know them. They've been caught smoking grass a few times behind the equipment shed. Their names have been bandied about in the teacher's lounge concerning skipping school and causing trouble. Why? Are they the ones who ransacked the lockers?"

Durst nodded. "Well, they've stepped in it this time. Bonnie and Clyde's stealing ways are about to end. Tell your boys they'll get their stuff back. Take care of yourself, Mitch."

"Thanks, Bruce. Say hi to the chief for me."

Durst got in the cruiser and drove off. He was heading back to the station to file a report, when a radio transmission came from One Police Plaza.

Police Dispatch:
Officer Harding, possible leg fracture. Ambulance and tow truck on site. Location, Walnut Creek.

Officer Durst:
This is Officer Durst. I'm leaving Titicut High now. Is help required? I'm only five minutes out from Trader's Bluff.

Police Dispatch:
Not at this time, Officer Durst. Officer Harding has been extracted from the vehicle and is on his way to Morton Medical. A tow truck driver is on scene. He has over a hundred feet of steel cable and is lowering it into the creek now. He says they should have the cruiser out in about twenty. You can head back in.

Officer Durst:
Copy that. Over.

"Holy hell," Durst said. "How the Christ do you end up at the bottom of Walnut Creek?" He turned his thoughts back to Cam and Randy. "I don't know how an officer ends up at the bottom of a creek, but I sure as hell know I'm going to get both of you sons of bitches."

CHAPTER 11
COUNTERINTELLIGENCE

Inside his office, Hicks leaned back in his chair, kicked his boots up on his walnut desk, and radioed to Sergeant Guthrie:

"Guthrie here, go ahead, Chief."

"Sergeant get on down to the Tri-Stop. When Carl Jenkins arrives, I want you to keep an eye on him and make sure he makes it on home."

"Copy that Chief. Tri-Stop. On my way."

Hicks picked up the phone and dialed the officer at the front desk. He asked not to be disturbed and to hold all his calls. He then drew down the shade, reached inside his desk for a bottle of Jim Beam, and poured himself a drink.

***

Carl made it to the rear of the parking lot at One Police Plaza and found his car where Sonny left it. He drove off, lit a smoke, and tried like hell to shake off Hicks.

The El Camino pulled hard to the right when he turned onto Post Road and it made a hideous screech of metal on metal. Just around the corner, a young woman pushing a baby carriage (one of those designer jobs that every uppity, new mother had to have, who preferred style over form) stopped dead in her tracks at the dreadful noise, throwing Carl a hysterical grimace.

Carl immediately wound up like Dennis Eckersley in the ninth and delivered his best fastball on a three/two count, "Fuck you bitch!" The mother's face twisted up in horror trying to cover the infant's ears.

"Not in front of the baby!" she cried. "Not in front of the baby! What kind of beast are you?"

Carl drove on, not sure where he found the strength or nerve after going a round with Hicks. He could hear the mother's shrieks of anger behind him.

"You disgusting pig of a man. You belong behind bars. You're horrible. What kind of animal are you—"

Carl straightened up in his seat and flashed a bony, middle finger over his right shoulder. He said, "Fuck you and the horse you rode in on!" Conjuring up his best Vincent Price voice, he muttered, "And they say I am the one who is possessed by the darkness."

Carl shook his head and pulled the ring tab off a warm Narragansett. His lips stretched back into a thin slit, surprising himself at such an uncharacteristic outburst, but it felt damn good.

Up ahead was the Tri-Stop, where each morning after working the night shift Carl would stop in for the dollar special before heading home. You could set your watch by it: two fried eggs, three strips of bacon, and hash browns with plenty of gristle.

The Tri-Stop was a fixture in town for as long as anyone could remember. It had been owned and operated by the same family since before the "Great One." What started out as little more than a counter service, became a full-service diner offering the best breakfast at the best price in town. The faded sandwich board of Betty out front, seen in her famous blue apron crossing her lumberjack-sized forearms, said so.

Carl pulled into the parking lot and swung into his normal spot. Before exiting, he noticed through the window Sergeant Guthrie sitting in his cruiser near the back entrance. He watched Guthrie glare at him through reflective shades as he stepped out of the cruiser, never breaking his stare.

An uneasy feeling came over Carl. Guthrie had mirrored sunglasses on, but Carl was damn sure Guthrie was watching him.

Carl drew a cigarette from his pack, closed the door, and knelt down beside the wheel well with his profile facing Guthrie. Striking a wooden match along the pavement, he lit the cigarette and inhaled deeply. Through the smoke, out from the corner of his eye, he could see Guthrie wave at him before he announced in a friendly voice, "A beautiful, September day, eh Carl Jenkins? Yes sir, nothing I enjoy more than sitting down to a warm piece of Betty's strudel on such a beautiful, September day. Mm, mmm, mmm...."

In stride, Guthrie tipped his peaked hat and passed through the rear door of the Tri-Stop.

Carl rose to his feet and passed his eyes over the parking lot, glancing into the sky: *It's as if he was waiting for me. But why would he? If the chief wanted me back in custody, Guthrie would have arrested me.*

He mulled things over, stamped out his smoke, and passed through the front entrance.

"Pay up, Bobby Jakes!" Betty said, like she hit the trifecta at the dog races. "I win. I knew he'd be here."

"Dammit, Carl!" Jakes began, "I had a five-spot riding you wouldn't show."

Carl closed the door behind him and took his normal stool.

"A little late," Betty announced triumphantly, "but my money always looked good. Never a doubt in my mind Carl Jenkins would show. Good to see you, Carl."

Snapping on her gum, Betty had a Pay-Up-Or-Else kind of look in her eyes.

"Yeah, yeah, yeah," Jakes said, reaching for his wallet reluctantly and shaking his head. "You cost me some good money, Carl Jenkins. Yes, sir, I thought I had it in the bag when the hand went nine."

Carl raised an eyebrow in his direction, while Betty poured him a hot cup of black coffee.

"Well, time's a wasting," Jakes said. "I gotta get all them deliveries done by four." Jakes got off his stool and fixed his wallet down inside the pocket of his trousers. "Hey Carl, by the way," he said, placing a hand on Carl's shoulder. "You hear about them kids that robbed the high school?"

Carl had a blank look on his face. Jakes continued. "And I hear, somehow, Officer Harding ended up at the bottom of Walnut Creek. Now, how you suppose he managed that? Damn hoodlums, right Carl?" With two quick slaps on Carl's shoulder, Jakes left some loose change on the counter and made his way to the door. Before he passed through, Betty rolled up the five-spot in her apron and said, "Nice doing business with ya, Bobby Jakes. See you tomorrow."

"Yeah, yeah, yeah." The door closed behind him.

Carl held the cup of coffee in both hands before taking a sip. The heat felt good, working its way through his tired joints and aching bones. He glanced over his left shoulder to see Guthrie sitting in a back booth giving a waitress his order.

In the foreground, only five stools down from Carl, a gentleman sat wearing a herringbone sport jacket and reading the newspaper while eating breakfast. Carl did not recognize him, as he watched him fork through a mess of scrambled eggs, but the gentleman noticed Carl was eyeing him and tipped his head.

"Good morning," the gentleman said, catching Betty's attention. "When you get a chance, can I get another cup?"

Betty turned from the counter with a piping hot brew in one hand and the dollar plate special in the other. "There you go, sugar," Betty said, setting down the gentleman's cup and sliding Carl his plate.

"What's your name darling? I haven't seen you around here before."

"Williams," the gentleman said, dabbing his mouth. "Don Williams."

"Well, Mr. Don Williams, it sure is nice to see a new face around here. Are you down here on business or just passing through?"

"I'm a writer."

"A writer?" Betty's curiosity piqued. "What, like books and novels? I bet a young, handsome guy like yourself writes them romance novels. What my husband calls 'Trash For Trailer-Parkers.'"

Don choked on some eggs trying to hold back a laugh. "No, ma'am." He covered his mouth with a napkin. "I'm a reporter."

"A reporter? Like for the evening news? Human interest stories? That kind of thing?"

Don grinned and took a sip of coffee. "No, crime reporter."

"Well, I'll be. You hear that Carl Jenkins? You best behave yourself and stay out of trouble. We got ourselves a regular Joe Friday here in Titicut."

Carl did hear. He looked down at the black coffee swirling in his cup and could not help but think: *What kind of trouble was Cam in now. Nothing he'd done before ever rose to a level higher than a few mentions in the police blog of the Titicut Independent. A couple fights, a little grass, busted for speeding ... What did Bobby Jakes say? Robbery at the high school? Officer Harding at the bottom of Walnut creek?*

He lifted his head from his thoughts and noticed Guthrie looking straight at him with a face like quarried stone. Carl averted his eyes when he noticed the reporter rustling through a folder of papers rather hurriedly. He was thumbing through the pages when his hand stopped and lifted from the folder a single sheet of paper with handwritten notes and shot his finger halfway down the page.

1973: Hockomock Swamp: Three disappeared: One survivor
John Hooke—Titicut—Disappeared
Paul Andrews—Titicut—Disappeared
Mark 'Scottie' Fuller—Titicut—Disappeared
Carl Jenkins—Titicut—*Lone* Survivor

Williams snapped back on his stool straighter than a young recruit in basic training. "Are you Carl Jenkins? Carl with a C?"

Carl nodded.

"Well, I'll be. When I heard the name Carl Jenkins, I knew I had seen that name before. Listen, I'm down here working a cold case. Would you be willing to answer some questions for me?"

Carl hesitated. "What questions?"

"Questions that will hopefully yield some answers on the contents of this folder."

Williams said in disbelief, "You know it's not often, but sometimes good things fall right into a reporter's lap. The only man who made it out of the swamp alive that night in 1973, is sitting right next to me."

Carl's stomach rolled. His eyes waved over the thick file of notes and his head began to spin. "Are you alright, Carl?" Carl's face turned pale, and his breathing became labored.

"Can I get you a glass of water?"

Watching the commotion, Guthrie peeled himself from the booth and made his way over to the counter.

"Here Carl," Betty said, placing the glass down. "Drink slow and breathe deep." She looked at Williams. "He'll be all right. Sometimes he gets these spells."

Carl sipped the water and began to regain his breath when a sudden crash of silverware rattled off the counter. Guthrie's large hand came down like an anvil, his body acting as a wall between Williams and Jenkins.

"Betty's right," Guthrie said, "Carl has been known to get these spells from time to time. There's no telling when they'll come on." Guthrie stepped back, making passive eye contact with the young reporter. "Nightmares from the past, is all. And you are?"

"Williams," Don said, offering his hand to shake Sergeant Guthrie's. Guthrie's hand remained by his side. He had a flat, static look for a beat taking measure of the young reporter. Then said, "Having served in Vietnam can sure mess with a man's head. Flashbacks and the like. Terrible. Causing a man to see things that aren't there. Ain't that right Carl?"

Carl placed the water down on the counter, his eyes affixed to his handprints fading on the glass.

"I know full well about flashbacks from the war," Don said, looking at his badge. "Officer?"

"That's Sergeant to you," Guthrie interjected. "Sergeant Guthrie, Mr. Williams."

"All right, Sergeant. No offense. If I could just have a few minutes of Carl's time, in private, I would like to ask him about the 1973—"

"You're not from around here, Mr. Williams," Guthrie said, "but you should know that we don't take kindly to outsiders snooping around. It's nothing personal, you understand. It's just the way it's always been."

Don stood silent.

"And right now, Carl needs his rest. And I'm here to see that he gets it. Come on Carl, let's get you on home. You don't want to disappoint the chief."

He grabbed Jenkins under one elbow and guided him off the stool. He then turned like a well-oiled gear and said, "Oh, Mr. Williams, just one more thing. It might do you some good to realize that people around here don't like talking to strangers, much. They, ah, like to keep to themselves, mostly. Call it a 'generational distrust of outsiders,' if you like. I would suggest you do yourself a favor and go on home. You won't find what you're looking for here."

CHAPTER 12
GETTING WARMER

Don Williams dropped two singles on the counter and spun off his stool.

"Thank you kindly," Betty said. "Don't be a stranger. You're welcome here anytime."

"Can I use your phone?" Don asked in haste.

"Sure, the pay phone is right outside, next to the ice—" Before she could finish, Don was out the door.

With the cold case file tucked under his arm and his hand searching his pockets for loose change, Williams shot around the corner of the building and saw the red letters *"ICE"* painted on the side of the ice machine next to the phone.

He balanced the receiver between his ear and shoulder and dumped a couple of quarters into the coin slot and dialed the city number.

"Hello, you have reached the City Dispatch, how may I direct your call?"

"Yeah, put me through to Metro Desk. I want to speak to Harry." Don adjusted the file up under his arm and looked down at his watch.

"Metro Desk, Harry Fletcher."

"Harry, Don Williams here. Listen, I think I've got something on this cold case, but I'm gonna need more time."

"Where are you?"

"I'm outside a restaurant called the Tri-Stop, down here in Titicut, off Route 24."

"You mean, you actually found someone who will talk to you? Someone who will be quoted and go on the record?"

"Yes and no. Not exactly—but, I'm working that out. Listen Harry, not ten minutes ago, a one, Carl Jenkins, sat down next to me at the restaurant eating breakfast."

"Carl Jenkins? That name sounds familiar."

"Yes, you'll know why in a second. Open up the duplicate file, the one marked 'Hockomock.'"

"Where the hell is it?"

"It should be in the file cabinet next to the water cooler. Under 'BT' I believe."

Harry thumbed through the files under 'BT' and came to one in the back. It was bound in twine with the word 'Hockomock' printed on the front.

"I got it. Why under 'BT?'"

"I'm not sure. The last guy to work this case was a reporter named Gerry Mulrooney. He had it filed that way. Notes with his name on it are all through the reports."

"Mulrooney ..." Fletcher uttered, thinking a moment. "Yeah, Irish guy out of Dorchester. It's been about ten years now since I've heard that name. Strange the way he left."

"Strange how?"

"Well, I was a beat reporter at the time, did not know him, but word got around that Mulrooney called the paper one day, out of the blue, and said he wouldn't be in again. Something to the effect that he had taken a new job and had to leave right away."

"Moved away? Where to?"

"Well, that's the strange thing about it. When he was asked if he was coming in to pick up his last check and clear his desk, the phone clicked and went dead. Payroll never got an address, and no one ever heard from him again."

Don sighed. "Harry, I think there's even more to this case than meets the eye. I want to stay down here a little longer. Have a one-on-one with Carl, and follow up any leads."

"I agree," Harry said. "Well, you wanted to work something different, now is your chance."

"Thank you, Harry. Now, as for Carl Jenkins, open up the file and flip to the back."

"Got it open."

"Okay, do you see the divider there? Look for the green tab."

"Yeah, I see it."

"Flip a few pages in and you will see a sleeve of loose notes and scraps of paper, some fastened with paperclips and some not."

"Right. Here it is."

"Good. Now take out the loose papers, should be near the top, and look for the heading of the note written as:

1973: Hockomock Swamp: Three disappeared: One survivor

John Hooke—Titicut—Disappeared

Paul Andrews—Titicut—Disappeared

Mark 'Scottie' Fuller—Titicut—Disappeared

Carl Jenkins—Titicut—Survivor

"I got it."

"Skim your eyes down to the last name." Fletcher's eyes followed his index finger down the page 'til it found the name Carl Jenkins.

"Well, I'll be. You sure this is the guy that sat down next to you at the restaurant?"

"I'm sure. One and the same. Oh, and Harry, you should get a load of this police officer that was at the diner, introduced himself as Sergeant Guthrie. Went out of his way to inform me I'm wasting my time down here and I won't find what I'm looking for. Something about distrusting outsiders. He was none too happy I was talking to Jenkins. Sergeant Psycho if you ask me."

"All right. Take all the time you need, but keep me posted. If you can get Jenkins talking, keep him talking and the ice just may begin to crack. And for God's sakes, tread lightly."

"Thanks, Harry. I'll check in with you in a bit. I'm gonna find a room over on the other side of town. This cold case is getting warm."

"Let me know if you need anything. I can have a crew down there within the hour. By the way, what about the file I'm looking at? Don't you need it?"

"I ran copies of everything I needed late last night. Fran helped me collate."

"I bet she did." Harry pulled a pen from behind his ear and made a few notes inside the file's binder. "All right, Don. Let's pick this up later. But remember, tread lightly. These people never talk, especially to outsiders. They've got some kind of hair across their ass, especially city guys like you."

"Right, Harry." Don hung up the phone and jumped in his car. Things were beginning to happen. He got approval to continue to investigate. He would find out where Jenkins lives and speak with him further. And Harry just offered to dispatch a crew if he needed the extra help.

As he drove across town, two thoughts crossed his mind. The first was: *this could be the story I was looking for.* The second was: *I need to buy some office supplies for a makeshift command center.*

CHAPTER 13
OVER THE FIELDS AND FAR AWAY

Sergeant Guthrie had seen Carl home and headed back to the station. And like clockwork, Carl passed out in his chair with the TV on after knocking back a six-pack of cold Narragansett.

It was a routine Carl fell into, ever since his release from Titicut State Hospital for the criminally insane and was greeted by a handwritten note penned in a familiar hand when he returned home.

A good wife to the end.

Beer in the fridge.

The ever efficient, two-line missive summed up quite nicely the woman Cam's mother was. Direct and dutiful. Not even a signature.

Cam checked over Carl to reassure himself that he was alive, as he sometimes did when he was around and had not seen him in a few days. He could see his chest rise and fall, and could smell the beer whistle through the premature, gray hairs in his nose. Everything appeared normal. Not a shabby curtain or worn rug out of place.

"Come on, let's get out of here," Cam said, "I just wanted to check on him since we were here."

Randy nodded. "Yeah, the plugs on the bikes won't replace themselves. We need to get that done before Darrah and Niki show up."

They were about to exit the door and head back to the barn when Randy said, "Wait. Do you hear that?"

"Hear what?"

"Listen…" Whitey's ears perked up and began growling at the door. A short distance away you could hear an engine rumbling and getting louder. There was now a smattering of voices heard hooting and hollering above the engine's roar. They ran outside on the porch.

"Over there!" Cam said, pointing across the field towards the barn. "Right there." Randy shot his eyes across and saw a pickup truck barreling through.

"What the fuck are they doing?" Randy said.

"Get ready boys!" Stillson said as they sped up the equipment road, while Jake and Dirk held onto the Molotov cocktails in the bed of the truck making sure the gasoline did not spill from the glass jars.

Paul Cannon hung out the passenger door and hollered, "Just up ahead, maybe three hundred yards." Tanner and Hopkins stood and found their balance; they clutched at their Louisville Sluggers and the readymade gasoline bombs with tight fists ready to strike.

"I can see their fucking bikes," Hopkins said. "I know they're here. Step on it."

"Jesus, Cam. They're heading for the barn. They're wearing football jackets, school colors." Whitey leapt off the porch and took off running. "Hold!" Cam said, "stay boy!" Whitey pulled up and huffed in frustration, patrolling in a tight circle.

"God dammit. How'd they find out?"

"I don't know," Cam said. "Shit! I can see a flame. They're lighting something. There's no way we can stop them in time."

"Cam, where does Carl keep his keys?"

"In the ignition. Come on."

They jumped over the porch railing and ran towards Carl's truck. The El Camino was not there. Cam opened the driver side door while Randy slid over the hood, jerking open the passenger side. Whitey hopped in the back.

"Let's go," Randy said. "We can catch 'em."

Cam turned the key and gave it some gas, but nothing. "Come on, Cam!" It sputtered and backfired; nothing but a strong smell of gasoline and the impotent whine of a battery dying. "Fuck! It's flooded! Shit!" Cam threw open the door and popped the hood. "Jesus, Cam, there's no time. We got to—"

Before Randy got out the words, a '79 Trans Am, jet-black, with a gold phoenix blazoned across the hood flew by the house faster than Burt Reynolds outrunning Sheriff Justice on Highway 54. It was Darrah and Nicole.

CHAPTER 14
PIED PIPER OF JENKINS FIELD

With bats and Molotov cocktails in hand, Tanner and Hopkins swung down off the side of the truck and made for the barn, while Stillson drove on a wide sweep, taunting Cam and Randy, thought to be inside.

"We know you're in there. Come on out or we're coming in!"

Seeing and hearing no sign of them, Tanner and Hopkins burst through the barn doors swinging their bats. "Come on out you faggots!" Lifting the bat high above his head, Tanner brought it down with enormous force like a strongman ringing the bell at the county fair. On contact, the workbench exploded into matchwood.

Hopkins quickly covered the inside of the barn. He began tossing and smashing old barrels, knocking over tables and workhorses, and looking under old tarps and drop cloths. He flew up the rickety ladder to the loft and searched every corner.

"They're not here," he said. "Where the fuck are, they?"

"Shit!" Tanner said.

Completely unaware, Darrah flew by the house and gunned it down the equipment road accelerating through the overgrown field.

"Hey," Cam said, waving his arms. "Stop!"

He dropped the hood of the El Camino and took off running.

"Cam, wait!" Randy said.

"Come on, Randy. We got to stop them."

"You can't catch a Trans Am."

"You got any better ideas?"

"Does Carl have a gun?"

"No, the cops took them away years ago."

"Shit!"

Accelerating through the field down the access road, Niki pulled back the tab of her beer and swung her tanned leg over the center console.

"Randy is going to love my painted toes. Don't you think?"

"Yeah, he will," Darrah said, "I know I do."

Just up ahead, but still out of view, Jake and Dirk hurled their Molotov cocktails and watched them explode against the barn walls—KAFLUMPF! The flames roared up the walls of the barn. It sounded like the air was tearing in half as the fire raged past the roofline, licking above the cupola.

Jake and Dirk turned and ran for the truck, diving headfirst onto the speeding tailgate.

"Hold on!" Stillson hollered. He banked hard left and drove straight for the dirt bikes, a wicked grin widening across his face.

"I got this!" Tanner blurted out. With one golf-like swing, the barrel of the bat caught the underside of Cam's dirt bike, knocking it clear over on top of Randy's bike.

"Yeah! Straight through the sweet spot, assholes," Tanner said.

"Let's find where these rats are hiding!" Stillson shouted. "They're not getting away that easy." As they made for the access road, laughing like blood-thirsty hyenas, they watched the flames behind them sweep over the roof.

Looking inside the shed for anything they could use as a weapon, Cam and Randy armed themselves with a shovel and a pitchfork. They slung them over their shoulder and took off behind the shed, making for the tree line.

They did not get far before they stopped cold. The smoke spiraling above the barn's roofline caught them flatfooted.

"What the hell," Randy said, "they lit the barn on fire."

Cam looked on in horror and remembered there was a fire extinguisher inside the shed.

"Where are you going?" Randy said.

"Hold on!" Cam ran to the shed and grabbed the extinguisher. "We got to hurry before it burns to the ground."

"Look out!" Niki screamed. Darrah cut the wheel, narrowly avoiding a head-on collision with Stillson's truck barreling towards them from the opposite direction. The car's rear end slid sideways through the tall grass, but she kept the vehicle upright, spinning it on a one-eighty. They watched as two guys in the back of the truck bounced like rag dolls before being thrown against the cab when the truck skidded to a sudden stop.

"Holy shit!" Stillson said. "That Trans Am came out of nowhere. Who the fuck was that?"

"I don't know," Cannon said. "All I saw was black paint and a flash of skin. The next thing I knew we were spinning sideways."

"I know who it is," Tanner said, wincing from the pain in his shoulder. "I know exactly who it is."

"Who?" Stillson asked. "Who the fuck ran us off the road?"

"Darrah Ryder and Nicole Guthrie."

"D. Ryder and Niki G," Cannon said. "I know them. Nicole's father is a cop."

"Yeah, Sergeant Guthrie," said Hopkins.

"So, what," Stillson added, "I don't care if her father is Ronald Fuckin' Reagan. They ran us off the road."

"It doesn't mean shit to me either," Tanner agreed. "These dirt bags aren't getting away with it."

"Then what are we waiting for? Let's get them."

Hopkins and Tanner held on for dear life; their arms snapped back tight as Stillson stepped on the gas and made a beeline directly toward the Trans Am.

"Step on it!" Tanner yelled.

"I've got it buried!" Stillson hollered. "But it's dragging some." Hopkins and Gannon looked worried. They escaped death once, nearly being flattened by a head on collision, and now they were tempting fate again. They failed to see the wisdom in fucking with Sergeant Guthrie's daughter.

Seeing the truck lurch forward, Darrah buried the gas pedal and spun the Trans Am around hightailing it thru the field when an idea came to mind. She would lead them, like the Pied Piper of Hamelin, straight toward the old well Cam showed her on the property. *Drown them like the rats they are*, Darrah thought.

"Buckle yourself down, Nik. The fox is in the henhouse. Four chickens are about to blink."

CHAPTER 15
HERE'S JOHNNY!!

A mile away, driving his wrecker down that long, country road, Sonny chewed on a spit of hay and was whistling along to Ramblin' Man. He was on his way to see Carl Jenkins. He had a good deal brewing and was feeling right.

"Carl Jenkins," he said aloud, palming a shiny, new fuel pump in his right hand. "Sure, as hell you got no money, but I know you've been holding on to that Johnny Popper. I've had my eye on that tractor for years. Rear wheels alone are worth four fuel pumps, rusted and all."

He turned down Old Foundry Street, whistling the words ...

Lord, I was born a rambling man
Trying to make a living and doing the best I can

"Yes, sir," he continued, "even if that Popper is seized up tighter than an ole maid and the carburetor is slicked black with varnish, the parts alone will fetch me a handsome price. You can bet your sweet bippy on that one."

Sonny flipped out his blade and carved off a thick cut of sweet Applejack tobacco and thumbed it tight inside his cavernous jaw. The acidic bite stretched his lips back into a freakish smile.

Feeling the wind on his face and that Johnny Popper vibe, he continued whistling and humming over the building spit. As he drove by Hanson Farm on the left, he slowed down before rounding the next corner. The Jenkins' driveway was set back and overgrown by oak trees, making it difficult for those unfamiliar with the property to locate the main house. Even those who knew the property had a hard time, often missing the driveway completely. That was just fine with Carl.

Going into the turn, there was a kind of leap of faith one took no one was approaching from the opposite direction. The road was hairpin and narrow; often times it was slick from wet leaves. Being an old country road, however, it was perhaps one chance in fifty that two vehicles would converge fighting over what amounted to be a single passable lane.

Sonny dropped his speed and crept along, holding tight to the shoulder. As he came out of the curve, he could see Carl's 57 Chevy pickup parked out front, and that sweet Johnny Popper tractor beneath the chestnut tree. "Ah, there she is. You'll be coming home with me, Johnny."

***

Randy and Whitey stood back and watched Cam punch out the flames. He hustled to the other side of the barn and snuffed out a flare fighting to reach a bough of pine hanging down on the roof.

"Randy, the bikes!" Cam said. Randy turned around to find them tipped over and leaking gas; he could see a large dent under the tank. He hurried them away from the sparks. "I'm going to kill those fucking bastards; I'm going to kill those fucking bastards."

He turned around in white-hot anger when his eyes locked on the Trans Am speeding through the field with the truck close behind. "Cam, check it out." Cam jumped up on some stacked cinder blocks for a better look. Darrah had them chasing. Like a Border Collie rounding sheep, she began to close the wide circle—a kind of high-speed corralling of human livestock—before leading them straight to the slaughterhouse. Niki looked over her shoulder and could see them closing the gap.

"Darrah, they are getting closer."

"Just where I want them, Nik. Keep watching. Tell me when they're at five car lengths.

"Darrah, they're at eight... now seven ... They're at six. Okay wait, wait... they're at five!"

"Niki, see the standpipe up ahead?"

"I see it!"

"Brace yourself. When we pass it on the left, I'm going to cut the wheel hard to the right."

"Darrah, they're on top of us! They're at four; they're at three. Shit, they're right behind us!"

"Hold on, Nick!"

Struggling against the wind, Jake Tanner lit a Molotov cocktail and cocked his arm back in a throwing position.

"I got them right where I want them!" Tanner said.

"We are right on top of them," Stillson said. "So, close I can see their tan lines. Get ready!"

"Now!" Niki said. Darrah cut it hard right, spinning the ass end out behind her.

Stillson panicked and jerked the wheel, knocking Tanner back on his ass. Thousands of pounds of pressure dove the truck's nose forward while pulling the rear end higher, curling up a massive wave of dirt like a plow blade on a snow truck. The rear wheels lifted off the ground before it flipped and slammed down into the muck.

As the truck took on water and began to sink, Jake, Dirk, Greg, and Paul were concussed in stunned silence. They noticed a single black dot sitting oddly above them at the farthest reaches of a brilliant, blue sky. Just sitting there, before it seemed to wink at them as they slipped from consciousness. It would be the last thing they would ever see before they were swallowed, and everything went dark.

CHAPTER 16
THE NATIVES ARE GETTING RESTLESS

Officer Durst pulled into One Police Plaza. He grabbed the report and made his way to the secure entrance at the rear of the building and punched in the code: The electronic door emitted a low hum and released the lock.

"Hey Bruce," Sergeant Guthrie said, crossing directly in front of him. "How did you make out down at the high school? Coach Daniels try to convince you the team's going the distance this year?"

Durst huffed, "You kidding. Those narrow-shouldered, momma's boys don't stand a chance."

Guthrie belched a hearty laugh while pouring a cup of hot coffee and handing it to Durst. Durst took a hard swallow; his face grimaced only slightly from the piping-hot liquid.

"You got any leads?" Guthrie asked.

"Better than that. I know the punk-ass sons-of-bitches who pulled it off."

"Where are you hiding 'em?" Guthrie smirked. "I don't see them behind bars."

Durst raised the cup to his lips. "Chief's gonna want to hear about this first." He finished his coffee on his next swallow and crushed the foam cup.

"By the way," Durst said, turning toward his desk. "Have you heard on Officer Harding's condition?"

"Word is," Guthrie began, "he's got a fractured leg. That, a few cuts, and bruised ego."

"How the hell did he end up in Walnut Creek?"

"Two punks on dirt bikes drew him into a trap, he says, then left him for dead. First responders said he was damn lucky that the police cruisers had been outfitted with air bags. That stretch along there, near Turner's Pass, has a thirty-foot drop."

"Two punks on dirt bikes? Well, well..." Durst grinned, glancing up at Guthrie. "Seems our boys have been busy. First the high school, then running Harding into the creek."

"Wait," Guthrie said, "you telling me these are the same punk-ass kids? Hold on. I want Stevens to hear this. Stevens, come over here. You gotta hear this."

Stevens walked over, grabbing the last Boston cream donut.

"What can I do you for?" Stevens asked.

"You know the incident down at the high school? And the one at Walnut Creek?"

"Aye yup."

"Same perps. And Bruce here is about to tell us who Bonnie and Clyde are."

"Randy Coltair and Cam Jenkins. ... Carl's boy."

"Carl?" Stevens said. "I brought him in this morning. The chief had a sit-down with him—"

Just then Hicks stepped out from behind his office door and gestured towards the officers. "Guthrie and Durst, can I see you a moment?" Hicks shook his head, watching Stevens scarf down a donut. He grinned and raised his voice so the entire station could hear. "Oh, and one more thing. Officer Stevens, wipe that cream filling off your chin. You look like an old whore." The station erupted in laughter, including a snicker from Hicks. He then retreated inside his office and waited for Guthrie and Durst to file in.

"Come in and take a seat. Close the door behind you."

The officers sat down exchanging glances at one another. They sensed Hicks's demeanor was about to change.

"I'll get right to the point," Hicks said, leaning forward and glancing at the clock on the wall. "Earlier this morning, after my sit-down with Carl Jenkins, I called for The Keepers to meet this evening, seven thirty prompt. Reports of 'activity' have been on the increase and unrest is building. Not since 1973 have we seen such odious levels."

Hicks set his eyes firmly on both officers and continued. "Being Chief of this town and elder of The Keepers, it is my sworn duty and responsibility to keep the public safe. For over three hundred years, each one of my predecessors has executed that responsibility without fail. Samuel Hicks, my 6th great-grandfather, shouldered the duties as elder back in 1694. And in all that time The Keepers managed a relative peace."

Hicks lifted from his chair and peered out the window. "Sergeant Guthrie see to it that all the necessary arrangements are made and confirm with the members. That is all."

The officers rose from their chairs and made for the door. Guthrie stopped and addressed Hicks. "Chief, we could have a problem. That trouble down at the high school and Walnut Creek points to Cam Jenkins, Carl's son. Bruce confirmed it."

Hicks turned from the window and stepped to his desk. He sat down in his chair and opened the top drawer. "Anything else?" he asked, unzipping a leather pouch.

"There's one other thing. Down at the Tri-Stop this morning, a reporter, a young city guy, made his acquaintance with Carl Jenkins and started asking questions. A fella by the name of, Don Williams."

The chief tamped down a thumb of tobacco in the bowl of his pipe and struck a wooden match against the sole of his boot. He guided the crackling stick of sulfur to the bowl's rim and drew the flame into the pack with a gentle pull of air.

Guthrie cleared his throat as he watched a blue ring spiral upward. An orange glow flared inside the chamber as Hicks dipped his chin and drew down on the stem. "What about Cam Jenkins, Chief?"

"For the time being leave it be. I need everyone's focus on tonight. After we meet this evening, I'll issue an arrest warrant against Cam Jenkins. He will be charged and held on bail by the book. But if he gives you any kind of trouble, I'll slap a Section 35 petition against him. I'll have his ass in Titicut State Hospital, just like we'd done his old man years ago."

Hicks lifted his chin, chuckling around the stem of his pipe. "Yes, sir, Sergeant Guthrie, any trouble at all and that boy will be strapped to a gurney and drooling into a government-issue cup faster than you can say 'Jack Robinson.'"

Guthrie smiled thinly, then snickered.

"Will there be anything else, Chief?"

"Keep an eye on this reporter fella, Williams. I want to know his comings and goings."

"Right, Chief." Guthrie turned and exited, shutting the door behind him. He grunted as he made his way to his desk. It was going to be a long night.

CHAPTER 17
BARK AT THE MOON

"That'll be sixty-five dollars and thirty-seven cents," the store clerk said. Don Williams reached for his wallet and thumbed through three twenties and a ten and handed it to the cashier.

"Say," Don asked, "the motel just off the exit on 24, do you know if it's a good place to stay?"

"Just off 24 you say?" The cashier took hold of his chin and gave it some quiet thought. The only sound heard was the rhythmic breathing from his nose and mouth. "Ah yes, on 24. The Wampan Inn. Fine establishment. You'll have no trouble finding a room neither."

"Why's that? Off-season?" Again, silence and breathing; Williams fixed his eyes on the coarse, gray hairs jetting from the cashier's nostrils on each exhale.

"Well, I can't say that I know," the cashier said, handing back the change. "I haven't given it much thought till now."

"Thank you," Don said, tucking his wallet inside his coat pocket. "Well, you have a nice day."

"You as well ... Mr. Williams."

Don stopped. He smiled oddly and turned back toward the cashier. "You just called me, Mr. Williams."

"It's a fine name. Welsh if I'm not mistaken."

Don shook his head. "Yes, but how did you know my name? I paid in cash, not a credit card."

"I don't know. Lucky guess, I guess. You kinda look like a Williams. Well, enjoy your stay over at the Wampan Inn. Say hello to Henry for me."

"Henry?"

"The proprietor is an old friend of mine. When you see him, tell him the fleshing knives he was asking about have just arrived. He'd want to know."

With a blank stare Don carried out the purchased items and loaded them into the trunk of his '77 Buick: cork bulletin board, a spool of wire, thumbtacks, a ream of 20-lb paper, Post-it notes, marking pens, fold-out maps of the surrounding area, mucking boots, and a couple of long-handled sickles with serrated blades. Don thought, as he held the thick-handled sickle dubiously in his soft hand, the blade resembled that of a medieval torture device used for purposes of disembowelment. A practice, he recalled, exacted on those found guilty of high treason in the middle ages whereby the condemned, still alive, would be slit open with all the skill of a surgeon. The organs would be carefully removed, making sure to keep the condemned alive as long as possible to maximize pain. He dropped the sickle hastily and closed the trunk.

Backing out of the parking space, Don turned and looked over his right shoulder. There, just below the sign, Burt's Hardware and Farm Supply, he could see the ashen face of the store clerk peer listlessly from behind the window and felt the hairs on the back of his neck stand up. He dipped his eyes a moment to shift into drive, then looked over his shoulder once again to see the face behind the glass fade from view like a smoke ring losing shape. Don squinted and shook it off as being nothing more than reflective glare.

He drove out of the parking lot and followed along Route 104. Glancing at the map, the Wampan Inn was only about five miles ahead by the 24 overpass. As he sped along, thoughts of the cold case flooded his mind.

Why did the Mulrooney file sit gathering dust for ten years? Why did Gerry Mulrooney, the reporter on this story, need to leave town so quickly and never bothered clearing his desk or picking up his last paycheck? And why then, when asked about his check, did the phone go dead before he answered? And why did Carl Jenkins look like he was going to piss himself when I asked him about the swamp back in '73? And then there's Sergeant Psycho. So quick to step in and act like Carl's correction officer, eager to get his inmate back to his padded cell and run me out of town?

It would be slow going and difficult to cut through the stacks of notes, names, locations, clippings, etc., etc.; but Don knew the answers were in the thick, Mulrooney file somewhere, and in the recollections of Carl Jenkins' mind, however scattered it may be.

If he could only speak to Carl, alone, gain his trust, get him to open up about that fateful night in '73, he knew he could find out what really happened to those three men, John Hooke, Paul Andrews, and Mark Fuller. He could find out why Carl was the only one who walked out of the swamp that night. And perhaps, just perhaps, help bring those responsible for their disappearance to justice and deliver some measure of peace to the victims' families. Making a name for himself would not hurt either.

"Route 24 just ahead," Don said aloud. "The Wampan Inn should be just beyond the next bend."

As he looped around the soft curve, the orange burn of a fluorescent light caught his eye. It glared in shades of red just above the 'vacancy' sign flickering *"Wampan Inn."* As he drove beneath the 24 overpass, he slowed down before turning into the parking lot. Thoughts of the case were still running through his mind.

Sergeant Psycho is watching Jenkins like a hawk. Getting to Carl won't be easy. But when I do, if I do, I only hope he is stable enough to answer my questions. The file talks of Carl suffering from flashbacks and from a nervous condition. 'Wackadoodle,' is what my mom called these types.... Vietnam, heavy booze, his wife leaving him, a stint at Titicut State Hospital. That's a heavy load. And with people surrounding him like Sergeant Guthrie, I guess I'd be crazy too.

Don parked in front by the main office door and stepped out of the car. He noticed only a pickup truck and a late-model Chevy four-door parked in front of room number seven.

Next to the pay phone, beneath a Simpson Spring soda sign, garbage spilled from a dumpster onto the ground. He could see the tail of what looked like a racoon, or perhaps an overgrown rat, jet between torn bags of loose trash squeaking and clicking.

Frowning, Don glanced skeptically over the property before he walked up to the office door. There was a cardboard sign taped to the inside glass which read 'Welcome. Your home away from home. Come on in.' In smaller, handwritten print, just below, it read: 'The door sometimes sticks. Management.'

Don turned the doorknob three-quarters releasing the latch from the strike plate, swinging the door open into the small office. "That was easy enough," Don said under his breath, as he stepped across the threshold, the boards creaking beneath his shoes. "Maybe this won't be so bad."

The tiny abode of an office looked like a hybrid between a Native American museum and one of those tourist traps so common down the Cape, where storefronts sell everything from cigar store Indians to novelty cans of Cape Cod air.

Closing the door behind him, his eyes traveled over the walls, the ceiling, and the floor; every square inch of the space was covered by hooks, wires, frames, and shelves. Old cabinets, and even older trunks were filled with toy Indians, plastic tomahawks, bows & arrows with rubber points, headdresses, smokeless pipes adorned with colored feathers, drums, moccasins, and breech clouts designed to wear over a boy's clothes.

In the corner stood a small replica of a teepee made of lightweight, bleached canvas. Complete with a plastic-log campfire and a flickering, red light plugged into a wall socket. It was every young boy's dream; all who had spent much of their youth running through the woods whooping up war chants and beating their hands over their mouths with alarming ferocity.

Don's eyes returned to the front desk where a tarnished bell lined with fringe sat on the counter. Taped beneath was an index card that read 'Ring for Service.' Don tapped down on the bell twice. The sound was louder and tinnier than he imagined it would be and he began to pace like he had just done something wrong.

He leaned his elbows on the desk, nervously, and studied the items hanging on the wall behind the register. His eyes were drawn to the two, feather headdresses. One in white, and the larger of the two in black. Flanked on either side of the headdresses, a pair of wooden objects with fringe on the handle and a gourd like object near the top hung at right angles. Just above, his eyes settled on a long staff made of dark wood which had a triangular-shaped point on one end with three, black and white feathers hanging loosely near its tip. The other end of the staff was worn down. Presumably from being handled over the years. Handled how many times and for what purpose? God only knew.

Growing a little impatient, Don rang the bell twice more and called out. "Hello. Is anybody here?" A second passed, then another, before he heard a dull grunt followed by a heavy, muffled thud. The sound appeared to be coming from outdoors just behind the office. He walked to the end of the front desk and leaned over to see a partially open rear door leading outside. He stretched over farther still, and could see through the narrow opening a human figure with his back towards the office, standing with hunched shoulders and his head angled downward, looking at whatever was before him.

"Hello," Don said, "are you the manager?" The figure snapped his head around his left shoulder.

"Sure am. One and only. I'll be right with you, if you please, and I'll get you set with the BEST room in the house, or my name ain't Henry James."

His voice was like bagpipes over broken glass. It rasped and shrilled with a kind of plantation twang. Yet there was a musical quality to it, with highs and lows, like jumbled notes tumbling down a river.

A little startled, Don fell back a bit from the man's sudden turn. His unique voice and his enormous smile set in the deep lines of his face caught him off guard.

"No problem, Mr. James," Don replied. "Take your time."

"Always do!" Henry James said. "Ain't no use in hurrying life, I always say, we all get there soon enough." His voice became louder as Henry passed from the outside in and stepped through the rear door. He was wiping down his enormous hands against the bloodstained front of a full-length rubber apron draped around his neck and cinched at the waist. It was the kind of apron worn by farm hands to slaughter pigs.

"Now," Henry continued, "let's get you setup with a room, Mr? ..."

"Williams," Don replied. "Don Williams."

"Good name. Strong Christian name," Henry said, extending his hand. "Pleazed to meet you Mr. Williams." Don reached for Henry's hand, but stopped at the sight of his bloodstained apron. Henry threw his head back, slightly embarrassed, the angles of his face more pronounced.

"Now, where are your manners at?" Henry huffed to himself, removing the smeared, rubber apron from his wiry body. "Forgive my appearance, Mr. Williams. One moment." Henry hung the apron on a back hook, out of view, and ran his long fingers over his shiny, bald head. "Now, that's betta. I don't wanna go scaring off any customers before they had a chance to sign on the dotted line."

Don smiled and reached his hand across the counter to meet Henry's.

"Pleased to meet you," Don said. "You are, Henry James?"

"I am," he said, his smile brighter than the sun. "However, the good folks of Titicut know me as Moonshine."

Don's upper lip curled into what could pass for a smile, his eyes looking deeper into the man's face. *Hmm, Moonshine, ha? Bloodshot eyes? Raspy voice? No stranger to the bottle, I'm sure.*

"Well, Moonshine, may I call you that?"

"I insist ya do, or my name ain't Henry James. Now then…" Henry flipped open a registry book and traced his finger down the page.

"Looks like you're in luck. We got several rums available. How long you plan on stayin' with us, here, at the Wampan Inn?"

Don shook his head indecisively. "Could be a day or ten. Depends how long it takes to find answers. That, and how long the paper continues to pick up the bill."

"Paper? You a newsman?" Henry asked, his eyes never lifting from the registry.

"Yeah, I'm down here chasing a story. Also, do you have a room that would accommodate a few more people, perhaps one with a hot plate and an icebox? It's possible that a crew will come down here to join me. I'll be setting up the room to be used as a command post."

Still maintaining eye contact with the registry, Henry's finger travelled up the page and turned it. He then lifted his head with a beaming smile and said, "I've got just the one. Rum sixteen. Bigger than the rest and more private. I can bring over an icebox and a hot plate, have it set up for ya in no time at all."

Before Don could reply, he heard what sounded like a voice softer than a whisper. Don had just pulled out his wallet and placed his credit card on the desk when he stopped and looked at Henry. "Did you hear that?"

Henry took an imprint of the card and asked for Don's signature before replying.

"Hear what, Mr. Williams?"

"A sound, a whisper. I don't know. I couldn't make it out, but I heard something."

Henry waved his hand. "Naah, it's nothing. Back in these woods, the way that wind comes off the swamp, people around here get used to all kinds of strange sounds. Don't pay 'em no mind at all."

Don finished signing the carbon receipt and took a copy and placed it in his pocket.

"Much obliged, Mr. Williams. Now, you just go out here and walk to the end of the building and go around back. Rum sixteen is at the rear."

"Got it," Don said. "Say, Henry—"

"Please, call me Moonshine."

"Right, Moonshine. The two headdresses on the wall, are they authentic?"

"Sure is," Henry replied proudly, turning to look them over.

"Where did you get them? I'd love to get my hands on a headdress like that. Having one in my apartment would be a great conversation piece. The guys would love it on poker night."

Henry laughed, shaking his head. "I s'pects you might find a replica that would suit you, Mr. Williams, but not like this. No-sir... These here have been passed down through the generations. Story is, they've been in my family long before the James's were fishing that river down in Virginia."

"How old are they? And why is one white and the other black?"

"Well, my daddy pulled me aside, when I was just a boy, and tells me, 'Henry, the black headdress is old and very special, but the white one, the white one, he says, was long old before the King of England ever planted his hands in the rich Virginia soil.'"

Don listened with interest. His face went quiet and leaned in closer, sensing Henry had more to tell. After pausing and partly closing his eyelids, Henry's voice went somber, no longer carrying a friendly musical twang.

"Then he says to me, 'Henry, there are two nations. People of the Early Dawn and People of the Fallen Night. The death of one gave rise to the other. Both are your story; both are your people.'"

"That sounds ominous. What did he mean the death of one gave rise to the other?"

"Well, it's never talked about. And most folks never heard of it, I reckon cause some things are better left buried and unsaid, but the first men were defeated in the war of 1675. The last of the tribe were killed right here in this swamp."

"My senior year in high school I wrote a paper on King Philip's War," Don said. "It was more like a massacre, an annihilation of a people."

"It surely was, but what the newcomers didn't know is the first men knew the swamp and this land like the back of their hand. And some of them survived their musket fire and could live within the swamp's black waters undetected." Henry smiled wide. "And their descendants live today. Enuff of that, Mr. Williams, here are your keys. Rum sixteen, just round back."

Don took the keys and turned toward the door when he heard Henry laugh out and say, "You know, Mr. Williams, that is a common enough misconception, why they call me that."

Don stopped and turned around. "Call you what?"

"Moonshine. People like yourself think because of who I am and how I look, the name Moonshine must be because I drink." A chill of air waved over Don, drawing up pea-size gooseflesh all over his skin. His lips parted, searching for the words.

"But I never said—"

"I never touch the stuff myself," Henry said, cutting him off. "Demon alcohol. Fire water. Never had a drop of the, how they say? White man's poison."

Don, feeling the gooseflesh harden like thumbtacks said, "How did you come by the name?"

"Over these many years, when the night skies are brightest, the townsfolk hear howling coming out these woods right behind here. I hear it too. But if you ask me, it sounds more like a yelp than a howl. Anyway, since I was the only one at the time that had any property along this stretch of swamp, they'd say, 'ole Henry must be howling at the moon again.' I've been known as Moonshine ever since. ARH-WOOOOOOOOOOOOOOOOOOOOOO." Henry cackled. "I still got it." He walked over to the hook and looped the rubber apron back on over his head. "I'll be over shortly with your icebox and hot plate. Thank you, Mr. Williams, for choosing the Wampan Inn. Enjoy your stay."

With a nod of his head, Henry turned and walked out the rear door of his office, whistling a tune.

Don stood there pale faced. He was both fascinated and spooked all at the same time. He could not help but think:

If I run into a dead-end chasing ghosts from the past, no worries. My story is right here in Henry James, Moonshine. Not only would he fill a ten-thousand- word Exposé in the newspaper, but this man is a walking, Stephen King novel ready to be written.

CHAPTER 18
NOW YOU SEE IT, NOW YOU DON'T

The thick, dark smoke that had blanketed Jenkins' field, had lifted and thinned to blue skies. The roar of engines and the terrified screams of one's last moments on earth had gone quiet. Only the pastoral sounds of grass rustling and the sharp trill of bush crickets could be heard. It was as before, yet somehow more still, the air more heavy. Like the quiet before a storm where the atmosphere is so volatile one hesitates to move or even breath for fear of being electrocuted. And then.

"Jesus, Cam. What the hell just happened?"

"I don't know." Cam was shaken and his head felt a dull ache. His eyes focused on the field in the distance.

"I can see the Trans Am," Cam said

"I see it too, but I don't see the truck. Where did those assholes go?"

"I don't know. They were right behind them."

Darrah and Niki were shaken. Everything happened so fast and then there was nothing. They sat stunned until Niki asked, "Darrah, are you okay?"

"I think so." Darrah's lip quivered as she turned to face Niki. "What just happened?"

Niki shook her head, bewildered. She slowly lifted from the seat, and looked behind only to see tire tracks and turned up dirt, but there was no evidence of the truck anywhere. It's as if it had vanished. She dropped back in her seat and said, "I don't know."

Frightened, they slowly turned their heads towards each other, their mouths hanging open. They could hear excited barking coming from behind and saw Whitey appear.

"Oh my god Nik, it's Whitey." Darrah stepped out of the car followed by Niki and knelt down beside Whitey patting his head.

"Are you all right?" Cam and Randy said, running up behind them. Cam cupped Darrah's face and kissed her on the mouth. "You scared the hell out of me," he said, rushing out the words. Her bottom lip parted into a tender smile as she lifted her hand and ran her fingers through his long hair. "I'm okay," she said. "I don't know what happened, but Niki and I are okay."

He had a look in his eyes, the look that spoke the words most girls long to hear, but his eyes held hers in unbroken silence until a wet sloppy tongue drew up the side of his face and killed the moment. Cam fell over on his back with Whitey glued to his chest.

"Jealous much?" Darrah said, her eyebrow raised at Whitey. "Both of us can share him you know."

"Did you hear that, boy?" Cam said, "Darrah is feeling jealous and left out."

Nicole laughed, but it turned into an uneasy smile as she stood and looked in the standpipe's direction, replaying the events in her mind. She doubted herself and questioned if what she just witnessed wasn't a hallucination of a pickled brain. She was still drinking, having just finished her umpteenth beer of the day, and still felt the effects of being drunk the night before. So drunk in fact, she woke up naked not knowing where here pants were, and almost made a deal with God but chose the devil instead.

But I know what I saw, Nicole thought, *before everything went black. There were four assholes in a truck chasing us through the field. And now they're gone.*

She looked up at the wide sky and felt a biting cold pass over her. Her nerves felt raw at her coming awareness. Scanning the field of blue above her head, she rubbed out the chill with the palm of her hands and looked for something, anything, that might explain what happened. She had seen it, plain as day. She knew she did. But did they?

"Who wants a beer?" Niki asked, turning back from her thoughts, bending over the cooler in the back seat of the Trans Am.

"Mm, mmm, I think I want something else," Randy cracked.

"Give it up, Randy," Niki replied, her hand on an exaggerated hip. "Just help me with this cooler."

"Yes, ma'am." Randy jumped to his feet, brushing off his jeans and grabbed an end.

"I'll take a beer," Cam said.

"Wine cooler for me, Nik," Darrah said, sitting up with tousled hair.

Randy underhanded Cam a beer and passed a wine cooler to Darrah. They all sat Indian style with Whitey sprawled out in the center of them like the hub of a wheel feeling content and restful.

Each cracked their drinks open and looked at each other like they all shared a secret they did not want to face, until Niki said, "All right. We all know what's going on. Tell me you saw what I saw. If I'm crazy, that's okay, then I'm crazy, but I'd rather be crazy together and not alone."

Heads turned and eyes darted. "I'm not sure how crazy you are Nik," Darrah began, "but you're not alone. I saw everything too. You saw it. I saw it."

Both Randy and Cam shook their heads in agreement. "Yeah, Same here," Cam said, lighting a cigarette. "Randy and I had just put out the fire and watched the truck vanish right behind you."

"See, Nik, we all saw it. So, if you're crazy, we're all crazy."

"What are we going to do?" Niki's uneasiness began to mount. She flashed a look at Cam and Randy. "What the fuck did you guys do now? Why were they here, lighting the barn on fire?"

"Those dicks," Randy spit, "they just showed up out of nowhere."

"Yeah, we were at the house when it happened," Cam explained, "and by the time we got outside to find out what was going on, we saw the barn in flames."

"Uh huh, so, you didn't do anything? They just decided hey, I know, let's go burn down Cam's barn for no reason?"

Cam and Randy looked at each other, knowing Niki would not let it go.

"Okay," Randy said, "we pulled a job down at the high school. It was a pretty good pull, too. Even scored some AC/DC tickets."

"Shit, Randy. My father is a cop, remember?"

"How'd they know it was you?" Darrah asked. "Did they catch you?"

"Our faces were completely covered," Randy said. "They never got a look at us."

"Randy's right," Cam said. "We were hitting the lockers when they came in on us, but there's no way they would have known it was us. We were out the window as soon as they came in."

"Fuck!" Niki said. "How many others know you robbed the school?"

"I'm telling you, there's no way they knew. I have no fucking idea how—"

"Cool it," Cam said, blowing out a smoke ring and rising to his feet. "We've got bigger problems. We don't know how they knew, and we don't know how many others might know, but we all just saw what happened. They did not just decide to drive off. They were right behind you Darrah, and then they weren't. They just vanished, poof! And they disappeared. When the cops come snooping, and they'll come, how do we explain a missing three-thousand-pound truck and four, missing, two-hundred-pound football players?"

"We don't, man," Randy said. "We just dummy up, all of us. Hear no evil, see no evil, bro."

"Randy is right," Darrah said. "We play it cool, like nothing ever happened. We can easily explain the fire as accidental, smoking in the barn, etc. And the truck? The jocks? What truck? What jocks? There's no evidence they were ever here, Cam. The tire tracks all blend together, and can be easily explained. If ever asked, you can say you were driving Carl's truck through the field, horsing around, or you were blasting through on your bikes. We are the only ones who saw what happened. The only ones who know the truth."

Cam paced back and forth and weighed his options. He wasn't convinced that all they had to do was dummy up and remain quiet and all would be fine, but it was the best option they had. The trouble is, he knew, it was hard enough for two people to keep a secret, never mind four.

CHAPTER 19
MY ONLY FRIEND, THE END

Ten miles south of Jenkins' Farm, in a town bordering Titicut, a woman in her mid-fifties set the receiver down next to the telephone. She had contacted the visiting nurse and informed her she would not be in need of her services today. An old friend, she said, would come by in the afternoon for lunch and agreed to help her fold linens and change her oxygen.

She lifted from her chair beside the credenza. The kettle on the burner was whistling. Rolling the tank behind her, she labored across the parlor, wistfully looking at the framed pictures of her son hanging on the wall.

Taking up the kettle in her arthritic hands, she poured the boiling water over the tea-bag and lowered a spoonful of honey into the steaming liquid. She gave it a few gentle swirls before she wrapped her bluish fingers around the mug and brought it to her lips.

The sweet hot goodness warmed her aching bones and swollen joints, but did little for her pained heart. A heart gone cold, burdened by a paralyzing sorrow.

It had been ten years since he was stolen from me, she thought, as she trained her eyes through the kitchen window at the frayed tire swing hanging from the oak. Despite official reports listing him as a missing person and despite the fact police reported multiple sightings over the years from so called 'reliable sources,' she knew he was long dead. She knew he was never coming home.

How terribly cruel it had been in the beginning, she recalled, *sightings of him springing up from time to time in the New England area, the descriptions near perfect. A mother's hopes raised only to be shoved back down into the pit of her stomach, realizing in sudden and sickening horror the reports must have been that of an evil trickster. A repugnancy of the most foul kind. ... It was all too heavy, all too hard to live with, but when you find the truth is far more savage, more terrible than anyone could have imagined, you give in to those voices pounding in your head; the ones telling you it is utterly hopeless. Telling you, it's a lost cause. Shouting you'll never know justice. Screaming you will never, ever, see your boy again. The voices well knew she was all alone, and so did she. Powerless in the face of the machine.*

She allowed the last bit of honey to trail down from the bottom of the cup and onto her tongue before she set the teacup down and looked once more out her kitchen window. It was time, she knew. Her long nightmare would soon be over.

Turning from the window, she stepped out from the kitchen and back into the narrow hall, passing through the parlor leading to her bedroom. She would take only two items with her: her favorite framed picture of him and the snub-nosed revolver kept in the drawer next to her sickbed.

Her heart paced at the realness of it. What she had thought of doing more times than she can remember was here and now. Decide on something and see it through, she always told her son, and once she had decided on something it was done. There was no turning back. Before her body failed her, before she felt too weak to carry on, she would exact what measure of justice she could at the end of a 38.

Holding the revolver in her hand and inserting bullets into the cylinder, sent a surge of nervous energy through her frailty. Anticipation grew and her breathing became excited as she tucked the framed picture of her son inside the front of her jacket and placed the revolver into the zipped lining of her pocket.

She reached down to crank the valve allowing for more oxygen to flow up through the inserted tubing in her nose. Her nerves were jumping. Not from the fear of getting caught, but from the fear of not succeeding. *They will know my pain. They will know my loss. They will suffer as I have suffered.* Weighed down with two pressurized tanks of oxygen, she wheeled the dolly behind her out of doors by the waiting car. Using what precious leg strength she had left, she lifted the awkward metal contraption up on the driver's seat with a series of ugly grunts. Struggling and huffing, thick mucus bubbling in her nose, she balanced her weight on the handle for a moment, before grabbing onto the steering wheel and hoisting herself in.

Short frenzied bursts of air gaped her mouth, panting as an old dog, screwing up her face like a grim reflection in a funhouse mirror. Beads of sweat danced and dripped from her blotched forehead, wetting her bony fingers trembling on the wheel.

She peeled her hands away and braced her aching ribs, strained and bruised, her lungs starving for air. Her fingers travelled down over her abdomen and found the corners of the picture frame. She prayed as tears welled up in her eyes repeating, "Their life for yours. Their life for yours."

After a few moments of repose, her fingers tracing the worn corners of the frame, she backed out of the driveway and drove the two-mile country road to I-495 north. It was the quickest way to travel the nine miles to Titicut Township and time was of the essence. And even though she had an extra tank of oxygen, it only took you so far, lasted only so long. Each minute counted in successfully carrying out her plan, the plan she thought about, alone, during the long days and even longer nights. There was no tomorrow, she knew. There would be no second chances. She would carry out her mission today, the day a price would be paid for taking away from her, her only son.

How many times since 1973 had she driven this road, she wondered, yet today was the first time she had noticed her surroundings. The sky was an early autumn blue dotted with white clouds like puffs of cotton sitting dreamily on a wide blanket. They appeared to float above the fields of shaded green as though they were colored in a children's book. The trees of oak and elm and red maple were glorious filling her windows, their branches like living fingers of God reaching for the heavens, where red-tailed hawks drift effortlessly on sweet currents of air. With a clarity of vision, she took in the natural world around her, soaking up the beauty that had always been there, she reasoned, but had never noticed before.

They stole so much. First my beloved son, then my faith in God. I have looked for you, as I have looked for Him. I have prayed as fools pray in the church of Your Father. I am broken and beyond His hand.

As she slowed to take the Titicut exit, she thought it funny and ironic, that of all the days, 'the day she would see her plan through,' was the day she saw clear signs of Him. She wondered, was it His way of sending her a wake-up call that what she was about to do was commit a crime against His laws? Or was it His way of affirming her plan with an Almighty smile of retribution? What Matthew 5:38 called "An eye for an eye, and a tooth for a tooth."

She smirked at how little it mattered now, but preferred to think it was the latter. She turned the crank down on her oxygen tank as she felt an unexpected calm wash over her. Her breathing felt light and effortless. A peaceful sense of purpose filled her aching heart with abundant joy — the joy a heretic on the cross must feel, she suspected, being born again and absolved of all sin, moments before they meet their maker.

She turned off the ramp into Titicut and drove that barren stretch of road to her place of vigil. It was a place along the western edge of the swamp where she and the others would meet for prayer, comfort, and the lighting of candles. It was a solemn place, a cut between the asphalt and the swamp, where her son and the others were known to have been last seen. It would be the place she would park today, but not to light candles of hope as she had done countless times before, but to flame a beacon of vengeance.

The metal dolly freed itself with relative ease as she yanked back on the handle and allowed gravity to send it to the ground with a clunking thud. She then reached inside her jacket and secured the picture before she felt over her pocket to make sure the revolver was in place. She affixed the oxygen mask snug to her face and secured the tubing in her nose. She was ready.

The walk into the thick underbrush and over the gnarled roots of the swamp's bed would be strenuous. It was critical she make it to the clearing in time before the police came to find her. They always came. She surveyed the long stretch of road and realized it would not be long now. They always knew when she was there, and they always came looking for her. It was like clockwork. They would find her, as they always did, but this time she had no plans to leave with them peacefully. She had no plans to leave at all.

As she disappeared behind the swamp's thick curtain, it was the first time in years she could see her way home.

CHAPTER 20
SEE NO EVIL,
HEAR NO EVIL,
SPEAK NO EVIL

"You're right, Darrah," Cam said, "there is no evidence around the standpipe. The only tire tracks I saw were chewed-up earth on the way to nowhere. And the fire can easily be explained by saying I fell asleep with a cigarette in my mouth. The cops have nothing. We are the only ones that know the truth. But what if—?"

"But what?" Randy asked. Cam hesitated. He was concerned that eventually one of the three would talk. Either by police duress, or by telling tales while shit-faced. Then Cam had an idea. He pulled out a jackknife and pressed it to his palm.

"Let's make a pact, together, and swear we'll keep this secret forever. All four of us, right now."

"I'm cool with that," Randy said, "Niki?"

"Yeah, I guess. But can't we agree without cutting ourselves?"

"I'm with Nik," Darrah said, holding up the back of her hand and wiggling her fingers. "Scars may be cool for guys, but I think it would clash with my painted nails. Can't we all just promise not to say anything? None of us are going to talk."

Cam thought about it, closing his jackknife, and tucking it in the pocket of his jeans. Their eyes all searched each other's faces, their expressions leaving him unconvinced.

"Look, I know we all trust each other. We've been tight a long time. But how about this? I've seen in movies where they use smoke in ceremonies, like in rituals and shit like that."

"I'm cool with it," Randy said. "Niki? Darrah?"

The girls both looked at each other and smiled. "Yeah, I guess. We're cool."

After some discussion, they decided each would stand before the others and recite words upon which they all agreed. After completing the simple oath, the oath taker would be bathed in ceremonial smoke whereby the others would bear full witness to the sworn offering.

Cam volunteered first and stood in the center with Randy, Darrah, and Niki at three equidistant points forming a triangle around him. Each lit their cigarette in preparation and waited for Cam to signal he was ready. Once ready, the three would draw back on their cigarettes and hold in the smoke until Cam finished reciting the words and extended his arms.

He gave a nod and began, "Bathed in smoke before the spirits, I pledge this oath of brotherhood. My word is my eternal bond, and I will remain forever silent from this day until my last."

Darrah, Nicole, and Randy exhaled together as they watched the cloud of smoke drift up around Cam's head and cover his face. The smoke wrapped around his shoulders and circled his waist. It then trailed up from his knees and swirled his outstretched arms, curling around his fingertips. His body was immersed in 'spirit smoke,' blanketing his entire being in a ritualistic cloud of brotherhood.

Each would follow suit, doing exactly as Cam did, all pledging to an eternal bond and promising to take their secret to the grave. Darrah was the last to take the pledge. As the cloud of smoke began to thin and peel from her body, a voice was heard shouting across the field.

"Hey, Cam! That you?"

"Who's that?" Randy asked, all of them shooting their eyes toward the voice. Cam squinted beneath a cupped hand and looked over the field towards the house. He could see a man waving his hand frantically, the other hand hung down by his side holding on to a tool.

"Shit. I think that's Sonny," Cam said.

"Who's Sonny?" Randy asked.

"He's a friend of Carl's." Cam gave Sonny a wave.

"What are you doing?" Randy said.

"He knew I saw him, Randy. He was looking right at me."

"Cam, you got a minute?" Sonny said.

"Dammit. Come on." Cam turned his head around and looked at the girls.

"Go on, baby," Darrah reassured him. "Deal with him now and find out what he knows. And remember the oath. Act as if nothing ever happened."

Cam nodded as he and Randy made their way across the field.

"This guy Sonny," Randy asked, "who is he?"

Cam struck a match and lit a cigarette. "Old high school buddy of Carl's. They served together in Vietnam. Carl used to hang out at his garage, talk cars, engines, shit like that. Back in the day, him and Carl, and a few other guys, used to hunt on weekends. There'd be times they'd head out on a Friday night and you wouldn't smell him till Sunday. Ripe with swamp water, sweat, and booze."

"Drinking by a fire and doing some hunting, I get," Randy said. "But swatting mosquitoes covered in swamp water. What's up with that?" Never breaking stride, Cam crushed his smoke out under his foot. "I guess it reminded him of Nam..."

Slowing down, they passed the standpipe on the left. Deep gouges could be seen cut into the field, fanning into a wider stretch of freshly overturned dirt. Brackish water lay still beneath thick locks of grass and weeds. But for a cloud of insects hovering just above the surface, there were no signs of life at all. A seemingly undisturbed wetland shrouded by a field of grass, hiding as the Venus flytrap hides to capture and swallow unsuspecting prey.

Sonny stepped out from the side of the house and passed under the branches of the apple tree. He spat out a dingy load of tobacco, black and slippery like the bottom of an oil drum.

"Friend-of-yours?" Sonny asked, his words running together as a single utterance.

"Randy," Cam said, "this is Sonny, one of Carl's friends." Sonny's sleeves were rolled up to the elbows; mechanic's grease smeared over the length of his arms. He pulled a red hanky from his back pocket and began to wipe the length of his fingers and hands, hands that reminded Randy of overcooked hamburger.

"Come again?" Sonny fired back.

"Randy," Cam said, "Randy Coltair."

"Pleazed to meet you, Randy." Randy gave Sonny a quick handshake, immediately reaching for the back of his leg to wipe the grease from his hand. Sonny cackled, his mouth wrenching to the side. "A little plug and grease won't hurt you none. Holy hell. It was a lot worse in Nam you know, Charlie was everywhere. Trouble is, you couldn't hardly see them until they drew ya into the bush and plunged one in your side."

Randy and Cam snickered as they glanced over Sonny's face trying to get a read of the man. But it was like staring into the face of someone who'd been zapped by 240 volts. Strands of hair standing on end. Red-faced. His eyes brighter than two glass marbles rolling in watery sockets. Reading him was like reading the face of a circus carney.

"You talk to Carl?" Cam asked.

"Can't say that I have. I gave the door a knock, but—what the hell? Is that your Trans Am out there? Looks like a '78. No, wait one goddamn minute, that's a '79."

Sonny spat excitedly and flailed around like a monkey. His voice was like a hillbilly's on helium. "Betcha she got a HEMI shifter, that 4-banging bitch of a smoke-show has a Super T-10 tranny with 400 in the throat. Damn boy! No trouble outrunning Charlie round these parts. Ain't like Nam, you know."

"I guess not," Cam quipped.

"Come again?" Sonny spit. The dazed face of a carny looked straight through Cam; his hand cupped around his right ear. Cam and Randy snickered, relieved that this guy knew jack shit to nothing. And if he knew anything, who the fuck would believe him.

"Want me to get Carl for you?"

"HELL NO," Sonny said. "Clear as a bell he told me. Don't knock twice. Once, but not twice. Just tell him I got that utility truck of his running. Dropped in a fuel pump. Even-Steven. Just need you boys to give me a hand loading up that sweet Johnny Popper."

Cam and Randy looked at each other with blank faces. "Holy hell, boys," Sonny said. "The Johnny Popper? That tractor rusting out under the chestnut tree? Chop, chop, gotta get. Not like Nam, you know."

CHAPTER 21
A ROOM WITHOUT A VIEW

After grabbing a coffee at Mary Lou's in the town square, Sergeant Guthrie circled the center green and headed out on Plymouth County Road, a few miles from the 24 overpass, and hopped on the radio.

"Officer Durst, come in, over." Guthrie set the mic of his police radio on his knee and took a sip of coffee, wiping his mustache with the back of his hand. He radioed again: "Officer Durst, this is Sergeant Guthrie, come—"

"Yeah, Sergeant, Durst here, over."

"Bruce, after you finish up, make sure you report to the chief."

"Will do. All but two have confirmed they'll be there tonight at the old meeting house, seven-thirty sharp. Still waiting on Thomas Prence and Walt Bradford."

Guthrie chuckled. "Old Walt's probably chasing that blonde receptionist of his. All right, I'm sure you'll hear from them soon. Check in when you do."

"Consider it done Sarge. Say, have you heard from Stevens?"

"Heard from him about ten minutes ago. Said he was on his way over to the Tri-Stop for a slice of Betty's rhubarb pie. Damn that woman can cook. All right, Bruce. Keep me updated."

"10-4 Sergeant. I'll radio in when I hear back from Prence and Bradford. ... Say, one other thing, Sarge."

"Go ahead, Durst."

"Switch over to your closed channel 22."

Sergeant Guthrie switched to channel 22 and waited a second for a sharp click.

"Channel 22, over, go ahead, Bruce."

"You think Officer Stevens will make it?"

"The chief thinks so. Up to this point, Stevens has kept his nose clean, always follows orders to the letter, has done all that's been asked of him. He has been fully vetted and cleared. Chief said we should know for certain by night's end if the council members will go forward and extend him an invitation."

"I remember my invitation," Durst recalled, "and the ceremony to follow. It wasn't until the 'lighting of the pipe' that I realized just how little I knew, what it takes to keep the peace."

"It hits most of us the same," Guthrie said, "like a diamond bullet shot through the forehead. By tomorrow, we could be welcoming a new brother to the order. Check back later, Bruce. Over and out."

Guthrie rested the mic down by his side. As he drove under the 24 overpass and approached the Wampan Inn, a familiar-looking Buick caught his eye parked near the corner of the building. He pulled into a dirt clearing and drove back behind the lot, passing slowly noting the plate number as he picked up the mic.

"Polly, can you run a plate: 9, 4, 7, J," Guthrie suddenly stopped. "Hold that plate a second, Polly."

"Sure thing, Sarge..."

At that moment, a white van rounded the corner and swung into the parking lot of the Wampan Inn and came to a screeching stop. The door slid open. A young man, no more than 21 or 22 years of age, maybe one hundred and forty pounds soaking wet, hopped out with all the enthusiasm of Bugs Bunny. He turned and leaned in through the door to grab a box, while the driver-side and passenger-side doors sprung open at the same time.

Behind the wheel, a man perhaps in his late twenties and just as spindly, shot down from his seat in a pair of High-Top sneakers while the passenger, a youngster with a fattish boyish face and belly to match, performed more of a careful slide until his unlaced shoes found the ground beneath him.

Guthrie observed the three men make their way over to room number 16. Before they knocked, the door opened in a whirl, spinning up a cloud of smoke as Don Williams stepped out. He was wearing a navy-blue Boston Red Sox T-shirt over faded jeans, a cigarette bounced between his lips while he spoke.

"Yeah, yeah, I know," Don said, feigning regret, "I know I shouldn't smoke, but I'm onto something big. The synapses are firing into overdrive."

The three young men glanced at each other and shrugged their shoulders. "Cool with us," the driver said. "Where do you want us to start?"

"First," Don said, "let's grab the gear. Did Harry have you bring down the audio/video equipment?"

"It's all in there," Brett Myers said, the spindly driver with the high tops. "Plus, some other goodies."

"Goodies?" Don asked, with a slight cock of the head.

"Stuff for the outdoors," Albert Cunningham said, the chubby-faced co-pilot with unlaced shoes. "You can't be too prepared, Mr. Williams. I'm not too fond of the outdoors. It gives me the creeps. Especially swamps and stuff."

Without saying a word, Don raised his brow and thought, *The kid should have picked another education/work co-op at Northeastern University.* Don reached in through the van's door and grabbed an open box. He could see canteens, repellent, flashlights, glow sticks, galoshes, mosquito netting to be worn around the head, and what looked like a folded-up piece of scrap metal with some kind of wide blade tucked underneath.

"What's this?" Don asked.

"It's a cat shovel, Mr. Williams," Albert said. "You know, if you're out in the woods and you have to go to the bathroom really bad."

Squinting his eyes through the smoke, Don stared at the bespeckled, red-cheeked kid. "You know we're here covering a story, not going camping?" Albert smiled and shrugged his shoulders, pushing his glasses back on his nose.

Sergeant Guthrie took a long swallow of coffee and sat alert, watching Don Williams and the crew unload boxes of gear and haul them into room 16. He set the cup back in its holder and picked up the mic, "Polly, put me through to the chief."

"One minute, Sarge." While Guthrie waited, he observed Henry James pass through the office door at the far end of the building wearing a slick, black apron. He disappeared behind a stretch of picket fence that led to the outbuilding where Henry kept the inn's supplies and maintenance equipment.

"Chief Hicks is on. Go Sergeant."

"Chief, I just got off with Durst. Only Thomas Prence and Walt Bradford need to acknowledge. The council chamber is all set for tonight."

"Keep on them. Let me know if you don't hear within the hour."

"Copy that. One more thing Chief, looks like our newspaper fella, Don Williams, is in town for at least awhile. He took a room over at the Wampan Inn, Room 16. Has a few friends along for the ride."

A throaty chuckle passed through the radio. "The Wampan Inn?" the chief said in wild disbelief. "And our boy hasn't taken off for the hills? Even folks around here run at the sight of old Henry, never mind outsiders."

Guthrie grinned. "You want me to stay on him?"

"Yeah, I do. I had something else for you, but I want you to stay on Williams. Find out what you can from Henry and alert me if Williams goes on the move, or if anyone else leaves that motel room."

"Right, Chief. What did you have for me?"

"The Hooke woman, Priscilla, showed up west of the swamp again. Parked along the side of the road where she always parks. I'm going to send Boo Stevens over there."

"Are you sure you want to send Boo?"

"He'll be fine. Hell, he brought in Carl Jenkins this morning, he can handle this. It will look good on his summons for invitation by the council members, if The Keepers decide to take it that far."

"Right, Chief. Copy that. Over and out."

CHAPTER 22
ONE IS FLIRTING TWO IS CHEATING

Betty leaned her elbows on the counter and propped up her smiling cheeks with her hands. "Well, what do you think, Boo?" Already knowing the answer, her smile grew into a big, toothy, gum snapping grin. She watched in delight as Officer Boo Stevens withdrew the fork from his smiling mouth, his face an expression of orgiastic pleasure under closed dreamy eyes.

His fork hit the plate and leaned back on his stool, his tongue working back and forth over his teeth.

"Well, Officer Stevens?"

Boo's eyelids opened in half-slits, his overall expression was that of a stoner after taking a massive hit on a water bong.

"Mm, mm, mm, mm…. Heaven on earth. Better than my Barb's on Thanksgiving, but don't you dare tell her that. You have outdone yourself again Betty. Let me tell you if I weren't married."

"Oh, go on," Betty said, lifting off her elbows and hitting him playfully with a dish linen on the shoulder. "Is there room in there for another slice?" She smiled, circling her finger toward his generous waistline. "Just fresh out of the oven."

Boo pitched back on the stool with his hands across his stomach. "I better stop it there. Two slices of your pie would be damn near cheating, Betty. Besides, my Barb is cooking up a special, birthday dinner for me. A leg of lamb with all the trimmings. 'So sweet and succulent,' Barb says, 'I won't even want the mint jelly.' God, I love that woman."

Betty sighed. "Aww, you are just the sweetest man. She is lucky to have you, Officer Stevens. There is just something about a man that loves his wife's cooking."

From his pocket, Stevens retrieved the folded-up note Barb had included in his birthday gift. He smiled as he fondly read Betty the words.

Happy Birthday my big and burly LOVE MUFFIN. Got my apron on and making your favorite tonight. Get on home when you can... Love, your CREAM PUFF Barb... P.S. You might need a bigger drawer.

"You know that woman had a birthday gift for me on the front seat of my cruiser this morning. A Lawrence Welk tape along with this note. She has been writing notes like this since we were kids in junior high school. I have kept each one of them, too." He chuckled as he lifted his eyes to Betty's. "The drawer in the workbench can't hold them anymore. That's where I keep them all." Betty sighed again and crossed her hands over her heart. "You are a dear, dear, man. Why do you keep them in the garage Boo?"

"Well, that started up years ago when we first moved into the house. I went out to the garage to unpack boxes and found all the notes and letters she had written, tucked inside several notebooks. I couldn't believe just how many there were. Anyway, I began to read through them, and the next thing I knew it was dark outside and not a single box unpacked. So, I stuffed all the notes and letters into the top drawer of the workbench and ran up the stairs to the breezeway and made my way into the kitchen. I thought Barb would be in a huff. But when I went inside the house, she wasn't in a huff at all, in fact she seemed happy and bubbly...

"Turns out, that woman was watching me read all her notes through the breezeway window. The roast she was going to cook was still in plastic wrap next to some unchopped vegetables. Well, my smile turned into an enormous grin, is all, and we both giggled like a couple of teenage girls. The afternoon got away from her too. Neither one of us got a single thing done." Boo smiled and glanced down at the note. "Ever since that day, each additional note or letter she'd write would go in that special drawer. And whenever I got a chance, I would say I was heading out to the garage to work on the lawn mower, change the oil in the car, or work on building birdhouses, and I could feel Barb's presence watching and smiling through the window as I sat on the stool beside the drawer and pulled out one of her love letters to read. Those afternoons always ended up with Barb ordering two large pizzas delivered just in time to snuggle up together and watch *The Movie Loft* with Dana Hersey. The roast would just keep in the freezer for another day. No, I'm the one who's lucky, Betty."

Stevens folded up the note and tucked it back inside his pocket when a call came in over his walkie-talkie. "Officer Stevens, come in. I got the chief on the line."

"Time to hit the road, Betty." Stevens leaned forward and reached for his wallet. "How much do I owe you?"

Betty smiled that Betty smile. "It's on the house. Happy birthday Boo."

With a tip of his peaked cap, Stevens turned off his stool and grabbed the walkie-talkie from his belt. "Stevens here, go ahead, Polly." He paced towards the exit and looked behind, smiling at Betty. She smiled in kind and gave a wave before the door closed behind him.

"Go ahead, Chief," Polly transmitted. "Officer Stevens is on the line."

"Boo, we've got a situation on the west side of the swamp. About a mile east of the 104 exit."

"What kind of situation, Chief?"

"Possible trespassing and disturbing the peace. Get on over there and secure the vehicle and bring in the suspect. I need to speak to her."

"Her? A female suspect has been confirmed?"

"It's been confirmed, Officer Stevens. Bring her in."

"Right, Chief."

"Oh, and one more thing. This woman has a history of insubordination and holds the law in arrogant contempt. I just want you to be aware, she could be trouble."

"Right, Chief. I'll have her in custody within the hour."

CHAPTER 23
SAY GOODBYE DON'T FOLLOW

Stevens drove out of the Tri-Stop and sped across town. He knew what "holding the law in arrogant contempt meant." They all did. The chief was the law, and the law was the chief. Those who were in open rebellion to the law, were in open rebellion against him. That could never stand. Come hell or high water, those who posed a threat to his town would come to know his wrath as he stomped them into the dirt and silenced them forever.

As he drove on, thoughts of his father drifted in his head and the words that still haunted him.

A seed of contempt allowed to be sown is a brutish weed upon the landscape. It strangles and chokes off one's roots. Roots of a common faith and common blood under a common purpose. Always keep the trust; always defend the faithful. Battle the evil forces of insurrection and wage war against all nonbelievers. Damn the insurgents of truth. Damn those of bitter lies. Blacken their eyes with hot pitch and cut out their treacherous tongues. Damn them all to hell.

Upsetting words for a young boy to happen upon in his father's study while searching for hidden Christmas presents inside a drawer never meant to be left unlocked. But those words had far more weight now. They were deeply disturbing and chilling words, dark and biblical. What could they have possibly meant? And why would his loving father, a man he looked up to, be in possession of such documents? Boo never found his way back into his father's study. His mother made him promise never to tell his father what he had seen. No problem there. That was the easiest promise Boo ever made. Mrs. Stevens made sure the study was exactly as it was and told Boo never to speak of it.

There was a part of Stevens that wished not to carry on in the tradition of his father, and all his fathers before him. He had always wondered when the day would come, if it ever would, that he would be asked to join the order. And he believed now, more than ever, the time drew near. It was a feeling deep within his bones that a summons of invitation had his name on it and that he would be brought to stand before The Keepers.

The truth is he knew almost nothing of them, which was the lot of family members of inductees, but he knew of its existence, and knew it dealt in matters of great importance. He remembered the day when he was still just a boy and his father left home. His father kissed his mother, then called him over and gave him a firm handshake like he was the man of the house. He remembered it well, but what really left an imprint on his brain was the strange, fantastical look on his father's face when he returned home three days later. It was not so much an angry face or even a troubled face, but a face somehow more discerning, more perceptive. There was something in those eyes that always stayed with him. He had the look of a man who had faced and accepted a truth beyond the pale of human understanding and who contemplated, gravely, the burdens that came with it. It reminded him of the movie, *The Ten Commandments*, and the look on Charlton Heston's face when he came down from Mount Sinai revealing two stone tablets to the Israelites.

Driving over the next rise, Stevens noticed the reported vehicle parked off the shoulder with its driver door ajar. As he got closer, it appeared as though the vehicle was abandoned. He saw no signs of the woman.

Pulling over into the breakdown lane, he drove a hundred yards or so before he passed over the shoulder and into the cut. He slowed the cruiser to a soft roll and turned up on an angle in front of the abandoned vehicle, blocking it from the main road.

Questions popped into his mind as he observed no signs of life through the vehicle's windshield. *Why was the door open and the engine running? Did the driver have a heart attack and try to find help?* He secured his nightstick before he stepped out of the cruiser and poised his hand just above his sidearm. As was standard protocol, he made his approach as if someone was in the car. "Ma'am, this is the police. I am Officer Boo Stevens. If you are in the vehicle, please step out so I can see you. Step out now, nice and slow." There was no response. "You are not in trouble with the law. The chief just wants to have a word with you." He stepped forward and placed his hand on the hood and peered into the interior. His eyes glanced over the bench style seat and saw no one from his partially obscured vantage point. The chief's voice echoed in his head: *She has a history of insubordination and holds the law in arrogant contempt. Bring her to me, now.*

Unsnapping his holster, he carefully removed his revolver and held the barrel low to the ground. He thought, *the suspect is possibly hiding under the dash or flat down on the floorboards.* Stevens straightened out and took a scan of the surrounding area, but saw nothing. He took a breath, and with one sudden move, he made two, gaping strides and lurched for the vehicle's door handle, swinging himself around with the barrel of the gun trained on the inside. "Don't Move! Put your hands over your head!" The gun darted rapidly over all points, but there was no one there. He bent over, breathing hard, again the chief's voice running through his head.

He reached his hand in, removed the keys from the ignition, and shut the door. He looked across the two-lane road at the service station, and wondered if she went there, but he knew the station would have called it in. *Still, an attendant might have seen her.* He turned around and eyed the Suds & Tubs car wash a quarter of a mile up 104. *She could have walked there to make a phone call. But why walk if she could drive? And why leave the car running and the doors wide open? It didn't make sense, ... unless?*

He remembered past reports of suicides involving bridge jumping, the ones that made the evening news. He was thinking in particular of the Tobin Bridge jumpers in Boston. Often times, a victim would park their vehicle and simply leave it running in traffic before jumping to their death in the Mystic River below. The vehicle would be found running, doors wide open, purses, belongings, whatever they had on them just left on the seat before they decided to check out and do their best Greg Louganis imitation.

Stevens turned around from the road, his eyes drawn to the miles of dense wetlands and heavy tree cover of the swamp. He stepped to the cut's edge and noticed newly snapped branches and fresh footprints in the dank peat. *She went into the swamp?* He did not know. What he knew is he had to find her and bring her in. The chief's orders reverberated inside his head like a plucked guitar string. There was no calling for backup or leaving the scene. There was only wading into the unknown and retrieving the suspect. No excuses. The chief wasn't kind on excuses.

With extended nightstick held tight within his grip, Stevens knocked back the underbrush and made his way through its thick, tangled wall. The branches of young saplings bent over and snapped back like rubber bands as he passed around and through them. Using his heavy police boots, he stamped down weeds and briars and maneuvered his way, pushing through its frontage.

Looking over his shoulder, he had already lost sight of the road and the cruiser behind him as a tangle of scrub closed in. Turning back to face the thicket, he trekked forward cutting his way through. Step by careful step, he pushed onward until he could see through the low, hanging boughs and rotted stumps a clearing up ahead. It sat just beyond the gnarled roots, jetting above the surface moisture.

She is close, I can feel it. He stepped over the low, hanging branches, being careful not to lose his footing on the slick surface of the bark when that familiar feeling overcame him like being drawn in by an unseen force, how vertigo feels when it first grips you. He remembered being thirteen years old gazing over the edge of Mount Monadnock and admiring a canopy of spruce when it happened. An unexplainable, magnetic-like force driving him flat to the rock face. His arms and legs splayed in a death grip with the cold of the rock pressed deep into the hollow of his cheek. And the thin, distant voices echoing over him in waves of distortion.

He stopped. Found his center. And continued on. He moved between the heavy roots and looked down to keep his foot aligned with the ground before displacing his weight fully with each step. He noticed what looked like fresh tire marks imprinted in the mud, something very unusual. The marks ran together side-by-side with a very narrow track. He did not recognize those kinds of markings, but he knew it wasn't the markings of a wheelbarrow, a ten speed, or a dirt bike, nor was it a tricycle, a wagon, or a wheelchair. He only knew they were marks, freshly made, and that he was close, real close.

The thicket of low, hanging branches, rotted stumps, and dense vegetation, thinned and opened before him giving way to daylight washing over the clearing ahead.

He unsnapped his holster and gripped the handle of his pistol and lengthened his strides with soft heels, careful to hide in the swamp's quiet and not give himself away.

Keeping low, he made his way behind a large northern white cedar and hugged up against its trunk, bending his head down between the branches for a clear line of sight. In the low water of the swamp, he could see an outcropping of smaller rocks fronting a large boulder where a singular female sat atop holding something to her chest with her left hand; her right hand appeared to be tucked inside her pocket. He noticed clear plastic tubes trailing down from her nose to an oxygen tank strapped to a metal dolly. He could not see the bottom of the dolly, it was behind a tuft of weeds, but he was convinced it was supported by two wheels with a narrow track.

Placing the gun back in his holster, his lips pinched together somewhat sympathetically, and stepped out from behind the tree. He was about to address the woman when he looked down at his heel. And there in the muck, behind the green stem of a starflower, a pressurized, cylindrical tank of oxygen stood upright.

He bent over to pick up the tank, when he heard a thin voice struggle over labored breathing. "Thank you, officer." Stevens cradled the tank in his arm against his chest and straightened up to make eye contact with the woman for the first time.

"Ma'am, I'm going to need you to step down from there. Chief Hicks wants to speak to you." She nodded her head in agreement and gestured with her index finger, asking for a moment.

She removed her right hand from her pocket, and with both arms, leaned over and grabbed low on the rigid tubing and lifted the tank from the dolly's platform and hoisted it up by her side. She cranked back on the valve and held the mask tightly to her mouth, taking in huge gasps of precious oxygen to ease her aching lungs.

"Ma'am, do you need any help?" Stevens began to approach, when she shook her head no and held out the flat of her palm in his direction, signaling him to stop before she pulled the mask down from her lips.

"I knew you would come." She took two more deep pulls of oxygen. "But I thought he'd send the others."

"What others?" Stevens inquired. She convulsed and managed to snicker, bending over and clutching at her pained lungs. "You don't know, do you?"

"Know what? ... Ma'am, If I could just help you down, we can be on our—"

"I will come quietly, but I ask that you allow me to say a prayer before I do so."

Officer Stevens hesitated as he observed her pained struggles to breathe and watched her lift a framed picture from inside her jacket and kiss the glass face gently.

"Sure, ma'am, I'll give you a moment." Stevens removed his hat and began to turn away from her.

"Officer, please, don't turn away ... Bear witness to my words. Know that I am a woman of God who has suffered a great loss."

Stevens was a man of God, too. He had known loss. He knew the healing power of prayer and he believed in the convalescence of Christian fellowship. He turned back to face her. With a nod of his head, he locked his fingers beneath the tank and closed his eyes. The woman held the picture over her heart, took two, deep pulls of oxygen, then looked to the heavens and began to recite the Lord's Prayer.

Our Father, who art in heaven,
Hallowed be thy Name.
Thy Kingdom come.
Thy will be done in earth,

She stopped. There were no more words. ... Officer Stevens lifted his head and opened his eyes; his face was a quiet reflection.

"Ma'am, do you need some time?" He noticed a gentle and peaceful smile come over her. Her face was warm and friendly. Her eyes were like two pools of tranquility, almost cheerful.

"Officer, did you happen to notice this morning how glorious the sky was and how beautiful the leaves were, like colorful fingers of god reaching for the heavens?"

"Why, yes ma'am, beautiful, the change came early this year."

She nodded her head and said, "Yes, there is beauty in change. My John always loved this time of year before the years were taken from him."

Officer Stevens cleared his throat. "Take all the time you need, ma'am, and finish your prayer. Then we'll get on out of here and see the chief." Stevens closed his eyes and prayed silently as he listened to the words:

Thy will be done in earth,
As it is in heaven
Give us this day our daily bread
And forgive me
For I am broken and can never be saved

Stevens jerked his head up to see a brilliant flash of firelight explode from a gun's chamber. Kaboom! The bullet pierced the ready-made bomb cradled in his arms, detonating the oxygen tank on impact. Chunks of meat and bone rocketed through the air, spraying bits and pieces of Stevens high into the sky.

Thrown against the rocks, Priscilla hugged the mask tight against her mouth and watched as Stevens rained back to earth, splashing down and bobbing up in the black water, like some kind of rancid stew.

As the echoes of the explosion began to quiet, she could hear the raspy, wet sound of rapid breathing filling her plastic mask. She opened the oxygen canister fully, draining nearly the rest of the tank and breathed deeply until her nerves settled down. There was one more thing she had to do. She had to get it right.

Before this long-awaited day had finally arrived, Priscilla Hooke practiced tossing a short-handled, grub hoe (a garden tool equal in weight to her snub-nosed revolver), at a fixed point in her backyard measuring exactly fifty feet. She practiced repeatedly, at first with eyes wide open, then with eyes firmly shut, repeating the movement a hundred times until she could hit the intended target repeatedly in her sleep.

She found her balance and faced east, took two slow pulls of air, and aimed at the lone birch tree by the water's edge. Exactly fifty feet. Like she had practiced a hundred times before, she drew back her arm and tossed the revolver underhand in the tree's direction and watched it land softly in the underbrush right at the base, all according to plan. Perfect.

She had accomplished much, but there was one act left. Her final act. Tears welled in her eyes as her body rocked, clutching the framed picture of her son, John Hooke, against her bosom. "I love you son," she said, kissing his forehead. "I'm almost there."

She drew in hard against the mask and then managed to turn over on the rock and lie flat on her back. *The sky,* she thought, *looked like a beautiful, celestial painting, a graceful hand to the heavens waiting to cradle her.*

She looked into the deep blue, beyond the clouds, and watched as a flock of geese took flight and organized themselves in the instinctual V pattern according to their nature.

Parents are not to outlive their children according to our nature, she thought, *but sometimes a rogue force mutates those laws and changes the whole of the game.*

With his framed picture resting like a halo on the swell of her chest, Priscilla Hooke, beloved mother of John, removed the mask from her face and pulled the tubes from her nose. Quiet became her. The relentless hiss of oxygen had been replaced by a triumphant chorus of angels reveling in her ear. ... It was then she knew. God revealed the truth. Her eyes went dark, her lips turned a cold mazarine, then silence. She was home.

CHAPTER 24
HELLO. IS THERE ANYONE THERE?

Jolted from his feet, sixteen-year-old Alex Feely dropped like an anchor, spilling gasoline all over his jeans. "Holy crap! What was that?" He slowly stood and grabbed some paper towels from the dispenser and returned the pump handle. Wiping down his pants, he looked toward what sounded like an explosion, perhaps a sudden clap of thunder, but there were only blue skies and barely a cloud.

He thought it strange, as he gazed across the street, a lone police cruiser sat just off the shoulder parked in front of another vehicle. Both seemed to be unattended.

He ran inside the station and found the clerk behind the counter talking on the phone. With a wave of his finger, the clerk gestured he'd be a moment. Alex pulled a five from his wallet and listened in on the conversation.

"Right. An explosion," the clerk said, glancing at Alex then looking outside through the station window. "That's right. Mutual Gas over on 104. I heard an explosion of some kind directly across from the station. ... Yeah, I'll hold." Again, the clerk asked Alex for a moment. "Um ... where do I live? I live at the Belmont Arms, apartment 20b. Why do you want to know?" Click — "Hello? Hello? Is anyone there?" The clerk hung up the phone. "I guess we got disconnected."

"Was that the police?" Alex asked.

"Yeah, I called them and reported whatever that loud bang was. There's nothing in those woods, but swampland, as far as I know. Last year there was a loud bang—dude, you smell like gas!

"I know I do. It spilled on me when I was knocked down from the explosion."

The clerk made a face.

"So, last year there was a loud bang?" Alex pressed.

"A transformer blew. It made a hell of a bang, but that shut off all the power to the businesses along this stretch. So, I don't think it's that. Unless there is some kind of electrical grid in the swamp I don't know about."

"I don't know either," Alex said, shaking his head and laying his five on the counter. "I heard it, but I saw nothing. What the cops say?"

"Get this. They said it was probably natural gas pockets. Apparently, pockets of gas build up over time and get trapped in the swamp's peat. They said even though it's rare, the sun's angle can cause the trapped pockets of gas to explode." He pursed his lips. "I never heard of such a thing."

"Me either. Say, can I get a pack of gum? Juicy Fruit?" The clerk grabbed a pack from the overhead bin and placed it on the counter. "That's 35 cents. Anyway, after they told me about the trapped pockets of gas, they asked if I knew anyone else who saw or heard anything. They were quite adamant about it."

"Did you tell them I heard it?"

"I didn't know that until you walked through the door."

"Oh."

"Anyway, they asked where I lived and then we got disconnected."

"Thanks," Alex said, pulling a stick of gum from the wrapper. "Well, I saw nothing, but I heard it alright. Knocked me clear off my feet, spilling gas all over my new jeans. So, if the cops want to talk to me, I'm over at Roller World. I work the concession stand there two to close."

Chewing on his gum, Alex began to smile. "Sally Matthews, the girl who rents the skates, she would be so impressed if the cops came down to question me. She would have to notice me then. Be sure to tell the cops where I work. Thanks."

"Whatever. I'm thinking you might want to change your pants."

CHAPTER 25
CARL AND THE MAGIC CARPET RIDE

"Thanks, fellas for the hand," Sonny said, grinning ear to ear. "She sure is a beauty, ain't she? Once I give her a bore and put in new pistons and rings, OOOH DOGGIE! Good as the day she came off the factory floor."

"What are you going to do with it," Cam said, "once you get it running?"

Sonny tightened down the chain around the axle and slid it through the eye hook on the flatbed. "Well, I should have her ready to go for harvest. Old man Button pays cash on the barrelhead. I'll test the waters come early spring, see what the Yankee Swapper will bring me."

"Harvest corn?" Randy asked.

"Hell no, cranberries. From mid-September through early November, them bogs will be picked clean. Not a berry left on the vine, sunshine. Not like Nam, you know. Well, that about does it." Sonny cranked back the come-along and tightened down the latch. He then wiped his mouth and brow with his hanky and tucked it in the back pocket of his Dickies.

"Time to get a move on, boys." And like a wiry cat, he pounced through the driver-side door of the wrecker and sat behind the wheel. "Tell your old man I'll be at the Tri-Stop later, if he wants to stop by for a shooter and a beer."

Cam nodded. "Thanks for helping Carl get his truck back running."

"Ain't no trouble at all. He's saved my ass more than once."

"Saved your ass?" Cam asked. "You mean back in Nam?"

Sonny turned over the ignition and reached for his pocketknife for a cut of chew. His eyes looked off for a second, then down at his knife. ... "Yeah, he did, but I s'pect Carl never told you."

"He never told me anything about Nam."

"Yeah, well, that's Carl. Back in '69, your dad and I and another fella named Eddie Maxwell from West Virginia. We called him Mad Max—served together on special ops."

"Why'd you call him Mad Max?" Randy asked.

Sonny bladed off a cut of plug and lodged it in his cheek. "It was those eyes of his. Far-off blue. There, but not there, you know? Like they was looking right through you. Anyway, Mad Max played the harmonica like he was possessed. He'd go until his lungs bled out if ya gave him enough air. And he knew how to handle his rifle even better than he could play. I've never seen someone shoot like that. With that new army issue M21, he could drop a tin can full of baked beans at 800 yards. He called his gun, Lucille. Slept with it every night like it was his woman.

"Lucille?" Cam asked, smiling.

"Ah yup. He said he loved that M21 more than his girl back home. It always came through for him when he had an itch and no back talk." Cam and Randy both laughed and bent out of the way from Sonny's oily spit.

"For a short stretch, we were positioned on a hillside along the Mekong Delta. Our job was to survey the paddy field below. VC were grabbing workers from the fields, mostly children, and strapping them with explosives. You'd see fifty work the field one day, the next day maybe forty. The day after that thirty-five. They seemed to disappear without a trace. POOF GONE! Could never figure it out either. We had our eyes trained on them like hawks. Anyway, one afternoon, hotter than hell, Mad Max was wailing on that harmonica and I told him to put it away. Told him he was going to give away our position and the last thing we fucking needed was for Charlie to firebomb our hill." Sonny cocked his head back and scratched his Adam's apple. Cam and Randy were on the edge of their Timberlands wanting to hear more.

"Come on, Sonny, what the hell happened?" Sonny's head bounced back down like a tire jack and continued. "Well, Mad Max didn't take too kindly to that. Maybe it was the heat. Maybe it was malaria. Maybe it was jungle rot. Hell, it could've been that agent orange shit they all talk about now, or the fact he was crazier than all hell with them far-off, blue eyes of his, or it might have just been that Goddamn swamp of a jungle shit VIETNAM! Because that night, after we ate our C-Ration, it was my turn to take the hill and keep watch while Carl and Max got some shuteye. Lying prone, my rifle fixed on its bipod, I scoped the paddy field below, observing nothing but shadows. The only sound I heard was a damn mosquito buzzing around my ear looking for fresh blood, until I heard hot, wet, breathing, and quick pipes of air. It sent chills up my spine. But before I had a chance to peel my eye from the scope and turn my head, I heard what sounded like someone cracking their knuckles, you know that rapid, awful, crackling sound. I immediately tucked and rolled onto my back, and right there, standing over me like some kind of jungle warlord, Carl had Max's lifeless body slung over his right shoulder. Max looked like one of them rag dolls, you know, all limp like, his arms and legs bouncing. I then watched your dad carry him down to the bottom of the rise like it was nothing. I'll never forget those glazed-over eyes of his, and the way Max's head bobbed up and down like a striped bass tugging on a fishing line.

"Shit," Cam said, "I never heard that story."

"No way," Randy followed, "what badass. Was Max going to shoot you?"

"No, sir, Max wanted it up close and personal. He wanted to shave me dry with his Western Bowie Knife. Thank Christ, Carl woke up to take a squirt when he did. He told me he just opened his eyes, and saw a glint of steel peek out from Max's fist. Boys, I know the army trained us to be quick and lethal, but not like this. Carl was faster than a jackrabbit. Before I knew what happened, he broke Mad Max's neck and tossed him over his shoulder like he was a roll of carpet, then hauled him away like trash. If it wasn't for your old man, I would have been one of them names etched on that wall down in D.C."

Cam and Randy were stunned. Their mouths hung open with surprise.

"He never told me," Cam said. "He never talked about it."

"No, I s'pect not. Most of us were just kids thrown into a meat grinder. We spent our time trying to forget, the ones who made it back." Sonny let loose a sour spit of chew and wiped his mouth with the back of his hand. "Well, boys, I gotta get this Johnny Popper back to the shop. Take care, you hear. Oh, by-the-way, I wouldn't worry about that truck."

"Thanks again, Sonny, you really came through in the clutch. I know Carl is going to be happy to get his truck back. Thanks for fixing it."

"Yeah, he will, but I wasn't talking about Carl's truck, I was talking about the other truck that disappeared in the field. The one with them four pissants, hooting and hollering, dogging that sweet '79 before POOF, Now You See It and now you don't."

An awkward moment of silence passed. Sonny knew exactly what had happened. Cam and Randy looked at each other searching for words.

"Listen," Sonny said, "this place is kind of like Vietnam. People have been disappearing around here for years. Carl probably never told you about that either. You'd see a fella one day, and the next day he was gone. Just disappears, and no one asks questions. Like it's expected. I bet you dollars to donuts, no one will ever see that truck again and nobody will come looking for it either. And if they ever do, hells bells, they're as good as gone too."

Sonny's lips tightened on his gums and passed his eyes over Cam and Randy. He then beeped the horn twice and drove away.

Cam and Randy stood slack-jawed with their mouths hanging loose. As they turned and faced the field, they heard 'Ramblin Man' fade in the distance behind them.

CHAPTER 26
BILLIE JEAN IS NOT MY LOVER

The large, double-glass, revolving doors opened to the front lobby of Morton Hospital, where rookie police officer, Harvey Pierce, sat curbside nervously tapping his fingers on the wheel waiting for Officer Harding to be released.

He'd been on the job four months, riding a desk, mostly, and ran into Harding only once, he recalled. He remembered Harding grunted at him and remembered how his square face and broad shoulders were even more intimidating than his height.

He knew Harding commanded respect at the station, or was it fear? Perhaps it was both, but what did that matter? Harding was an officer who got the job done. "A good soldier," Chief called him. "A man you can count on to do a tough job." He had been lauded by his fellow officers as a criminal's worst nightmare and law enforcement's best friend. Loyal to the end.

Officer Harding stepped through the lobby doors on a decisive limp. His left leg, below the knee, was fitted with a cast and walking heel. *He looked like Long John Silver, Ol' Peg-Leg*, Pierce thought, as he hitched towards the cruiser. Only Harding did not have a parrot on his shoulder, just a chip the size of Mount Washington.

He was surprised by Harding's strong gait and how nimble he moved with his leg bound in plaster. It was as if the walking cast was just part of him, and not something trying to stabilize and mend a newly broken leg which needed time to heal.

Pierce pulled his eyes back as Harding approached and hurried out from behind the wheel. He darted around the nose of the cruiser and popped open the passenger side door, standing like a bellhop.

"Be careful, Officer Harding. Watch yourself, I'll get the door behind you." Harding stopped mid-stride. "Rookie Officer Pierce is it?"

"Harvey Pierce, at your service."

Harding sneered and swung his leg in and sat down. He looked up at the fresh-faced officer still standing there.

"Unless you plan on wiping my chin or changing my diaper, rookie Officer Pierce, I suggest you get in and drive." Pierce swallowed hard; he could see his own Adam's apple ripple in the mirrored reflection of Harding's sunglasses.

"N-no sir. I didn't mean to suggest—" Before Pierce could get it all out, Harding shut the door.

Pulling out of the parking lot of Morton Hospital, Pierce headed towards the highway. He drove in mock silence, shifting in his seat, his hands fidgeting on the steering wheel. He found his lips parting several times, struggling to find the right words to break the tension, but they remained caught in his throat, masked by discomforting sighs leaking from a closing windpipe until the tension spilled over into a clumsy, "S-O-O-O-H, you want to listen to music? Are you a Michael Jackson fan?" Like a mouth full of lemon juice squirting from a firehose, the linings of his cheeks sucked back into his throat. Hot and bitter.

What the hell is wrong with me? Did I really just ask, Officer Long John Hardass, his head the size of an anvil, if he liked Michael Jackson? Jesus, no. Harding's going to think I'm a momma's boy, or worse, gay ... He'll tell the entire station. What was I thinking? I know, I wasn't thinking ... This guy looks like he would be listening to Merle Haggard if he weren't marching in military formation to John Philip Sousa. Maybe he didn't hear me. He's not moving. I see no reaction. His black, mirrored glasses are still pointing straight ahead. Yeah, that's it. He didn't hear me. ... Of course, he heard you, rookie Officer Pierce. You said it. You heard it. He heard it. Maybe the very question sickened him. Maybe I'm just a recruit, and he doesn't want to dignify it with an answer with the likes of me. Maybe my only claim to fame was playing tuba, first chair, in the high school orchestra, while he was out hunting bears with his bare hands. Yeah, that's it. That has got to be it. If it wasn't, he would have ...

"You got *Thriller* rookie?" Pierce was stunned to hear a voice, a not entirely unpleasant voice from his stone-faced passenger. On a strong exhale, Pierce's hunched-over shoulders, bound up tighter than thumb screws, broke free from their vise and returned relaxed against the back of his seat. He peeled his hand from the steering wheel and reached into his pocket to pull out a tape. With measured confidence, he held the tape up by his right ear. "Yes, I believe I do."

"Cool," Harding said, still sitting square like an oak table, his black, mirrored eyes poised straight ahead. "Play Billie Jean. ... rookie." Like a curtain rising for an opening performance, the corners of Pierce's mouth lifted into a high grin before he inserted the tape into the player and said, "That's my favorite, too."

Pierce stepped on the gas and took the ramp to Route 24. He rolled his window down to feel the rush of cool wind wave over him as the familiar pop beat of 'Billie Jean' thumped from the cruiser with seismic intensity. The music blared throughout the interior reverberating in a sweet, falsetto pitch: Daring not to sing, Pierce mouthed along to the words, his head pecking back and forth like a rooster. He noticed that his stone-faced passenger was tapping his left knee with his index finger, when a radio call came in from One Police Plaza:

"Officer Pierce, come in. Come in, Officer Pierce, this is Chief Hicks." Pierce killed the volume and brought the handset to his mouth.

"Pierce here Chief."

"Is Harding with you?"

"Affirmative."

"Are you heading in?"

"ETA fifteen minutes. On Route 24, about to take the 104 exit."

"Good. You're less than five minutes from the scene. Put Harding on."

"Go Chief."

"Get to the closed channel, Officer Harding, and put your earpiece in."

"Copy that. Over."

"Minutes ago, across from Mutual Gas on 104, we all know that site well, it was reported by the station's clerk that an explosion occurred somewhere deep inside the swamp. Are you fit for duty?"

"I won't be running the Boston Marathon anytime soon, but I'm fit."

"I don't know what you'll find there, but an hour before the reported explosion, I dispatched Boo Stevens to pick up Priscilla Hooke and bring her in, she was back visiting the roadside memorial again."

"Is Priscilla in custody?"

"We are unable to confirm that. Stevens never radioed in. Not uncommon in that area, I know, but I need you to canvass, secure, and report back to me right away.

"Copy that, Chief."

"I've sent Durst to meet you. Once you meet up with Durst, cut Pierce loose and send him back."

"Copy that, Chief."

"We'll talk about what happened at the creek when you report in. Durst will fill you in on another matter concerning tonight."

"Right, Chief. Harding out."

Pierce stiffened in his seat; his fingers clutched the wheel tighter as he took the Route 104 off-ramp and followed west. He glanced at Harding, then the road as he rounded the loop, the Mutual Gas Station sign was now coming into view.

"Over there," Harding said with a commanding tone, pointing at two, parked vehicles a few hundred yards up the road. Pierce crossed over the two-lane road and reduced his speed to about thirty-five miles an hour. He drove in the breakdown lane and passed over into the cut of grass.

"Pull behind the cruiser," Harding said, his hand on the door handle ready to get out. "Bring it in tight." Pierce brought the nose in close and threw it in park. With their hands by their holsters, Harding and Pierce swung open the doors and stepped out. "Look over the suspect's vehicle and secure it," Harding said, as he humped it over to Stevens' cruiser and looked through the window.

"Anything?" Harding said.

"All clear." Harding slammed the roof with his hand and ratcheted his body to face the swamp, then spun his eyes across the road towards the gas station when Officer Durst pulled in front of him and rolled down his window.

"Head back to the station, Pierce. Chief's orders."

Pierce nodded and made his way back to the cruiser. "And Pierce," Durst said, "don't talk to anyone until the chief has had a sit-down with you. Is that clear?"

Pierce's eyes darted from Durst to Harding and then back to Durst. "Straight to the station," Pierce responded. "Talk to no one."

Holding two machetes in his hands, Durst got out of the cruiser and paced quickly over to Harding, his eyes drawn to his cast. "Officer Stevens still hasn't radioed in," Durst said, electing not to comment on Harding's leg. "We better talk while we hack our way in, but first..." Durst tossed Harding a whetstone. "Cut a sharp edge on that blade. The machetes are duller than piss from the last time we hacked through this mess.

CHAPTER 27
FLIGHT OF THE BLACK CONDOR

Inside room 16 of the Wampan Inn, Don Williams was on the phone and penciling in his notepad. "Yeah, okay. Good. Where's Dave's Pizza located…? Corner of Union and Plymouth street? Right. Got it. Look for the Miller Beer sign with a pool cue. Okay, I'll see you there." Don hung up the phone and turned towards the map of the swamp hanging on the bulletin board.

"Where are we on collating points of activity?"

"Albert is poring through the file," Brett Myers said, "and feeding me the coordinates."

"Good. Why the different color pushpins?"

"The black pins," Albert said, "represent reported sightings of unnatural occurrences. The Mulrooney file has entries on several of these types."

"What occurrences?" Don asked, studying the map.

"They represent strange sightings, the unexplained, weird phenomena and so forth," Brett said.

"And over here," Albert continued. "you can see a cluster of activity. I pored through the file going back decades and found a high number of incidents in this area."

"Some witnesses," Brett said, "described seeing a Bigfoot-like creature bounding through the dense underbrush."

"And that's not all, Mr. Williams," Albert interjected, in the excited tone of a child. "There are entries in the file that describe sightings of a giant, bird-like creature, dark and scary." Albert licked his thumb and flipped through some pages. "Right here. Back in 1967, a ten-year-old boy, Benjamin Church, was in the swamp looking for minnows, when he described seeing a humongous shadow pass overhead. He said he felt a strong wind and heard branches and leaves crackling. Here is the super part." Albert's excitement grew. "Ready for this?"

Brett and Don shook their heads.

"Go on," Don said.

"Okay, okay, ... when Benjamin Church looked up, he said, and I quote, 'I couldn't believe my eyes, I just saw The Black Condor.' End quote." Albert's cheeks reddened with delight. "Can you believe it? The Black Condor, guys, the Black Condor."

Don, Brett, and Scott Provost, the equipment engineer, who looked up from the fax machine, all stared at each other with blank faces. Albert's demeanor turned to comical disbelief. "The Black Condor, guys. Comic book superhero? Could fly super-fast, was super cool, and had telekinetic powers?" Albert shook his head and pulled a comic book from his backpack. "See, ... this is what he described seeing." Don, Brett, and Scott gazed at the comic book held in Albert's hand. On the cover, what appeared to be a powerfully built man in all black, with red laser eyes and the wings of a thunderbird, spanned across the cover flying high above the city.

Don realized, of course, through the eyes of a ten-year-old boy, and possibly Albert, the eyewitness account provided by Benjamin Church was that of a child's comic book hero, not what Don immediately thought of as a creature more prehistoric in form. Something more animal, something more sinister, something more heavily feathered and reptilian like.

Don remembered back in college one night, he and some friends got together in his dorm room for some drinks, when one of the girls began to tell ghost stories. He did not recall what town she was from, but he knew her to be from somewhere on the South Shore of Massachusetts. The story she told turned his skin to gooseflesh. Like most ghost stories, she set the scene so very carefully with affected language and impregnated pauses to build fear and suspense. But the way she described the creature, blacker than coal-fired dust, and larger than a battleship soaring high in the night skies and swooping low on the horizon to snatch livestock and unsuspecting humans with its razor-sharp talons, was terrifying. But what was beyond terrifying, what stayed with Don all these years, was how she finished her story. She got quiet and her countenance changed; her eyes no longer held the joy of a storyteller. She said, "There was no need to fabricate the story I just shared with you, because it is all true. And because I have seen the creature myself."

Don realized the creature on the cover of Albert's comic book fit what she described. It was only a comic book, but it was enough to call up the fear he felt years ago. And now, buried deep within the Mulrooney file, a ten-year-old boy had described the creature to a tee, albeit from the fantastical mind of a child and likely dismissed.

"Benjamin Church described seeing this?" Williams asked.

"To a tee," Albert said, pushing up his glasses around his smiling cheeks.

"I think he'd be about twenty-five or twenty-six years old now," Don said. "We need to track him down and talk to him."

"And there have been others," Albert said, facing the map and pointing. "All have reported seeing the same creature. Different people, different times, but all in this immediate area."

"Holy shit," Don said.

Albert snickered. "Holy doody, Mr. Williams. The Black Condor really does exist."

"Good work," Don said, "Put Benjamin Church on the short list. What about the red and blue pins?"

"The blue pins represents areas of reported power failures," Brett said. "Flashlights, metal detectors, cameras, things like that have all gone dead without explanation. There was a news crew down here just two years ago in '81, covering a story of swamp runoff flooding the streets of a bordering town, when suddenly their cameras went dead. They changed out their batteries and ran checks, but the equipment never worked."

"I am continuing to tabulate names," Albert said.

"Good," Don said. "We'll reach out to them and cross reference accounts of their stories. What about the red pins?"

"The red pins represent disappearances," Bret said, pointing to a grouping of four in the western quadrant of the map. "This grouping of four represent John Hooke, Paul Andrews, Mark Fuller, and Carl Jenkins."

"Carl Jenkins?" Don said, "I just got off the phone with his son, Cam. He's agreed to talk to me and I'm meeting up with him later."

"What about Carl?" Scott asked. "The file says Carl made it out alive. Is he still around?"

"He is. I plan on catching him at work later tonight, at a place called Taunton River Mill. Okay, good work guys. Stay on this. Is the fax machine up and running?"

"I'm sending a test fax now," Scott said.

"Good. Send one to Harry's direct line and ask him to send one back."

"Mr. Williams?"

"Yes, Albert, please call me Don."

"Sorry, Mr. Williams, is the manager bringing over the icebox and hot plate? I've got snacks and stuff."

"I'll check on that," Don said. "Moonshine told me he would come by and set us up, but that was a while ago."

"Moonshine? Who's Moonshine?"

"Henry James," Don said. "The one and only. He's the manager and proprietor of this fine establishment."

"Mr. Williams—sorry Don," asked Albert. "Why do they call him Moonshine?" Don shook his head before he opened the door and stepped outside. "That's a story for another time. Right now, I need to find him."

CHAPTER 28
PICK UP THE PIECES AND GO HOME

Like a pit on a pendulum, Harding swung the machete through the underbrush, clearing a path as he and Officer Durst drudged farther into the swamp.

"How far back?" Harding asked.

"The clerk across the street thinks he heard the blast a few hundred yards in. It's strange though. The old gal never went into the swamp before. She always just visited roadside, either alone or with the others."

Harding continued swinging the machete with tremendous force, the blade whistling through the air. "I'm surprised the chief dispatched Stevens here," Harding said.

"About Stevens," Durst said, stepping firmly around some decayed stumps. "The chief thinks it's time. He believes Stevens will be brought before the council soon. As early as tonight." The crunching and splintering of dead wood was heard under foot with each powerful hitch of Harding's cast. His walking heel plowed through the dirt like the tusks of a wild boar, churning and uprooting all in its wake.

"Tonight?" Harding asked. "What time?"

"Seven-thirty this evening the small council meets in chambers." Durst stopped and grabbed Harding's attention, resting his machete by his side. "The chief is worried about the building unrest. And frankly I am too. He called for The Keepers to meet right after he had a chat with Carl Jenkins. And wouldn't you know it? It was his son, Cam and his buddy, Randall Coltaire, that led you into the creek."

Had it been a colder day, piping steam would have been visible rising from Harding's enormous forehead. "That son of a bitch Cam is going to get his." Harding drove his left boot into the ground to brace himself and wielded his blade with two hands through a six-inch maple, cutting it in two. "I'm going to

119

pound his skinny ass into the fucking dirt. Him and that red-headed boyfriend of his."

"I don't blame you a bit… but—"

"But what?" Durst dropped his head and then lifted it to meet Harding's bulging eyes. "The chief has plans for the boy."

"What plans?" Harding said, as he bludgeoned through a bough of dead pine using his forearm like a medieval war hammer.

"After council tonight," Durst said, "he plans on having the boy arrested and held on bail. Then he'll be sent up to Titicut State Hospital, just like the chief did his old man."

A deep crease cut a line through Harding's brow. His face twisted into a hard grimace, revealing a set of incisors that would be the envy of an Eastern mountain wild cat. Using the back of his hand, he wiped his gaping mouth and said. "Not if I get to him first."

"Don't do anything stupid. I don't have to tell you what happens if someone crosses the chief. Forget about the boy. He'll get his. Come on, we've got more to canvass."

Durst turned from Harding's mounting anger and pressed forward. Behind him, he could hear Harding sputter in between the whistling sound of steel cutting air, when in the distance, something caught his eye behind an outcropping of rocks. He waved his arm furiously at Harding to keep back, as they both quickly took cover.

"What is it?" Harding asked, kneeling below some brushwood.

"Something, someone, I can't be sure … behind the rocks … I saw something move I thought then it was gone."

"You probably saw a rodent. This place is swarming with them."

"No, not this. What I saw had shape and substantial weight. At first, I thought it could be Stevens, but it disappeared as fast as I saw it. Didn't get a good look at it. I suppose it could have been a fisher cat. I've seen them as big as dogs and a lot meaner."

"I tell you what," Harding said, "I've come upon fisher cats a few times checking traps in the state forest." Durst canvassed the area while Harding went on. "Last fall I heard one of them weasels screaming, you know that blood-curdling scream of theirs, but this scream was different. Pained and brutal. I drew my weapon and ran into the pine following the scream. And there it was, the biggest, damn, fisher cat I'd ever seen. It was back on his hind-legs and huge. That son of a bitch looked right at me and lunged."

"He came at you?" Durst asked.

"I thought he was, so I got off a shot, but it trailed wide. Before I had a chance to pull the trigger again, he had lunged his head with full force towards the ground. It was the most God-awful sound you ever heard. I advanced on it and unloaded. It took three to drop him."

"Jesus, three?"

Harding nodded. "Three rounds it took. When I walked up and kicked over his carcass, I saw what he was lunging at. A bobcat was caught in the steel teeth of a varmint trap with his stomach ripped open. Nothing but chewed up organs spilled all over the bed of pine needles. Gruesome." Harding reached for his gun and lifted from a crouched position, his eyes scoping through the low, hanging branches. He scanned the clearing the best he could, but could not make out anything definitively from the obstructed view.

"I can't see anything from here," Harding said. "We need to flush out whatever you saw and secure the area. Draw your weapon and let's move."

Trained at a forty-five, both officers gripped their service revolvers with both hands and bound towards the clearing, shielding themselves behind trees as they went. Harding motioned to Durst about a felled Atlantic white cedar twenty-five yards ahead. Durst motioned back, dipping his weapon in that direction, and humped it over. The branches snapped back as he came in low and hard at the base of the large cedar.

Quickly turning around, they dug their heels into the soft ground and pushed their backs tight up against the furrowed bark of the tree, low enough to create a wall between them and the clearing beyond.

"Alright," Harding said, looking down at the open cylinder of his service revolver. "We have a clear sightline from here. Keep your eyes forward and alert. We need to—" Harding suddenly stopped. He noticed the back of Durst's uniform was covered in something thick and kidney red.

"Jesus Christ!" Harding said. "Don't move." He swiped the tips of his fingers through the tacky substance.

"What?" Durst huffed. "What the hell is it?" Harding passed his fingers under his nose. It had a hot, coppery smell, and it was sticky like pine pitch. Bits of white, like chopped up cauliflower, ran through the smear.

"It's blood," Harding stated.

"Jesus Christ, blood," Durst said, furiously kneeling over trying to reach the back of his own shirt when a flash of gold caught his eye. There in the dirt, beneath the trunk of the cedar, Durst reached for the shiny metal object.

"What is it?" Harding asked. Durst could not answer. He buckled at the waist and lurched forward. The pungent smell of vomit filled Harding's nostrils bending him supine when he saw what caused Durst to retch. Harding crawled underneath the trunk to get a better look at a gold watch wrapped around a man's wrist attached to a severed arm. Tendons and shredded tissue, bruised and burnt, bubbled over the unmistakable, blue cuff of a policeman's uniform. "No, no. Shit." Covering his trembling mouth with his left hand, Harding grabbed a branch with his right, and used it to hook the limb, awkwardly dragging it towards him.

Durst lifted into a kneeling position and weakly hung his head to his side. He reached for his hanky and wiped down his vomit smeared mouth. He dropped his shoulders, turned around to face Harding, holding something hairy, bloody, and concave in his hand.

At first look, it appeared to Harding to be part of an animal carcass. You could see what looked like matted fur poke out from underneath Durst's knuckles. But when he tossed it underhand towards Harding, it came to settle right-side up revealing its true nature. It was a piece of shattered skull belonging to Officer Stevens. You could see a hint of jawbone protrude beneath the cranium where black hair oddly fell from the scalp into a neat part.

Both men were sickened by the sight. Harding picked up the severed arm and turned the watch face over to see an inscription on the back which read: Forever your cream puff. A sinking feeling hit him like being crushed under a drum of concrete. The two men, their mouths alive with horror, looked at each other before Harding broke his silence first.

"It's Stevens's watch. What in God's name happened here?" Still wiping around his mouth and chin, Durst's head clicked back and forth like a gear in a timepiece, his eyes vacant. "I don't know. I don't know."

"We need to call this in," Harding said. "Chief is going to want to know right away." Durst closed his eyes a moment indicating he agreed before they both lifted warily to their feet. Harding took a moment to holster his revolver, while Durst turned towards the clearing. Then, like staring into the oncoming headlights of an eighteen-wheeler, his face stretched in horror.

"What's wrong?" Harding said, spinning, and drawing his weapon. It took a second to register, but what he saw turned his blood to ice water. Perched on a rock like a ceremonial offering, lay the lifeless body of Priscilla Hooke. At the base of the crude altar, spanning out on a wide arc like a shadow from a sundial, swamp dogs were stacked in a tight circle. One by one, side by side, they fell in like a battalion of soldiers and faced the body with their muzzles angled skyward, their lusty eyes fervently fixed on the descending blackness.

Harding and Durst dare not move. Their eyes were drawn above at what held the dogs gaze. They were at ground zero and there was no escaping the revenant shadow, enormous in scale, falling towards the earth. An ensemble of maniacal howls rang out as the encircling horde kicked up and threw down, wrenching their necks and bodies like rodeo bulls, their jaws twisting back and forth in gleeful fits of rage. Their excitement boiled over in a sort of black-hearted tribal, war dance as they flashed a dizzying array of teeth, spitting and frothing.

Angling towards earth, the descending blackness sliced through the air; its massive wingspan eclipsed the sun, blocking out all light and casting black shadows over the landscape. Durst and Harding fell to their knees. They covered their heads from the debris churning up from an upsurge of wind. The frenzied horde howled in wretched unison, their bone-chilling cacophony beyond deafening as the creature swooped down, alighting at the body of Priscilla Hooke.

Behind the felled cedar, Harding and Durst watched in stark terror. The creature began to shape-shift. Its mammoth wingspan retracted from the sky, allowing the walled-off sun to flood its heinous form with unnerving light, revealing its true nature. It was heavily chested and black feathered. Its beak profound and hideous. The razor-sharp talons morphed before their eyes into a discernible form of human arms before it bent at the waist and tenderly lifted the body of Priscilla Hooke and cradled it lovingly to its breast.

Durst and Harding were dead silent. They watched as the creature unfurled its claw-like hand and touched Priscilla's scalp with a long and crooked finger, seemingly observing, examining. Then, as quickly as it appeared, holding her body protectively, the creature turned east and lifted from the rocks. The frenzied pack of dogs fell in behind in a sort of carnivorous gauntlet and together moved over the swale in a commanding wave, thrashing and snarling, vanishing into the murky depths.

Neither man said a word. They felt their legs give way, dropping them to the swamp floor. What evil had they seen? What horror had they witnessed? The lifeless body of Priscilla Hooke, lain beneath the sky in her natural sarcophagus, was no longer there. The outcropping of rocks no longer served as a crude altar to the creature and its canine dwellers. All that remained was a disorienting sense of terror, and the bits and pieces of Officer Stevens, a close friend and comrade, scattered in blood and bone.

CHAPTER 29
HIDE AND SEEK

Sergeant Guthrie sat behind the wheel of his police cruiser, his face turning a pale and sickly color. He continued to observe Room 16, but found his mind drifting. He just got off the radio with Hicks and was having trouble processing the events that occurred in the swamp. *What must it have been like in Boo's final moments? Did he suffer? Did he know it was coming? How will Barb, his loving wife, ever handle such devastating news?*

His mind squirmed and his stomach soured. Finding pieces of Boo's skull, body, and limbs the way Durst and Harding did left a bitter taste in Guthrie's mouth. Although the chief was short and direct, Guthrie knew him well enough, by the slight tremor in his voice, that he was deeply disturbed. *I will fill you in later,* the chief said, *but know I have ordered a clean sweep.*

Behind the picket fence near the maintenance shed, Guthrie could hear Henry James exerting himself. His breathing was heavily labored. They were short, quick gasps in between strong grunts, but he paid it little mind as his thoughts were preoccupied with the loss of his fellow officer and childhood friend. Fond memories of fishing and barbecuing, being best man at his and Barb's wedding, showing Boo the ropes as a young officer, and more recently helping groom him for the day The Keepers might extend him an invitation to join the order. That day might have even come today, but now his life's purpose resides in the hands of God.

Guthrie noticed Don Williams exit Room 16 and pace towards the rear of the maintenance shed. He shook out of his listless stare and watched as Henry James revealed himself from behind the picket fence with an enormous grin. Guthrie noticed Henry's black apron was shiny and beads of sweat clung to his forehead. A large blade, slightly curved with an angled hook, hung by his side dripping red; it appeared smaller than it actually was clutched in Henry's mammoth fingers.

"Nice day, Mr. Williams," Henry said, cleaning the blade across the front of his apron. "Having a pleasant stay?" Don quickly jerked his head away. Seeing bright- red blood caught him off guard and tripped a gag reflex closing his throat. Henry looked over his shoulder at the work stump, then glanced down the front of his rubber slicker.

"Sorry, Mr. Williams. I forget most folks from the city aren't used to this kind of thing."

"It took me by surprise, that's all," Don said, wiping spit from his lower lip. "I'm fine, really. I'm sorry for appearing rude." Don's eyes shot past Henry and focused on a large, animal carcass slumped over a tree stump. Half the animal appeared skinned. It was pinkish and white. The muzzle, chest, and front haunches were covered in a thick coat of barbed wire-like fur, gray and black, folded back on itself.

"Don't pay that any mind, Mr. Williams. Some things just need doing."

"What kind of animal is it?" Don asked. "It looks like a bear."

"He's as big as one, I'll grant you that." Henry turned towards the animal. "No, this fella is an American jackal, or coyote if you prefer. I call them swamp dogs. Some folks call 'em prairie wolves, though I can't imagine why, there's not a prairie to be found round here. Nothin' but black water and woods."

Don swallowed hard, staring at the gruesome sight.

"Want to have a closer look at him?" Henry asked. "I Could use some help to get 'em over on his side."

"Well, um, I need to—"

Henry threw his head back and cackled. "He ain't gonna bite ya none. Not after I took most of his hide." Don's fingers twitched for a cigarette, managing to get one to his lips. He then fumbled looking for a lighter patting down his front and back pockets.

"Here, I got a match for ya." Henry sauntered over by an open steel drum and grabbed a box of Ohio Blue Tips. The box sat next to a blowtorch on a makeshift bench made from a plank of wood supported by two, upside-down milk crates.

"Here ya are, Mr. Williams." Using his thumbnail, Henry struck the match head and lit Don's cigarette.

"Thank you Moonshine." Henry bobbed his head in acknowledgement flashing his oversized teeth. Don took a drag and said, "I wanted to check with you on that icebox and hot plate. Can we—"

"Dammit!" Henry snarled, snapping his fingers. "I forgot all about that. Get absent minded sometimes working a hide. Yes sir, right away. I bring it right over."

"I appreciate it Moonshine. Thanks." Don turned, and made his way back to Room 16, while Guthrie watched Henry remove his apron and glance in his direction. He stood and held Guthrie's eyes a moment, before smiling and passing through the office door.

CHAPTER 30
SOME THINGS JUST NEED A DOING

"Got your hot plate and icebox," Moonshine said. "I brought ya a coffee machine with some filters and fresh grounds too."

"Thanks, Moonshine," Don said, greeting Henry at the door. "I have been dying for a cup."

"I feel bad is all, I hadn't brought the hot plate and icebox like I promised you." Don opened the door wider and called over his shoulder. "Hey Guys, this is Henry James. Moonshine." Henry greeted Brett, Scott, and Albert with a friendly hello as he walked in pulling a small wagon behind him. His eyes traveled the room, bouncing from maps, to boxes, to papers and files, and to some kind of headgear that looked like miner's hats laid out on the bed next to a couple of long, curved blades.

As Henry unloaded the wagon, he could hear them plotting pins in the map and discussing what areas of the swamp they should explore first. They talked of trekking in after dark, the time when most occurrences happened. They spoke of making sure their lights, compasses, and glow sticks were ready. They discussed the proper dress, including meshing, and how to wear it about the head and neck, and to make sure they bring enough mosquito repellant.

After Henry plugged in the icebox and set up the coffee maker and hot plate, he passed between them and stopped in front of the bulletin board. "Fellas, forgive me, but I couldn't help overhearing ... it sounds like you plan on going back in them woods after dark?"

"Most of the activity we're investigating," Albert began, "has occurred at night."

"And with our lights and cameras," Brett said, "we hope to witness and record any unnatural events."

"We would like to talk to you," Don said, "about what you know of or heard of over the years, Moonshine. You could be a big help to our investigation."

"I keep to myself mostly," Henry said, looking over the entire room. "Not sure what kind of help I can be, Mr. Williams. Is all this part of the story you're working on?"

"We're working on the 1973 disappearances of three men that were never found. Right here." Don pointed at a grouping of red pins. "This is the area the men were last seen. From what we've gathered on this case so far, the reports say that you may have knowledge about the disappearances, but I know the police can intimidate and can cause potential witnesses to not remember or remember incorrectly. So, if we could have a sit-down, I think maybe we could revisit—"

"The police sure can be," Henry interjected, "but folks around here keep quiet, mostly. They don't like to involve themselves in other folks' business."

"I'm getting that feeling," Don said.

"Look, you're a friendly bunch of fellas," Henry said, with a forced smile. "But them woods are no place for outsiders, especially at night, even with lights and fancy equipment. Listen, I know these woods better than anyone, and I know what areas to avoid. You don't want to go in there blind and make a wrong step. Not out there. The peat beneath the swamp waters is deep. No one knows just how deep either. There is just no way of telling. But one wrong step and it will swallow you like quicksand, and there ain't no way of getting yourself out, just like them animals."

"Animals? What animals?" Don asked.

"Every spring after the snows melt, animals are found out there in the swamp stuck in the peat. Kind of like those ash people of Pompeii I've seen in the National Geographic. The ones flash frozen like they never saw it coming."

The guys hung on every word. Each looked at the other and then watched in silence as Moonshine's head drifted over the map. His large fingers trailed slightly ahead of his hypnotic eyes; they moved with steady pressure like a planchette on a Ouija board, beginning in the west and moving towards the east. He surveyed the map as his fingers traversed north to south, hovering and circling around the grouping of pins in a predetermined pattern.

Henry withdrew his hands and stepped back. Then, as if coming out of a trance, his lips stretched wide into a full grin, his eyes clear.

"I know every square inch of them woods like the back of my hand, Mr. Williams. When night comes, I'll take you back in there ... I wouldn't feel right letting ya go in by yourself." Henry turned and scanned their hanging faces. "I sure want to help ya find what you're looking for. There's no tellin' what I might remember speaking to friendly faces like you fellas. A lot friendlier than the police, I can tell you."

"Thank you, Moonshine," Don said, glancing at Albert, Brett, and Scott. "That settles it then. You'll lead our party out there tonight. I got to leave in a bit and meet up with someone, Cam Jenkins, at a place called Dave's, but once I'm back, we'll head into the swamp together."

"Alright then," Henry said, slapping his knee. "I guess that settles it then. When night falls, I'll come knocking. Between now and then, just ask me if ya need anything else. See you round fellas..."

"Mr. James, wait." Albert said. "We don't have and extra light or sickle or mesh netting for you to wear when we go back in the swamp. If—"

"Now, don't go worrying yourself. Albert, is it?"

"Yes, Mr. James."

"Well, Albert, the weatherman says it's gonna be a clear night, I'll be able to see by the light of the moon. And mosquitos? They don't bother me none. I bite them before they bite me."

"What about a sickle?"

"I've got my own blade for that. I prefer a one-handed, Hudson Bay Axe. Light enough to swing with one hand for underbrush and saplings, but hefty enough to cave in a coyote's chest, if he comes charging after ya." Henry could see Albert's cheeks turn a deeper shade of red. The others had a worried look on their face.

"Nothing to be scared of," Henry said. "It hardly ever happens. But now and then, one of them loses his way and turns against its nature. And when that happens, POW! Some things just need a doing."

Henry turned towards the door with his back facing the crew and reached inside the front of his shirt. He lifted a red necklace, strung with deerskin, and brought it to his lips, whispering. So quiet a whisper, it went without hearing. He then opened the door and passed through pulling his wagon behind him.

Sergeant Guthrie saw Henry emerge and got out of the cruiser. He walked from the back of the parking lot towards the maintenance shed when he caught Henry's attention.

"Afternoon, Sergeant Guthrie," Henry said, slipping the apron on over his head. "Give me a hand getting him on his side." Guthrie stared down at the half-skinned carcass slumped over the work stump. He slipped on some heavy rubber gloves and lifted under the animal while Henry tugged back on the folded hide, turning him over on his left flank.

"So, what they got brewing in there?" Guthrie asked, watching Henry draw the blade under the skin to work the animal.

"They plan on going back in them woods tonight," Henry replied, never taking his eyes off the carcass.

"Chief's not going to like that," Guthrie replied. Being careful of its hide, Henry moved the fleshing knife with precision around the haunches, neck, and skull. Then, working his way around the animal's head like a surgeon, he cut around the eye sockets, ears, and nose, freeing the hide from its sinew. Henry smiled and placed the fleshing knife on the stump and looked at Guthrie.

"I s'pect the chief won't. Tell him, Mr. Williams is gonna be heading over to Dave's tonight to speak to Cam Jenkins. I'll let you know when he leaves."

Both men looked at each other with an understanding between them. It was an understanding that didn't require explanation or clarification. And with silent retreat, Guthrie turned and paced back to the cruiser. Henry returned to his work stump. The pelt was almost ready.

CHAPTER 31
THE TIES THAT BIND US

At One Police Plaza, rookie Officer Harvey Pierce sat in the chief's office opposite his desk. He stared down into his curled, wrapped fingers fidgeting in his lap and tried to process the one-sided conversation Hicks was having with him when the phone rang.

"This is Hicks. ... Uh hum ... right. Thank you, Smitty."

Hicks hung up the phone and reached for his pipe. He struck a match and held the flame over the bowl, regarding a moment the confirmation he just received that Boo Stevens's police cruiser and Priscilla Hooke's sedan had been taken care of by Smitty's Iron Works and Smelting. The job was done without issue. Both had been crushed and lowered into the smelting furnace, turning them into a river of liquified ore. Not a trace of them would ever be found.

With a few quick draws on the stem, a ring of blue smoke wafted into the air as he fell back in his chair and returned his attention to Pierce.

"We are all one family here, Pierce. I hope I've made myself clear how things have always been and how things must always be. Is that understood?"

"Yes, Chief."

"Good. You are dismissed. Send in Durst and Harding."

Pierce lifted slowly from his chair and paced through the door; his demeanor was that of a man in possession of a horrible truth he was not prepared to hold, but one he knew he must hold and take to his grave.

Durst and Harding watched as Pierce approached, his face grave.

"The chief will see you now."

"Don't worry, rookie," Harding said. "It's all part of being on the same team. We are all on the same team here, understand?" Acknowledging Harding with a nod, Pierce returned to his desk.

"Take a seat," the chief said, his eyes trained on some paperwork. As Durst and Harding took their chairs, Hicks got up and closed the door and drew down the blinds. He then picked up the phone and dialed the front desk. "Hold all my calls." Choosing to have a more intimate conversation, he came around to the front of his desk and sat on the corner, face to face.

Durst and Harding waited for the chief to speak first, as was standard protocol. He was not a man to waste time and preferred to get right to the point. But taking measure of his own thoughts, a few strained seconds passed before the chief spoke.

"This is the first time on my watch an officer of the law has been killed in the line of duty. Boo Stevens was a good man, a family man and loyal comrade to all his fellow officers. Until his life was tragically cut down today, Boo carried on the tradition of his father, and his father before him. Boo senior was a comrade of mine and an outstanding officer in every way. He was a great asset to the department and to the order and was a man who understood duty, who understood with clarity and without hesitation what must be done and never questioned the methods of execution. And now, bless his soul, his son will never have that chance, he'll never have the privilege of carrying forward that proud tradition as his fathers before him." Hicks was visibly troubled. He gazed off toward the woods. "They are restless. Very restless. I can feel it in my bones. What happened out there today was no freak accident. Stevens was drawn in and killed. Brutalized in a monstrous, targeted way. Knowing Priscilla Hooke, the way I do, what happened out there today was meant for us. I don't believe she even knew Boo."

Hicks sighed and turned back from the window and continued. "Contempt for the law and this department threaten all within the territories. God help us all if balance and order are not restored."

Durst and Harding hung on every word. The loss of their friend and comrade hit them hard. They were still shocked and sickened by their gruesome discovery and were mystified at what unfolded before their eyes. They knew of the creature and feared it. And at times they even spoke of it in their secret meetings, but they had never seen it before. To witness its presence, a menacing and terrible presence of part man, part condor, and part reptile, was a sobering reality. Recorded in the first documents over three hundred years ago, the tribal leader of the first men, having been cut down by a hail of musket fire, had returned to his native land from the realm of spirits as was foretold.

To be so close, within its reach, as Harding and Durst were, watching as it hovered, as it scanned, as it surveyed a congregation of bloodthirsty, swamp dogs was paralyzing.

The chief continued to peer out the rear office window; he watched the trees sway, blanketed in afternoon cloud cover, while he contemplated his enormous responsibilities and then continued.

"The spirits are restless. They are agitated and they are getting louder." He returned his firm-set eyes behind a face of stone, his voice low and deliberate.

"Did it see you? Did it ... confront you?"

The men looked at each other before Harding began tapping the heel of his walking cast, his face tightening and reddening. Durst swallowed and wiped his drying mouth with the back of his hand and said, "We believe it looked at us. Not fifty yards away, it was performing some kind of ritualistic ceremony."

"And Chief," Harding began, "I don't know if they were wolves, jackals, or coyotes, but a pack of them, more than I could count, were in a frenzy. I mean they were crazed. And before this creature, this thing descended from the sky, they were all looking up at it. It's as if they knew it was coming."

"It did not confront us, exactly," Durst said, "but it knew we were there. There was no mistaking those eyes. It felt like they took hold of you."

"We were crouched down behind a felled tree," Harding said. "But it didn't matter. Like Durst said, it knew we were there."

"The, the next thing we knew," Durst stuttered, "only a few seconds later, it cradled the dead body of Priscilla Hooke to its chest, glanced over at us, and took off. All of them just disappeared into the swamp."

The chief listened intently to their account. He himself had only seen the creature in ceremony. Not in a physical dimension. Not under its own power. It was only through the Skinwalker, the one who roams the plains and soars the skies, channeled by smoke and incantation, had he ever seen the creature traversing over the landscape or flying high above the territories.

Not since 1676, since the earliest recordings of the first documents, had credible evidence ever surfaced of the creature's existence in a physical dimension corroborated by honest, reliable witnesses.

At the end of King Philip's War, 'His Rise' as it was named by some, or 'First Encounter' as it was written by the elders, was the only time in over three centuries, as was foretold by the chief of the first men before succumbing to his death, that he would reappear on the third day after being slain by the newcomers' muskets.

Over the last three centuries, accounts of the creature had always existed, of course, but they were always vague and witnessed alone, unsure of exactly what the witness saw, heard, or felt. Generally, these were nothing more than dark shadows and images conjured up in the wilds of imagination. Nothing more than a product of blinding terror and human embellishments. Other accounts were usually by men taking to the woods under the influence of heavy drink, claiming to have witnessed something, a creature of some kind, and then going on to spew their ghost stories at the local watering hole.

The chief and the order knew of these accounts and knew of the tales townspeople shared with each other, as was their business, and even monitored a few whose details seemed to break from the pattern, but largely they never did. Not the details that could lead back to them. The reports only ever varied in the description of the creature, nothing that would suggest anything of importance that would lead to their exposure. And this is just how they wanted it. Tales of the creature helped provide cover for them by diverting the populace's attention and by creating plausible deniability allowing them to carry out their true creed that would perhaps otherwise be scrutinized.

So, the stories went on and were allowed to fester; in fact, they would even help fan the flames by actively leaking false information, creating bogus accounts, producing fake witnesses and fake testimonies, creating diversions and suspicions, all to keep a curious and naïve public focused on a straw man. It was a classic diversion technique, a sleight-of-hand designed to keep a populace's eye trained on the left-hand side of something, so they would never suspect what might be happening on the right.

But today, witnessed in the physical realm and not in the altered state of ceremony, the creature appeared before them in a massed form, an anatomy of shape and weight and movement descending from high above the earth. It had revealed itself as a physical entity and not in the shadow of folklore, or the channeling of the Skinwalker in closed council.

The chief feared what was coming. As alderman of The Keepers, it was his charge to appease the warring spirits and to protect the faithful. It was the same enormity of responsibility shouldered by all the aldermen that came before him. To hear accounts of the creature's return, witnessed and confirmed by two of his best officers, was bone-chilling.

Part II

CHAPTER 32
OUR FOREFATHERS WHO ART IN HEAVEN

The Compact of the Covenant (a sacred agreement between the six elders of the six original territories), was a written document agreed upon in secret by the elders. It was based on the terrifying and unholy events they witnessed in 1676 where before their incredulous eyes the leader of the first men, in a form not altogether human, rose from the dead three days after he was cut down and killed by their muskets.

Recorded in the documents, the first men who had lived on their native land for more than twelve-thousand years, found themselves locked in the depths of the swamp and surrounded by a god-fearing militia who came to drive a stake through their collective pagan heart. They had been rounded up and most of them killed; some, including the chief's wife and son, were chained like rabid dogs and taken into custody before they were bartered and sold into slavery.

One nation destroyed gave rise to another; a foreign usurper of Anglo-Saxon extraction who sought a new land to escape religious persecution came to worship freely in God's name, to evangelize His good word, to plant the seed of faith in tilled and fertile ground, to sing His thankful praises, and to bear unflinching testament. They came to defend mankind's savior by holy sword against the savages of wind, rain, earth, and fire, and to thrive and prosper in an unforgiving, ungodly wilderness, cutting those down in open rebellion to the light of truth by a congregation of the willing.

Theirs would be an unprecedented expansion. From a small plantation in Southern New England, their industry in God's name spread their growing population across the vast wilderness. The newcomers gave little thought to a nation of Godless pagans they massacred, gone to the forgotten peoples. They were doing God's work.

Counter to their core beliefs, the blasphemous truth of the leader's resurrection, witnessed by the six elders only three days after he was killed by musket fire, had the power to fracture the very foundation of their Christian faith and to destroy their burgeoning society. A truth so mammoth in scale, so heretical, it could never be allowed to get out among the faithful.

To speak such words that the leader of the first men lived again after being sent to his death, would cast themselves as apostates. The elders knew they would be charged with courting evil and bearing false witness by the congregants; they would be accused of succumbing to the unclean presence and charged with heresies.

These men of God, the newcomers who crossed an unforgiving sea, who faced untold hardships, and who planted roots in a new world to build a congregation of the faithful steadfast upon His rock of truth, would have never heeded such wicked words from the elders' lips. Only the Lord himself was eternal life. Only He had the power of life after death. Even the mere suggestion that any man, never mind a pagan savage, lived again in flesh and blood after being sent to their grave was blasphemy of the highest order. Such testimony would have exposed the elders to harsh, public ridicule. They would have been forced to confess their sins; they would have been forced to root out all who fell under Satan's spell. They would have been forced to defend themselves against the practice of witchcraft, and would have been forced to charge their own family members, as innocent as they were, with heresy and succumbing to the beast before they were summarily charged and shamed in the public square and put to death in the most horrific of ways. This could not be. The knowledge the elders possessed must be buried and hidden forever.

For more than three hundred years, the Compact of the Covenant had been safeguarded and its tenets carried out zealously by the reigning alderman. It was the alderman's solemn duty to ensure the accord of peace and to protect the duality of nations (those in the realm of spirits, and those in the realm of the living) by eliminating all insurgents and destroying all threats.

On that day in 1676, after the first men had been rounded up like cattle in the depths of the swamp, the chief of the first men said, "Tears overflow. They crest our great rivers; they fill our great lakes; they fall as streams, never leaving our swamps dry and in want of rain. Today, by the usurper's musket, no longer will my people of the early dawn hunt or pray in the land of our ancestors, but will leave this realm for another in the Great Mystery's cathedral of solitude."

The elder militia paid the chief's words little mind as they rounded up the last of the first men and instructed the pagans, in the fiery language of their faith, to fall in and prepare for what was to come.

Men, women, and children, unprotesting and subservient, with a look of peaceful resignation on their faces, filed in two columns of perfect quiet and were marched two abreast deep into the bowels of the swamp. They moved in silent prayer, as was their custom, embracing the Great Mystery in peaceful contemplation. They were seemingly impervious to the stern reading of scripture by Thankful Brewster, elder and pastor of one of the six original territories, as they trekked deeper into the wooded swamp.

What must have sounded like a reveler in God's army in the captives' ears, Brewster's scornful words of admonition and condemnation rang out loud and shrill as the silent herd of first men paraded on to their deaths. They heard:

Jesus said unto him, I am the way, the truth, and the life: no man cometh unto the Father, but by me. He who sacrifices to any god, other than to the LORD alone, shall be utterly destroyed.

The Lord says, do not start following pagan religious practices. Do not be in awe of signs that occur in the sky even though the nations hold them in awe. The Lord rebukes all pagans. He condemns all false Gods. He sentences all to a fiery hell, all who dance as fools at the altar of the beast. May their judgement be swift and everlasting.

Written in the hand of the elders, the first documents describe their last walk as treading unawares and unrepentant. Forsaking God's laws with each step closer to death. Only a people cloaked in evil would not ask for God's forgiveness and God's mercy facing eternal damnation. Only the children of Satan would, in their final hour, reject God's testament and welcome eternal hell fires. Only by destroying evil in His name, wherever it has taken root, can God's light shine bright upon the world.

After finishing his readings, the elder militia turned and faced the black waters with closed eyes and began in unison to recite the Lord's prayer. To a man, each feared the pagans' presence, but they were resolute in God's grace and in God's truth to confront the evil lurking before them.

With muskets raised, the militia turned back with open eyes and gestured for the leader to step forward. He moved with grace and with the lightness of an eagle feather, floating above the heavily rooted ground.

Humble and reflective in tone, the chief confessed in hushed, deliberate words at the insistence of his captors. He said, as it was written, "I confess to the Great Spirit: Sun, Earth, Wind and Air, whose giving hand touches all things. From a single blade of grass to the primeval forest, from an inching beetle to the mighty grizzly, from morning dew to mountain waterfalls, and from a mother's womb to a tribal elder, I confess only my people's tears. When I am brought before the Great Spirit, I will beseech him to forgive you and your unjust God, for you know not what you do."

The written accounts of that day describe the chief's words as blasphemous and unrepentant. It was further proof of the pagans' open rebellion against God's truth and God's law. "Evil begets evil," was written by an elder. "It must be faced and destroyed, leaving no seeds to sow in the hearts of men."

The newcomers believed all swamp areas to be places of evil, where dwellers of the underworld took up residence in its black waters. They believed the black waters to be gateways to hell, a portal used by its condemned residents to transport freely between the underworld and the living.

Since the beginning of time, Satan, through insidious trickery and deception, cloaked in his many forms of disguise, behind his many faces, had always sought to destroy God's creation and put to the test God's righteous followers. This, the elders knew. God was the creator of all things, including Satan and his evil works. And it was only by His perfection that he permitted the dark one to test God's flock and to root out heretics.

Two-by-two, the men, women, and children of the early dawn passed their captors in silence, each wading into the depths of the black water without fear or hesitation until their heads dipped below the water's crest and were lost forever.

The elder militia looked on in bewilderment at the way they entered the water with a sense of peace, each with a face almost grinning. They took to their final destination as natural as a bear in winter takes to his cave, or how birds flock to the south, a natural, instinctual movement of predestination. The first men had fulfilled the visions of their ancestors without doubt or trepidation, or without protesting the truth of their ancestor's prophecy who foretold of the newcomers arrival and the demise of their people.

After his people had dipped below the black water, the leader was asked if he had any last words before he would take his last walk. He lifted his head from prayer and looked towards the heavens and said, "Three days from now, in this our final resting place, the dead shall rise from the black water as your God rose from His stone tomb. They will be led into the realm of ancestral spirits, to reunite in brotherhood before the Great Mystery. We will dwell in his light, a nation free from the newcomers, whose God rejects all 'people of the early dawn' who have hunted and fished and lived in harmonious peace for thousands of years in his native lands before the usurpers prophesied arrival. Let no man of your world forsake ours. For you have dominion over the land as we have dominion in the realm of spirits. Let them not disturb or disparage our name, for it would be perilous for him and his kind to do so. Committing such acts would break a sacred trust I make with you today in the cathedral of the Great Mystery. Let the elders of your race not be foolhardy and take for granted my words, for the wrath of our ancestral spirits will ascend from the depths of the black water and haunt your children, and your children's children. I say to you today, 'Honor ours and fear not and we both will live in an accord of peace. Dishonor ours and fear everything.'"

Sickened by the leader's blasphemous words, the militia lashed out with the butt plates of their heavy muskets, striking the great leader about the head and shoulders. They bludgeoned him with repeated blows and shouted scripture at him until his feet breached the black water and he waded in. The elders were shaken and angered at what they heard, to listen to such ungodly filth and such lies from the mouth of a pagan was so profanely disturbing, that they each knelt and prayed and asked for God's strength as they watched the black water circle up around the chief's waist—before he stopped and walked no farther.

Quickly, the militia trained their muskets on him and watched as he angled his head back with splayed arms and looked toward the sky. The blood from his deep wounds flowed over his mountain-like shoulders and down the stillness of his back, rolling off like rainwater dripping from the rim of a barrel.

His head began to sway as he intoned in his native tongue, raising his outstretched arms upward until it formed a tight V facing the sun. The elders admonished him harshly. They charged him to stop speaking the devil's tongue and to keep moving like all the others before him.

The intonation ceased, but the great leader did not proceed as all the others; he turned to face the elders and recited scripture in the words of their own God:

"Do not judge, and God said you will not be judged. Do not condemn, and God said you will not be condemned. Forgive, and God said you will be forgiven. Do none of these things, and God said salvation shall not be yours, only contempt and eternal damnation."

Like sustained claps of thunder, musket fire exploded, hurling balls of lead through the great leader's chest, shoulders, and abdomen. The sudden blast cut him down and sent him to his knees, clutching at his wounds.

Before he descended to his watery grave, he managed to utter some last words through the blood building in his throat. "Three days ... I rise. In three days, I rise again." Succumbing to his fatal injuries, his mighty shoulders slumped forward, and his head dipped below the water's crest.

CHAPTER 33
DO YOU SEE WHAT I SEE?

Curled up on a blanket over a fresh bed of hay, Whitey was fast asleep, gently snoring while Cam and Randy finished cleaning inside the barn.

"Cam, what time is it?" Randy asked, dumping a shovel full of smoking debris inside a barrel.

"Cold beer and shooting pool time. That's what time it is."

"Yeah, it is. I'm starving man. Dave's pizza sounds about right. When are we meeting Darrah and Niki?"

"An hour forty-five, but I want to get there early and get a practice game in or two."

"They smoked us the last time we played," Randy said. "Darrah owned the table."

"Whenever she needs quick cash," Cam replied, "she heads to Norton or Halifax or someplace that doesn't know her and pads her jeans with winnings. Twenty bucks a game. Straight eight-ball."

"No shit?"

"Rick Ryder, her brother, was a legend. From Bangor to Providence and every pool hall in between he'd clean house, but not here, he never hustled his home table."

"Why's that?" Randy asked. "That would be an easy score."

"Yeah, but the money dries up once the house knows a shark swims too close to shore. Listen, you're hungry, I'm thirsty and I always play better on a pitcher of beer. Let's get out of here."

With Whitey in tow, Cam and Randy made their way across the field, keeping back from the standpipe and the black waters beneath. As they passed, they were startled at Whitey growling behind them. They looked over their shoulder to see him baring teeth.

"Come on, boy," Cam said. "Get away from there." The muscles tensed beneath Whitey's fur as he dipped his head lower, his snout an inch from the water's surface.

"Shit Cam, he's not moving."

"Whitey get away from there. Come on, boy, it's not safe." Whitey was more agitated. He hissed and snarled and batted his paws at the water.

"Come on, Randy," Cam said.

"Come on, what?"

"Help me get him away from there."

Randy followed behind Cam as they both tried to get Whitey's attention. "Come on, boy, come on," Cam said, repeating the words, but it's as if Whitey did not hear or see them. He paced back and forth with quick, jerky moves; his eyes and teeth popping from his skull, oblivious to anything outside his narrow scope of vision.

"I'm just going to get up behind him," Cam said.

"Jesus, Cam. You saw what happened."

"I know, I know. As long as I don't touch the water. 'Don't get near the water, Carl always said.'"

"Cam don't be stupid—"

"I don't have a choice, Randy. Help me get him."

With his snout low, partially obscured from sight, Whitey cut back and forth skirting the water's edge.

"If I can get close enough, make him see me," Cam said.

"Go ahead Cam, I've got my finger hooked through your belt loop." They shuffled forward until they could see the water peeking through the tall grass. Cam inched closer. He could feel Randy's breath and hear his voice race the back of his neck. He shuffled to within a hair of the water's edge, standing tall enough now to look straight down into the watery pit. He examined the surface and tried to peer below, but he could not see what was agitating Whitey; he could only see the dull grey of standing water beneath the growth. But Whitey did see something, something Cam and Randy could not see. From the far-reaching depths, like a distorted image caught on mirrored glass, four, dark reflections of human form stared back hauntingly from their watery grave.

Cam lunged and grabbed at Whitey's back legs, his hands missing and splashing down. "Shit!" He quickly pulled his hands from the water and wiped them in the grass. With his head still low, Whitey snarled and skirted the edge one more time when he halted. He lifted his snout from the ground and his tail began to wag. The tensed muscles rising from his fur relaxed. And his deep brown eyes returned in a friendly matter. Whitey retreated from the water's edge and happily bounced over to Cam and licked his face.

"Atta boy," Randy said, kneeling beside Whitey and running his hand through his coat. Cam tried to speak, but Whitey's sloppy, frantic tongue prevented him from doing so.

Randy lifted to his feet, grabbed Cam's hand, and pulled him off the ground. "I thought I lost you there," Cam said. "What made you do that, boy?" A soft whimper was met with Whitey's head cocking to the side. Cam brought his face in close and spoke to him. "You know to keep away from there, right? There is nothing in there." Cam patted him on the head and reassured him. So did Randy.

"All right," Randy said. "I'm ready for beer, pool, and pizza man, let's head to Dave's."

"Come on, Whitey," Cam said, scratching him behind his ears. "You heard the man; you want to come with us and ride in the back of the truck?" Whitey spun in a tight circle, his tail wagging fast. "Good boy. Let's go."

With all the excitement of a child going to Disney World, Whitey shot across the field faster than a greyhound, and in a single bound leapt into the back of Carl's truck and spun around tighter than Dorothy Hamill trying to pull off a triple-salchow.

"I don't know, Randy," Cam said sarcastically, "you think he wants to go?" Randy shook his head and smiled. "I'm not sure man, the kid lacks enthusiasm." They both lit up a smoke and watched as Whitey stared at them with his tongue hanging out like what are you waiting for?

"I think someone wants to get out of here, Cam."

"Yeah, come on, let's head to Dave's."

CHAPTER 34
A VOICE OF REASON

As cited in the verbal warrant issued by the chief, the meeting of the small council would be carried out this evening. It was imperative that all preparations were made and without delay. Hicks knew the threats within the swamp were real and they were mounting.

Having destroyed all files on Carl Jenkins, having ordered a clean sweep, and having ordered the arrest of Cam Jenkins following the ceremony, all of these, including the threat level posed by the reporter and his crew, had been carefully weighed and considered.

As alderman, the responsibility lay square on Hicks's shoulders to carry through what was entrusted to him when he swore an oath before the order ten years ago: To appease the warring spirits in the realm of the dead, and to protect the faithful from Satan's works. After conversing at length with Harding and Durst, the chief dismissed them, each knowing their role and responsibility for tonight's small council meeting. The last time The Keepers met had been only weeks after Hicks was sworn in as alderman and the trouble that occurred in 1973, but the preparations and protocols all remained the same.

The chief walked across his office and over to the bookcases. There on the center wall, an early American painting hung depicting newcomers and the first men feasting around a common table and communicating through a native translator.

He reached behind the painting and slid open a panel to a combination safe. Turning his fingers slowly, he listened to the pattern of clicks when he heard the tongue slide and the door open. He reached inside and retrieved an intricate metal key; it was fashioned with five points resembling that of a star, when the private line in his office rang.

"Hicks," the chief said.

"I know..." a quiet voice spoke, sounding distant.

"Who is this?" the chief shot back. "Know what?"

"The Six, the Order, the meeting of the small council. Disband now before it's too late." The phone went dead before Hicks had a chance to press further. He bounced the receiver in his hand a few times, gazing pensively at the metal ring in his hand before he placed the receiver back on the hook and closed up the safe.

CHAPTER 35
VIRGINIA MAN GONE DONE US WRONG

From his police cruiser, Officer Durst radioed to Sergeant Guthrie. "Sergeant Guthrie, come in. Over ..."

"This is Sergeant Guthrie, go ahead, Bruce."

"ETA in about thirty minutes. You know how traffic is Friday after quitting time, all that Cape backup on 495."

"Roger that. Thanks for the heads-up, Bruce. Over."

Durst sped ahead, winding through the quiet neighborhood streets to avoid all the major thoroughfares. The small council would begin at seven-thirty this evening and arriving late was not an option. He and Guthrie needed to speak.

Parked under a shady oak tree at the Titicut center green, Sergeant Guthrie thought about Boo Stevens and how he needed to act when he spoke to Barb, his loving wife, about why Boo would not be coming home this evening. He knew exactly what to say, as was prepared in the script by the chief, but it would be hard this time to sell a lie about someone he knew and well liked, one of their own.

Running a hand over his mustache, Guthrie unfastened his seatbelt and began to open the door when a transmission came over the radio from Polly.

"Come in, Sergeant Guthrie. I need to patch a call through to you on your closed channel. Man says it's urgent..."

Guthrie reached in for the radio. "Who's on, Polly?"

"Don't know, Sarge, he wouldn't say, but he did say you knew who he was, and you were expecting his call. He has kind of funny twang and asked if I knew there was going to be a full moon tonight."

Guthrie groaned and sat back in his seat. "Put him through."

"Copy that, Sarge, here he is."

"Go ahead, Moonshine."

"Mr. Williams is on the move."

"What about the crew, Henry?"

"Just like I s'pected, they are staying put. They are working on their map and preparing to go into them woods tonight." Guthrie noticed Durst circling around the green and unlatched the door. "Thanks for keeping me posted, Henry. You know what to do. We'll take care of Mr. Williams. I gotta run."

Henry hung up the phone in his office and made his way through the rear door. He walked behind the fence, passing his work stump, and made his way over to the animal hide drying in the sun. Drawing his large hand along the inside of the pelt, he checked for remaining pockets of fat and sinew in need of hoeing. With an exaggerated smile of teeth and gums, Henry nodded in prideful understanding of a good day's work.

Turning back from the hide, he lifted the bald carcass off his work stump, slung it over his shoulder, and hitched over to the oversized, metal, oil drum. He leaned forward and watched as the heavily muscled animal slid off and thumped into the barrel.

Henry stretched back and gazed at the dipping sun; he would have only a couple of hours before he would escort the news crew back into the swamp. It was more than enough time to make final preparations.

He lifted the necklace from around his neck and removed three, peyote, mescal buttons and placed them inside a metal bowl. Then, using the butt-end of his fleshing knife, he sat down beside his work stump and began to grind up the buttons into a fine powder humming the words to an ancient song.

In-dhin-ga-ye ... in-dhin-ga-ye
Virginia man came to our land, taking more, tobacco hand
King and river two by name, sold it back to where they came
In-dhin-ga-ye ... in-dhin-ga-ye
The river runs up sacred ground, red it runs til native found
1622, fire and blade, send 'em back to where they came
In-dhin-ga-ye ... in-dhin-ga-ye
Defeat in battle but not in war, the white man stakes his claim goes forth.

Quiet his drum it beats no more, red man falls a distant shore.
In-dhin-ga-ye ... in-dhin-ga-ye
Now we hum this same old song, lost in time, forever gone.
Now we hum this same old song, Virginia man gone done us wrong.
Virginia man gone done us wrong.

CHAPTER 36
REHEARSAL OF LIES

Guthrie stepped out of the cruiser and made his way across the center green. He could see Officer Durst sitting on the park bench by the gazebo and walked over to him, his face grim behind a pair of dark sunglasses.

Guthrie sat down on the end of the bench and mindlessly stroked his mustache. Both men appeared as strangers for a moment, before Guthrie leaned forward, staring at the ground, and uttered the name, "Boo Stevens. ..."

A quiet second passed as Durst shifted in his seat. He then said, "Had I not seen it with my own eyes, I would not believe it. Still not sure I do. What Harding and I saw. ..." He shook his head in stunned silence.

Guthrie sat up with a straight back and gazed off across the green for a moment, tapping his fingers, keeping his feelings close to the vest. He watched a squirrel gather acorns and said, "Bruce, once we're through here, the chief is sending me to see Barb Stevens and take care of things with her before heading over to the old meetinghouse tonight. What did you find out at the high school?"

"Coach Daniels says four of his players missed double-session. They practiced in the morning, but never returned for the afternoon practice. A couple of the parents were down at the field looking for them, trying to find out what they could. I thought hell, being the end of summer, it was just some players letting off some steam, you know, but the parents insist they wouldn't do that. There is just too much on the line, they said, scouting and scholarships. They fear something has happened to them."

Guthrie dropped his head and nodded. "I heard from Harding. The situation at Mutual Gas on 104 has been cleaned. Alex Feely, the boy at Roller World, was apparently more difficult, but in the end, he was dealt with."

"What about Priscilla Hooke?" Durst asked.

"Ms. Hooke's residence has been cleaned. All anyone will ever find, if they come looking, is a note left on her bedside chair in the forger's handwriting:

I am tired of my illness and miss him more than I can bear. I always wanted to go west before I die, perhaps see the Grand Teton, perhaps not ... However far the oxygen and my gas tank will take me ... Goodbye to an unjust world. Signed, P.

"Apparently, Priscilla signed most things by just her first initial. Anyway, about Harding, what's his state of mind? I'm worried about him."

"Worried about what?" Durst said.

"Well, when I spoke to him, there was a strained anger in his voice. He sounded unhinged."

"Finding Boo Stevens, the way we did, didn't sit well. And I know he didn't like the chief telling him to lay off Cam Jenkins. When I told Harding, the chief ordered Cam Jenkins arrested, he told me, 'not if I get to him first. I'm going to bury that punk's ass in that creek.'"

Guthrie sighed and shifted in his seat, stroking down on his mustache again.

"I'll have a talk with him. We can't have him going off the reservation."

"He'll listen to you, Sergeant," Durst said. "It will mean something coming from you."

Without saying another word, Sergeant Guthrie got up from the bench, adjusted his peaked hat and stood true, his eyes taking in the expanse of the green. With quiet acknowledgement, he turned and faced Durst before walking back to the cruiser.

As he sped off driving east towards Boo Stevens's place, Guthrie knew the consequences if a member of the order could no longer be trusted. He needed to speak to Harding before he did anything stupid, before he went down a path that could only end badly for him.

"Officer Harding, this is Sergeant Guthrie, come in, Officer Harding ... Officer Harding, pick up your radio. ... Come in, Officer Harding ... Polly, patch me through to Harding."

"He called off duty, Sarge. Complained about the pain in his leg."

Guthrie paused a moment, his concern mounting. "Roger that, Polly, Guthrie out." He hung up the receiver and took a few deep breaths. For the moment, he placed Harding at the back of his thoughts and went over the script in his head about what he needed to say to Barb Stevens, and to remind himself to avoid her eyes. Never make contact with the eyes, a survival skill he learned back in Vietnam if ever he were captured and interrogated. Focus on their forehead and disassociate. Never give yourself away.

CHAPTER 37
STANDING TALL AGAINST IT ALL

Sleeping one off became a late morning ritual for Carl Jenkins. Day after day was the same: work the night shift down at the mill, eat breakfast at the Tri-Stop, drink beer in his favorite chair until passing out in front of the television set, and then wake hours later with an industrial sized headache and do it all again. But today he woke with more than a headache, it felt like he barely survived a ten-car pileup as a tremor crept up his arm and he convulsed. His foot kicked and bounced as his eyeballs darted behind closed lids. He could no longer outrun the dark visions. His legs had failed him, seizing like the propeller of a research vessel caught in an ice-shelf. He was trapped, exhausted, and hopeless. His mouth fell agape, and his lips stretched back from the gums, hollowing his cheeks like an old man's in advanced rigor.

He yelped out squashed and frightened cries; not cries of terror exactly, but cries more despondent in nature, more wretched and morose like an animal trapped in a sewer drain.

His tongue went big and loose and hung from his mouth. It stretched his face beyond normal human proportions, packing his throat with thick strings of bile pooling at his bottom lip. Then, as if being thrown through from a speeding car's windshield, he was jettisoned from the nightmare and thrown on the floor. Veins popped from his forehead. His ribs were sore like someone kicked them with steel-toed, work boots. He was in agony and tried to stand, but his lungs spasmed. It bent him in half and buckled him where the last of the bile drained from his mouth.

With a throbbing head, sore lungs, and a burning throat, he convalesced a moment, thinking only of how he desperately needed a drink. Not beer; the hard stuff. It was getting to be evening, and like all evenings the cloud of beer gave way to the fog of whiskey.

Lifting his splitting head and getting to his feet was hard, but not as hard as the thought of delaying his thirst a gallon of cold spring water could not pacify. And that's okay. Cold spring water was the last thing on his mind.

Hitching toward the kitchen, he set his course on the icebox and made an ugly approach. With a gnarled-up hand twisted up tighter than a stubborn root, he swung at the latch of the icebox with all the dexterity of a blunted stump. Clumsily, his fingers trembled around the latch, failing to bend at the joints.

He began to panic. Beads of cold sweat dotted his forehead like water-pocked measles. His throat felt coarse and burnt. The nose, lips, and tongue a swollen tomato. The mad craving for a swallow of corn whiskey tightened down his jaw on aching teeth, contorting his face into something monstrous, something unrecognizable.

His fingers were rendered useless. It was like trying to pick a lock with two glazed hams. The savage mania pounding his brain was too much to handle and he damn well needed a belt of whiskey and he needed it now. Right fucking now.

With the face of a deranged lunatic, he stepped back and swung his heavy boot into the lock, kicking and thrusting his heel at the latch in rapid fire. He kicked and flailed until the mangled lid ripped off its hinges, exposing a single bottle of pure, Kentucky nectar.

Jamming his fist and arm through the ice, he grabbed the bottle, spun off the cap, and held the bottle high over his head like an eyedropper and gulped down swallow after burning swallow. The liquid fire lit his tongue and throat with a healing bite.

Bloody ice-water dripped down his arm and chin as he drank greedily, barely noticing the sharp cuts on his knuckles and wrist from the jagged ice. As the river of alcohol flowed, he began to come down from the teetering edge, setting him right like a shot of heroin sets a junkie.

The violent storm had blown out to sea. It took with it a few more splinters of wood from its damaged hull, but it had passed all the same, allowing the calming waters to wash over him and set his compass true.

Wiping his mouth and chin with the back of his sleeve, he set down the bottle next to his Mason Jar—his preferred way of drinking whiskey—and noticed under the jar a handwritten note stained with his own blood. It read:

Sonny fixed the fuel pump. Said he'd be at the Tri-Stop later.
Off to Dave's shooting pool, borrowed the truck,
Cam.

Rubbing his eyes, he focused on the note and only now realized the extent of his cuts as the blood dripped from his hand and wrist pooling on the floor. Carl shot his eyes around the kitchen, looking for something to wrap his hand with, when he heard the door swing open followed by a loud, squeaky voice.

"Jesus, Carl, are you, all right? What the hell happened? Looks like ya caught your hand in the garbage disposal."

"Help me find something to wrap this with."

Mighty Mouse turned and found a shop rag stuffed inside a coffee can full of nuts and bolts. He then grabbed Carl's hand and shoved it in the sink under running water. Mighty Mouse glanced over the floor, the counter, the icebox, and saw fresh blood scattered and dripping everywhere. He turned back to the sink, shut off the tap, and wrapped the shop rag around Carl's fist the best he could.

"What the hell happened, Carl?"

"I cut my hand on the damn icebox." Carl's hand throbbed as he poured whiskey into the Mason Jar. He noticed Mighty Mouse glancing at the mangled lid.

"Damn thing was broken," Carl said. "I couldn't get the latch open."

"I can see that," Mighty Mouse said. "But it looks like you used a sledgehammer to get her open."

Carl grunted and fixed his drink the way he always did. He reached inside the breadbox and fished out a bottle of Pepto-Bismol and poured the liquid over the whiskey like a pink blanket.

He steadied himself against the counter and looked at Mighty Mouse with bloodshot eyes. His upper lip quivered into something that might pass for a smile and said, "I should be asking you the same thing, Earl, what the hell happened to you?"

Earl Winston, otherwise known as Mighty Mouse, tugged back on his neck brace from the uncomfortable itching and winced from the pain in his left shoulder.

"Son-of-a-bitch water tank slipped off the dolly when I was moving it down at the high school, landed right on top of me."

Carl swirled his jar and took a swallow. "Earl, if it wasn't for bad luck, you'd have no luck at all."

"Could say the same about you, if—"

"What is it you want?" Carl interjected, looking at the clock on the wall. "I could use a couple hours sleep before I head to the mill.

"I'm looking for Cam, know where he is?"

"He said he was heading down to Dave's shooting pool. He left this note. Why, what kind of trouble is he in now?"

Mighty Mouse did not want to tell Carl the police were looking for Cam, so he made up a story. "He fouled the plug on his bike riding this morning. I told him I had some high-performance plugs at my garage for him."

Carl grunted, then stepped over to the refrigerator and opened the door. In between a line of beers, he grabbed a large, glass jar full of pickled eggs and set them on the counter.

"Head down to Dave's," Carl said. "You'll find him there."

"All right Carl. Careful with that hand now." Earl pursed his lips together and left, closing the door behind him.

Carl unscrewed the lid and dipped his hand into the pickled brine and pulled out three, rubbery eggs. He sprinkled the saltshaker over one egg before eating half, sprinkled again, and swallowed the rest as his eyes fell across the overgrown field and noticed the trees. The branches were swaying gently at first before shaking violently. A powerful gust of wind came out of nowhere and rustled the leaves back on the branches. The trees looked like giant umbrellas turned inside out.

The winds shifted suddenly and reversed direction. The trees creaked and groaned, bending over slowly like an aging actor at curtain call. Carl was terrified. He watched in horror as the tips of the trees aimed straight for the house. For one blinding moment of terror, he thought the trees would uproot themselves and shoot through the air like arrows. But thankfully they held their position until... the Mason Jar slipped from Carl's hand and smashed on the floor. A sudden burst of wind roared out like a freight train. It barreled across the field and flattened the grass as Carl collapsed in a ball of terror curled up in shards of glass.

Bracing himself, with his arms tight over his head, he felt his heart in his throat and heard the panes of window glass rattle loose in their wood frames. He reached down and held on tight as the sound pounded his eardrums, the room turning pitch-black. The only light was a single, kitchen bulb swinging round from the ceiling. It spun like the blades of a helicopter when a loud, metallic sound rang out. Ping! Black water burst from the faucet and slammed his nostrils with a pungent odor. He reached behind the sink and held on to the waste-pipe and braced against the back draft.

Lifting off the ground, his legs flowed out behind him when suddenly he felt a powerful jolt and was dropped to the floor. Silence.

As Carl sat huddled and trembling, he no longer heard the sounds of whipping wind and rattling windows. The black water bursting from the faucet and the house creaking on its foundation had stopped. All he could hear now was a muffled echo like the sound of a conch shell held over one's ear.

When he pulled his head out from beneath his arms and examined his surroundings, he chuckled defiantly at the sight of his whiskey bottle standing tall and unharmed. "Well, I'll be Goddamned," he said aloud. And with a quick swipe of his hand, he grabbed the bottle of whiskey by the neck and walked up the back-staircase, muttering, "You haven't killed me yet."

CHAPTER 38
ALFRED HITCHCOCK, I PRESUME

Don Williams took a right onto Plymouth Street and glanced down at his scribbled notes: *Dave's—Corner of Union and Plymouth. Look for the Miller beer sign with a pool cue.* He trained his eyes on the passing street signs, "Corner of Union and Plymouth, Union and Plymouth. Ahh, the Miller sign, there it is."

He swung into the parking lot and pulled into a spot beside the payphone. He parked, grabbed his notes, and dialed Harry Fletcher. As he waited for the city desk to pick up, he glanced over the parking lot at the many trucks, hot rods, and motorcycles. Two bikers opened the door and stumbled out in a cloud of smoke. He could hear Bob Seger belt out from the jukebox. *A real roadhouse bar kind of place,* Don thought. *I should have worn some boots and torn jeans.*

"City desk, can I help you?"

"Evelyn, Don Williams here. Can you patch me through to Harry please?"

"Sure thing, one moment ..."

"Don, Harry here. Where are you calling from?"

"I'm outside a place called Dave's in Titicut, corner of Union and Plymouth Street.

"I can hear Seger in the background. Sounds like my kind of place. Listen, I called over at the Wampan Inn after I received your fax. The crew told me you were following up with Jenkins."

"I'm meeting up with Cam now. He's agreed to talk."

"Good," Harry said, securing the phone under his chin and sorting through some mail. "What about Carl?"

"Not yet. Cam tells me the best chance to catch him is when he clocks on shift tonight, when he's somewhat sober."

"When he's sober, hah. When and where?"

"He works the midnight to eight shift at a place called Taunton River Mill. I'm heading down there later tonight."

"All right, see what you can find out from the kid. We'll touch base after you speak with Carl."

"Right, Harry..."

"Oh, one more thing. How's the crew managing? Has Albert started to complain about all the damn mosquitoes down there?"

"Albert is Albert," Don laughed. "Prepared for anything that flies, crawls, bites, and slithers. It's a little tight in the room, but they are managing fine. Right now, they are working up a map of sightings, disappearances, disturbances, etc. And get this, after I finish up here with Jenkins, the manager of the Wampan Inn, calls himself Moonshine, is going to lead us into the swamp and walk us through some of the hot areas, including the spot on the western boundary where the men disappeared in '73."

"Going back in there at night?"

"Activity levels have been highest at night. It's our best opportunity to witness and record any disturbances. Besides, he says he knows the place like the back of his hand and that we are far safer with him at night, then on our own during the day. I tend to believe this guy, Harry. He's been living in these woods for God knows how long. You should see this guy, Harry, a genuine character, an early American throwback to pre-colonial times."

"Yeah, I know the type," Harry responded, "talks and fancies himself a Pilgrim. Claims his ancestors came over on the Mayflower."

Don laughed. "I know the type too, Harry, but not in this case. I mean early American as in Indian early American. All right, Harry, quarter is about to run out. I'll check in later."

After hanging up the phone, Harry noticed an odd, shaped envelope in the pile of correspondence and daily mail. It was simply addressed to: *"Gerry Mulrooney, City Desk, 1973."*

Harry's pulse quickened, like he'd seen a ghost. Until today, he had not thought about the name Gerry Mulrooney in a long time, and now after speaking to Don about the case and seeing Gerry's name on the envelope, that's all he could think about.

He picked up the envelope and noticed on the back the sender's name and address: *"Priscilla Hooke, 37 Mount Hope Street, Middleboro, MA, 02344."* That's all he needed to read to make the little, white hairs stand on the back of his neck.

***

Walking into Dave's was like walking into any Southern New England bar. Pictures of Boston sports teams and autographed photos of legends of the game adorned the walls, including Bobby Orr's flying goal in Game 4 of the 1970 Stanley Cup Final. It was signed in black pen: *"To Dave's, best pizza in town, Bobby Orr."*

Directly to the left was the kitchen, where the cook was busily making ten-inch bar pizza's for thirsty patrons and for phone order pickups. To the right, regulars stood up against the wall drinking beer and talking sports. Don could hear a guy shout out with a muscular voice, "You're crazy! He's long past his prime. He had a great run, but it's time Yaz retired."

Directly in front of him was the main bar crafted from heavily varnished slabs of oak in a classic horseshoe shape. It was surrounded by occupied barstools with old timers trading in "not in my day" stories and gulping ale. On the serving side of the bar, two, corralled, female bartenders were kept busy mixing drinks, draughting beer, and working tips with just enough suggestive bending to keep the old timers spending.

The mouth-watering smells of oven-baked dough, cheese, sauce, and charred pepperoni permeated the thick air and reminded Don how hungry he was. The only thing he had to eat was the breakfast special down at the Tri-Stop and some dried- up Wampan Inn, vending-machine crackers. Not enough to allow the sour underpinnings of stale beer and dirty dishrags deter him from wanting to eat.

Beyond the bar in the backroom, he could see two pool tables and a dart board; both were surrounded by the after-work crowd drinking and smoking. Some were bobbing their head to Seger and chalking up their cues; others were leaning forward, focusing through glazed eyes at the dartboard looking for an inner bullseye. None of them, however, fit the description of Cam Jenkins.

Seeing an empty barstool on the other side of the horseshoe, Don rounded the acre of varnished oak to claim the seat; he could feel the suspicious eyes of locals heavily upon him as he found his way.

As he sat down, he glanced over his right shoulder into the backroom for any signs of Cam, but he would just have to wait it out. Having a few beers and a Dave's, famous, 10-inch bar pizza—Bobby Orr approved, as the picture proudly stated—would take the edge off before his face-to-face with Cam.

Don waved his hand to get a bartender's attention, but to no use; each one ignored him as they worked the bar, passing by him a few times without even a look. He let his arm down and slid over an ashtray lighting up a cigarette.

Glancing to his right, a man getting on in years, sat on the stool next to him making no attempt to hide his overt staring. Other than his eyes boring a hole straight through Don's forehead, the first thing he noticed about the man was his cheeks. They were red and bouncy like balloon-shaped, slices of bologna that swallowed up around his chin. His eyes were small and lively, partially obscured under thick brow and heavy lids.

Don crooked his head towards the man when their eyes locked, but he quickly averted them, mostly from the awkwardness of catching someone staring at you, but also because it immediately struck him how sorely out of place the gentleman seemed to be.

Everyone in here is in jeans, work boots, T-shirts, and leather jackets, Don thought. *Town-bred, the after-work crowd, here on a Friday looking to spend their week's pay, but this guy looked like an English birder right down to his wellies ...*

Feeling uncomfortable, like discovering your fly is down and wondering for how long, Don spoke first in hopes of breaking the man's peculiar gaze.

"What's a guy need to do to get a drink around here? Am I right?" A gassy cackle sounded from the English birder's rather large, misshapen lips.

"It's nothing personal, mind you, just the way it's always been round here."

Alfred Hitchcock! I knew he reminded me of someone. Only this man wore a scally cap over a head larger than what I imagined Hitchcock's being, and Hitchcock would have never worn a rumpled, wool jacket with a tie that struggled to fit around his fleshy neck.

"Been like what?" Don asked.

"An outlander, of course," the man said, sipping his dark lager. "From beyond the territories, if you like." He drained the rest of his lager and set the empty pint down, smacking the foam from the corners of his mouth. "Not quite satisfying, not like the porter of old, eh?" The man could see the puzzlement on Don's face and knew he was being provincial and cryptic. "I do apologize," the man said. "It's not the first time I've elicited that sort of look, and it certainly won't be the last. Lest, of course, I up and die within the hour."

"That is quite all right," Don said, feeling less apprehensive. "It's no trouble."

"What I meant to say," the man continued, his cheeks flexing with each hard syllable, "obviously worded poorly the first go around, is they all know you to be an outsider, not a local. Things being the way they are, the moment you walked in here we all knew that. Have a look around you."

"Tell me about it," Don said, glancing the width of the bar. "Since I've been in town, the message has been loud and clear. I know now what it feels like to be a slithering bug pinned under an entomologist's microscope."

The man cackled, "I suppose generations of cloistered families nesting on top of one another like fire ants breed unhealthy suspicions. A tradition not easily broken, I'm afraid."

"Beyond the territories?" Don asked, "is that some local, archaic reference?"

"Not thought about that before, but I suppose it would be to an outlander."

The man held up his empty pint to flag the bartender. "Dave, if you please, and if you could get ... ah, what's your name, gent?"

"Williams, Don Williams..."

"What are you drinking, Mr. Williams?"

"Miller draft," Don said, his face turned towards the bartender. "And can I place an order for a ten-inch pepperoni? And put Mr.?" Don flashed a look at the odd, but friendly fellow.

"Fogg. Bletchley Fogg," he said.

"Put Mr. Fogg's order on my tab."

Dave stared down his rather-long skeptical nose at the unfamiliar face. "No tabs, cash on the barrelhead, bub."

Don shot him a glance before he reached into his wallet and thumbed out a twenty. "Say, do you know a, Cam Jenkins?" Dave cashed the twenty in his drawer and placed the change down, grabbing hold of the bar.

"Yeah, I know him, everyone here knows him. He's a regular you might say ... but you're not." He jerked back his arms and grabbed two-pint glasses, and began to fill them under the taps.

"Look, I get it. All I'm asking is—"

Before Don could finish his thought, Fogg said, "Jenkins? It's an old name you speak of, Mr. Williams. A name of historical significance in the colony's founding." Fogg's tone and cadence reminded Don of a professor he had in his freshman year of college. "Newcomers," Fogg continued, "is how we in the 'territories' refer to families like Jenkins. They've been here since the beginning.

Samuel Jenkins was the first of theirs to arrive. He ferried over on the Fortune in 1621."

"What about you, Mr. Fogg, are you a newcomer?"

"Yes, but you'd get a different answer depending on who you ask." Fogg shifted on his stool and grabbed at the loose knot in his tie. "Nathaniel Fogg, the first of ours to arrive was the ship's cooper and not a puritan forefather. A fact considered regrettable in certain circles. But in 1623, he ferried into the territories on the Little James all the same, which technically makes Nathaniel a newcomer, and by extension, all the Fogg's since. An inconvenient fact for the inner circle I'm afraid, but I assure you, Mr. Williams, the name 'Fogg' is on the original manifest. There's no disputing that!"

"So, why would some around here, the inner circle, not consider you a newcomer? All your papers seem to be in order."

"One would think, but you see Mr. Williams, with Nathaniel's ship being the last of the original four to arrive, and the fact that Nathaniel was asked on to make the journey to the new world as a barrel maker and not a puritan, a member of the vaunted flock as it were, we simply don't enjoy the same celebrity afforded those on the Mayflower." Bletchley dipped his head towards Don and held up a stubby finger to his brow. "That privileged lot looks at us with a jaundiced eye. Among their own, they like to whisper and point it out every blooming chance they get, and without the slightest effort made to hide their pomposity. It's putting on airs if you ask me. You'd think I was an outlander the way they've been known to carry on. Disgusting is what it is."

The clank of two draft beers landed on the bar. "Pizza will be up in five."

"Ahh, a poor man's stout," Bletchley remarked with twinkling eyes, his tongue fat on his bottom lip. "But still better than nothing at all, eh Mr. Williams? Cheers."

Don lifted his Miller draft and returned the gesture. He wondered, as he proceeded to drain his pint in a single go, if Fogg really was Hitchcock and if he, Don Williams, city reporter and outsider, was just an unwitting character in an episode of The Twilight Zone.

CHAPTER 39
TELL ME LIES, TELL ME SWEET LITTLE LIES

Barb Stevens was a fun-loving gal, big-boned and lots of smiles. There was something pretty about her, perhaps not classically so, but in an organic hometown sort of way. Freckles sat atop her apple cheeks and seemed to wink at you whenever she laughed. Her golden locks bounced and shimmered whenever she took a step, and her shapely calves, exposed beneath her baker's apron, held the ground firm with open-toed, summer sandals and painted nails.

She was clear of voice with a seducing, friendly pitch, and the way she drew down on certain words was musical foreplay. Her giving nature and larger-than-life personality pulled you in; the scents wafting from her kitchen made any man want to stay. Barb Stevens was a special woman, small-town attractive and the wife to one of Guthrie's closest friends. That made it all the harder the lie he was about to tell.

After pulling into the Stevens' driveway, Sergeant Guthrie sat a moment to gather his nerves, reminding himself to act normally and to remember the script. *And whatever you do, don't look directly into her eyes. Look just above her brow. Keep natural and keep focused.*

He stepped out of the cruiser and walked through the open garage to the breezeway door and knocked. As he waited for an answer, he cocked his head around and glanced over his shoulder. He could not help but notice a half-completed birdhouse on the workbench with wood glue, sandpaper, and an open trade's magazine beside. A stool sat behind the bench with a red baseball cap with the letters "*H F*" on the front bill. It was the official cap of the Harvest Fair committee members gave out to all the pie-eating contestants last year.

A wistful smile formed on Guthrie's lips as he remembered taking the blue ribbon with Stevens coming in a close second. He would never forget Boo pulling his face from the pie when the bell rang, blueberry filling smeared over his cheeks crying out, "Did I win? Did I win?" And then to see Barb, a smile as wide as the Grand Canyon, hop up on the platform, sit in Boo's lap and proceed to lick the filling off his face.

"Coming love muffin," announced the cheerful voice of Barb Stevens from behind the door. Guthrie took a breath and exhaled slowly. He could hear the soft clack of sandals stop when the door swung open.

"Hon, did you forget your house keys—Oh, Sergeant Guthrie, what a pleasant surprise." A savory mix of home cooking and the light scent of perfumed skin greeted him. Presenting a measured smile, Guthrie removed his hat. "Thank you, Barb, that smells delicious."

"It's Boo's favorite. Leg of lamb with all the trimmings. Silly me, where's my manners. Come on in Sergeant and pull up a chair, just need to set this lamb back in the oven to keep it succulent for my big, strapping man. It's his birthday you know."

Guthrie let himself in and sat at the end chair of the kitchen table, resting his hat on his knee. Using her heel, Barb curled up her leg behind her and closed the oven door with all the grace and dexterity of a ballroom dancer. Without missing a beat, she did a half twirl about the counter, unlaced her apron, and landed a perfect smile. "There we are. It will be just perfect when Boo gets home. Which should be..." Barb looked at the hands of the clock. "Well, anytime now. You know Sergeant, you're a man that looks like he could use a cup of coffee and a slice of pecan pie."

"Thank you, but I'll have to take a raincheck. I'm overdue at the station and need to be getting back soon."

"Well, all right, Sergeant. The pie is fresh from the oven." Barb had a way of tilting her head and lilting her voice which was quite disarming. On any other day, Guthrie certainly would've made time for coffee and a slice of her famous pecan pie.

She sashayed across the floor and sat down next to Guthrie, crossing her legs just so, as if rehearsed, and placed her hand lightly on his arm. "You know, Sergeant, I probably shouldn't tell you this because it would probably embarrass my man to death, being an officer of the law and all, but I think I can share this with you. Would you indulge me?" She squeezed his arm as her eyes traveled over his face. Guthrie was careful not to meet them directly. He kept looking for the right time to tell her what he came to tell her, but it wasn't now. He knew she was eager to share a story about Boo and he was compelled to let her. He would tell her soon enough.

"Well, it's just that my heart pitter-patters whenever that man walks through the door, Sergeant, and you know it's been that way ever since we've been married. Actually, even before that. Don't tell anyone, but Boo and I lived in sin together for a short time at the Hollywood Apartments soon after we both graduated high school. We were just a couple of kids, broke and in love, and could not afford to get married right away. But Boo's hormones were in overdrive and, well, the buds of my springtime were feeling summer heat. You know, I do see how most folks look at us Sergeant, like we are still on our honeymoon and wonder when will those two ever grow up."

She looked off a moment daydreaming, her calf bouncing just so over her crossed leg. "All I can say to them, Sergeant Guthrie, 'You all just missing the point. The first thing that man does when he gets home is wrap me up in his big strong arms and plants a kiss square on my mouth. He then picks me clear off the ground and sings in a booming voice: Cream puff, cream puff, powdery sweet, sticky buns so good to eat.'" She burst out giggling and gently swatted Guthrie's shoulder with a dish linen. "That man could surely be fresh sometimes. Speaking of my man, he should be home by now." She glanced at the clock, but when she did so, she had the misfortune of reading Guthrie's expression when his eyes looked away. Barb went quiet and her sunny disposition turned gray. "Sergeant Guthrie, why are you here? Where's my husband?"

CHAPTER 40
IN THROUGH THE OUT DOOR

"Niki, turn that up," Darrah said, as she blackened her eyelashes thick and long with perfect strokes, admiring her image in the mirror as a painter gazes upon the finished canvas.

"What?" Niki said, turning off the hair dryer in her bedroom.

"I love this song," Darrah replied. "Turn it up."

Niki rolled over on her four-poster bed to the Pioneer stereo on her bureau and turned up the volume. Niki and Darrah sang "Shadows of the Night" as they finished painting their faces and nails and juiced up their lips with gloss. They held each other's hair off the other's shoulders and applied fat dollops of Coppertone lotion over the neck, back, and thighs. They used big circular motions, working the lotion over every inch of skin, making sure to cover the calves, shins, and toes. By the end of this summer ritual, every square inch of sun-bronzed skin was supple and fragrant with coconut.

"Almost ready Darrah," Niki said, in a breathless Marilyn Monroe voice. "I just need to squeeze into a tube." Sitting up laughing with her black hair gathered off her shoulders, Darrah struck a pose in front of the mirror and admired the shapely curves of her body as she thought of what to wear.

"God, I'm so jealous," Niki said. "You have that savage tan guys like."

"Nik, you have beautiful skin."

"I guess, Randy likes it, but yours is like cocoa butter all year." Smiling at Niki in the mirror, she continued to gaze at herself, presenting distinct looks.

"This hair and skin come from my mother, but my personality? I'm my father's daughter, all the way. Nik, can I borrow your yellow tube?"

"Sure, I was going to wear the pink one, anyway. I'll check the laundry downstairs. Back in a flash ..."

Barely a shimmy, her perky, young boobs lead the way as Niki sprang from the bed like a jackrabbit and ran downstairs. Darrah fell back against the plush pillows, lit a cigarette, and grabbed the recent issue of Cosmo. A photo of a nearly naked Christie Brinkley donned the cover with barely enough gold draping to cover her privates. A thread less, she would have been on the cover of Playboy.

Just above Christie's left shoulder, an article caught Darrah's eye. She turned down the radio and said, "Hey Nik, did you read this article in Cosmo? The one on boob surgery?"

"Yeah, I can't believe it. It says women are getting surgery to increase the size of their boobs. One woman, from Detroit I believe, said she went in with a 32C and asked for the Dolly Parton package."

"Really? You've got to be kidding me?"

"She said it saved her marriage, but with all the extra attention she's getting now from other men, she wonders if she even wants to."

Darrah shook her head and tossed the magazine. "Crazy ass bitch. Hey, Niki? Speaking of someone's Dolly Parton's, mine are getting cold. Did you find the yellow tube?"

"Hold on. I know it's here somewhere." Niki looked through the stack of folded clothes and rifled through the laundry basket on the floor. "Where the fuck is it?" She opened up the dryer door and peered inside and then lifted the washer lid. "Shit!" She thought a moment and then it hit her. *The couch!* She ran into the finished rec room and over to the couch, quickly looking behind the pillows and feeling under the cushions, running her fingers between the length of the seams. She searched every corner and crevice, but came up empty. "Shit. Where the hell is it?" In frustration, she plopped her ass down on the floor and stretched back on the carpet and said, "Darrah, I can't find it!" She then turned her head and right there under the couch, up against the wall, she saw a tiny, yellow garment balled up like a lemon.

Bronzed and topless, Darrah flew down the stairs and looked on, placing her hand on an exaggerated hip. "Niki, what are you doing under there?"

"Keep your panties on, Darrah, I found the tube. I just remembered Randy was over last Thursday and we fooled around on the couch. Give me a sec, I think I can reach it..."

With her head to the ground, she reached back as far as she could and snagged the tube top with her finger. "I got it!" As she started to pull her arm back, her eyes were drawn beneath the couch towards a finger of light peeking out behind her father's office door. She found it more than odd the light was on when Sergeant Guthrie wasn't home. His office door was always closed, always locked, and the light was always off, unless he was in there working. But even then, it was only a soft desk lamp he ever used. He never turned on the bright overheads.

Niki gasped at what she saw next. A shadow behind the office door stepped into the finger of light then quickly broke. She slammed her hand over her mouth and shrieked silently. She jumped to her feet, stared at Darrah, and held a tight finger over her mouth. She mouthed the words "I think someone's in there."

"What?" Darrah mouthed back.

"There's someone in my father's office. No one is supposed to be in there. The door is always kept locked."

Darrah snatched the tube from Niki's hand and slipped it on over her head, tugging it down over her breasts. "I'll take care of this."

"Darrah, what are you going to do? Jesus, don't go in there."

Darrah stepped up to the office and slammed her fist against the door shouting, "Cut the shit! Whoever you—" Before she got out all the words, the door fell back awkwardly, teetering on bent hinges.

Caught by surprise, Darrah darted from the threshold and hugged up against the wall, pressing her face to the door's casing and glimpsed inside the office.

Niki dropped below the arm of the couch yelling, "Darrah, get back!"

Noticing an aluminum baseball bat leaning against the wall, Darrah grabbed the bat and burst in swinging. "Come on motherfucker!" The bat whirled through the air wildly missing everything, except the backside of a file cabinet.

Hearing the loud, metallic thump, Niki sprung to her feet and ran into the office. She found Darrah walking rather nonchalantly toward the window with the bat hanging loosely at the end of her fingertips.

"Darrah, are you alright?" Niki's eyes traveled the four corners of the office, glancing floor to ceiling, but nothing looked disturbed.

"My hands are vibrating a little," Darrah replied, "but I'm good."

Darrah reached behind the torn shade and found the sash four inches above the sill. There were scuff marks over the stained wood. "Nik, come look at this. This window was opened from the inside." Niki walked over to Darrah and looked at the open window. They both peered out over the backyard and treeline, but saw nothing. Whoever was in the office only minutes ago, was gone.

With trembling fingers, Niki locked up the window and drew the shade closed before she walked over to her father's desk and plopped down in his chair. "Sergeant Fucking Guthrie is going to freak!" she said, when she looked down at the desk and noticed gouge marks on the locked, paneled drawers, splinters of jagged wood shooting out from the sides.

"Darrah, come look. Whoever was here, was looking for something in my father's desk. These drawers have been pried open."

"Oh shit, are you going to call the police?"

"My father is the police," Niki said. "He would be pissed if I called the station and didn't go to him directly. But..."

"But what?" Darrah asked.

"He's going to be even more pissed when he finds out I was in his office."

"But somebody broke in. You were just trying—"

"'Never under any circumstances,' he said, 'do you ever enter this office?' And he made me promise."

Darrah smiled. "You know what? He's not going to find out."

"What are you talking about?"

"How's he going to know? We just make it like we were never here."

"Right. How would he know? We just pretend like nothing happened ... Wait, what about the dent in the side of the file cabinet?"

"Whoever broke in did that, right? There isn't anything in here that can't be explained by some dickhead burglar."

Niki smiled. "Right. Hear no evil; see no evil."

"Exactly, just like at Cam's. We didn't see or know a fucking thing."

Niki smiled and glanced at Darrah. "Sounds good. Just make sure you return the bat where you found it. He'll notice."

"Come on Nik, let's cruise over to Dave's. I think the guys have had just enough beer and practice time."

"Enough beer, no doubt, but never enough practice time. Darrah Ryder runs the table on everyone."

Getting up from the chair to follow Darrah out, Niki noticed inside the damaged drawer a handwritten note in black ink sitting atop some strewn items as if carefully placed there. It read.

'We know. The Keepers, the order, the compact, the meeting of the small council. Disband now before it's too late. There's very little time. We fear the situation is grave. Come forward and put an end to all this. We assure your anonymity will be protected. We'll be in further contact."

CHAPTER 41
GHOST WRITER

Sitting in his office, Harry Fletcher grabbed the Mulrooney file and opened it to the section Don had referred to:

1973: Hockomock Swamp: Three disappeared: One survivor

John Hooke—Titicut—Disappeared
Paul Andrews—Titicut—Disappeared
Mark 'Scottie' Fuller—Titicut—Disappeared
Carl Jenkins—Titicut—Survivor

There it was, John Hooke, the very first name. Harry sat back in his chair, chewed gently on the temple tip of his reading glasses, then fixed them back on his nose. He opened up Priscilla Hooke's envelope addressed to Gerry Mulrooney and found a handwritten note.

As he began to read, his heart sank at the despondent, hopeless nature of her words, but his investigative reporter's belly was stoked with fire at her damning accusations.

Could this be true? Is any of this true? He knew if even a portion of her allegations were true, there would be enough to launch criminal investigations into a whole host of federal and state felony charges: corruption, extortion, threats, conspiracy, arson, kidnapping, forgery, falsifying records and destroying legal documents, assault, and even murder. You name the charge; it was in there.

Harry's mind raced at the enormity of the claims. A picture began to form in his mind of a corrupt enterprise operating with impunity and in secrecy, leveraging fear to keep a community in a sort of numbed silence until now.

Though if Priscilla's letter was true, it took a mother suffering from the loss of her son and a debilitating illness to bring it all to light. It reminded Harry of 1979 when a team of reporters were investigating the methods of enforcement and obfuscation James Bulger employed as crime boss of the Winter Hill Gang when anyone got close.

As Harry mulled over the note, he knew it would not be easy to wrap his head around all of this, it never is, but this case in particular presented unique difficulties. The Mulrooney file was a ten-year-old hodgepodge of scattered notes and jumbled correspondences. There were names and places written throughout the documents and jotted in the margins. Dates, maps, charts, timetables, matchbook covers, newspaper clippings, etc., etc., strained the binder beyond its capacity in a kind of paper haystack of disorganized information, but information, nonetheless.

It would take time, Harry knew, to get a handle on it, but now was not it. He had just read the words of a distraught woman who left him gasping, prompting him to want to get to Titicut right away. He was compelled to confirm or deny Priscilla's accusations, and Don Williams needed to know about the gravity of the situation.

His eyes scanned up to the first paragraph where Priscilla detailed the means of her own demise and read through it again:

"On Friday, September 9th, 1983, I will take to the woods at his site of vigil. Cognizant and clear of faculty, under no immediate duress, I will pace back through the thicket and arrive at the clearing by the water's edge. It is there, surrounded by an outcropping of rocks, beneath a wide sky, where I shall lie in wait. Know that they always come.

"To this point, perhaps above all others, you must know is ironclad. They always come. They always know when I return to the site of my son John's disappearance. They are always watching and are always vigilant in protecting whatever evil happens there. This I know. This you must know.

"But this time, I will not be dragged away to be brought before Chief of Police, Hicks. This time, I will hold my ground in protest and leave this world on my own terms. This time, I will rejoice that my long nightmare is over and a reunion with my beloved son draws near. This time, I will finally make peace in this place of sorrows as I lay down and prepare for the journey ahead. And this time, I will hold them to account. I will face their wall of power and stand in open rebellion against their whole fucking order.

"But know this. All will happen without a single witness, a single police report, or a single shred of evidence. There will be no whispers or even rumors of what happened here. Believe me, if there ever were but a whisper, the perpetrators would be silenced. There will be no evidence my car was left roadside at the site of vigil, with keys left in the ignition and the door wide open. All of this will be swept clean and buried. I know how they operate; I do not know why.

"I'm not sure if anyone has ever come forward from the past. I'm not sure if anyone actually even knows the truth, other than those that surround him. But even they, how much do they know? How much does he allow them to know? Myself, I only know this. Forever the truth will be, regardless of the web of lies they'll spin, and the cover-ups they'll employ, that I willingly choose to end my life on this day: Friday, September 9th, 1983, by means of oxygen starvation. And that before I pull the tubes from my nose for the last time, I plan on taking with me his corrupt minions dispatched to bring me in.

"I have become quite comfortable firing my snub-nosed revolver. And although my hand isn't steady as it once was, I have practiced and learned how to shoot with deadly accuracy. Remember, it's not if they come, but when they come. They always come. I will not change my mind. I will not rethink my decision and back out at the last moment. Once I make a promise to my son, I always carry through.

"I have struggled over this for years, but now look forward to carrying out my plan with great urgency; I will not be robbed of the opportunity to see their faces when they're staring down the barrel of my gun. I have made this decision and I will follow through to the letter. No matter what any of them tell you, it's not true. If it wavers even a hair from what has been outlined in this testament, written in my hand, know their cover-up is underway. I know now this is the only way to force even the slightest chance that they will someday be brought to justice and will ultimately be destroyed. I owe that to my son, that he did not die in vain. And I owe that to myself and to all who have suffered as a result of their wicked crimes.

"All that will ever remain of this event is this letter, hopefully being read right now by someone who has the means to investigate and the courage to expose the truth once and for all. If all goes to plan, as proof that I was in the swamp on Friday, September 9th, 1983 you will find my gun, freshly fired. From the site of vigil, trek back through the woods until you see the outcropping of rocks by the water's edge. From there, look east. You will notice a single birch tree at fifty feet. It is the only one. There, at the base of the tree, somewhere in the dense undergrowth, you'll find my gun.

"I do not know how large their corrupt ring of injustice is. There have been other such happenings, disappearances, and so on over the years that mimic the same circumstances of my son's and others. All have vanished in the towns surrounding the Hockomock Swamp. They have always been explained away with manufactured stories, false witnesses, bogus documents, *forgeries, destruction of evidence, etc., etc., and have been swallowed and accepted by the populace as fact.*

"I realize this letter is futile. I sent it to your newspaper, knowing full well it's addressed to a ghost. Gerry Mulrooney did not have to drop the investigation, leave unexpectedly, and take a new position. I know better. I know they got to him. I write this letter, this unabashed plea, in the long hope that one day it will find someone's desk who will have the courage and sense of justice to hear my words…"

Harry withdrew his eyes from the note and sat back in his chair when an intern rolled in with a food cart.

"Mr. Fletcher, roast beef, pickles and mayo on rye, bag of chips, and a cola." Harry hesitated, rubbed his eyes in thought, then thumbed out a five-dollar bill from his wallet. "Thanks, Michael, keep the change. Say, Michael, do me a favor and grab me the Metro South map behind you. Right there next to the phone books."

Michael handed Harry the map while Harry moved his sandwich out of the way. He proceeded to unfold the map and spread it out over the table. "Dave's Pizza. Corner of Union and Plymouth street," Harry muttered, leaning in with his glasses. "Corner of Union and Plymouth." He placed his index finger over the map, noticing the Hockomock Swamp as he traced west to east along route 104. "Right there … Dave's Pizza." Using a highlighting pen, he traced from where Union and Plymouth intersected back to the highway off-ramp. He knew how to take the highway and look for 104.

Quickly gathering up the map, phonebook, Mulrooney file, and Priscilla's letter, Harry headed straight through the door.

"Mr. Fletcher!" Michael said. "What about your sandwich?" By the time Michael finished speaking, Harry was on the elevator descending to the lower level garage. He had to move fast.

CHAPTER 42
WHEN THE FOG BEGINS TO LIFT

"There, Mr. Williams, now that's a proper English stout, dark and dry with a royal crown for a head." Don lifted the glass and sniffed about the rim. "Go on," Bletchley urged, "have at it. I promise you won't start speaking with a funny accent or fancying a top hat."

"Cheers, Mr. Fogg." Don leaned his head in and took two protective sips and set the pint down.

"Never seen someone drink stout like it was piping hot tea before," Fogg chortled. "You know, Mr. Williams, stout needs time to set the tongue and lips before you swallow it, and that requires a full measure."

"Very well, Bletchley, when in Rome..." Don took a long swallow, then another, then craned his head back and tapped out the pint before he set the glass back down with redemptive authority.

"An effort worthy of the brew, eh, Mr. Williams? It's satisfying, if you ask me, to know six-hundred years of mastery and tradition is settling in the mass of your belly like kidney pie, rather than sloshing around looking for something to grab a hold of like your pale lagers or pilsners. There's just more on the bone."

Don struggled to speak over the building gas. "Feels more like I swallowed a six-hundred-pound, lead weight."

"Just takes a bit of getting used to, Mr. Williams," Bletchley said, his eyes twinkling with seasoned pride.

"Thank you for telling me." Don pulled the pencil from his ear and fixed his notepad against his leg. "Now," Don said, "you were about to say."

"Yes, I was about to say, before we got you sorted, if you were asking me what I think you were asking? Whether I believe the creature really exists?" Fogg's eyes grew sober and his voice became clipped. "That is what you are driving at, eh Mr. Williams?"

Don shifted on his barstool and glanced at his notes. He detected a change in Fogg's demeanor. He had become overly cautious and somewhat accusatory in his tone. Don took up his pencil and met Bletchley's eyes. "Yes, Mr. Fogg, that is precisely what I am asking. As I have mentioned, there are families without answers who still mourn the loss of loved ones. My only intention is to help bring some closure to them, if I can."

"And to get your name in the papers," Fogg quickly shot back. "I know this much, Mr. Williams, to bring closure, one must open doors that are better left closed. The chief will not look kindly on that sort of thing. That is a certainty."

Don lit a cigarette and sat back on his stool, flipping the book of matches pensively in his hand before he said to no one in particular. "It always goes back to the chief."

"How's that?" Bletchley asked, his fat fingers cupped around his ear. Don looked over his right shoulder into the pool hall, glancing past Bletchley, when he heard Bletchley speak in a quiet voice.

"You didn't hear this from me ... but—" Fogg's eyes darted from left to right then left again and reached for his pint. "But we have learned around here that some things are not worth knowing, if you catch my drift?"

Don waited for Bletchley to fix himself another sip, as he knew he had more to say. It's as if Bletchley needed courage to continue on, or at least take a few moments to weigh the consequences of his words. "I am retired, Mr. Williams, and have made it thus far following three, simple rules: One, never question the chief. And two, ignorance is bliss."

Don listened to Bletchley mention two of the rules and waited for the third, but heard only the sound of dark stout creeping over misshapen lips.

"What is the third rule, Bletchley? You mentioned there are three."

"Quite. It's easy enough to remember, it's the same as the first. Never question the chief."

Don balked in frustration and returned to the remainder of his pint, when he heard a sudden buzz of voices blaring over his right shoulder. "Cam my man!" "What's up, Randy? What's the good word boys?"

Cam and Randy had just entered through the back door with their pool cues in hand. They were red-eyed and feeling no pain as they sauntered in on a cloud of smoke laughing and joking and throwing out solids all around.

"Looks like the Jenkins boy has arrived," Bletchley said. Don pushed back his stool immediately and dropped a ten-dollar bill on the bar. He quickly drained his pint and acknowledged Bletchley with a nod before he excused himself and turned toward the back room.

"Truth is stranger than fiction, Mr. Williams," Fogg said, taking Don by the shoulder as he walked by. "We all see what we want to see and are blind to all the rest."

"Not all, Mr. Fogg. Some of us see things for what they really are and seek out the truth."

Bletchley drew his face in tighter to Don's ear. "Well, they don't live here, Mr. Williams, but I can tell you this much if you promise me it's off the record. You understand that none of this can lead back to me?"

Don nodded and said, "You have my word."

Bletchley exhaled and wiped his lips. "Very well. Those who have seen the creature describe it as terrifying, as monstrous. They say its breast and flank are black-feathered, blacker than chimney soot. They say it's covered in thick, oily scales that of a lizard, and it has a horrible, twisted-up beak. Over the years, some have described it as something prehistoric, something from another time. They say the wingspan is thrice that of a football field. So large, that if it ever appeared during the day, God help us, it would block out the whole of the sun and cast its menace over the land."

Don was astonished, but not entirely surprised; it fit the account he heard back in college and fit the account in the Mulrooney file about the Black Condor as described by the young, Benjamin Church. Hearing it from Fogg made it frighteningly more real.

"Still others describe it as something entirely different," Bletchley went on, his eyes darting again both left and right.

"Different, how?" Don pressed. "How do the others describe it?"

"You didn't hear this from me, but some describe it as being more human than creature, standing six-foot-four with a badge on its chest." Fogg needn't say the name, Don knew who he was talking about.

"Thank you for your time, Mr. Fogg," Don said. "It was a pleasure making your acquaintance."

"Bletchley, Mr. Williams, call me Bletchley." With a slight nod, Don made his way across the bar and entered the back room.

CHAPTER 43
HONOR OURS AND FEAR NOT

Along the winding banks of the Titicut River, built on the same ground just north of the first meeting house where newcomers first gathered during the earliest settlement, the small council building has stood since 1676.

At the conclusion of King Philip's War, official records state that the new meetinghouse—known today as the small council building — was to be built as a meetinghouse in typical, early colonial fashion, where church services, town business, and court sessions were all to be conducted as normal. But the newly proposed structure would be built with an elevated fortification in mind. Bolstering its defenses and bettering its lookouts would be paramount in its construction.

Throughout the territories, many lives were lost during the year-long hostilities between the first men and newcomers. The congregation's numbers were significantly reduced, killed by the pagans, leaving many grieving widows. The new structure would ensure that God's chosen would never be caught unawares again. They would be protected from the savages.

Within the records, the building plans called for high walls, watchtowers, fortified windows, additional points of egress, etc., etc., all made of the strongest oak. But nowhere in the archived papers was there ever mention of secret underground bunkers and secret tunnels to be built below the new meetinghouse.

By war's end, the first men had been annihilated, but it was argued by the territorial elders that the new meetinghouse was prudent and part of God's plan. It was needed protection against future attacks by nomadic, pagan tribes seeking a claim of land, or perhaps worse, seeking retribution for their fallen brethren.

It was predestination that God's faithful would be saved from the wickedness of the damned, but it would be their God-given gifts of industry and prudence that would ensure their survival.

Unbeknownst to church and government leaders, as well as congregants and settlers in the territories, the elders, as was witnessed and stipulated under oath in the tenets of the Covenant in 1676, required a place to carry out its true purpose. They needed a secret and protected place to ensure that the leader of the first men's ominous, last words, voiced minutes before his death, never fell on deaf ears.

"Let no man of your world forsake ours. For you have dominion over the land as we have dominion in the realm of spirits. Let them not disturb or disparage our people, for it would be perilous for him and his kind to do so. Committing such acts would break a sacred trust I make with you today in the cathedral of the Great Mystery. Let him not be foolhardy and take for granted my words, for the wrath of our ancestral spirits will rise from the depths of the black water. Honor ours and fear not… and we both shall live in an accord of peace. Dishonor ours … and fear everything.

The small council building was rarely used anymore, as matters of town business were conducted at the Titicut Township Municipal Building on the center green. Annual town meetings and the calling of special town meetings, as warranted, were held at the Titicut Middle School to accommodate the growing census.

For townspeople and local historians, the small council building was a landmark of historical significance and a symbol of the earliest democratic principles carried forth by their forefathers. For The Keepers and its protective bulwark, The Order, it had been the place where the alderman gathered his council and presided over matters concerning the Compact of the Covenant for more than three-hundred years.

Sergeant Guthrie turned down Brewster Mills Road and drove the mile and a half towards the small council building. Ever since leaving Barb Stevens's place, he felt deathly ill. His mouth and throat were dry, and his forehead felt feverish. His stomach, lungs, and the rest of his internal organs felt as if they were decaying in a liquified toxic sludge.

Lying to Barb Stevens, the way he had, made him feel like an accomplice to a conspiracy against one of their own. Concealing the truth about Boo Stevens was hard to take.

The way her mouth hung open, Guthrie thought, *the way her eyes went big before her eyelids closed and began to tear,* tore him up inside. It was the first time he'd ever seen Barb Stevens cry. But what made him feel worse than a possum three days dead, is he knew it would not be the last of the lies. Telling Barb that Boo was undercover, working at the behest of the chief in a clandestine operation coordinated by the State Police and the DEA to take down a drug trafficking ring, and that he could not break radio silence was only the first part of the script, the first part of the story.

Eventually she would find out the rest of the tale, so carefully crafted to insulate the police against all claims of suspicion and wrongdoing. That tale was yet to come. When and how were known only to the chief. Although she would never know the real story, Guthrie knew, it would be real enough when days bled into weeks, and weeks bled into months, and still no sign of Boo. At some point she would realize, regardless of what the official reports will say, that she would never see him again.

Guthrie turned down the heavily wooded dirt road and drove five hundred feet until he arrived at a police barricade flanked by two, uniformed officers. The officer standing on Guthrie's side, motioned with his hand to roll down the window.

"Evening, Charlie," Guthrie said in a friendly manner belying his countenance. "How are the wife and kids?"

"Better than my fishing," the officer replied, "can't catch nothing down at Lake Nippenicket anymore worth eating. Seems the only thing that bites, nowadays, is those good for nothing yellow perch, forget bass or walleye."

Guthrie manufactured a snicker. "Yeah, well, you just gonna have to head down to McMenamy's Fish Mart like the rest of us and buy it by the pound. Better yet, open that wallet of yours and take the wife out to that new fish house down on Broad Street. It will do your ego a world of good."

"Yeah, how's that?"

"The fish can't laugh at you served hot on a plate..."

"Yeah, yeah, go on through Sergeant."

"Thank you, Charlie. I'm serious about that fish house, you hear?"

Guthrie rolled up the window and drove past, blotting his mouth and forehead with a hanky. He did the best he could to hide his severe discomfort. He was good at hiding, but he wondered if it was good enough. *Thank God, Charlie was still wearing his police-issue sunglasses,* Guthrie thought, *and didn't notice I was white as a sheet about to puke.* He looked in his rearview mirror and watched the officers fixing the barricade back into place and saw Charlie speaking with the other officer in a relaxed manner.

"Sergeant Guthrie, come in. This is rookie Officer Pierce. Come in, Sergeant."

"This is Guthrie, over."

"Sergeant, what's your ETA?"

"My ETA, rookie?"

"Sorry Sarge. The chief ordered me to find out if you're on your way. Everyone has reported to the small council building. Everyone, but Officer Harding and yourself."

Shit, Guthrie thought, *I hope to hell Harding hasn't flown the chicken coop and disobeyed the chief. God help him if he has.* "I just pulled in, Pierce. I'm rounding the east tower and will be there in a minute, over."

Where the hell was Harding? And why is rookie Officer Pierce here?

Guthrie pulled to the west side of the building and parked the cruiser. He gobbled down some Tic Tacs from the glove box and exited. As he made his approach, he could see police cruisers, a few off-road trucks, and the vehicles belonging to the Six parked on the south side of the building hidden behind the structure. All had apparently arrived; all except for Officer Harding.

Guthrie walked across the small lot and ascended the grass hill.

"Evening, Sergeant Guthrie," Pierce said. "They are all assembled and nearly ready to enter the lower chamber."

Guthrie passed through the heavy oak door and spoke in a hushed tone.

"Still no Harding?"

"No Sergeant, he's not answering his radio either. He's MIA at the moment." With a nod, Guthrie removed his hat and made his way with Pierce, passing officers and other members of the Order on their flank. In the back and to the right, the door to the inner chamber was closed and in session. The chief's booming voice could be heard from behind the door. He was reciting from the Psalms.

"What is the chief reciting, anyway?" Pierce asked. "Sounds like some kind of sermon in there."

With a dubious look on his face, Guthrie said, "The chief is reading from the Psalms… Look, I don't know how much you know, Officer Pierce. Frankly, I'm surprised you're even here—" Guthrie's words were clipped by the sound of a steel bolt sliding back against its strike-plate when the door opened, and Officer Durst emerged from the inner chamber. "It's time," he said. On Officer Durst's announcement, all within the meetinghouse moved determinedly into position; not in a hurried or panicked way, but moved with the sure-footedness of purpose like a column of soldiers on the march. Some moved to east and west entrances; others took positions as lookouts surrounding the grounds, and along the outer treeline at water's edge. Still others climbed the back stairwell to the rooftop position and stood guard with weapons drawn along the embattlements where seventeenth century saker cannons jutted out from the ramparts like eight-hundred-pound gargoyles.

While Officer Durst motioned for Guthrie, Pierce fell in behind the members exiting the western entrance, taking positions at various locations along the perimeter. Guthrie stood beside Durst and waited for the room to clear before the men exchanged words.

"All preparations have been made," Durst began. "After they complete final prayers and face east in a moment of silence, the ceremony will begin. By the way, how did it go with Barb Stevens?"

Guthrie opened his mouth to speak, but reached for his hanky and blotted his head and mouth. He felt his stomach turn sour. "My part is done. Any word from Harding?"

Durst shook his head. "He better have a damn good reason for not being here, for his sake. If he had a mind to go after Cam, god help him."

Guthrie felt a chill climb up his spine. "Did anyone go check on him?"

"Chief sent an officer to his apartment, but no one answered."

"Did they knock loud enough? Polly said his leg was in pain and he took the afternoon off. If he's on heavy meds, maybe he fell asleep."

"Well, Sergeant, if that's true, then someone stole his truck and took it for a joy ride. It wasn't there."

"Jesus H. Christ," Guthrie uttered under his foul breath. "Is that why Pierce is here?"

"All I know is when Harding didn't report, the chief had Pierce show up and help the order cut boughs of pine and cedar and tie up some sage, but he is not allowed into the lower chamber. Chief's orders. He's only to stand perimeter duty."

They heard the door unlatch and open. They were ready. Chief Hicks and the six had completed their prayers and stood now in an altered state of collective solitude, prepared for ceremony, waiting to descend into the lower chamber. Guthrie and Durst exchanged tight glances before they secured their peaked hats under their arms and passed over the threshold.

CHAPTER 44
LOOSE LIPS SINK SHIPS

With a pool cue in one hand and drink in the other, Niki stepped back from the jukebox, her cheeks lit red from alcohol, and sang out with Pat Benatar.

We're running with the shadows of the night, so baby take my hand, it'll be all right. Surrender all your dreams to me tonight, they'll come true in the end.

Sporting big hair, neon headbands and dungaree jackets, some girls joined Niki around the pool table and sang out:

You can cry tough, baby It's all right, You can let me down easy, But not tonight….

The music blared on. It was the Friday night leading into the last weekend of summer and Dave's was getting packed. Partiers, burnouts, jocks, dweebs, and dorks filed on in. Everyone from freshmen to seniors showed up in hopes of seeing those they had not seen all summer long. Who had a killer tan? Who was boinking who? Who grew a set of boobs since Memorial Day? All pressing questions that hormone raging teens needed answers to.

Getting together over the last weekend of summer became a tradition, and Dave's had always been the local bar to kick it off. At two-for-one pitchers and dollar Cape Codders, a ten-spot would see you drunk as a skunk—that and a slice.

Dave's was a typical South Shore bar, a place for townies to commiserate over the Red Sox's chances while they wolfed pizza and gulped beer. It was a working man's stop, a watering hole for day laborers, construction workers, truck drivers, and ex-high school athletes who liked to revel in their past glories while trying to forget that soft inner-tube bulging around their waist twenty some-odd years in the making.

But on nights like this, the Friday night on the last weekend before the start of school, and other select dates throughout the year: Thanksgiving eve, New Year's Eve, and the Sunday night before Patriots' Day, Dave's became a mosh pit of imbibing youth. For Don Williams, it became the launching point into a night of evil; it would be his *Where were you when President John F. Kennedy was shot?* kind of moment—a time and place that he would never forget, one that would carry with him like his ink-stained fingers from his Olympia typewriter.

"Call it!" Cam said, flipping a quarter high above the pool table. With a sweet movement of her hips, Darrah turned and arched her back. Her jet-black hair waved past her shoulders as she playfully pointed to her curvaceous derriere and mouthed the word "tails" before the coin hit the table.

"Tails again..." Randy said. "Fuck."

"Damn woman," Cam sighed, "your break."

Darrah removed the rack from the stacked balls and strutted to the head of the table. "What can I say?" she teased. With an irresistible shrug of the shoulders, she grinned with cunning and bent into position. She sighted her cue, lined her shot, and drew back on her stick. And like a jaguar lying in wait, she remained poised and ready to strike. Only her eyes moved as they turned up from their laser-like focus, flashed over Randy and Cam, and without so much as a flinch said, "I guess I just have one lucky tail, boys." By the time she said "tail," fifteen balls exploded across the table sinking four.

Don Williams' mouth stretched open like a circus clown. He had played pool in college and once in a while got together with friends for a game, but never had he seen such a powerful break delivered in such style. Randy was smiling at Cam and pointing at Don.

"What's the matter?" Cam asked. "You never seen a girl break like that?"

"Not in this lifetime."

"Stick around my man, she's only getting warmed up."

Don wanted to introduce himself to Cam and start asking questions, but he was taken by Darrah's presence. The way she broke. The way she surveyed the table, examining the lines and angles, moving around the field of green like a lioness circling an antelope, taking careful measure before executing her next move. It reminded Don of chess players back in school, the way they examined the board, planned several moves ahead, before a player would ever shift a piece. Only he did not recall any chess players that looked like her.

"Four Cape Codders, a pitcher of Bud, and two shots of Jack," announced the young waitress, jarring Don from his trance-like gaze as she placed the serving tray on the table.

"Right here!" Randy exclaimed. "A shot of Jack followed by a beer chaser."

"One of those Codders is mine," Cam said, forking out a few singles from his clip.

"Put it away," Don said, "it's been taken care of."

"Taken care of, what do you mean?"

"Keep your money," Don said. "I'll be expensing it back to the paper."

"The paper? Wait, are you the guy that called me earlier?"

"Don Williams, pleased to meet you. Can we talk —"

"Well, all right, man," Cam said, slapping his shoulder and stepping away, seemingly not hearing Don's question.

Holding the stick behind her neck, Darrah made her way over to get her drink. Without breaking form, she bent at the waist, holding back her hair, and wrapped her lips around the straw. She sucked down the alcohol with wanton talent. Wearing her best smile, she thanked Don and tapped Niki on the shoulder.

"Nik, we're stripes. Eleven in the side pocket."

"You got it, Darrah. Bury that sucker with just enough English and line up the seven."

Don watched Darrah unfurl the stick from behind her neck and sink the eleven in one fluid movement. The cue ball spun out with a quirky hop and lined itself beautifully behind the seven.

"Nice fucking shot!" Niki said.

Don caught the waitress walking by and thumbed a few singles in her tip jar. He told her to circle back often and that he liked to tip. He knew he was gambling on how much a guy like Cam could drink, before he would be too shit-faced to divulge any worthwhile information, but Cam had been standoffish when they first met and was reluctant to talk. *Hell, everyone in this town is reluctant to talk*, Don knew, but he also knew if he was ever going to break through with Cam, Cam would need to be flying high and feeling no pain. How high? Don wasn't sure, but after that Cape Cod, a shot of Jack, a few beers, and God knows much weed Cam smoked, Don knew he was well on his way.

With a cigarette hanging haphazardly from his lips, seemingly defying gravity, Cam thanked Don for the drinks in a friendly matter. That was progress. It was a far cry from, "What do you fucking want, anyway?" The greeting Don received when he first spoke to Cam.

"Loose lips, sink ships," as the saying goes. And there was no better way to get Cam loose than to feed him free booze and make him a friend. Asking the right questions and pushing the right buttons would not hurt either. *But what were they?*

CHAPTER 45
LIVE LONG, SEE FAR, KNOW MUCH

Behind the Wampan Inn, a mile from Dave's as the crow flies, flames roared out from an oil drum in a blistering torrent. The fire consumed the animal's carcass as the heat dried out the animal's hide that had been stretched taut like the sail of a ship.

The peyote buttons had been pulverized into a fine powder, boiled down, and cooked into a paste before it was readily consumed. Twilight had given way to night, and the interlopers were right where they were supposed to be.

It had begun. A seismic heat licked inside Henry's brain and all things began to melt away into an alternate reality; all except for one singular, pulsating focus—room number 16 and its meddlesome occupants.

Honoring his people of the fallen night, Henry's incantation rang out hauntingly between the whirl of flames as he sat beside his work stump and pedaled his grinding stone set between two wooden sawhorses.

With just the right amount of pressure, Henry drew his one-handed, Hudson Bay Axe across the spinning wheel, passing it back and forth, widening the bit and forging the steel head into a razor-sharp edge. So sharp, that one good swing could chop through meat and bone like a machete blade through a head of lettuce.

His chants grew louder and more tribal. Beads of sweat bubbled on his forehead. He pedaled the wheel faster and applied more pressure on the axe blade as he gazed through the shooting sparks of metal.

Through the kaleidoscope of flaring colors, he felt the spirit fill him, dwell within him, and he praised the Great Mystery for gifting him sight. To see above, behind, and through. To perceive, foretell, and know. To see far without losing sight of what was right in front of him like one's vision passing through the glass of a snow globe, seeing everything with utter clarity leaving the occupants blind to his knowing.

Behind the closed door of Room 16, Henry knew their every movement; he knew their every word. He knew them to be unlocking clues, working theories, and uncovering mysteries lay hidden for hundreds of years. He knew them to be curious about their findings and eager to share their growing knowledge. He could see the equipment being checked and rechecked, making sure the listening and recording devices were in all good, working order. Boxes of mesh netting, flashlights, glow sticks, compasses, repellant, etc., were being readied and being packed. He could see their working map hanging from the wall. He could see it dotted with colored pins and symbols. Arrows connected by lines forming triangles inside of other triangles spanned the entire area.

Henry saw all and knew all, but what was most disturbing to his mind's eye were their handwritten notes jotted inside the marked triangles. It revealed a burgeoning knowledge, a growing understanding of things that had remained secret for more than three-hundred-years and beyond. And he knew one more thing; they were more determined than ever to get into the swamp.

That could never be. To allow that knowledge to breathe outside that room and become anything more than what it was, was to risk exposing the order and the sacred covenant. It must not be allowed to transpire. It must be destroyed and forever entombed with the heretics conspiring behind the door.

Like a willing volunteer who gazes into the sway of the hypnotist's watch, Henry's eyes fell upon the spinning wheel. The time was now. The task at hand was known. But only when the creature appeared high above the black water would he do what must be done.

CHAPTER 46
WATER, EARTH, AIR, FIRE, SPIRIT

Inside the chamber, a stone slab lay hidden below the minister's lectern. Beneath, a passageway barely larger than a mineshaft led down to a labyrinth of tunnels by rounding a series of stone steps. As alderman, only Chief Elias Hicks was in possession of the key. The five-pointed round of metal, wrought before their coming, was designed to insert in the eyelet of the slab before being turned counterclockwise with slow and steady pressure.

Hicks removed the key from his pocket and aligned the northern point with the northern marking carved in stone. He then rotated it as the sun rises until a succession of clicks released the iron tongues from their flutes.

Following behind Hicks, the members made their way into the passageway as a singular progression and descended into the bowels beneath the meetinghouse. Lit only by a fiery beacon, one by one the men stepped down into the circular well where the darkened tunnels came to light in flickering shadow.

The well was built with a mixture of clay, stone, and timber and served as a stronghold feeding the extensive network of passages. Many of the passages ran straight until the ground fell away into nothingness. Some of them were built to nowhere with impassable sealed walls. Others were a construct of mystifying corridors which maneuvered through an entanglement of crosscuts and channels leading right back to where they started.

However, their design, all were built in secret by the founding elders, and all were perilous if unknowing entities happened upon them. Only The Keepers were privy to the one significant tunnel built within the maze of others that served their needs for more than three-hundred years.

It was believed that black spirits—crafty, demonic tricksters, but devoid of logic—would be riddled and confused if they were drawn into a tangled maze of tunnels. It was further thought that the first men—believed to be Godless pagans in both form and belief—traded in both realms between the living and the dead and would find themselves trapped between both worlds in eternal darkness if ever they happened upon the labyrinth.

Since the beginning, the tunnel they would follow, as their predecessors before them, was due North. It was referred to as Prana—meaning "Life Force" or "Vital Principle." To the first men it meant "Aether" or "Spirit" and was held as the most sacred of all the elements: water, earth, air, fire, and spirit—the five pillars. But only when the Spirit combined with the other sacred elements: water, earth, air, and fire, did it complete the five-pointed star known as the Pagan Triad.

The *Trilogy of Life*, as it was otherwise known, was a series of perpetual threes found repeatedly in both the spirit and natural worlds in its many forms: creator, redeemer, sustainer: beginning, middle, end: past, present, future: birth, life, death: body, mind, spirit: expiration, transition, resurrection, etc.

Throughout the known world the rule of threes has been revered. To the first men, the rule of threes was deified and worshipped. The Pagan Triad, a series of three interconnected triangles forming a five-pointed star, was invoked in silent prayer and celebrated in tribal dance. It was their guiding principle. It captured the very essence of who they were as a people, a people who believed that all things are connected to all other things in both the physical and spiritual worlds.

When separated from Prana, the sacred elements of the natural world exist only as elements unto themselves, building blocks lying dormant in a cloistered, unconscious existence. When joined with Prana, the life force awakens. Elements organize and triangulate in harmonious balance, perfect in conception and design. The triumvirate becomes conscious. Water becomes blood; earth becomes flesh; air becomes spirit; and fire becomes reverence. All give rise to the "Great Mystery." The grantor of life and the spirit to all things.

Gathered in the pattern of the crescent, The Keepers stood in silent rumination awaiting the alderman to make his way to the center of the well where a vaulted chest lay interned. Given his position within the order, it was customary for Sergeant Guthrie to be the one to retrieve the sacred chest from its chamber. He stepped forward, as first order, and bowed his head while the alderman recited a quiet prayer before inserting the key.

After hearing a series of clicks releasing the capstone, Guthrie reached in and retrieved the cedar chest. He grabbed one end of the box while Durst took hold of the other. Together they secured the chest between them as they retreated back from the center. No more than an arm's length between them, the order fell in behind Hicks and moved as a single column toward the northernmost corridor.

As they advanced forward, they crossed several adjacent tunnels, making note of how many steps they took. Once they achieved two-hundred paces, they all veered off into a sunken catacomb where the northern passage lay hidden.

This far into the passageway was disorienting. One might describe the feeling as being buried alive, leaving your eardrums packed and muffled in distorted silence. There was a damp, organic odor that penetrated the nostrils. So pungent at times, one could taste it in their fillings and the lining of their gums. If not for their common purpose and shared state of mind, one could not help feeling overwhelmed and frightened by an impending sense of doom.

Like their predecessors before them, they would take this journey to the pagan circle of five stones whenever the alderman called upon the small council. To this end, The Keepers had never abrogated their sworn oath. They held to this promise like scripture, adhering to the leader of the first men's words as if God himself spoke to them.

Honor ours and fear not… and we both shall live in an accord of peace.
Dishonor ours … and fear everything.

These were the bone chilling words from the pagan leader who met his end under a rain of heavy musket fire, his lifeless body claimed by the black water, or so they thought. What the elders witnessed three days following the leader's death, changed the course of providence in the new world. No longer would the newcomers colonize this land alone by God's willful hand. They would carry with them the long shadow of a bygone people.

Up ahead, a bluish-grey light filled the tunnel, casting the men's resolute faces with an ashen glow. It beamed in from a crevasse above like a train car passing through a mountain passage, illuminating the ceremonial ground with ambient light. The men fell in as a circle and took their places around the ancient stones. They sat in an ecliptic formation with crossed-legs and gazed skyward towards the crevasse, while select members of the order prepared the area with sage and cedar for burning.

Officer Durst and Sergeant Guthrie placed the trunk at the feet of Hicks and unlocked it under his watchful eye. The trunk was fashioned with pewter latches and bands which ran its length. Each were adorned with intricately carved designs depicting the newcomers voyage across the ocean and their encounter with the first men.

Inside the trunk were essential elements for ceremony. Each were necessary to alter the realm of the living and to open the portal to the realm of the dead as the compact directed. The items removed from the trunk were peyote, a feather fan, a smoke-stick, gourd rattles, eagle-bone whistle, skin drum, tobacco, calumet, and seven necklaces. The necklaces, crafted in 1676, were fashioned with teeth of the coyote, raven feathers, and mescal buttons. Each were strung together with rope skin made from the innards of the northern swamp snake.

As the tenets dictated, once Hicks delivered the invocation, they would light a fire of cedar and sage and the necklaces would be placed over the heads of The Keepers to be worn around the neck. Each man around the circle of five stones would then partake in the smoking of the filled-pipe and would drink from the peyote bowl. This brought on a restful, catatonic state, and would expand their minds with transcendental vision.

Out of the silence, the rhythmic beat of the skin-drum sounded, and the eagle-bone whistle began its spirit call. And like a king cobra rising to the snake charmer's flute, a thin wisp of purple smoke began to twist from the sage and cedar and turn above the stones. The ceremony had begun.

CHAPTER 47
IF IT QUACKS LIKE A DUCK, IT'S A DUCK.

While the girls racked up a few games on the boys, Don Williams racked up quite a bar bill. The alcohol was flowing—no problem there—but Don was reaching repeated dead-ends when pressing Cam with questions. He wasn't being outright belligerent anymore, as he had when Don and Cam first met, but he wasn't exactly saying anything of investigative value either. In fact, he barely knew anything more than Cam has a dog named Whitey and that he enjoys hanging out and drinking beer. And the only reason why he secured that bit of brilliant, investigative knowledge was that Cam dropped Whitey's name when he said he wanted to go out and check on him. That and take a piss.

Don watched as Cam palmed a Miller draft and two slices of pizza, and exited the rear entrance in curved, loopy strides. Before the door swung shut, Don slipped out through the exit just behind him and caught his attention.

"Hey, Cam, wait up?" Never breaking pace, Cam spun around and continued walking backwards, flashing a rubbery smile beneath almond-slit eyes.

"Don, my man," Cam said with animation. "I'll take a shooter of Jack and a pitcher of beer. And charge that to the paper."

"You got it, but I thought we might speak first before we head back in for that free cold beer and free Jack shooter." Don made sure to emphasize the word free.

"Whatever you say," Cam snickered. "Not sure what good it'll do. I know as much out here as I did in there. Which is nada."

The two walked over to the treeline where Cam parked the truck. Whenever Whitey would come along for the ride, Cam would always pull into the rear of the lot so the tailgate would face the woods. He did this so Whitey could curl up in the truck bed away from the noise, and to keep assholes away who think it's funny feeding a dog beer.

Before they reached the rear quarter panel, Whitey popped his head up and spun out from underneath the blanket with his tail wagging and his tongue bobbing wet between his canines.

"There's my boy!" Cam said, releasing the tailgate and burying his head in Whitey's fur. Somehow in his delirium, Whitey managed to reach his tongue around the crown of Cam's head and lick his face. "Hold these for a second," Cam said, as he handed Don the pizza, his words barely decipherable through a thicket of fur. "I'm under attack."

Don watched the two make canine/human love (so-to-speak) as man and man's best friend often do, but Don could tell there was something more. Something in the way in which they looked at each other, the way they interacted, was deeply emotional. It reminded Don about the stories you hear sometimes when WWII buddies get together after being separated for a number years, inextricably bonded by the shared experience few others could understand.

"Beautiful dog," Don said, "I don't think I've ever seen one with such a black coat."

"Dark as the dead of night," Cam replied, turning to unzip his fly. "If not for that single, white paw, shit, you'd never see him out here at night. You'd think he was O.J. as fast as he can run." Cam chuckled and looked over his shoulder. "Don't sweat it, Don. He's just hounding you for some pizza man. I need to drain the main vein, you know, make some room for more FREE booze."

"Are you sure it's, all right?" Don swallowed timidly.

"Don't bite the hand that feeds you, right?" Cam quipped, "Go ahead man, he won't take your arm off... unless I tell him."

Don took a slice and carefully held it to Whitey's snout and, like that, with a quick snap of the jaw, Whitey scarfed the entire slice. "Holy shit!" Don shrilled, jerking his arm back.

"Not the whole slice," Cam said, laughing hysterically and zipping up his fly. "Not supposed to give him the whole slice, just a piece at a time, man."

Don fumbled for a cigarette, and before he had time to reach for his lighter, Cam struck a match and lit Don's smoke. Don nodded as a gesture of thanks and took a deep drag, handing over the second slice of pizza.

"Piece by piece, my man," Cam said. "Now, watch. Sit, Whitey ... there, that's my boy." Through a cloud of smoke, Don watched as Whitey sat patiently with perfect posture, eating the smallest of pieces with all the refined culture of an English nobleman.

Don knew that if he was going to get anything out of Cam, it was now. Through the use of alcohol and Whitey's affections, that protective guard surrounding Cam had softened. And at least for the time being, he would not have to compete over loud rock music and shooters of Jack.

"Cam, when I asked you inside the bar, if you knew anything about the persons gone missing, I got the strong impression you were hiding something. It was only for a split second, but it looked like you froze. And I swear, Niki, Darrah, and Randy shot you a glance like you better not say anything. What are you afraid of? Do you know something about that?"

Cam's body tightened like a vise and his eyes turned sober. Fear seemed to choke off the flow of blood to his vital organs, turning his boozy, ruddy cheeks into a sickly shade of dried Elmer's Glue.

"Cam, are you all right? Are you going to be sick?"

Seemingly, vacant to Don's questions, Cam's eyes passed over him listlessly, rolling his head over the side of the truck.

"If you know something about the people gone missing, talk to me."

Without the will or inclination to respond, Cam struggled against a turning stomach as Whitey began to whimper and nuzzle up around the back of his neck. Cam's mind raced with panicked thoughts.

How could Don Williams know? How could he possibly know? Ok, focus. Breathe easy. Think straight. Remember the pact. He can't know. Then why is he asking about it? He has to know something. But how? Is he just fishing? There's nothing to worry about, Cam. You're drunk, but you know better. Play it cool. Cool like Darrah. Remember the pact. None of us saw anything or know anything. We all agreed. We all swore to honor the pact Till Death Do Us Part, and even then, don't say anything. Yes, play it cool like Darrah. "Erase it from your mind," she said, "and erase it from your life." Yes, that is the way to play it. But still? How? That truck full of jocks disappeared without a trace. Right before our very eyes. Gone. Poof. Adios. No jocks. No truck. No trace of them motherfuckers. But this guy knows. Shit! That's why he's pressing me. The police are going to fucking hang this on me... Who broke? Who couldn't keep their fucking mouth shut? Niki? Randy? Darrah? No, not Darrah. Absolutely not Darrah. Darrah plays it cool. Breathe easy. Think and breathe easy. It was none of them, you know that.... But how? How could he...

With Don's disembodied voice hauntingly at his back, Cam lurched forward as a violent stream of puke exploded from his mouth. Copious amounts of partially metabolized barley and hops, mixed with sour mash whiskey, sauce and dough, splattered against the trunk of a large pine tree with tremendous force. It clung to the tree like pancake batter, slowly pulling away in clumpy beads. It formed a pattern, oddly, that reminded Cam of the Rorschach test given to him by the school psychologist when he was just a boy. "A game of pictures," they had said. The shit one thinks about in moments of humiliation struck him as somewhat humorous.

Cam uncoiled his twisted body from its embarrassing contortion when a thought hit him like acute diarrhea brought on by consuming spoiled meat.

Sonny! Fucking Sonny! That crazy—not like Nam, you know—sonofabitch Sonny. It must have been him. No doubt that mofo mouthed-off during one of his purple-hazed, Vietnam flashbacks. Shit!

"Glad to see you back," Don said. "If nothing else, I think you broke the Guinness Book of World Records in the category of projectile vomiting, both for distance and velocity. Congratulations!"

Play it cool... Cam reminded himself as he gargled a mouth full of beer and spit it out. "I think the pizza did me in."

Don snorted at the absurdity of his statement. *Never blame it on the booze. A motto many teens lived by.* "Yeah, I mean what else could it be?" Don said. The sarcasm lost in teenage translation.

In his effort to comfort him, Whitey scooted forward as close to Cam as he could. He would have climbed inside of him if his bunting snout found a soft spot to enter. But with resigned agitation, he came to settle in Cam's lap resting his head on his leg.

Don looked down at the glow-in-the-dark hands of his watch and could see he was running late. "Dammit. I have to get going. I need to be back at the Wampan Inn."

"Wampan Inn?" Cam asked with surprise.

"Yeah, me and the crew are staying there. A guy named Henry James has offered to take us back into the swamp tonight and I'm running late."

"You mean Moonshine?"

"Yeah, Moonshine. You know him?"

"Yeah, I know him. Everyone around here knows him. He keeps to himself mostly, but everyone in this town has had a run in and a story to tell."

"I've known him only a day," Don said, "and I had an interesting run in with him."

"And I bet you have plenty of stories to tell, too?"

Cam threw up the tailgate and lit a smoke; he was still worried how much Don knew, but he felt better after evacuating himself. He leaned over and cupped Whitey's face in his hands. "Ok, boy, curl up under the blanket. I'll check you out later and bring you another slice. All right?"

Don and Cam started back across the parking lot when Don picked up the conversation where it left off. "Yeah, that man, Henry James, raised the hairs on the back of my neck. There are several stories old Moonshine told me, but the one story I wanted to hear about, the man shut down on me."

"Yeah, how's that?"

"Like you, when I asked him about the people that went missing ten years ago in the swamp, and why your dad was the only one that made it out, he went stone quiet. He said he didn't know anything about it and immediately changed the subject."

Cam stopped dead in his tracks. Like a cold ocean breeze on a hot summer day, sweet relief rushed over the surface of his skin.

"What's wrong?" Don asked. "Looks like you just saw a ghost."

Looking slightly down, the expression on Cam's face might be described as one of restrained jubilation. *Ten years ago?* Cam thought. *He's asking about ten years ago, not today. This guy doesn't know shit about today.*

He needed to keep his reaction in check. He knew Don was observant and did not want to give himself away on what really terrified him. It reminded him of the time when his girl told him she finally got her period and wasn't pregnant. He knew that if he performed cartwheels at that moment and sang Zip-a-Dee-Doo-Dah, he would not have conveyed the proper message; and quite possibly it could have resulted in a punch to the nose, or worse, a kick in the jewels. It's not so easy trying to hide your heart-pounding celebration when you know your girl is examining your reaction like a homicide detective, looking for any twitch of the eye or curl of the lip that could render you guilty in the "you only wanted sex, you never loved me" court of histrionic females.

"Cam, are you all right? You disappeared there for a second."

Cam smirked and ran his hand through his hair. His complexion returned to the reddish hue of the imbibed.

"Yeah, I'm cool. I just remembered something Darrah said to me last summer."

Don had his doubts, but dropped it in favor of getting out of there. He was late.

"Here's my card. I'm going to be at the Wampan Inn at least for the next couple of days. Call and ask for room sixteen if you remember anything, okay? I don't care how insignificant it might seem."

Don grabbed the pen behind his ear and wrote #16 on the back of the card and slipped it in the front pocket of Cam's dungaree jacket. Don then turned to walk away but stopped.

"Listen, Cam, there are families who desperately want to know what happened to those missing men. Not knowing tears families apart. You and Carl may be the only ones alive who can fill in the missing pieces. Because from what I've seen, I'm not going to get any help from the cops. They don't seem keen on an outsider poking around in their affairs."

"Yeah," Cam shot back with a quick reply. "Like they got something to hide, right?"

"Right. Like they got something to hide." The tone in Cam's voice suggested Don made a breakthrough.

"Tell me what you know? Even if you don't think it's important. Just tell me."

Cam dropped his smoke and ground it into the pavement with his size eleven Timberland's.

"Understand, I've never trusted cops. To me they've always been total dicks, always on our asses for one thing or another. But I never knew Carl to have any problems with them. In fact, he had a few buddies on the force back then. But after what went down ten years ago, it all went to shit. Night after night, Carl would go on and on about the cops being liars. He would be damned near passed out his chair, and then all of a sudden, like someone shoved a cattle prod up his ass, he would freak out screaming."

Don stepped in a little closer. "Go on. What else? Did he say anything more?"

"I don't know, maybe, but I can tell you it went on like that for a while until they straight-jacketed him and tossed his ass in the looney bin."

"Looney bin? Do you mean Titicut State Hospital?"

"That be the one. A funny farm for the criminally fucked and the maniacally insane." Cam had worked himself into a lather. He extended his hand, mockingly, as if to shake Don's hand and slurred out with biting sarcasm.

"Pleased to meet you, Don Williams, Cam Jenkins here, proud son of the town quack."

With his mouth slightly agape, Don fell silent. He knew of Titicut State Hospital and what horrors went on there. The abuses at the facility had been exposed in a 1967 documentary as well as hearings commissioned in 1968.

Over the years, he had heard a smattering of reports that the place was actually worse now. There had been a marked increase in population and tactics grew more inhumane. But each year, since the reports, the institution routinely passed state inspections and kept its certification finding no abuses. Don knew those reports were as corrupt as this town appeared to be, but somehow, they found a way to hide their dirty laundry. He also knew there were more memories sloshing around in the grey matter of Cam's pickled brain, and if he just had a little more time to press him, he might just succeed in vaporizing the impurities and release the floodgates.

"Titicut State Hospital...." Don uttered with quiet remorse, returning his eyes to Cam's. "I wouldn't wish that place on my worst enemy—"

Just then, a set of headlights belonging to a puke-color-green shitbox held together with duct tape and chicken wire swung in from the road and careened toward them like an oncoming freight train. Mighty Mouse was behind the wheel, shouting, "Cam! Hey, Cam!"

"Who the hell is that?" Don said, throwing up his hands in a defensive position against the blinding lights.

"Mighty Mouse," Cam said in a matter-of-fact sort of way.

"Did you say, Mighty Mouse?"

Cam nodded. "He hates being called that to his face, but some names just seem to fit."

Coming to a wrenching stop, the brakes squealed, and the car shimmied in a horrible sound of twisting metal.

"I wonder what's frosting his ass?" Cam said. "Why did he fly in here like a Bat Out of Hell?"

Being a fan of the comic series and a fan of the cartoon show, Don just couldn't resist. With a reluctant shrug of the shoulders, he squeaked, "He's come to save the day?"

CHAPTER 48
THE CALM BEFORE THE STORM

From their rooftop positions atop the old meeting house, the assigned officers maintained their posts and trained their attention on the swamp. Armed with top-grade, military, night vision devices (NVDs) with telescopic lenses, their duty was to surveil the night sky and report to One Police Plaza immediately when they saw the sign.

It was critical to get it right. Events to follow always unraveled at chaotic speeds and being out in front was imperative. "It's like a tsunami," as it was described by a member of the order, "that erupts suddenly from a violent tear in the ocean floor and waves out over the landscape with enormous force. There's no stopping it once unleashed, no putting the genie back in the bottle. The only hope is when it hits, you best be out of the way."

As it so often happens before a storm, there is a kind of strange, electric stillness that sets in. The air takes on a magnetic quality, humming and banding over the invisible cables of the atmosphere, rising the cadaver of quiet like Lazarus from his grave. Things that normally escape one's attention are suddenly exposed and amplified, thumping loudly inside the echo chamber of our minds where every breath becomes a gale and every heartbeat becomes a hammer blow. Even gooseflesh can be heard bubbling from dormancy, like a mountain range rising beneath the skin. Your senses try to fool you into pulling the trigger too soon. Only your skills and training as an officer keeps you on that razor's edge until it's time to move when the command is given.

"Go! Go! Go!" said an officer from the rampart, his NVD trained hard over the western sky. "I can see it turning! Take up your positions now and move out! Go!"

Quickly and efficiently the officers abandoned the first level, second level, and perimeter positions of the old meeting house, and hightailed it out of there in a fishtail of dirt. They dispersed with proficiency to their assigned zones covering every road, exit, and highway, patrolling their designated territories.

Through the eyepiece of the NVD, the sighting officer's eyeball held tight against the lens as he watched the thin and purple smoke build, and turn from the glade like a corkscrew twisting above the surrounding trees. He unsnapped the clasp on his hip and lifted the walkie-talkie to his mouth issuing the alert over the closed channel.

"One Police Plaza. One Police Plaza. Hockomock. Hockomock. It's a go!"

Situated at the rear of the station, towering up from the ground like the steel-cage scaffolding at Cape Canaveral, the communications speakers perched overhead blasted over the eastern, western, northern, and southern skies.

Bwaaaaaaaaaaaahhhhhhhhhhhhhhhhhhhhhhhhhhhhhhhhhhhhhhhhhhhhhhhhhhhhhhhhhhaaahh

The single blast ripped over the darkened landscape, bludgeoning the eardrums with an unapologetic scream. All civilians in the territories knew what the single blast meant. By order of the chief, they all knew what it meant, but what they did not know was how many blasts would follow.

Per standing order of the chief, a full lockdown drill had commenced. Citizens driving the back roads and throughways immediately pulled over with measured calm, locked their doors, and sought asylum at the nearest residence as the order required. Police set up roadblocks to off-ramps and lit flares at the exits. All highway traffic that flowed into the township was flagged by police and waved over to the soft shoulder to await further instructions.

All who were on foot, entering or exiting places of work, restaurants, schools, municipal buildings, shops, etc., etc., immediately and calmly retreated to the closest structure and remained behind closed doors. Children who were playing basketball under the lights, or riding their bikes home from their friends' houses, were under order to make their way home if they could do so within the stated time parameters, otherwise they were to report to the nearest residence, business, or structure and seek prompt asylum.

All went down without a hitch and in record time. The controlled bedlam of exercising the lockdown procedures gave way to vigilant calm. Those within the vicinity, confined to vehicles, turned their radios to 88.9 on the FM band and sat with a newspaper or relaxed with a cigarette. Those behind the closed doors of their homes, businesses, and common structures turned on the local channel as well, and sat listening, reading, or playing cards, awaiting almost systematically for the announcement the drill was over.

Under Chief Hicks, full lockdown drills had consistently improved. The order and efficiency in which it was executed was that of a military operation with all the hallmarks of population reassignment procedures drawn up by The International Atomic Energy Agency.

Even Cam and Randy took the drills somewhat seriously. They were punks and cynics to be sure, often mocking the loud blasts as "just the chief taking a shit," but they did so with cautious tones. They knew the seriousness of failing to carry out the order, so did they all, and the thought of not complying was a fool's game; a game they knew had no chance of winning. And given their history with the department, the last thing they needed was to be picked up by a hard-ass patrol officer trying to make sergeant and brought before Hicks.

"What the fuck was that?" Don said, immediately dropping to his knees, his hands shaking over his ears. "HOLY MOTHER OF GOD!"

"Warning blast," Cam said. "Chief's got us on lockdown." Cam quickly turned to Mighty Mouse and said, "Earl, park your car and lock it. We can still get inside."

Don's body was still vibrating. His head was in a slightly crooked position being shielded by his arms as he slowly struggled to his wobbly feet. He looked like someone in that moment of blinding terror, when out of the darkness a bat dive-bombs erratically at your head.

He found his balance and stood erect under his own power. He fixed his shirt, pushed his hair back in place, and cleared his throat.

"Lockdown?" Don asked. "It damn near blew my eardrums out. What do you mean the chief's got us on lockdown? Lockdown for what?"

"It's a preparation drill. In case one of those crazy motherfuckers escapes," Cam said.

"Escapes? Escapes from where?"

"Titicut State Hospital. Carl's alma mater... Come on, Earl!" Cam said. "Get a move on. We got to get inside."

"Yeah, Yeah," Earl barked, wincing from the pain in his shoulder. "Hold your horses." Earl shut his car door and stammered across the parking lot with a quick step, catching Don and Cam already in mid-stride heading for the back entrance at Dave's.

"Why the hell is the chief running another drill for, anyway?" Earl bitched. "I'd be damn angrier than a drunken clown, the way Chief runs those boys in blue with no overtime pay, but after this morning, Fuck 'em." Earl ended his diatribe and stopped. Cam was studying him.

"What the hell are you looking at?" he asked, his weaselly eyes darting from Cam to Don and back to Cam.

"A mouse that apparently got his ass kicked," Cam shot back. "Who'd you piss off this time?"

"Not me, smart-ass. You! You pissed someone off, and I paid for it. And dammit, you know I hate that name."

"That's a long list, Earl. Who'd I piss off?"

"The entire force, that's who," Earl huffed. "And at least four jocks that I know of. I saw them bake it out of the parking lot looking for your ass."

Don looked on with perverse interest. Earl Winston stood out for sure, but not in a good way. His voice, his greasy, black hair, and his dwarf-like build did render him a "human mouse" of sorts. Don stared, observing Earl like a kid examines a squashed bug under a magnifying glass. *Standing there looking like he was beaten within an inch of his life? Entire police force pissed at Cam? Four jocks looking for Cam's ass?*

Don broke his catatonic gaze and searched behind his ear and pockets for his pen and notebook. He desperately needed to update his notes with descriptions of Mighty Mouse and what he just said before he head back to the Wampan Inn.

"How long do these drills last?" Don asked. "I have to get out of here."

"Twenty or thirty minutes is about all," Earl said, jumping out in front of Cam. "Say, who are you anyhow? What kind of fella comes to a drinking man's bar with his school supplies?" With an offbeat laugh that sounded like a demented monkey, Earl flexed his cartoonish chin and followed with, "I'm talking to you, pencil boy."

"Come on, Earl," Cam said. "Cut the shit. We'll talk inside."

Just then, the door swung open with Randy standing in the threshold. "Jesus Cam, I thought you took off. Get in here before Dave locks down the door. Fuck man, another 30 seconds and you'd have patrols chasing your ass."

The bar was still packed as they made their way through the door, but it was remarkably more quiet. It sounded like a classy, white-tablecloth restaurant on a Saturday night where the low rumble of polite voices and the clinking of glasses is all you hear.

CHAPTER 49
CAN'T GET THERE FROM HERE.

Like a runaway ghost train without a man on the brake, Officer Harding opened up all four barrels of his Chevy Blazer and gunned it hard along the railroad tracks. He had just found Cam's note at the Jenkins' house, and knew he would be at Dave's getting drunk with his curly-haired partner in crime. And just like every other place in Titicut Township, Dave's was in full lockdown mode. Cam was trapped like a rat. Just the way Harding wanted it.

Harding knew these roads like the back of his monstrous hands and knew which ones to avoid when patrols were out covering their assigned grids. And even if he was flagged and stopped, or caught in a blind roadblock, he knew, being a fellow officer, he could bullshit his way out of it. And if not? He glanced down at his 10-gauge shotgun resting on the seat and checked his service revolver tucked inside his waistband. He had an answer for that too.

He would flush Cam out, so was the plan, and drag his ass into the swamp and empty two rounds in the back of his skull. Nice and clean. He cackled at the thought:

How sweet it will be. To blow out the back of that punk-ass kid's head, up close and personal, and no one the wiser—not after them blood-thirsty swamp dogs get through with him….

With the keen eye of a big game hunter, Harding focused at the steel rails of the railroad tracks filling up the windshield before they zipped beneath the Blazer's chassis repeating, "Jenkins is mine. Jenkins is all fucking mine."

Being the last Friday of summer break, Harding knew the booze would be flowing stronger than Niagara Falls and not one of them punks at Dave's would suspect any kind of foul play. Jenkins would be long dead before they shook off their hangovers.

Only minutes away, Harding passed underneath the Highway 24 overpass where Harry Fletcher was just above driving south. According to the map, Harry had driven the twenty-five miles out of Boston and was now looking for the Titicut exit when he noticed flashing blue lights and flares just ahead. Police were alerting drivers to keep moving past the exit with a 'Don't even think about getting off here' look on their faces.

"What the hell?" Harry barked, slowing down before pulling over onto the soft shoulder about a hundred yards before the exit. He double-checked the map with a penlight and looked ahead at the exit sign eerily flashing against the lights.

"Dammit!" Harry looked at his watch, then the map, then the sign, back to his watch, then the officers ... "Shit!"

The map showed an exit five miles ahead, but Harry estimated it would take him out of the way and along dark, winding roads he did not know. Tough enough during the day, he thought, almost impossible at night, considering many of those old country roads were not well marked nor well lit.

Just shy of the exit, he drove up the shoulder and parked the car. With map in hand, he exited the vehicle and made his approach to one of the officers standing on the nearside like a pillar of stone. He found himself oddly smiling, holding up the map like some kind of tourist about to stop a passerby for directions.

"Say officer, how long—"

"Sir, turn around and get back in your car."

Harry glanced over by his car, then back at the officer. "I just need to—"

"I'm not going to tell you again," the officer commanded with a strident voice. "Get back in your car and drive."

Harry dropped his head and turned back. Sometimes you know when challenging someone would not be in your best interest. As he walked along the shoulder in a somewhat deflated manner, he knew he would have to drive to the next exit and hope for the best. There was no turning around. He needed to get in touch with Don Williams tonight.

Just as Harry opened the car door and was about to slide into the seat, he noticed in the clearing below the highway a vehicle's headlights bouncing along a dirt road. He could not be sure, but it looked like one of those army trucks with a high canvas top.

To get a better look, he stepped up on the floorboard of his car and surveyed the entire area. His eyes passed from the town road, blocked off by police, and followed the sightline where the truck had emerged back to a large, metal structure.

Other trucks were beginning to roll out. As he studied the situation further, he noticed a parking lot at the rear of the structure lit up with overhead floods. It revealed the proximity to a rest area he drove by only minutes ago when the thought hit him. His frustrated grimace gave way to a triumphant grin.

Harry got back in his car and sped ahead. As he accelerated past the police roadblock, he gave a one-finger salute to the officers standing their post (doing so, of course, from the safety and anonymity of his car's darkened interior), and gunned it up to bang a U-turn. Harry saw a way in.

CHAPTER 50
GOOD FENCES MAKE GOOD NEIGHBORS

Like a black widow spider suspended in the eye of her web, Henry James clung to the back of the fence devoid of all bodily movement. Not even an involuntary blink of the eye would betray his stolid poise as he watched the occupants of Room 16 with inhuman vigilance.

The blast from the communications tower had shaken the heretics from their room. They were outside the property scampering like rats looking for the source of the noise. Their heads were darting left and right, and swiveling about their rubbery necks terrified at what was happening.

Henry watched with cat-like focus. He could hear fearful curiosity in their voices as Brett, Scott, and Albert stepped out from the dark and under the lit gable of the inn. Their attention was drawn to the crackling flames shooting up wildly from the oil drum only ten yards behind Henry's position.

"Look over there!" Albert said with concern. "There's a fire."

"Come on, let's go check it out," Brett said.

"Guys wait," Albert replied. "We need to be inside when Mr. Williams calls...."

"It will only take a minute, Albert," Scott said. "Come on."

From the heavy stench of smoke, they covered their noses and mouths and made their approach. Step by cautious step, they closed in to see what was burning beyond the fence.

Henry held steadfast, his eye strained thru the wooden slats. He felt his long fingers clamp around the axe handle like a vise, the weight balanced nicely in his ready hand.

Without making a sound, Henry crouched down as far as he could go with his legs cocked and ready to spring. He pressed his ear tight to the fence and listened closely to their every movement.

He heard footsteps walk in his direction when suddenly they stopped.

Henry heard a voice say, "Stay here. I'll see what's burning."

"Hurry, Brett, but be careful."

"Don't worry, Albert. It will only take a second."

Brett stepped toward the fence and paused. He took a deep breath and ran his hand over his mouth. As he moved closer to the fence line, he was suddenly roused with terror. He glimpsed through the bending flames at something monstrous. An animal's skull with enlarged hollow sockets seemed to hover atop the roaring flames like a spirit totem. Its teeth twisting and protruding from its distended jaw-line, and its fur bristling from the heat made it appear as though the hideous thing was alive. Wild in the fire's blaze.

Brett fell back in fright and lost his footing.

"Are you all right?" Albert cried. "What's wrong? What did you see?"

Fear shot up Brett's back and nearly stopped his heart. He quickly averted his eyes from the terrifying sight and scurried backwards, his legs buckling beneath him.

"What the hell did you see?" Scott panicked.

"A, a, monster," Brett stuttered. "It was a kind of animal. Ten feet tall. Its teeth are all twisted up; its muzzle advancing through the flames. It was staring right at me."

"What animal?" Scott pressed. "Are you sure?"

As Scott and Brett continued their back and forth, Albert smiled and adjusted the light on his miner's cap towards the flames. Without saying a word, Albert stepped to the fence line and propped himself up on a milk crate. Wrapping his sausage-like fingers over the top of the fence, he lifted himself up, so the bottom of his chin rested just above the pointed slats.

Henry remained still as a corpse. From his low place, his eyes traveled up the slats and fixed themselves on the fleshy underside of Albert's chin. He was close; too close. If not for the dark, the heretic's eyes surely would have discovered Henry's hiding place, just beneath. And if not for the rancid smell of smoke, the stench of acrid sweat purposing Henry's body would have certainly given him away.

Now is not the time, ran through Henry's head like a burning fever. *Only when the creature calls out from high above the black water, will I do what must be done.* From his squat position, not moving an inch, Henry well knew he need only to swing his axe, a mere flick of the wrist, to split the heretic's melon-sized head in two. But only when summoned would the deed be carried out.

With a quick resettling of his glasses, Albert confirmed his suspicions. It wasn't a monster at all. It was a pelt hung between two rods drying by the fire.

Albert giggled. He turned on the crate and said, "Hey, Brett, your monster is not a monster at all. In fact, it's not even alive, it's—"

"Boom!" The loudspeakers high above One Police Plaza cranked out two short blasts followed by a prolonged third. The deafening and sudden sound knocked Albert off the crate and onto his backside.

Scott and Brett fell to the ground, but quickly regained their feet and fled to Albert's side, lifting under his arms and propping him up.

"Come on, Albert, let's get inside!" All three covered their ears, instinctively ducking, and ran into Room 16 and closed the door, making sure to lock it.

They pressed themselves up against the windowpane and watched powerful bands of light beam out across the night sky and rotate like a giant carousel. The bands cut through the air like the blades of a propeller, creating a strobe-like effect which threw off their balance and sense of well-being. But what was most awful was the voice, if one could call it that, a voice that seemed to pursue you from high above the communications tower repeating repeatedly in a hollow metallic tone:

"Warning. Warning. This is not a drill. Repeat. This is not a drill. Remain indoors until further notice. Remain indoors until further notice."

"Warning. Warning. This is not a drill. Repeat. This is not a drill. Remain indoors until further notice. Remain indoors until further notice."

Covering his mouth and holding his stomach, Albert fell back from the window and cried, "I think I'm going to be sick." With hurried steps he fled into the bathroom and locked the door. Brett and Scott remained at the window and watched the sky in stunned silence while Henry rose from his low place and looked skyward through the flashing light. He watched the purple smoke twist tighter and faster; it corkscrewed upward with enormous force, fanning wider and stronger with each rotation and formed a funnel cloud that stretched high into the night sky.

Henry could feel the familiar tremor quake beneath his feet and grinned, knowing the swamp dogs had erupted from their putrid den. His lips stretched back into a horrid smile while his eyes gazed over his newly sharpened, Hudson Bay Axe. The creature was out. His work could now begin.

CHAPTER 51
VENGEANCE IS MINE

Officer Harding fishtailed his Blazer into Dave's parking lot, the ass end kicking out in a hail of baked rubber. With flashlight in hand, he rolled down the window and propped his elbow up on the Blazer's door, angling the light over every vehicle as he quickly motored past.

Having left Jenkins's Place only fifteen minutes ago, Harding knew he was looking for Carl's '57 pickup; and once he confirmed its presence, he would flush Jenkins out.

Running past rows of vehicles was a little tricky due to the disorienting lights propelling from One Police Plaza communications tower. His depth perception and sightline were askew and struggled to view the vehicles as he sped by. He nearly clipped a couple of cars racing down one row and up the next where he blindly ran over a parked Harley Davidson. It crunched under the Blazer's wheels and dragged beneath the chassis before Harding even noticed.

He turned down the last row that ran the treeline and watched the beam of his flashlight bounce off the hoods of the vehicles until a set of eyes, glowing red, fixed directly upon him. Harding slammed on the brakes. It was unmistakable. He had just passed Carl's '57 Chevy and saw a dog pacing back and forth. Cam's dog.

***

Dave's became alive again. Now that they knew they were in full lockdown mode, and had complied with the ordinance, the bar resumed its normal activities except for all the doors had been locked and a designee monitored the phone and radio. No one was to enter or leave the premises, per order of the chief.

Not until the lockdown was lifted, could anyone pass through the doors of whatever establishment they were held up in. To do so would directly violate the chief's order. Patrols were watching. Patrols were always watching.

The jukebox kicked up, and the drinks were flowing. Shooting pool and throwing darts were in full swing. The mood was one of being stuck with your friends some place, preferably a bar, when a winter storm hits, and the mundane realities of life cease to exist for the duration. A time when responsibilities of work and school are put on hold and appointments and obligations are given a pass, and all that's left is to hunker down and party like it's the last day on earth. For some it would be.

At the front, sitting and gathering around the bar were the older set. Most had been down this road before and most liked to argue the merits of drills and whether dispatching the many patrols was a smart use of taxpayer dollars. They felt comfortable enough to chin-wag and criticize openly the use of town funds as it was the town fathers, and not the chief, who approved budgets and emergency funds for such operations. It mattered not that behind their arguments, well-hidden with ardent voices, was the stark reality of who was actually in charge and thus better left unchallenged.

"No fewer than three drills," Bletchley said, holding three, stubby fingers up to Ted Parker, a townie on the barstool next to Bletchley.

"Three, I tell you! Three! With the third being a full lockdown today. All of which occurred in the same fiscal year, mind you." Bletchley shook his head in disgust and gulped down half a pint. With a quick wipe of his sleeve, he picked up where he left off. "There will be gross overages, Ted. Mark my words. I mean the nerve of these people, thinking we all have money sprouting up from pots and falling off of trees. And that Tommy Fulcrum, the way he parades himself around the town offices. I have it on good authority he's not even a newcomer, and yet he comports with such air. Assessments, re-evaluations, fund drives. Keep your wallet close to the vest, Ted, that's what I say, they'll be snooping about without nigh a care to shore up their coffers."

Bletchley finished off his pint and waved Dave over. "Dave, if you please. Another pint for Ted Parker, here. I'll have the same." As Bletchley turned to face Ted and continue his diatribe, the phone behind the cash register rang.

"Ted Parker, there's just no telling how long this lock down will last, but we'll do our stay as proper gentleman. Not like those hooligans carrying on in the back."

Dave turned from the taps and reached behind the register for the phone. He cupped his hand over his ear and said, "Dave's Pizza." Struggling to hear, he leaned in and pressed the phone tighter.

"You are going to need to speak a little louder. Officer who?"

"Officer Harding," the loud and unnerving voice said. "Badge number 02324."

Dave winced, pulling back the receiver. "I can hear you now."

"Good, listen carefully. I know Cam Jenkins is inside your establishment, but he is in violation of the chief's order. Send him outside at once."

"I assure you, Officer Harding," Dave urged, "Jenkins was behind closed doors when we locked down. He was accounted for. I saw him myself."

"The order requires that all are to report to the nearest domicile, no exceptions. This includes pets. Send his ass out here now."

"Pets?"

"Tell him patrol discovered Whitey wandering outside the premises and he's hurt really bad."

"Hurt?"

"He needs medical attention right away. Send out Cam now."

Dave hesitated for a second, then said with a timid voice, "If I send him out now then I'm in violation of the order. I don't want any more problems with the chief or the department. They've pulled my license before for far less—"

"Shut up and listen! I'm tired of repeating myself. Send Jenkins out now or I'll pull more than your fucking license. I'll pull out your teeth one-by-one by the roots. Do you understand me?"

"Hold on, hold on," Dave huffed in a panic. "Okay, I don't want any trouble. I'll send him out now. Just, just give me a minute and I'll find him."

"You've got thirty seconds. Now move!"

Visibly shaken, Dave clumsily placed the phone down and turned from the cash register and faced the bar. He appeared thick and distant and unaware of his surroundings.

Bletchley, ever aware, was tired of waiting. "I say it took less time to fix the pothole on my street than for the barkeep to serve up two pints to his most loyal, paying customers."

There was no reaction. Dave looked as though his eyelids were set on fishhooks. Bletchley watched as Dave just stood there.

"Are you feeling ill?" Bletchley asked.

Without saying a word, Dave snapped out of his stupor and quickly hustled off to find Cam leaving Bletchley unattended.

"I say, Dave, what about our pints?"

CHAPTER 52
I'LL HUFF,
AND I'LL PUFF,
AND I'LL BLOW YOUR HOUSE DOWN

While Albert had locked himself in the bathroom, Brett and Scott watched the lights chop through the night sky, mesmerized by the whir and holding them spellbound by the voice's hypnotic thrum—until a painful groan from behind the bathroom door woke them from their trance.

"Albert, are you, all right?" Brett said. "It sounds like you're dying in there."

"I have a stomachache. I think the lights made me dizzy."

"I told you not to eat those cupcakes from the vending machine."

"I know. I know. I was just so hungry. Did you speak to Mr. Williams yet?"

"No, Scott's trying to reach him now. Scott, any luck yet?"

"Hold on," Scott said, "I'm dialing Dave's Pizza. Dammit, they are not picking up. I keep getting a fast-busy signal."

"Try calling Harry, maybe Don checked in with him."

"Right," Scott said, reaching his hands in his pockets. "Does anyone have his number?"

"Hold on, I think I have it," Brett said.

"Check the fax transmission Mr. Fletcher sent to us earlier," Albert said from the bathroom. "His phone number will be listed there."

Brett stepped lively to the machine and pulled the fax from the tray. His eyes scanned down the page. "I got it, Albert, thanks."

After handing over the fax to Scott, Brett reached for a soda out of the icebox and went to check on Albert. Scott dialed Harry Fletcher's number when suddenly there were three rapid knocks at the door.

"I'll get it," Brett said, "that's probably Don now."

"Mr. Williams has a room key," Albert said. "It's probably Mr. James–I mean, Moonshine."

Without asking who was at the door, Brett turned the knob and opened it, but there was no one there. He stepped out and scanned the entire area, seeing only the closed doors of vacant rooms and the empty parking spaces flashing in and out of view from the strobing lights.

"There's no one there," Brett said, as he turned around to face Scott. But what Brett saw in Scott's face looked more like a scarecrow than human. The waxen figure before him appeared frozen like a Madame Tussauds's dummy of a frightful clown. Brett watched in confusion as the phone fell from Scott's ear and hit the floor.

"What's wrong?" Brett asked. Scott's mouth spasmed, trying to form words, as he lifted his arm and pointed over Brett's shoulder in the parking lot's direction. His lips moved slow and desperate. Breathless gasps escaped his mouth as he stumbled backwards like a fairground drunk stepping off a Tilt-a-Whirl.

The hairs stood up on the back of Brett's neck as he watched Scott writhe in terror, but what he heard approaching from behind turned his eyes to stone and his entrails to ice. The hard sound of an animal's nails scratching and clicking, and the sound of gnashing teeth drew up behind him like a ticking bomb. He was paralyzed to move; and even if he could, there was nowhere to turn. His legs, back, and posterior tingled. A strange sense of weightlessness overcame him. It felt as though a thousand tiny barbs laced with morphine prickled at his skin. Stimulating points, light as a lash, combed over his entire body from the crown of his head to the pads of his toes. It brought on an apathetic numbness where he felt a sensation as of floating above and watching himself suffer a psychotic break.

Hot feral breath and a wet snout blunted up against the back of his leg. It immediately jolted him off his feet and snapped his neck around to see what it was, but what he saw, before his head exploded in brilliant white light, was a creature of some kind, half man, half animal. It stood tall and strong, naked but for a crude bit of breechclout. It peered down at him with red eyes set in deep sockets. It had jagged teeth and a distended jaw-line whose coarse hide fell over its shoulders and down its back like a tribal chieftain's frock.

Before Brett could breathe his next breath, an axe swung down with tremendous force. The blade exploded his head like a swollen pomegranate. Blood and brain burst forth from his skull in a crimson spout, fouling the walls, ceiling, and floor. The creature caved in his chest and turned Brett's face into a bloodied chop of hamburger.

Scott tossed himself over the bed and started jerking at the bathroom door handle screaming, "Albert, Albert, let me in! Jesus, Albert, hurry! Unlock the door, Albert! Unlock the fucking door...."

The creature swung the axe high and hard, smashing lamps and crushing tables. It snarled at Scott and turned with a quick jerk and eyed the map, delivering the axe like a Kaiser blade, slicing through the air on a wide arc. The pins dotting the map exploded on contact, shooting through the air like colored stars. The creature hacked and cut with blinding speed, turning the axe into a one-armed, threshing machine, leaving everything in the room in shards and bits.

The creature's head snapped around, and with a powerful, catlike move it sprung through the air with the axe out in front. As its weight came down, it planted its hind legs with the assuredness of a mountain goat and passed the axe through the crown of Scott's head with jolly good surprise. A sickening thud was followed by a steaming splat. The axe split the cranium and passed through the neck like a stalk of celery, burying itself in a knot of shoulder meat.

Terrified beyond lunacy, Albert shot up from the toilet and dropped his glasses. He flailed his hands over the bathroom floor, but stepped on them clumsily, breaking the lenses and frame. He retrieved them and tried to fix them on his face, but was knocked back to the floor in sheer panic.

A blood-curdling snarl, wet and hollow, ripped out like a belching furnace and sent the bathroom door vibrating on its hinges. Albert kicked his feet and propped himself up by the toilet bowl. He tried to distance himself from the carnage on the other side of the door by throwing back the rings of the shower curtain and hiding behind the filthy plastic. The creature pitched down on its muscled haunches and waved its snout over Scott's phlebotomizing hump. The taste of fresh blood, thickening and kidney red pleased the creature, but there was unfinished work. Its gala feast would have to wait.

Using the butt-end of the axe, the creature caved in the bathroom door with a brutal swing. It busted through the splintered wood and forced its way in, its massive shoulders barely clearing the damaged frame. Seeing nothing but the sway of the shower curtain, the creature sneered. It swung the axe like a Gandy dancer drives a railroad spike, smashing down through the shower rod and tearing the curtain from its rings with surprising little resistance on the other side. The tub was empty; there was no meat or bone to deaden the swing. The only thing behind the crumpled shower curtain was the water-stained porcelain of an empty tub and an open window leading out to the parking lot. Albert was gone.

Pressing its snout against the window, the creature could see Albert stumbling down the road. He was waving his flailing arms at a car driving towards him when the brakes jammed on and stopped to let Albert in. Emitting a vile groan, the creature careened back in the tub, cracked its neck, and shape-shifted into a jackal. With a ferocious push from its hind quarters, it smashed through the window and bound after Albert at a savage pace, its jaw bulging and teeth advancing.

It got within three lengths of the chrome bumper until the car sped up and began to pull away. The creature stopped in the middle of the road and peered through the rear window of the fleeing car. It watched the car disappear around the bend before it snorted in frustration, turned, and followed its own bloody prints back to the Wampan Inn.

Albert was shaking and hyperventilating and took three blasts off his inhaler.

"He's gone!" Harry Fletcher said, as he pulled over and stopped. "It's okay, he's gone. Take deep breaths. Take long, deep breaths." Harry studied his rearview mirror while Albert tried to speak over his labored breathing. "It's okay," Harry said, trying to calm Albert down. "What the hell happened? Where's Brett and Scott? Talk to me, Albert. Whatever that thing was is gone. You are safe now. Tell me what happened? Can you speak?"

"Keep, keep, driving," Albert uttered through his inhaler, tears flowing down his flushed cheeks. "I don't know what happened exactly, but I think they're dead. Both of them were attacked. I could hear growling and things smashing—"

"Dead? Scott and Brett? What do you mean you think they're dead?"

Albert tried to answer, but he was sobbing uncontrollably, and his throat was closing. Albert wiped his mouth and eyes and steadied himself. He turned and said, "They are both dead. They must be both dead. I heard the whole thing from the bathroom. It was the most hideous sound I ever heard. Something I never want to hear again."

"What did you hear? Who killed them, Albert? Was it that thing chasing you?"

"I'm, I'm, not sure, I didn't see, but whatever it was had inhuman strength. Tables and chairs were being smashed and tossed around like toys. I could hear something whirring through the air and the sound of hard, crushing thuds. I don't know. I never want to know, Mr. Fletcher."

Harry Fletcher was sickened by what he heard. He focused on the street signs and reached down for the map beside him. "Listen Albert, I'm down here because I need to speak with Don right away. There are lots of things happening right now I don't understand. But first, we have to report whatever you heard or might of saw to the police. They need to get to the Wampam Inn right away." As soon as Harry said that, he saw the familiar lights of law enforcement flashing up ahead.

CHAPTER 53
COME OUT,
COME OUT,
WHEREVER YOU ARE

"Dammit to hell, Dave!" Mighty Mouse said. "My Goddamn arm!"

Dave bumped into Earl hard as he weaved his way through the throngs of shit-faced teens looking for Cam. He shot back at Mighty Mouse.

"Where's Cam? I gotta find him right away!"

"Jesus, you crushed my shoulder."

"Where is he?" Dave said, yanking Earl by the collar. "Tell me where he is, or I'll shut down your tab!"

"Okay, Christ almighty. The last I saw of him was over by the cigarette machine, with his girl."

Dave released his collar and gave him a shove. He swiftly maneuvered through the crowd like a seasoned waitress. He rounded the pool table and took the narrow corridor behind the back bar, which led directly to the cigarette machine by the men's room.

As Dave came through, he saw Darrah's backside. It was unmistakable. She was making out with Cam and getting into it, but there was no time for a bashful "excuse me." Dave forced his way in between Darrah and Cam.

"Hey," Darrah steamed, "what the fuck? Take your hands off me."

"Cam, you need to listen to me," Dave said. "Whitey's in trouble. He's hurt." Cam's eyes turned from glassy and lazy to sober and alert. It was as if he was a prizefighter hit with a dose of smelling salts.

"What do you mean he's fucking hurt? Where is he? What happened?"

"We need to get to my office now," Dave said, already shoving through the crowd with Cam at his elbow.

They moved through the throngs of teens with Darrah right behind. Don Williams stepped out of the men's room and immediately saw the back of Cam and Darrah's heads forcing their way through the crowd. As he watched them pass the tables, he saw Darrah mouth a few words to Niki, who immediately turned and grabbed Randy. Something was going down, and Don had to know.

All four of them were being hurried along into the kitchen. They passed by the pizza ovens and headed to Dave's private office in the back. Cam grew more concerned by the second. He was anxious to get to Whitey and was calling out his name and urging Dave to hurry and unlock the door.

"Listen," Dave said, as he unlocked the deadbolt. "Whitey's right outside with the police officer now. Go!" The moment the handle turned, Cam shoved his way through the door with Darrah about to follow, but Dave stepped in front of her and stopped her cold.

"Get out of my way," Darrah fumed, the whirring beams of light flashing against her face.

"You can't go," Dave said in an unapologetic tone.

"Cam needs me. He's going to fucking flip."

"Darrah, listen to me. You can't be out there. You know this. You can't violate the order. We are in full lockdown."

"But you just let Cam out. Isn't that breaking the order?"

"Only because the on-duty patrol officer demanded to see Cam, and no one else. Understand?"

Darrah could read people better than most, in part, it's what made her a great pool player, so it wasn't hard for her to notice the slight change in Dave's tone. Albeit subtle, there was a somber, somewhat distant cadence to his words now. She could see it in his eyes and face and could tell it was something more than Whitey being hurt, it was something more grave and irreparable, something underhanded. The thought had even crossed her mind Whitey wasn't hurt at all and that Cam was the target of a bait-and-switch. She looked Dave straight in his wavering eyes. "Cam's in danger, I can feel it. I know there's something you're not telling me. What's going on?"

Cam sprinted across the parking lot and headed straight for the truck. He was shouting Whitey's name as he leapt onto the truck's bed, immediately checking under the blanket, but finding nothing.

As Cam hollered out in anger, shouting for Whitey, he heard a high-pitched painful whimper. He jumped off the truck and rushed blindly towards the helpless cries when a powerful beam of light hit him in the face and froze him where he stood. Cam stiffened at the voice that followed.

"Hold it right there, cowboy. That's far enough."

"What are you doing with my dog? You better not fucking hurt him."

Whitey's bark was strained as the voice stepped out from the shadows and into the light. Cam was temporarily blinded. He could hear a hitching gait clicking toward him and could hear paws dragging on the blacktop.

"Whether I hurt this dog or not depends on you, cowboy," the voice said.

Cam's eyes began to adjust as the shadowy image of a man with a shotgun in one hand, and the back of Whitey's scruff clutched in the other revealed himself.

"You hurt one fucking hair on his head," Cam said, "and I'll kill you! You fucking hear me?!"

Cam lunged forward, but before he completed his second stride, officer Harding jerked back on Whitey's scruff and trained the barrel of the shotgun straight at Whitey's head.

"Another fucking inch and I'll kill this mutt. Then I'm gonna kill you." Cam froze. His eyes flashed from Whitey to the officer and back to Whitey.

"It's okay, boy. You'll be all right. Just hold —"

"Shut the fuck up and listen," Harding said. "Do as I say, and I won't kill him."

Harding had Cam's attention, at least for the moment. He stepped out a little to the left, where the light was more favorable, and studied the young face looking back at him. With a smirk Harding said, "You don't know who I am, do you punk?"

Cam cocked his head and immediately shot back, "A one-legged dickhead threatening to kill my dog?"

"Keep running your mouth, boy." Explosive anger rode on the edge of Harding's words. "But that mouth is gonna cost you plenty." Harding yanked on Whitey's collar with a hard tug and lifted his hind legs off the ground.

"Don't hurt him! Jesus fucking Christ! I'll do whatever you want, just don't hurt him." Harding eased off the collar, allowing Whitey's hind legs return to solid ground.

"I'll do whatever you want," Cam pressed. "Just let him go and I'll do whatever you want."

He watched Harding's grin twist into something horrible before he said,

"That's what I wanted to hear, you made the right choice, cowboy." With a quick jerk of his head towards the Chevy Blazer, Harding stepped towards the vehicle, still holding Whitey by the scruff, and opened the door.

"Get in cowboy. We have some unfinished business."

Cam took a couple of steps toward the Blazer, then stopped. "I'll get in, but release Whitey first."

"It doesn't work that way. Now, get your ass in and shut the fuck up. We are going for a ride." Cam knew to comply. Harding had a gun, and he had Whitey, and something told Cam he would not hesitate to use it. He approached slow but sure, entering the back-light of Harding's shadow, when Harding stepped in and said through clenched teeth, "But this time, when we drive out of here, I won't be taking a drive into Walnut Creek, shithead. I've got other plans for you."

The second Harding said it, Cam knew exactly who he was. His new awareness hit him like a two-by-four over the back of his head. Diverting his eyes with his head facing down, Cam approached the passenger door almost fatalistically, feeling vacant and numb with each step. He looked at Whitey and said, "It's okay, boy. I'll be okay. Go back to the truck and wait for Randy. He'll make sure to get you home."

"That's enough," Harding berated, slamming the door of the Blazer. "Now, shut the fuck up."

Cam's eyes immediately focused on the rearview mirror as he watched Harding drag Whitey off.

"Let him go! God dammit, you said you'd let him go!"

Cam watched in horror as Harding wrestled Whitey behind the dumpster.

"Whitey!!!—" In a flash of gunpowder, a high-velocity explosion went off tearing a hole through the center of Cam's heart. He screamed out for Whitey. Tears stung his cheeks, and he felt his eyes burn with hateful sorrow.

CHAPTER 54
MR. MAGOO, WHERE ARE YOU?

Down in the labyrinth of tunnels, gathered around the pagan circle of five stones, The Keepers had completed the rituals of ceremony—as the tenets of the compact require—allowing the people of the fallen night to transition from the realm of spirits to the realm of the living. It was an ancient practice the members feared. Each considered it a pagan ritual designed to court evil, but they feared even more not to do so.

Sergeant Guthrie, Officer Durst, and the others manned their radios and closely monitored the members for signs of dissociative detachment—a state by which a member breaks off completely and never returns.

They watched closely and observed the rapid eye movement of each member as they dipped their heads in unison and shifted their bodies in inhuman ways. It was their charge to keep a close-eye until they all returned safely, as was their sworn duty.

Although a dissociative detachment was extremely rare, there had been a few accounts over the last three hundred years: one in 1692, another in 1889, and the most recent case was in 1933.

The 1933 case was especially dreadful. Thomas Morton, a member of The Keepers, crossed over with the others during ceremony, but he disassociated and failed to return. Members appeared to get him back with a shot of adrenaline, but he suffered a seizure on reentry and violently died. It was said his eyeballs ruptured and his heart exploded from his chest cavity. No account exists on what happened to the body.

On 104 East, a couple of miles down from the Wampan Inn, police cruisers were parked across the road at two separate markers one hundred yards apart. Each marker formed a barricade; one faced East, the other faced West, together they both served as a protective wall, a gauntlet for what was to pass.

"Stand by!" one of the officers commanded. "I hear them coming." The patrols working the barricades turned their attention to the treeline facing south. Before they could see any movement in the dense thicket of woods, they could hear a dark chorus of yeasting throats and the thunderous ground as they approached.

"Train the lights down aways!" a patrolman said. "I want to get a good look at 'em when they come through!" A slew of lights turned on the south woods and lit up the treeline in haunting shadows. The throaty snarls bellowed with rage, when out of the darkness, like a freight train emerging from a mountain tunnel, a thick column of fur and teeth breached the treeline. They drove headlong into the bank of lights and crossed the street through the gauntlet of police cruisers.

"Don't you go trying to pet none!" a patrolman said, his voice cracking above the rolling thunder. "They'll take your arms at the shoulder! Ah HAHAHAHA. You hear me boys?" Still chuckling, the patrolman turned from the gauntlet and reached for the radio on his hip.

"Right on time, Sergeant. They crossed the first checkpoint and they're running hard."

"Roger that," Guthrie acknowledged. "Notify the other units."

"Aye, Sarge, copy that, over."

The patrolman fixed the radio back on his hip and looked up. That's when he noticed a car's headlights on fast approach.

"What the hell?" he groaned, jerking the radio to his mouth. "Stand by, Sergeant. I think we got trouble." He ran to his cruiser and flipped on the switch to the loudspeaker. "Halt right there!" he commanded, drawing his pistol. "Stop! Not an inch closer! Turn the ignition off and both of you step out of the car with your hands up. Nice and slow! Hands way up where I can see them."

"What's happening, Mr. Fletcher?" Albert asked, his poor vision making out only smudged images and a smear of lights.

"I don't know," Harry replied, almost whispering. "Something's not right. Stay here Albert and don't move. I'll be right back."

"Mr. Fletcher, wait! Don't—"

Harry had already stepped out of the car and closed the door, keeping his hands high over his head.

"I said both of you!" roared over the loudspeaker. "Both of you step out of the vehicle with both hands up. Do it now!"

"Albert, stay in the car!" Harry said over his shoulder. "Listen, officer, he can't see a thing without his glasses. The kid has already been traumatized enough tonight—"

"Shut up and place your hands on the hood and get your legs spread. Is that clear?"

"Did you hear what I said? Two colleagues of ours, we believe, were killed only minutes ago—"

"Shut up! Now, I'm not gonna tell you again. Get your hands on the hood and spread your legs!"

Harry heard the hammer cock on the officer's service revolver and knew things just went from bad to worse. How bad? He wasn't sure. But everything hit Harry all at once: Priscilla Hooke's letter, the Mulrooney file, what Don Williams said about Sergeant Guthrie, Carl Jenkins, Cam Jenkins, Henry James, the chief, Brett and Scott being killed, and now this. He had been around cops long enough in his career to know that what was happening now was off the books. There was no more pleading his case. He was certain, more than ever, that the officer training his sidearm on him had no interest in any murders other than perhaps his own. He was in it right up to his neck and felt helpless to escape the tightening noose.

Making like the Tin Man, Harry stiff-legged it toward the front of the car and turned. He bent at the waist and splayed his arms firmly against the hood. The heat of the engine began to bake his left cheek as he peered helplessly through the windshield at someone even more helpless.

"Hold that position!" the loudspeaker jarred. "Hug that front end like your life depends on it." Harry heard several boot heels clicking on the pavement and they were getting louder. Daring not to move his hands or arms or speak at all, he tried to communicate with Albert using only his eyes when everything went black.

Cars headlights, flashlights, radios, and the jarring speaker all went dead. The moon had disappeared, as if a thick curtain had been draped over the sky. For a few seconds, time seemed to be suspended and the air somehow changed; it was thicker and heavier, creating an atmosphere as though gravity was twice its normal strength.

Harry pried himself from the hood, his attention drawn skyward. There, far above the treeline, there was a presence, something inexplicable and beyond human understanding. By the time the moon showed itself again, Albert knew what it was. "It's the black condor!" Albert said.

Suddenly, Harry's feet were swept off the ground. The sound of screeching tires roared out as Harry wrapped a hand around the driver side mirror and used the other hand to brace against the hood. His arms immediately snapped back like ropes on a dropped anchor, his legs whipping out behind him.

"Albert, what are you doing? Stop the car, Albert!" Harry hung on desperately.

The nose of the car pulled hard to the left as gunshots ricocheted off the passenger side.

"Hold on, Mr. Fletcher! Hold on! Tell me which way to turn. I can't see the road."

"No shit! Just keep driving, Albert! They're shooting at us. Go! Go! Go!"

"I can't see!" Albert said, realizing he might as well be Mr. Magoo behind the wheel of a speeding car.

"A little to the right, Albert. That's it. All right, steady, keep it straight."

"My arms are shaking, Mr. Fletcher. I don't know if I can hold the wheel."

"You're doing fine, Albert. In about five-hundred feet there's a clearing leading to a field. Wait until I tell you to turn!" Suddenly all power had returned. Headlights and flashlights were back on, and the voice of the police officer was roaring out from the loudspeaker once again.

Albert jumped and his heart skipped as more gunfire rang out. He heard sirens cawing behind him like a murder of crows.

"They're coming," Harry said, "hold on and wait for my signal!"

Albert's hands slipped off the wheel causing the car to swerve.

"Keep it straight, Albert!"

"Sorry, Mr. Fletcher!"

"All right, Albert! In 50 feet, 40 feet, 30, ready?"

"READY, Mr. Fletcher…"

"Turn!"

Albert cut the wheel to the right. The car shot down a slight embankment and hurled back up to find the clearing.

"That's it, Albert, you got it! You got it, Albert!"

"Hold on, Mr. Fletcher. My hands are slipping."

"Just a little farther, Albert. Keep on the gas and keep it straight!"

As the car skipped along the clearing, heading for the field, an enormous, black shadow passed overhead, giving way to the warm glow of a Full Corn Moon. Harry could see acres and acres of tall grass before him like a dense, pine forest. He knew once they were in the middle of it, they could abandon the car, and not even Sherlock Holmes himself would be able to find them.

"All right, Albert, here we go. Once you feel the bumper hit the grass, bury your foot down on the pedal!" Harry was jubilant. Almost forgetting that creepy Barney Fife and his merry band of backwoods deputies were closing in. Not to mention forgetting a blind man, more boy than man, was behind the wheel of a speeding car in which he was the hood ornament.

"Here we go, Albert, drop the hammer!"

"What?"

"Stomp your foot on the gas pedal and hold it down!"

Albert braced himself and closed his eyes — not that it mattered — and dropped the pedal to the metal. "Hold on, Mr. Fletcher!" His voice was drowned out by the grass and wheat stocks whipping by as they cut into the grill and slapped over the hood like a car wash.

Using his arms and shoulders, Harry covered his head the best he could while he held onto the front hood with fingers growing weaker by the second.

"That's far enough, Albert! That's far enough!"

Albert could not hear a word over the deafening noise. He kept repeating to himself, "Keep your shaking hands on the wheel; keep the gas pedal buried. Keep your shaking hands on the wheel; keep the gas pedal buried." He kept repeating this until he heard a pounding on the roof and saw Harry's distorted face pressed up against the windshield like a squashed bug.

"That's far enough, Albert! Stop the car! Stop the car—"

The next thing Harry knew, he was rolling across the field like a carpet unfurling down a flight of stairs. He was tumbling too fast to notice anything until he noticed the sky cartwheeling overhead. His body tossed and bounced until he came to a complete and abrupt stop.

He lay there a moment, as his head continued spinning, and could hear the wail of sirens in the distance. He had to find Albert and find him fast. It was dark, and they were well afield hidden in the tall grass, but there was only so much time before the police would track them.

Harry could hear a rustling sound over his left shoulder, as his head spins gave way to a dull ache. Not footsteps, exactly, more like the sounds a giant tortoise would make crawling through the grass. Harry turned and then smiled.

"Mr. Fletcher, it's Albert, are you okay?"

CHAPTER 55
PARKING LOT PANDEMONIUM

Choking on his own spit and bile, simultaneously heartsick and enraged, Cam jumped from the Blazer and ran towards the dumpster. Darrah, frightened by the shotgun blast, knocked Dave to the ground and forced her way outside through the rear door. Seeing their opportunity, Randy, Niki, and Don ran out just behind.

"Jesus, Darrah! Wait!" Niki yelled. "Someone has a gun!"

Darrah ran towards the direction of the shotgun blast and heard Cam shouting, "Whitey, Whitey!" Cam rounded the dumpster, his face red and huge, and braced himself for what he might find, but what he saw sent a wave of relief through his body. Whitey was alive! His teeth were clamped down on Harding's arm like a vise, just above the wrist, preventing Harding from reaching for his shotgun. Cam leaned down to grab the shotgun and took off running with Whitey by his side.

"Drop the gun!" Harding said, struggling to sit while reaching for the service revolver tucked inside his waistband.

"Goddamn it!" Harding said, as he got his feet. "Drop the fucking gun! You are under arrest!" Watching them get farther away, Harding managed to draw his revolver from his waistband and stumble slowly toward them. "Last chance! Deal with me or deal with the chief! Your choice!" His arm was shaking and painful to move, but managed to raise his sightline and took aim.

"Run all you want to," Harding cackled. "It's not going to help you, or Carl for that matter. It's far too late." Without looking back, Cam slowed, almost stopping, before he and Whitey made their move and jumped in Carl's truck.

Harding's finger felt for the trigger, when out of nowhere a half-empty beer bottle whirled through the air and struck Harding on the back of the neck, causing him to drop his weapon.

"Yeah!!! You Sonofabitch!" Randy said. "Go Cam! Go!"

"Grab the gun Randy!" Darrah said.

"I got it," Don said, already in stride running past Randy. Harding saw Don coming and quickly shifted over on his hips and kicked out his leg, sending Don hard to the pavement.

Randy was right behind, trying to run past Harding, who was now crawling over the parking lot like a sand crab, desperate to get his weapon before Randy did.

"Not so fast, asshole!" Randy hollered, when the thought occurred to him that his best chance to keep the gun out of Harding's hand was to not break stride by bending over and trying to grab the gun, but to maintain speed and kick through the gun like attempting a field goal. If he did that, Harding would not have a chance; that is, if he could connect his steel-toed work boot square on the butt end of the gun handle. Not an easy task for a drunk punk.

With full momentum, Randy planted his left foot, and brought his right foot through with a strong leg and sent the gun skimming across the parking lot like a puck across pond ice.

"You sonofabitch!" Harding said. "I'm gonna get you!"

Just over Randy's right shoulder, Cam was fishtailing across the parking lot when Don Williams grabbed onto the truck's passenger side door and pulled himself through the window, dropping down beside Whitey.

Randy was on the far side of Harding, nearer the gun, and was now looking at the ass end of Cam's truck screeching by.

"Jump in with Darrah and Niki!" Cam said. "And get back to the house now! I think Carl's in trouble. Go! Go!"

"Come on, Niki!" Darrah said. "Get in the car."

Randy watched Harding regain himself and make towards the gun resting in the weeds. Randy knew he would not beat Harding to the gun this time and took off zigzagging across the parking lot in case bullets started to fly. He waved his arms as he ran and yelled out to get Darrah and Niki's attention.

"Niki! Darrah! Hold up!"

The wheels of the Trans AM baked across the parking lot, leaving a stretch of blue smoke as it swept toward Randy.

"Jump in!" Niki hollered. Randy sidestepped and swung ass-over-teakettle landing on Niki's lap. "Go, Darrah! Go!" he said, as Darrah steered out of the one-eighty and straightened out the nose making for the main road. She knew

Cam had maybe a thirty-second lead and knew she could easily close the gap. She also knew patrols would be everywhere, but like Cam, she knew the roads, byways, and cut-throughs better than anyone. And what she had under the hood, forget about anyone catching her.

Harding winced as he bent over and fished out the gun from the weeds. He struggled against the pain in his arm and his leg, but made it to the Blazer and gunned it out of the parking lot.

"That fucking dog!" Harding said. "I'm going to kill that mutt and kill Jenkins and leave their bodies in the swamp."

They won't get far, Harding thought, *Patrols are everywhere. And when they get stopped, I'll be there.* His tongue darted over his lips like a lizard, contorting his face into a sinister grin. He sat back in the seat, checked his revolver, and buried the hammer. "They're fucking mine!"

CHAPTER 56
THE DOGS OF DOOM ARE HOWLING MORE

Carl Jenkins woke before the alarm and stared listlessly at the ceiling. But for his eyes flitting along the exposed attic beams and drifting toward the gables, he remained lifeless as a corpse. It was a rarity on such nights, especially after heavy drinking, he would even stir in bed, and usually found himself comatose straight through the alarm; but tonight, he knew why he woke so early as his eyes settled on the rafters. They were here and there was no escape.

The once-terrifying, dark shadows, the ones that came for him at night, were no longer feared as they once were. The long nights of hauntings and the foreshadowing of evils yet to come, were over. It was here, and it was now. There would be no escaping or hiding or negotiating. And even if there was a way out, Carl Jenkins no longer cared. He wanted it all to end.

Like the sun rising in the east, or the force of gravity, or the immutable truth that all that lives must surely die, there were certain unbreakable scientific laws that governed the planet. There were also rogue laws that governed the underworld. As dark and incomprehensible as these laws may be, they exist and have always existed. They have cast their long shadow of condemnation since the beginning of time and have wielded enormous influence over mankind. And although not fully understood, the laws of demonic possession have been practiced over the millennia and were as sound today as Newton's laws themselves: when the realm of darkness stakes a claim of ownership on a poor soul, a thousand holy men the world over are powerless to stop it.

There are no miracles. There is no salvation. There are only immutable truths governing the realm of the living and the realm of the dead and the cheating of such truths are an impossibility. In the end, all that remains are unpaid debts and prayer offerings for the departed.

Carl lifted slowly and sat on the edge of the bed. His breathing was slow and deep, almost unconscious. As he looked blankly at the floor, a sense of amenable nonresistance took hold, melding with the thick cloud of despondency hanging over him.

He lifted his head and peered through the blackening window. The moon's light which had watched him to bed had been swallowed in a pit of darkness. As the creature's enormous shadow came to settle over the house, he sat there quiet a moment in the heavy pitch and weighed his final thoughts.

CHAPTER 57
THERE'S A KILLER ON THE ROAD ...

"Hold on!" Cam shouted, cutting the wheel hard to the left to make the turn.

"Holy shit!" Don said. "Did you see that sign?"

"What sign?"

"The one that says BRIDGE OUT AHEAD."

"That sign's been up for years."

"Okay, but is it true?"

The look in Cam's eyes revealed the answer. As Don held on for dear life, Cam fixed the driver-side mirror and wiped the glass down with his elbow, but still could not see.

"Don, look behind you. Do you see Darrah?"

Don reluctantly turned in his seat and stuck his head out the window.

"Not yet. But I see headlights through the trees. That has to be them."

"All right," Cam said, "they'll be making that turn any moment. Hold on to Whitey. This road is shit, and it only gets worse. But this is the only way back to the house if we want to avoid patrols. They never send patrols down here."

Cam reached his arm down and ran his hand through Whitey's fur. "It's all right now. It's all right..." He felt his eyes turn misty, but managed to fight back tears. He had thought the worst believing Whitey was killed by a shotgun blast, shot by a sick, son of a bitch cop that promised to let him go. The idea that someone could pull a gun on a dog with intent to kill sickened him. Knowing that if Whitey had not made a move on Harding when he did, Whitey would be dead. Feeling his anger grow, he swallowed and grit his teeth, and ran his hand through Whitey's fur again.

"I thought I lost you, boy. I thought I lost you. I'll never trust a fucking cop again."

Cam lit a cigarette and then fixed both hands on the wheel. "All right hold on. The road turns ugly on the other side of this rise. It's about to get a whole lot worse."

"Great," Don said. "Bad roads, no bridge."

"We don't need a bridge to get over that river," Cam smirked. "Just a set of balls and a shitload of horsepower."

Don held onto the dash with one hand and used the other to grab the window crank. He then drove both legs into the floorboards and braced himself.

"Hold on!" Cam shouted. The truck flew over the rise and immediately slid to the left, rutting the tires, kicking back up on the road, the rear end sliding out to the right. Whitey scooted up almost on Cam's lap while Don was bucking and bouncing like a drunk on a mechanical bull.

"Holy shit! How much longer?"

"Not long. On the other side of the river there is an access road. We just need to get there and then it's a straight shot for the house.

Don regained his balance as the truck evened out. He sat back in his seat and took a couple of deep breaths, regaining his composure.

"Hey," Don began, "what did that cop mean when he told you it was too late, that it had already begun. Is Carl in trouble?"

Cam just shook his head, uncertain of anything. He glanced at Don. "I know why the cop came after me, but Carl? I have no idea what the Christ he's talking about. But knowing the cops in this town, I believe it's something more than an officer just fucking with me. I gotta get there now!"

Reaching the bottom of the rise, Cam saw lights bouncing in his rearview mirror.

"I see Darrah. She just drove over the hill." Don looked behind to see headlights, when he turned back and noticed a strong smell of gasoline. "Do you smell that?" Before Cam could answer, the truck misfired, bucking them forward and jerking them back.

"Hold on!" Cam shouted, his right arm reaching out for Whitey, his left arm struggling against the shimmying wheel. "Shit! We're leaking gas like a sieve.... God dammit Sonny!"

The truck sputtered and choked, lurching forward as it skidded off the side of the road when the engine died.

"What the hell happened?" Don asked.

"Fucking, Sonny, that's what happened. The fuel pump shit the bed." Whitey was scared and pacing, but wasn't hurt. Cam looked over at Don.

"Are you all right?"

"I'm good," Don said, rubbing his left elbow and shoulder.

"All right. I have to flag down Darrah."

All three jumped out of the truck. Cam ran to the middle of the road waving his hands. The approaching headlights lit up their faces as the vehicle raced past the bottom of the hill. He and Don shielded against the bright glare as the vehicle barreled towards them, but suddenly stopped.

"Thank Christ," Cam said. "Shit, at her speed, I thought we were going to be ass-ended."

Don and Cam stared at the headlights as the vehicle sat idling.

"Why is she just sitting there?" Don asked.

"Darrah, come on!" Cam shouted, both hands cupped at his mouth. "Darrah! She doesn't want to take the Trans Am down this far." Cam gazed down at Whitey and noticed a trace of foam forming at his snout and thickening at the gumline. He knelt down and cupped his face.

"What's the matter?" Cam took his hand and tried to wipe away the foam, but Whitey was having none of it. He was far too worked up and unable to keep still for even a second.

Cam withdrew his hand and noticed Don stepping backwards with his mouth hanging open. He moved like a zombie in slow, hypnotic steps.

"Don, what the hell is going—" Before Don could answer, gunfire rang out, snapping the dirt at their feet like firecrackers.

"Get behind the trees!" Cam said. Whitey barked in a frenzy and turned towards the gunfire. Cam whistled twice and shouted his name, spinning Whitey around and putting his legs into high gear.

The three of them scrambled to the woods and took cover behind a fallen tree as another shot whizzed by their heads cutting through some branches.

"Jesus Christ," Cam said, "it's fucking Harding!" Cam and Don crouched below with Whitey beside, and kept down through the gunfire.

Other than the headlights, they were blind to see anything, but they could hear heavy footsteps which suddenly stopped.

"Listen," Cam whispered, "I can't hear him anymore. He's not moving." Don unfolded from the ground and positioned himself beside Cam. He lifted his nose to the level of the bark and trained his eyes on the headlights.

"Where is he?" Don said.

"I don't know, but we can't stay here. The man is hobbled. We can outrun him."

"Can you outrun a bullet?"

"Do you have any better ideas?"

"Shit! What about the shotgun you grabbed?"

"It's useless. There're no shells."

"Fuck!" Don said, louder than a whisper.

Thinking about their next move, Cam wrestled with the obvious question weighing heavy on his mind. What happened to Darrah, Niki, and Randy?

She was trailing behind us. There's not a faster car in this whole fucking town or a better driver than she is. It doesn't make any sense... Ran out of gas? Engine problems? Decided to turn back?

Running these scenarios through his head, he struggled with the one, unthinkable scenario, the one he did not want to enter his mind. But sometimes our worst fears have a way of muscling themselves to the forefront of our brains.

Jabbing at Cam's neck with a wet nose, Whitey attempted to grab his attention without making any noise.

"What is it, boy? What is it?"

"I think he wants us to make a run for it," Don said.

Whitey's head kept darting frantically towards the woods; back and forth, back and forth, his paws dancing like a foal's in a barn fire.

"Okay, boy, okay," Cam said. "Can you get us out of here?"

Whitey dipped his head and threw up his paw. Don and Cam smiled at each other and then heard Harding move.

"All right, boy, let's go. Lead the way."

Just as they were rising to their feet, the Blazer's engine roared and its headlights barreled forward. It lit up the trees and the surrounding space.

"Jesus Christ!" Cam said. "Go! Go! Go!"

With Whitey out in front, they followed him into the thicket. They could hear the sounds of tree saplings and branches crunch under the Blazer's tires and ran as fast as they could, weaving and ducking, desperately trying to hold to Whitey's path.

"Run, Don, run!" Cam said. "Don't look back!" A gunshot ricocheted off a tree, narrowly missing Don's leg. He quickly regained his balance and fell in line behind Cam.

"Are you all right?" Cam yelled over his shoulder.

"I'm not hit, keep going, he's gaining on us."

Whitey led them down to the river's bank. The Blazer was close behind and gaining on them. Cam could see the lights bouncing wildly and knew it would be tough for Harding to get off a shot. If they could just get on the other side of the riverbank, before Harding could level his gun, they would be home free.

Whitey turned on the jets and started upriver. The gorge along this point was far too steep and loose to scale it, but Whitey knew there was an outcropping of rocks around the next bend that could be used as a bridge to the other side. They just needed to get there before Harding did.

But getting across the river was only one issue, what Cam and Don did not realize was there was a far bigger issue up ahead. One they could not foresee and was heading straight for them.

Their adrenaline kept them moving ahead of Harding, but Harding was gaining fast. The Blazer's four-wheel drive powered over the bank's edge, barely holding to the wet, clumpy dirt, and cut down the side of the river like a downhill skier cuts through a mountain face.

He blasted ahead, closing the gap to about four car lengths when... *Slam!* Metal and glass exploded on contact, followed by steam bursting from the radiator louder than the blaring horn.

Whitey spun around and sidled up against Don and Cam who lost their footing and fell to the ground. They all turned to see the Blazer's front end perched atop a boulder and hissing like a snake.

But for Whitey, no one heard over the blaring horn and hissing steam what was coming from the other side of the river. Whitey frantically batted his snout under Cam's arm to get him on his feet, while Don struggled to stand.

Finding their balance and about to run, they watched the Blazer pitch over the boulder and slide down the bank. Somehow, before the two-and-a-half tons of twisted metal plunged into the river, Harding dropped from the driver's side window and rolled out of the way. He got to his knees and immediately ripped off two shots, blindly, as he watched them disappear around the bend.

Clumsily, his leg struggled to find solid ground, but Harding pushed forward, hitching his way along the banks and around the bend when there, high on the bluff, Harding saw Whitey's tail move.

He stopped and grinned, taking a few seconds to reload his service revolver, before he stepped forward in a calm and measured fashion, and made his way up the rock face.

With each step Harding took, Whitey remained still, never trying to hide or make a run for it. Harding thought he must be hurt or perhaps his leg was caught in between some rocks. He never considered, as he sighted his gun directly at Whitey's head, that he was being drawn into a trap, snared like a lamb when — breaking over the bank's crest like a runaway avalanche, a pack of swamp dogs ripped through Officer Harding's body like the high-speed blades of a Cuisinart slices through beets. Snapping teeth tore through Harding's flesh and bones as the dogs stormed over the riverbed, never breaking stride.

Cam and Don had just hoisted themselves up into a nearby tree and watched the brutal carnage play out below them; it was like watching the force of a tidal wave, powering forward, smashing and swallowing everything in sight. Harding never knew what hit him.

The dogs passed directly beneath the branch Cam and Don were standing on and disappeared into the darkness. Fast as the dogs appeared, they were gone, leaving nothing but a rooted-up swath of ground in their wake and the remains of Officer Harding splattered over the rocks.

Whitey knew the dogs were coming and knew they would pass over his position safely behind the rocks. When the dogs disappeared into the night, Whitey emerged from his hiding place and bound for the base of the tree.

Cam hung down from the bottom branch and dropped to the ground. He was pounced on immediately, licked from stem to stern. Noticing, however, another pair of feet had yet to hit the ground, Cam looked up to see Don motionless, hanging on for dear life.

"Come on, Don, jump! We have to get the fuck out of here! We need to hurry."

It had escaped Don's notice that his nails started to bleed from using them like pole spikes, and that sound pounding in his eardrums was his own heart beating.

He was in a state of disorientation, terrified to the core at the brutal carnage he just witnessed.

"Don, we got to go!"

Don managed to look down, and when he did, his eyes met Whitey's. He was struck by them. There was something about the way they resonated. There was a protective calm, and a sense of wellbeing in them. It's as if they were extending Don a guiding hand to join them on the only path ahead.

The next thing Don knew, his legs were moving faster than they ever had before. They were in perfect consort with Cam and Whitey's as they all made their way straight for Jenkins' Field.

CHAPTER 58
THIS IS THE END,
MY ONLY FRIEND, THE END

After climbing the attic stairs, Carl stooped beneath the workbench and retrieved his army footlocker. He unlatched the lid and placed a note inside addressed to Cam. He contemplated a moment, hoping he explained things well, as his eyes glanced at the thick rope hanging from the rafters, dropping through the open ceiling to his bedroom below. It was time.

Carl carried the footlocker down the stairs to his bedroom, knowing what he must do. It frightened him to hear the chorus of savage throats draw ever closer, the sounds of impending death ever louder. The bloodcurdling howls and thunderous wail of the dogs was terrifying and sent a tremor through his hands. Anxiety seized upon his frailty. The muscles in his legs and his arms failed him, collapsing his atrophied body to the floor. With his fingers curled into useless knots, he struggled to leverage his hands so he could slide the trunk under the noose.

Exhausted from his long fear this day would arrive, he collapsed overtop the footlocker with his arms wrapped around it, the way a man overboard wraps his arms around anything that floats. He could feel the cold metal hinge bore into his cheek as his breathing turned shallow and rapid. *God, help me find the strength.*

It was as if his limbs were that of a jellyfish, but somehow he got his legs underneath him and stepped on the trunk. He teetered, found his balance, then lifted on his toes and pushed his head through the waiting noose. His breaths came in quick, piping gasps as the coarse fibers burned into the soft flesh under his chin. His eyes strained from the lack of oxygen, but remained conscious enough to see a congregation of dogs gathering outside his window. It was even more terrifying than he had seen in his dark visions. All were spitting and snarling and howling overhead; they were throwing themselves up and wrenching their bodies into horrid shapes. A thousand savage throats braying at the night sky chattered the teeth in his head shimmying the noose even tighter.

The last image on earth Carl took with him before the rope snapped tight and crushed his windpipe, was the most hideous of creatures descending from the night sky and screeching out to its canine legion.

With his legs kicking and his body jerking, Carl hung on a few seconds in semi-consciousness, when he heard the windows explode from their wood frames and the gnashing of teeth echoing in his ear. His legs twitched once more, then went still, his body swinging on the rope like a cadaver on a butcher's hook.

For a brief moment Carl thought he had seen God, if only for a second, before the lights went out and everything went dark.... Wave after wave, the dogs took the house with blinding speed. Their lean-muscled bodies propelled them up and over each other with maniacal lunacy, and shot up the stairs to the second floor. Turning through the bedroom door, what they saw stopped them dead in their tracks. The first to burst through pulled up instantly when he saw Carl's lifeless body swinging from the rope. The others flooded in from behind and howled in the dank air. Some clawed up the walls to the rafters and hung from their perch like fruit bats.

They all watched Carl's face begin to bloat and the tongue turn blue as the pack leader paced forward to the hanging carcass. It rose on his hindquarters, extended its neck, and rammed its snout against Carl's rib cage. To its vexation, there was no response, just the awful sounds of bones snapping and the weight of a dead body swinging backward.

CHAPTER 59
TEARS FOR FEARS

Running through the acres of farmland, Cam and Don did their best not to fall too far behind Whitey, but by the time the barn came into view they were thoroughly exhausted and slowed to catch their breath. Suddenly two short blasts followed by a longer third ripped across the sky from the communications tower, leveling Don and Cam to the ground.

"Holy shit!" Don said.

"Come on, get up," Cam said, jumping to his feet. "We gotta move."

"Why'd the horn blast again?" Don asked.

"Lockdown is over, the chief shut it down. Come on man, we gotta go."

Keeping wide of the barn, Don could smell smoke as they ran by.

"Something's burning," Don said. "You smell that?"

"Yeah," Cam said, hesitating a moment, not wanting to reveal how the fire really started. "I'll explain later." Don caught a glimpse at the burnt exterior and knew, by the look and smell of the fire, that it had been recent.

About midfield, halfway between the barn and the house, Whitey became highly agitated and began growling and darting between Cam's legs.

"What's wrong, boy?" Cam asked.

"Look!" Don said, pointing at the house. Cam knew what Don was pointing at. The first-floor doors and windows looked like cavernous, black holes. There was not a pane of glass or door anywhere; all were completely blown out. It looked like a tornado slammed into it.

"What the hell happened?" Cam uttered to himself, trying to get a better view.

But for a single bulb casting a yellowish light, the entire house was dark.

"Wait!" Don said, trying to stop Cam running towards the house. "Don't go in there!" Without a second's hesitation, Cam and Whitey were already on the move.

"I gotta find Carl!" Cam said.

Don stood there flat-footed; his head swiveled around looking at the dark field and treeline and knew there were no good options. He thought of Harding being shred to pieces before his very eyes, and realized, as he stood there alone, acting as fresh bait was definitely the worst option.

"Cam, wait up!" Don said, as he kicked it into high gear.

Even before Cam and Whitey entered the house, Whitey's nose was working overtime; he had picked up a strong, animal scent wafting out from the doorless opening and was anxious to find the unwanted intruders and roust them from the house.

Cam told Whitey to stay by him as they entered. He knew Whitey was picking up a powerful scent and feared what was inside. Passing over the threshold, into the kitchen, he flipped the light switch on only to find it wasn't working. He remembered Carl kept a flashlight in the lower drawer of a toolbox inside the pantry and fetched it. He barely noticed his wet feet when he beamed the light over the ceilings, walls, and floors. There was water everywhere. Scattered debris and splintered wood were strewn about. Sections of flooring were ripped up. Deep gouges curled up the linoleum in jagged ribbons.

His heart sank and screamed out for Carl.

"Dad! Are you all right? ... Dad?"

There was no answer. Cam knelt down and cupped both hands around Whitey's face.

"Listen, I need you to stay here. Okay? I'll be right back. I have to check on Carl. It's okay, boy. I'll be right back." He got up and turned down the hall when Don entered.

"Cam, hold on. Where—" The damage to the kitchen shut Don up for a moment. His eyes focused on the deep gouges in the flooring when something else caught his eye. He bent down to pick up what looked like a tuft of coarse fur. Bringing it up close to his eyes, Cam stepped over and directed the flashlight as they both studied the clump.

"Jesus." Don grimaced as he glanced over the kitchen and noticed clumps everywhere. "Cam, they were here."

"And they still could be," Cam said, turning to open the basement door. "Quick, hide in the basement until I can clear the area. I'm going to check upstairs."

"Don't go up there alone," Don said. "They could be just waiting for you."

"I need you to stay down here with Whitey and warn me in case they come back. They could be watching the house right now."

"All right," Don agreed, "but get up there and come right down."

Cam started to turn away. "Wait," Don said, "does Carl have a gun? You can't go up there without a weapon."

"The cops took them all away," Cam said.

"Well, take this then." Don reached just inside the basement door where a spade hung from a hook and passed it to Cam.

"Stay here," Cam said. "And listen close. If you hear anything at all, bang on the coal chute at the foot of the basement steps. I'll hear it loud and clear. But don't open this door unless you know it's me. Got it?"

"Got it." Don said. "Good luck."

Cam threw the spade over his shoulder and moved from the kitchen down the narrow front hall. He could not believe how much damage there was. The floors and walls were all chewed up and the only two pictures that used to hang on the wall were smashed on the ground. He noticed the front windows, the frames, and the front door were blown out just like the back of the house.

He stepped through the foyer and began to walk up the staircase, calling out for Carl. "Dad? Are you up there? Wake up! Dad? Answer me?"

Before he got to the second-floor landing, Cam noticed clumps of fur strewn over the steps. As he waved the flashlight, he noticed something else that shot a cold chill up his spine: clumps of oily, black feathers and the large remains of what looked like the skin of a snake. It was paper thin with raised, etched scales and it had a translucency about it. It scared him to think how large an animal would have to be to leave a skin behind like this, twice that of a giant anaconda. But what really terrified him was why they were here in the first place, and was Carl all right.

Too big to step around, Cam hacked through the skin with the spade and crunched his way through the hallway and into Carl's room. Passing through the door, the horrific sight that met his eyes punched a hole through his heart and buckled him over. He cried out in heavy yelps and ran wildly to his father. He jumped up to reach the noose and knocked the trunk over, spilling the contents over the floor which included some baseball cards, a metal ring, a Buck knife Carl carried with him in Vietnam, and a yellow piece of paper addressed to him.

He pushed his hand through the items and grabbed the note first, tucking it firmly inside his pocket. He then reached for the knife, and with one quick move set the trunk upright and stepped up to cut down the body. He used his left shoulder to press underneath Carl's chest to create some slack, and then used his right hand and sawed through the rope until it snapped, dropping them both in a heap.

Cam struggled to a sitting position. He propped Carl's lifeless body up against his chest and began rocking him back and forth like a mother rocks her child. Every few seconds, Cam nervously reached inside his pocket, making sure the note was still there, and continued to rock.

Whatever words were written in Carl's final moments, they were precious words for Cam and Cam only. And although he was desperate to know what they said, he was terrified to know what they might reveal. Tears formed his eyes as he held his father's lifeless body with loving care. He was overcome with grief, but felt an anger building like a forest fire gulping air.

CHAPTER 60
BIRDS OF A FEATHER

"Thank you, Betty," Sonny said, drinking the last of his coffee. "I gotta make the rounds."

"Did you ever hear from Carl?" Betty asked.

"Never did. I suppose he thought better of it unless he got caught up in the lockdown and had to hold up somewhere. Anyway, I'm glad it's over. Time to make some money."

Sonny glanced at his watch and headed for the door. He turned before he exited. "I think I'll take a run by the house, but if you see Carl in the meantime, let him know I was here and I'm looking for him."

"Will do, Sonny," Betty replied. "Be careful out there."

Sonny cut off a plug of tobacco and turned on the two-way radio. Shifting into drive, he listened to dispatch recite all the vehicles' license plate numbers and their locations in need of towing. This was typical. There were always vehicles forcibly stopped and left abandoned during lockdown, per order of the chief, that were now in need of confiscation and impoundment. It was important that violators of the lockdown not only pay an admonishment, the chief would say, but also pay in the pocketbook to get their vehicles back.

Sonny tuned the channel and listened to Polly's running transmission: "Late model pickup, black on silver, on the south side of Long Pond Road, plate number three, seven, nine, Alpha, Zulu. Chevy Impala, white on white, located east side of Conant Street by Green and Summer, plate number Victor, Foxtrot, Whiskey, six, six, two. '78 or `79 Trans Am, black on black, spoiler, T-Top located Old Post Road, a mile before Hanson Farm. Plate number—"

"Holy hell!" Sonny picked up the CB. "Polly, I'll hook that 79 Trans Am. That screaming chicken is mine - I'm only two miles out - just leaving the Tri-Stop now."

"10-4, Sonny," Polly transmitted. "Hook it and book it."

Polly continued rattling off plate numbers as Sonny stepped on the gas when a screech of tires and a set of bouncing headlights damn near blinded him.

"What the hell?" He squinted through the grimy windshield, barely making out Mighty Mouse behind the wheel.

"Say, Sonny, have you seen Cam Jenkins?"

"Nope. I haven't seen him. Listen, Earl, I've got a hookup on Old Post Road, I got no time to chinwag."

"What about that girlfriend of his, Darrah Ryder? You see her?"

"I can't say that I have. What you want with them anyhow?"

"They're missing. Darrah, Nicole, Cam, and Randy."

"Missing? What do you mean missing?"

"They were at Dave's during lockdown, along with half the town, and then they just disappeared. No one knows what happened. We all heard what sounded like a gunshot outside, but not sure what happened after that. I tried to ask Dave about it, but he just walked right on past me like he'd seen a ghost."

"I'll keep a look out for them," Sonny replied, "but I have to get going." Sonny did not let on that it was Darrah's Trans Am he was on his way to hook. It wasn't unusual for vehicles to be abandoned during lockdown, of course, but the owners of those vehicles were mostly accounted for. They were brought into the station so they could pay the chief.

If they were at Dave's during lockdown, how did their car end up abandoned on Old Post Road? He did not like the sound of it, considering what he witnessed at Jenkin's Field earlier in the day, and he certainly did not want that loudmouth Mighty Mouse to know.

Turning on his flashing yellows, Sonny had a bad feeling about Carl and what he might find at the house. *It's typical for Carl to not answer his phone or not show up somewhere, but when you take into account his boy, Darrah, his buddy Randy, and Sergeant Guthrie's daughter all unaccounted for. Shit.*

Turning onto Old Post Road, that bad feeling was working its way into full-blown heartburn. He rolled down the window, turned his head, and wretched out a wad of stringy tobacco, swiping across his mouth with the back of his flannel sleeve. When his eyes returned to the dark road, he saw what he was looking for, but not what he expected. The Trans Am was clearly abandoned, as expected, but it was in the middle of the road with both the driver side and passenger doors wide open. The exterior and interior lights were all on, and as he got closer, he could hear the radio playing and the engine running.

Sonny quickly parked the truck and set some hazard cones. With his flashlight in hand, he walked around the car and examined the exterior and interior. He reached inside and turned the engine off. As his eyes traveled over every square inch, what shocked him more than anything is he noticed a lipstick-marked cigarette, still burning, resting in the ashtray. He saw a few, empty beer cans strewn throughout the interior, but a bottle of Miller, still cold, stood upright on the rear floorboard like someone sitting in the back just cracked one open and balanced the bottle between his feet. *What the hell happened here?* He pulled back from the vehicle and flashed his light over the road and along the treeline in both directions. None of it made any sense, but he had no time to figure it out now, he just needed to hook it quickly and get on over to Carl's.

He dropped the inclined bed, hooked the front end, and winched the vehicle up high enough to chain down the back wheels. Walking around to the rear, a flash of bright silver across the T-top caught his eye. He could see bare, metal scratches shoot in all directions; and there were deep gouges clawed through the roofline like someone attacked it with an iron rake. Flashing his light over the top, he leaned in for a closer look. A single, black feather, stemming from the roof, twisted and fluttered in the breeze. It hung there just a moment before it was swept away on the night winds.

CHAPTER 61
DUDLEY DO-RIGHT ALWAYS GETS HIS MAN

Whitey was restless and began whimpering in low, broken cries.

"It's okay," Don reassured him. "Cam will be back any second."

Spinning on the basement stairwell, Whitey pushed his snout under Don's arm and then ran down the basement stairs.

"Whitey get back here. Where are you going? Whitey?"

Don flew down the stairs after him and followed him to the open window by the coal chute. He was frantic, trying to draw Don's attention.

"What? The window? What's out there?"

Whitey persisted until Don jumped up on some old crates and peered out. What he saw through the thick spider webs looked like when Boston PD honor a fallen hero. A line of cruisers were rolling into the driveway in tight formation, two-by-two, as if following a memorial protocol on the way to a cemetery.

This isn't right, Don thought, *unless they are being extremely careful because they heard reports of the dogs..... But they couldn't possibly know about the dogs unless they were already here. But how could that be? We had only just arrived minutes after the dogs came and went. There was no sign of the police anywhere.*

Don realized it did not matter anymore. He just wanted it all to end and get the hell out of town. If he could just explain the situation to the police, there must be someone on the force that would have to listen.

Don stepped down from the crates and turned to Whitey.

"You've got good ears, boy. The police are right outside."

Whitey's frantic behavior did not let up. He seemed to be even more agitated. "Don't worry boy. Even if those mutant dogs return, they would face a heavily armed police force ready to take them out. You're safe. You can come or stay if you want, but I have to find a cop out there who is willing to listen, okay?"

Don ran his hand across Whitey's head. "I can see why Cam loves you boy, but I gotta go. I'll leave the door open." Don looked into his troubled but soulful eyes and fled up the basement stairs. When he reached the top, before he even had a chance to open the door, a bank of spotlights powered on and lit up the entire house. It was so bright that even from the dark basement it appeared like the house was engulfed in flames.

Don cowered behind the door and listened as a thunder of boots stormed the house. It advanced like an army regiment under direct orders to take an enemy position. And it was now parading up the second-floor stairs.

Don swung open the door, raising his arms immediately in a defensive position against the assailing light. He could barely see the last of the officers making their way up the stairs and had to move fast. He needed to explain things before Cam had a chance to speak.

"Officers!" Don said, running through the kitchen and turning through the foyer. "Hold on, I need to speak to you."

As Don ran up the top of the stairwell, he could see a few policemen standing guard outside Carl's bedroom door. They swung around immediately and trained their weapons on Don.

"Halt! Not a step closer."

Don recoiled. "Don't shoot. Don't shoot. Put your weapons down. I just need to talk."

"Turn and grab the wall and get your hands up. Who are you?"

"Don Williams. I'm a reporter down here doing a story. I'm here to meet with Carl Jenkins—"

"That's not possible." The officer grimaced.

"What are you talking about?"

The officer took a step closer and leaned in. "Carl Jenkins is dead."

"Dead?" Don was afraid to ask. His instincts told him not to say another word. There was a look in the officer's eyes that suggested he believed Don had something to do with Carl's death. The officer grunted and took Don by the elbow.

"This way, Mr. Williams, the chief's gonna want to have a word with you."

"Where are you taking me? I don't know anything about Carl's death. Have you spoken to Cam yet? Where's Cam?"

"Right this way, Mr. Williams."

The officer strong-armed Don into the bedroom. There, just inside, police officers, including Sergeant Guthrie, were standing by a crouching Chief Hicks who was shining a flashlight into the bruised and swollen face of Carl Jenkins.

Upon seeing Don Williams enter, Guthrie bent down and spoke into the chief's ear. "That reporter I was telling you about, the one I had words with down at the Tri-Stop, he just walked through the door." Hicks was stone faced, deeply troubled at what happened to Carl Jenkins. He knew something had gone wrong during the ceremony. Jenkins's act of suicide, a shameful death, was not what he expected.

Looking over at the dead body of Carl Jenkins, Don lost his breath. He had seen a dead body before, but not one whose head and facial features were bruised and swollen and dark blue.

Hicks lifted to his feet and turned from the dead body. He stepped into Don and forced his baton under his chin.

"What's the matter, Mr. Williams, never seen a dead man before?"

Don tried to answer, but the baton pressed against his Adam's apple turned his words into crushed gasps.

"I'll take that as a no." Hicks yanked back the baton and chuckled as he watched Don clutch at his throat.

"You are looking at a long and hard night, Mr. Williams. Just how long and how hard? Well, that's up to you. Now, you look like a reasonably smart man, so I'm sure you will cooperate fully and answer all of my questions, and not waste my valuable time. Do I make myself clear?"

Don Williams nodded in agreement, while Hicks shared a laugh with the other officers.

"You see that," Hicks said, "we have us a smart, city boy. I just knew Mr. Williams would understand. But you know what I think? I think you're just another smart-ass outsider, a malcontent who thinks he knows more than we locals do, who thinks he can pile up some dirt on Podunk, USA, for the amusement of his highfalutin readers. That's what I think, Mr. Williams."

Guthrie, Durst, Pierce, and the rest of the officers laughed along with Hicks when Hicks suddenly wound back, planted his boot, and struck Don with two powerful blows with his nightstick. The first caught his kidney and lower ribs, buckling him over and sending him hard to the floor; the second was a downward blow striking the back of his legs, laying him out in blinding pain at the boot-heels of Hicks. Hicks grabbed Don by the collar and jerked his head back.

"Now, you think you're in pain? You lie to me, city boy, and I promise you'll know what pain really is. Now, tell me where Cam Jenkins is?"

Although his voice sounded distant, somewhere behind the throbbing waves of pain, Don knew it was Hicks interrogating him. He also knew that if he did not provide an answer toot sweet, he was sure to meet with Hicks's nightstick once again. But this time he feared it would be much worse.

Don struggled to lift his head to speak, terrified at what was coming, but the words failed to form his convulsing mouth.

"I swear to God, city boy, I'm gonna split your head wide open! Now speak, God dammit!"

As Hicks wrenched the nightstick high above his head, a voice shouted from above the attic rafters.

"Hicks! You want me, you got me!"

Stopping mid swing, the chief shot a look over his head and commanded, "Bring that sonofabitch to me now!" He clipped the nightstick to his belt and peered down at the contorted body.

"Looks like your lucky day, Mr. Williams," the chief mocked. "Your partner in crime has just saved you one helluva headache. Now, get your ass up!"

Hicks grabbed Don by his belt and collar and jerked him to his feet. He snapped his head back by the hair and leaned in.

"Before the night is through, one way or another, you're going to tell me everything I need to know. But I am a fair man, Mr. Williams. If you come clean and tell the truth, it could be a relatively brief night for you. I'll spring you from custody in time to catch last call at Dave's. But if you lie to me, speak in half-truths, or spin any fancy, city crap ... well, well, well, it will be an awfully long night indeed." Hicks flashed a look over the dead body of Carl Jenkins, then back to Don. "As long a night as ole Carl Jenkins had. I promise you that."

Fully understanding, but too weak to speak, Don nodded with a whimpering cry. Hicks, who was tapping the nightstick against the palm of his hand, directed his scorn at Cam now being ushered front and center by Pierce and Durst.

Cam looked down at his father's bruised and lifeless body, and collapsed like a paper doll between the arms of Pierce and Durst, his legs now being dragged behind him.

"Get him on his feet," Hicks charged. "Haul him up by his fucking neck, if you have to."

"We can't get a hold of him Chief," Durst said.

"God dammit!" Moving over Cam like a mountain cloud, the chief grabbed Cam by the neck and yanked him to his feet.

"Now, this is how this works. I ask the questions, and you answer me everything, truthfully. You lie to me, or leave anything out, and this will be the longest night of your life."

Cam already had an idea how this worked. Although he lacked the nerve to read the entirety of the note, his father left him, he had stolen a glance before he stuffed it back in his pocket and hid in the attic before the police found him. At the top of the note, written in crude, capital letters, it read.

DON'T TRUST HICKS
DON'T TRUST THE POLICE
THEY ALWAYS GET YOU IN THE END

Cam mustered his strength, glanced at his father's body, and said, "What's there to talk about? You killed him. You know you did. And nothing's gonna change that."

A vicious blow to Cam's rib cage bent him in half.

"You're dumber than your reporter friend. Sergeant Guthrie, place Cam Jenkins under arrest for breaking and entering Titicut High, for burglary, for possession of stolen goods, for endangering the life of an officer of the law, and…" He made sure Cam's eyes met his. "And place him under arrest for the murder of his dearly departed father, Carl Jenkins."

"You fucking bastard!" Cam said, struggling to lift his head. "You won't get away with it. Not this time!"

The chief leaned in with a sinister grimace. "I run this town and everything in it. I'm gonna enjoy seeing them doctors fry your brain, just like they did your old man in that booby hatch."

"Fuck you!"

Just when Hicks was ready to deliver another blow, Whitey burst up the stairs, turned down the hall, and stormed past the gauntlet of officers. He was barking wildly, cutting left and right, dodging the outstretched arms of officers trying to reel him in.

"Get that dog!" Hicks said.

"Whitey!" Cam said. "Get out of here! Run! Run!" Whitey was wild with panic; he had to get to Cam, but there was an officer at every turn. He slipped through the legs of one officer, and lunged at another coming towards him, knocking him clear to the floor. The officers closed around Whitey leaving no path for escape. He made one last turn, but slammed into a human wall. It was Hicks.

"Don't hurt him!" Cam said. "You've got me Goddamnit! Let him go! He can't hurt anybody. Just let him go. Goddamnit, Hicks!"

Whitey struggled mightily in Hicks's arms, trying to fit his jaws somehow around his arms, chest, anywhere he could grab hold. But it would be no use. Hicks was too large and too strong.

"Don't worry son, I'm not the kind of man to hurt a dog. Rookie Officer Pierce?"

"Aye, Chief," Pierce responded, stepping forward.

"Take care of this dog."

"Chief?"

"Find a shovel, a pickaxe, a grub hoe, I don't care which, and take care of him, you got that?"

"Don't hurt him!" Cam raged. "Don't fucking hurt him! Whitey! I swear to Christ—"

With one punch to the head, Hicks knocked Cam unconscious. "Sergeant Guthrie, officer Durst, take both of these subversives back to the station and lock them up in separate cells. The rest of you tape off the house and then turn this place upside down. You all know what we're looking for. Find anything that Carl left behind that might reveal what he knows about the swamp, and us. And somebody, get that stiff out of here and down to the morgue."

After they were cuffed, Durst and Guthrie hauled Jenkins and Williams to the squad car, while Pierce wrestled Whitey under his control before dragging him outside.

Hicks remained behind, alone, and paced the room in thought. He had always followed the tenets of the compact, like all the aldermen that came before him. He had considered closely his enormous responsibility, and weighed every contingency—except for one thing: Jenkins took his own life and possibly the secrets of his survival of ten years ago, with him. What did the people of the fallen night want? What were they after? Hicks knew it was more than common revenge. They had always been appeased before, restoring calm in the realm of spirits, but this was different. Hicks could feel it in his bones. They wanted something and Carl Jenkins, now dead, was the key.

Hicks moved to the bedroom window, trembling, and looked out over the reach. His eyes scanned the acreage and followed the tree line heading in the swamp's direction. He peered into the dark sky and ran his thumb along the beads of his ceremonial necklace. He prayed in silence.

CHAPTER 62
INVASION OF THE BODY SNATCHERS

Leaving Old Post Road with the Trans Am loaded on his flatbed, Sonny would head to impound located directly behind One Police Plaza, but first he needed to check on Carl.

He wasn't scared exactly, as his eyes glazed over the narrow dark road, barely thinking of where he was heading, but finding the Trans Am the way he did really picked at his brain.

It was straight out of Close Encounters of the Third Kind. Like aliens abducted them in their spaceship and whirred them away to some faraway galaxy. Abandoned in the middle of the road? Lights all on? Engine running? Cigarette burning? Cold beer barely touched?... What the hell happened? Other than them scratches and gouges on the roof, the Trans Am was pristine, undisturbed, like it was flash frozen in time. Weird. It was like they were still in the car, but they weren't.

Sonny cursed and spit; his eyes darting wildly. "I'm either head tripping or I'm back in Nam and Charlie's about to snatch me."

Turning down Foundry Street, Sonny spotted a convoy of cruisers about a mile past Hanson Farm. They were moving at a good clip with their lights flashing and heading in his direction. One by one, they zoomed by with their sirens blaring. He could not be sure, because of the oncoming headlights, but he thought he saw two figures in the back seat of one of the cruisers. Even though they would have to face Hicks, whoever they were, Sonny hoped it was Cam and Darrah. Anything was better than being snatched by aliens.

Passing Hanson Farm, he slowed into the corner and drove cautiously past the large oak trees that hugged the road. Straightening out as he came out of the turn, his headlights flashed over streams of yellow tape surrounding the entire Jenkins' house. He could see red signs staked in the front yard and could see a sign nailed next to where the front door should have been.

He parked on the side of the road and ran up to the house, ducking beneath the police tape as he went. Stepping over the shattered glass, he passed over the front door threshold and read the sign: CONDEMNED: DANGER - KEEP OUT - POLICE ORDER.

Clutching the flashlight in his hand like a weapon, he stepped past the stairwell leading to the second floor and shined his light down the hall into the kitchen. "What the hell?" He stepped back and beamed the light over his right shoulder into the parlor, up the staircase, and bounced the light over the blown-out windows on all sides of the house. He could not believe the damage. It reminded him of a bomb structure they used during explosives training in boot camp.

He shouted up the stairs, "Carl! You there? Carl! ... Carl!"

Suddenly, the sound of an animal's nails, turning and spinning rapidly, tore across the kitchen floor like a tornado. Sonny fell back against the wall and beamed his flashlight at the fast-approaching animal. The light caught a shiny black coat and a single white paw lunging toward him. It was Whitey.

"Holy Hell!" Sonny blurted. "You scared the piss out of me."

Whitey barked frantically, batting his nose into Sonny's chest and legs, jerking his head toward the kitchen.

"What's going on boy? Where is everybody?" Whitey kept batting him and wrenching his neck back toward the kitchen.

"What you looking at, boy? Is something out there?"

Just then, a young police officer, no older than twenty-two or three, walked into the light. He was holding a shovel in one hand and gripping a service pistol with the other. His face was deadpan. His eyes resembled the black dots at the bottom of two question marks and looked through Sonny like he wasn't there.

"Now, just hold on there, officer," Sonny began, "what the hell went on here? Where's Carl?"

Officer Pierce's lips began to move like he was talking to himself. Still gripping the shovel and pistol, he paced down the hall toward Sonny.

"What you got a gun and shovel for?" Sonny stared into the officer's eyes and snapped his fingers. "Hey, what's the matter with you?" There was no response. It was like speaking to the whitetail deer head above his mantelpiece. Sonny had seen that same look in the young officer's eyes plenty of times before; and although the officer was too young to serve in Vietnam, he knew he was staring into the eyes of a man who was shell-shocked all the same.

Officer Pierce stepped by listlessly until he reached the front entry and stopped. He stood there motionless, overlooking the front yard like a lawn jockey keeping watch.

Whitey whimpered and barked, trading looks between Sonny and Officer Pierce. Sonny watched Pierce carefully, knowing not to trust a disturbed man with a loaded gun. He knew he could take Pierce out before he turned around, but ultimately it was suicide. The last thing he wanted was to have Hicks and the police target him for attacking one of their own. He had a good thing going, making cash on the barrelhead hooking vehicles for the department. As long as he kept himself to himself, he could avoid the wrath of Hicks.

Then, without provocation, Officer Pierce turned around on his own accord, his hand gripping the gun handle tightly.

"I, I, just couldn't," stuttered Pierce.

"Couldn't what?" Sonny urged. "What are you talking about?"

"Barely out of the academy," Pierce continued, speaking as if uttering a soliloquy. "I disobeyed a direct order."

Squinting, Sonny's eyes bore through him. "What direct order?"

"My dad was so proud when I graduated. 'Carrying on a fine tradition,' he said, 'a proud institution served by a proud line of Pierce men.' It was the first time in my life I had my dad's respect, but now…"

Sonny could clearly see Pierce was despondent. He was brushed back when the young officer, inadvertently, waved the gun in his direction.

"Now, hold on one sec," Sonny said, "we can work this thing out. Put that gun down, so no one gets hurt."

"The dog is supposed to be dead and buried," Pierce said with a peculiar smile, his countenance heavy. "A direct order…. I disobeyed a direct order. No one disobeys the chief." Pierce craned his neck back and pressed the muzzle under his chin.

"No! Don't do it!" Sonny said.

Pierce's lips thinned into a seeping grin before he took four rapid pipes of air and pulled the trigger.

Sonny leapt off his feet as the gun exploded. His hands were reaching around his ears and shaking, his eyes wild with disbelief; but they did not deceive him, he'd seen men take that way before. The force of the gunshot blast laid out Officer Pierce's body with his legs and arms bent in all directions. He looked like a mannequin dropped from a ten-story building. Officer Pierce was dead.

CHAPTER 63
EVERY END IS A NEW BEGINNING

Tuesday, September 13th, 7:49 am: Four days later.
Behind the closed door of his office, Sergeant Guthrie sat at his desk in the still air of contemplation. He gazed down at the framed picture in his hands and struggled over how things went so horribly wrong. And although there were no forensics to confirm her death, he knew his daughter, Nicole, went the way of so many others before her, all finding themselves on an official list of missing persons, none of which have ever been found or would ever be.

Nicole, and the others gone missing that night, would have a file on them with a carefully crafted narrative; each one would be documented with falsified statements, compromised evidence, and bogus witnesses.

From time to time, for example, it would be falsely reported by members of The Keepers, posing as witnesses, that the missing person was seen with an unidentified man or woman in Boston, or seen stepping off a ferry down the Cape, or seen hitching on I-70 just south of Topeka.

Whatever the particular case, a file would be built on each one of them creating a paper trail infused with false statements, unidentified witnesses, and nonexistent leads that would lend the appearance of legitimacy. If anyone from the outside world ever became curious and decided to look into it themselves, the police were more than cooperative. They knew the file would lead an outsider down a rabbit hole of smoke and mirrors, exhausting resources long before each lead was sufficiently followed up. It was important to appear above board and to demonstrate the police were a dutiful servant of the public. It provided sufficient cover, and it allowed The Keepers to enforce their mandate. And it was good PR.

This was the way of things, the way things had always been, but it sickened Sergeant Guthrie to think that now he was an accomplice in his own daughter's coverup, never mind his good friend and fellow officer, Boo Stevens.

Being a teen, with Nicole's wild background, Guthrie knew all too well how Nicole's file would read. They would smear his little girl as a whore who fled town in search of drugs, or perhaps left her "small-town boring life" behind on the back of a gang leader's Harley. It was all too much to bear.

Nicole was what Hicks called "residual." It was a term used to classify all collateral fallout from pre and post ceremony; it included all items that would need addressing like plausible explanations of missing persons and any such related evidence with extreme vigilance and discretion. All was done to indemnify the police and The Keepers from outsiders sniffing around where their noses did not belong. All measures were taken, regardless of how seemingly trivial, to guard against exposure.

Everything is lost, Guthrie thought, *my only daughter was taken from me and I was powerless to stop it. And now, as always, I will be expected to follow the script. I was too scared to go against Hicks and The Keepers and scared beyond hell not knowing what revenge the swamp would take. We all are. But my daughter is as good as dead, probably dead, I'll never know. I only know I will never see her again and I am the cause.*

He fought back tears remembering Nicole's childhood. As a little girl, Guthrie recalled how she would run to him when he came through the door at night, her blonde pigtails bouncing as she leapt into his arms shouting, "Daddy, Daddy, did you catch the bad guys?" He recalled just how much she loved sitting in his lap while he drove his cruiser really fast and allowed her to flash the blues when he knew it was safe to do so. Years later, when he made sergeant, he remembered just how proud she was of him, and how she used to call him, "My protector."

"You are my little girl," Guthrie said aloud, his eyes heavy on the picture.

A tear rolled down his cheek while he held the picture closer as if he were speaking to her directly.

"I always promised to protect you from harm, to catch the bad guys, but I failed in that promise. I failed as an officer of the law and failed you as a father. I won't ask you for forgiveness, because I deserve none, but it's time I face what I've done."

He placed her picture back on his desk and took a few deep breaths, bouncing his eyes from his wristwatch to the clock on the wall, both faces reading 7:59. He had a minute or less before he had to decide, but he already knew what his answer would be.

Tapping his fingers nervously on the desk, he watched for the light on his phone and again looked at his watch. He was on edge, feeling anxious, and wanted to get it over with before he had time to change his mind. So quiet the room, so heightened his senses, he never noticed before just how loud the ticking hands on the clock were. He wondered, as loud as they were, how it was possible his heart pounding in his chest was even louder — until the phone rang like a leaden bell and the light on his private line glared red.

"Guthrie," he said, his eyes darting over the squad room from behind the plated window.

"It is time, Sergeant Nathaniel Guthrie," said the voice on the phone. "We need your answer."

"The terms of my immunity, are they as we discussed?"

"The District Attorney and his liaison at the Federal Bureau of Investigation have agreed upon all terms. You will be placed into witness protection under an assumed name and will be immune to all federal and state charges in perpetuity. You will have a new life, but as the terms state, you will never serve as an officer of the law, or serve in any capacity of law enforcement, whatsoever, again."

"Where will I be relocated?"

"I am not at liberty to say, Sergeant. Those details are privileged and known only to the bureau. All details will be disclosed to you at the appropriate hour. Time's running out, Sergeant Guthrie, what should I tell them?"

Guthrie hesitated, not because he was undecided, but because of the gravity of the situation. Acting as an informant for the Feds and realizing how everything was about to change weighed heavy, and although he had learned the FBI had been investigating Hicks and the force for some time, the evidence they had gathered was flimsy, circumstantial at best. They needed someone on the inside with intimate knowledge, someone who knew where all the bodies were buried, and someone to disclose evidence. That someone was him.

The thought of it chilled him to the bone. In over three-hundred-years, it would be the first time there was a real possibility of bringing down The Keepers, exposing their secrets, and destroying the entire, clandestine organization he had pledged his life to uphold. It's not every day you realize your actions, forthcoming, will be responsible for breaking a sacred trust and sending your colleagues to prison; and the real possibility of waking the dead and unleashing hell on earth.

Over the last few days, Guthrie learned whose voice it was; it was the same one behind the note left in the drawer of his desk. And as he learned through their closed conversations, the voice was someone with deep knowledge of the first men, their demise, and what will restore peace within the territories.

From those conversations, Guthrie held onto a small measure of hope, that if he just "had faith," as the professor urged, all of it would come to a peaceful accord.

It was terrifying to think about, but what terrified him more than anything was Hicks himself. He knew the man well enough to know it was only a matter of time he would find out who the rat was. Witness protection or not, prison walls hardly presented a logistics problem for someone like Hicks, even if and when Hicks found himself behind bars. His influence was vast. Just how vast? No one knew for certain, but everyone knew, especially Guthrie, if Hicks wanted you, he had you.

Hicks would use his power to root out his hiding place and take him the first chance he had. As he saw it, however, Guthrie knew witness protection was his only way out. It offered him the only chance to escape jail time, atone in some measure for his daughter, and to extricate himself from a poisonous town cursed by singular beliefs and a generational distrust of outsiders. The way he looked at it, he would never survive prison. The inmates had his number, and so would Hicks.

Guthrie leaned into the phone, breathing heavily.

"Tell them I agree to the terms and that I will cooperate fully. I'm ready to end this."

"You made the right choice, Sergeant. Remember, when they show, act as normal, and as surprised as anyone. I will be right behind."

"How long?"

"Ten minutes, no longer. What of the boy?"

"He's in tough shape. Hicks worked him over pretty good, but he'll live. He is due to be transferred, along with the others, at 9:00 am to Titicut State Hospital."

"Ending this as we will," the professor said, "and protecting that boy's health is all that matters now. As his court-appointed guardian, he'll be under my care from this day forward. I'll see to it he receives the best medical attention. You made the right choice, Sergeant, for you, and for us all. Remember, ten minutes."

After the professor hung up, Guthrie placed the receiver down and sat back in his chair, sliding open the top drawer. He reached for a pack of stale Winston's and lit up a cigarette. He coughed harshly as the smoke filled his rising lungs. He rarely smoked, in fact, almost never, but when he did, it was usually accompanied by a tall glass of Kentucky rye. As he braced himself and weighed what was to come, he wished he had a bottle now.

Glancing down at his watch, he tamped out the cigarette butt and walked to the window which overlooked the parking lot. It was 8:10. The professor struck him as a punctual man, a man who did not suffer tardiness in others and in himself. And although Guthrie found him somewhat eccentric, his measure of him was a man of purpose and integrity. A man who meant ten minutes when he said ten minutes.

Guthrie glanced again at his wristwatch. As his eyes returned to the parking lot, he saw a fleet of black sedans pull into the plaza like a presidential motorcade. Bringing up the rear, at more than one hundred yards, a gray, Lincoln Town Car with tinted windows followed close behind. Guthrie easily recognized it as the professor's.

"Right on time," Guthrie said matter-of-factly, still looking on like a captain who has resigned himself to the coming wave. And then he looked and saw something else, almost accidentally as he turned from the window. A large, female hawk, twice that of the male, hung flat against the sky. It appeared to be suspended, as a cloud-bank suspends itself in still air before it vanished and was lost to the ether.

"Cease and desist! Cease and desist!" a voice said as a pack of mirrored sunglasses stormed through the front entrance of One Police Plaza. "I am Federal Agent, Ken Driscoll. Stop what you're doing, put your hands up, and stand against the wall!" Driscoll immediately grabbed the cord to the paper shredder and yanked it from the outlet. "Officer, step back from the machine and get against the wall. And you!" He flashed a hard look at the rotund officer behind the desk. "Hang up the phone and step away. Do it now."

The officers made for the wall in a stiff-legged gait, their eyes reaching behind their heads. With guns drawn, the gang of suits looked on as Agent Driscoll held the warrant over his head.

"Don't move and listen up. The Honorable Walter T. Stewart, United States Federal Judge, has ordered a search and seizure of all property as outlined in the warrant. The 'Police Misconduct Provision' (42 U.S.C. 4141), otherwise known as "Section 1983," covers all violations of police dereliction, including, but not limited to: excessive force, discriminatory harassment, false arrests, falsified reports, destroying evidence, unlawful stops, unlawful search and seizures, and of course, murder."

"At this moment, as sure as I'm speaking to you now, every fax machine, every phone, every file, every table, every chair, desk, pen, and or paper clip, and of course, all of you, is under federal jurisdiction. Meaning, you belong to me. If anyone is caught destroying, altering, or hiding any property for any reason, the officer or related personnel will be in direct violation of the order and will be prosecuted to the full extent of the law. If you so much as blow gas, without my consent, you will be hit with an obstruction charge faster than any of you bumpkins know how to bait a hook. Do I make myself clear?"

The officers and administrative personnel stood slack-jawed, stunned at events rapidly unfolding. They remained motionless as they listened to Driscoll bite off their ears with a series of crimes and violations.

Now that Driscoll had their attention, he turned to his agents. "Bring me Hicks. And bring me anyone else you find back there wearing a badge or picking their teeth with a spit of hay."

On Driscoll's command, the agents flooded the station searching the long hallways, changing lockers, interrogation rooms, broom closets, and the break room.

Behind the glass of his office door, Guthrie could hear the FBI agents trampling through the station and closing in. For strength and validation, He glanced at the framed picture of Nicole as he listened to his fellow officers being rounded up and ushered outside.

Guthrie was anxious, but he felt an odd sense of relief when his office door swung open with a hard bang.

"Hold it right there, Sergeant," the agent commanded, giving Guthrie a wink. "Step away from the desk and lock your hands above your head."

Guthrie gestured with a nod and did exactly as instructed.

"Eyes forward, Sergeant and step towards me. Keep your hands on your head where I can see them."

The agent took hold of Guthrie at the threshold and ushered him to the front desk.

On Agent Driscoll's instructions, Polly dispatched a message to all patrols to head back to the station immediately, Chief's orders. Driscoll knew from Hicks's file, not a single officer would question the order. All would report to headquarters at once.

Driscoll stood tall with an authoritative posture. He examined the officers with disdain as they were escorted front and center.

"What the hell is going on?" Officer Durst snapped with anger.

"And who the hell are you?" Sergeant Guthrie said in a convincing tone.

Driscoll leaned into Guthrie, clenching his disgust between his teeth and jaw. "I'm Federal Agent Ken Driscoll, Sergeant. That makes me the worst case of fucking hemorrhoids your fat ass has ever bent over for. Now, step back."

Driscoll looked over the officers. He counted heads and studied faces and knew one was missing. "Where's Hicks? Where the hell is Chief Hicks?"

"He's not in his office," an agent said. "I pounded on his door, but there was no answer. I also checked the back lockers and cells, and he's not there either. I can confirm, however, some of those on the missing persons list are being held in the rear cells, including Cam Jenkins."

"All right," Driscoll said, "other than Cam Jenkins, release the others being held, but hold them for a debriefing. Sergeant Guthrie is going to take me to Hicks."

"You heard the agent," Guthrie said, "he's not in his office."

"I can't confirm that," the reporting agent said. "I can only confirm that his door remained closed and there was no answer."

Driscoll smiled. "We've been tailing Hicks for the last few days, Sergeant. He's in there all right, and you're going to help me get him out."

Guthrie stared down Driscoll in silence, before he dropped his head and was pushed toward Hicks's office. As they made their way to the rear of the station, Driscoll gazed into the holding cells where Harry Fletcher, Don Williams, and Albert Cunningham where being held separately from Cam Jenkins. He hoped they were okay.

"Okay Sergeant," Driscoll said, "Open up Hicks's door."

"I have the keys to every office, but Hicks. And even if I did have a master key, you'd still have to get past the electromagnetic lock first."

Driscoll lowered his voice and addressed Guthrie. "Are you telling me you can't override the system, Sergeant?" Guthrie just shook his head.

"All right, Hicks," Driscoll said, raising his voice. "This is your last chance. Come out now. Here's the story. You are completely surrounded and there's no way out. You must understand there are very few options and none of them are very good, but if you cooperate, we can end this thing with no one else getting hurt." All they heard was silence in return.

"Where's the station's fire axe, Sergeant?"

"We keep one behind glass by the rear entrance."

"All right, go get it."

Driscoll waited for Guthrie to step away. He then drew his weapon and shot through the locking mechanism three times. The door flung open revealing an empty office.

"He's on the run!" Driscoll said, jerking his head around to meet Guthrie. "And you're going to help me find him."

"I don't know where he is. He should be in his office—"

"Not good enough, Sergeant. You better know where he is, or the deal is off. No Hicks, no witness protection. But first, you're going to give me a hand with Jenkins. He looks like he's going to need help off the floor." Driscoll looked at Guthrie suspiciously. "That young man better be all right."

"He'll be all right. The boy is tough, it's just that…"

"Just what?" Driscoll shot back.

"He's disoriented, listless. He had a breakdown of sorts during his interrogations, and well… the benzodiazepine we administered left him legless."

Driscoll's face turned red. Harry Fletcher, Don Williams, and Albert Cunningham could walk from their cells under their own capacity, but Jenkins was another story. He was face down and foaming at the mouth.

"What did you do to him?" Driscoll asked, picking up under Cam's left arm while Guthrie took up his right.

"It's a common reaction to the drugs," Guthrie said. "Just keep his head up so he doesn't bite through his tongue."

After Cam was carried out of the cell, he was taken outside to a waiting Lincoln Town Car. A man, perhaps in his late fifties with jet-black hair, stood like a totem on the passenger-side of the vehicle. On visual confirmation that it was, indeed, Cam Jenkins, the man with black hair opened the door for the attentively waiting occupant. The occupant exited the back seat and set his walking cane firmly to the pavement. His appearance was slightly disheveled, yet dignified. He had a thicket of gray hair that fell over his brow with finger-sized locks, framing his deep-set, intelligent eyes. His face was kind and familiar, yet cultivated in the way of an English gentleman with a whimsical sense of humor and striking, keen wit.

For a moment, Professor Julian Banning did not speak; his examination of the boy's well-being left him utterly silent, concerned.

"Sergeant, Agent Driscoll," the professor began, addressing them both. "I can see the boy is in need of care. I'll make sure he gets the proper medical attention immediately."

"You do that Professor Banning," Driscoll said. "I've got a fugitive on the run and the Sergeant here is going to help me find him."

"Wait," the professor urged. "You did the right thing, Sergeant, but before you chase down your fugitive, let me first take this opportunity to apologize the way my driver, Ahkee, broke into your home office and left you a note in such a clandestine manner. It was crude, but I think you can see now the matter at hand was most urgent. Without your cooperation, we would never hope to succeed in bringing down this corrupt enterprise and its dangerous liaison with the dark realm."

The professor glanced at Cam, then back to Guthrie. "Can he hear me?"

"He can hear you," Guthrie said, "but know he's coming off heavy tranquilizers. Speak slow and direct."

"We'll leave you to it professor," Driscoll said, turning away and radioing in an APB on the chief. "We have a fugitive to catch."

Banning stepped forward. "Son, I am Professor Julian Banning. My colleagues know me as Professor Banning; my friends know me as Jules. I would prefer you address me as Jules."

In a weakened voice, Cam said, "What's going on?"

"For now," the professor said, "you need only concern yourself with two things: first, know that you are under my custodial care; and second, no longer will you suffer the indignities and harsh treatment of the local police."

The professor turned to his driver and gave a nod, then said, "But before we depart, however, there is just one other thing."

When Ahkee opened the opposite door, a burst of black fur sporting a single white paw leapt from the back seat and pounced onto Cam.

Professor Banning could see Cam manage a smile and mouth the words of personal affection, a clear cognizance of Whitey and his lively presence.

There was much that lie ahead and much to do, the professor understood, but for now he looked upon the joyful reunion as a father might look upon his infant son about to take his very first step.

THE END

THE PAGAN TRIAD: BOOK II
COMING SOON!

Chief Elias Hicks is on the run and the FBI are following up every lead, but Professor Julian Banning knows they are chasing a red herring and time has run out. The urgency of their pursuit, he pleads, should be tightly focused on the swamp, what the people of the fallen night call "the place where spirits dwell."

Cam Jenkins blames Chief Hicks for his father's death and wants revenge. Under the professor's custodial care, Cam begins to trust the professor who convinces him they can find and bring Chief Hicks to justice, but only with Cam's help.

Banning is the only one who knows that Jenkins's land holds the key to restoring calm within the territories. He believes that somewhere in the labyrinth of tunnels beneath the old meeting house, the same tunnels built by the founding elders, there lies a passageway between the living and the dead which led Carl Jenkins safely out of the swamp and back home in 1973.

When FBI agent, Ken Driscoll, is finally convinced by the professor, he refocuses his man hunt to try to save Titicut before it's too late. Will the territories escape their fate? Or will the ominous words spoken by the leader of the first men, *dishonor ours and fear everything*, be forever carved on Titicut's headstone?

If you enjoyed *The Keepers* and want to find out, you won't want to miss book II: *The Pagan Triad.*

ACKNOWLEDGEMENTS

My good friend and fellow writer, Deborah Wynne, author of the *Pirouette and Promises* series, gave her time generously and used her gifted talents and expertise as my level one, beta reader. Her keen eye lifted my words, paragraphs, and pages above what I could ever have expected. She helped make *The Keepers* the best book it could be. And I will always be grateful.

I want to thank, Andi Marchal, fellow writer/poet/friend, author of *Vykup*, for her encouragement and friendship. Her daily support has been steadfast. Thank you for being an early reader, and for your exciting review of *The Keepers*. I will always be thankful.

I want to thank my Twitter writing family, especially the #vss365 crew, for all their love and support. I have met fellow writers and poets who amaze me with their talents — yeah, that's right, you know who you are. Many have become good friends, and all have been very supportive and welcoming, something I never expected.

I want to thank my parents, Edward and Alma Burns, for always being there for me and for providing me with support and guidance. Stay the course and good things await.

I would like to thank Mark Schultz, wordsmith extraordinaire, for his expertise in extricating and polishing all spelling, grammar, and usage faux pas that helped make the manuscript shine. https://www.wordrefiner.com

Many of the characters in *The Keepers* were born in the compost of imagination. I want to thank my hometown, North Easton Massachusetts, Oliver Ames High School, Bridgewater Massachusetts, and the local watering holes where I spent much of my early adulthood. All have served as nitrogen rich fertilizer for creative and fertile ground. Raised in the New England countryside, you meet the most unique and peculiarly wonderful people. I will always be thankful.

Lastly, I would like to thank Black Rose Writing for believing in *The Keepers* and giving me a chance. Wow, never could I believe. I'm still not sure that I do.

SPECIAL THANKS

None of this would matter without the love and support of my wife and best friend, Ann Stewart Burns, author of *The Pink Parasol and The French Confection*. I am literally writing these words twenty-five years to the month we were married. I can think of no better celebration on *The Keepers* completion, than a silver anniversary with the woman I love. I will always be thankful that she believed in my writing, even when I didn't. She is my love, my life, and my inspiration. Thank you for everything you do. You will always be my First Reader.

ABOUT THE AUTHOR

Chris Burns writes under his pen name, Tan Van Huizen. Van Huizen is a phonetic variation of the name "Van Husum" his 8th times great-grandfather's name. Van Husum was a sailor for the Dutch West India Co., and the first of Tan's maternal line to arrive in America, 1639.

When Tan's not writing, he enjoys researching family history, hiking, travel, driving "The Beast" his souped-up F-150 truck, and hanging out with his best friend and wife, Ann Stewart Burns. He and Ann live in Southeastern Massachusetts.

NOTE FROM THE AUTHOR

Word-of-mouth is crucial for any author to succeed. If you enjoyed *The Keepers*, please leave a review online—anywhere you are able. Even if it's just a sentence or two. It would make all the difference and would be very much appreciated.

Thanks!
Tan Van Huizen

We hope you enjoyed reading this title from:

BLACK ROSE
writing™

www.blackrosewriting.com

Subscribe to our mailing list – *The Rosevine* – and receive **FREE** books, daily deals, and stay current with news about upcoming releases and our hottest authors.
Scan the QR code below to sign up.

Already a subscriber? Please accept a sincere thank you for being a fan of Black Rose Writing authors.

View other Black Rose Writing titles at www.blackrosewriting.com/books and use promo code **PRINT** to receive a **20% discount** when purchasing.

www.ingramcontent.com/pod-product-compliance
Lightning Source LLC
Chambersburg PA
CBHW010729100726
47899CB00009B/2985